OPHELIA

Afterworld Book One

OPHELIA

K.M. RICE

WILDLING
SPIRIT

Library of Congress Control Number: 2018903706
ISBN: 978-1-947944-05-3

For my little sister Alexandra. You are my other half and I love you with all my heart.

He ne'er is crown'd
With immortality, who fears to follow
Where airy voices lead...

John Keats, *Endymion*

Ophelia Brighton was three-years old and in the bath when she looked her father in the eye and told him that she was happy to be there, because it wasn't always that way.

"What do you mean?" he asked, wringing out a washcloth.

"I went to a big bedroom. The man opened the door," she whispered, as if gossiping at a stuffed animal tea party. "He wanted to hurt me, so he did."

Her father let the washcloth drip in his grip as he watched his daughter with the big brown eyes and natural curls lie down on her tummy, luxuriating in the warm water. Though he did his best to control what she watched, he worried she had seen a violent scene on TV.

"Where did you hear that?" he asked, straightening on the closed toilet seat.

"Someone gone." Ophelia began blowing raspberries in the water. "Nowhere."

Her father relaxed, knowing he had his little girl back.

*O*phelia was an average child, if not a little timid and prone to tantrums. There was a boy at her pre-school with shining eyes and a broad smile called Jack. She loved to make him laugh.

"Let's play house," she said to Jack.

"I'm the dog," Jack announced before crawling under the play kitchen's table. He had a funny way of speaking that had nothing to do with his lisp. For the most part, Ophelia could understand him, but when she asked him to repeat a word, he often shouted it.

Ophelia gazed down at him, her brown hair bound in two braids. "You're the daddy."

Jack snarled in response then yapped.

Ophelia decided that his choice of dog over human was a small sacrifice if it still meant they were in the house together. *Together.* For she hadn't seen Jack all weekend, and a weekend was a terribly long time for the three-year-olds. Jack's laughter made her feel filled up to the brim inside, like she was a night sky full of twinkling stars, or even just two brightly glowing ones.

As she stirred the imaginary soup, the play kitchen faded and she saw a ballroom full of dancers waltzing elegantly to a stringed tune. The women were in long gowns and the men looked like penguins with their suit tails. Across the room was a beautiful lady with chestnut curls who smiled at her like someone from a fairy tale. The images slipped away as fluidly as they had formed.

"Puppy?" Ophelia asked, kneeling down beside Jack with her spoon and imaginary soup. "Are you hungry?"

She held out the plastic cutlery and he licked it with a happy whimper then cowered, hiding his face with wounded paws and sad sounds.

"What's wrong, puppy?" she asked.

"I'm sad," he whined. "You were gone so long, Opeelia."

"I was at work," she replied, imitating her mother's voice as she rested on her side and laid a hand on his arm. "I'm home now, puppy."

"Nooo," he whined, and when he peeked up, she was startled by the tears in his eyes. "Much longer than that."

"Don't cry," Ophelia whispered.

"I saw one of the Gone People hurting you."

"It's okay, puppy." She patted her thigh. "I'm here now."

Jack scooted towards her, dragging his legs as if he couldn't use them, then burrowed his head into her stomach. She cooed and petted his dark curls, her voice so high that neither could understand the words she said.

"I'm still sad," he whined with a sigh, dragging a finger over the coarse carpet in spiral shapes.

Ophelia stroked his head and kissed his cheek.

Jack's eyes widened and he immediately let out a loud, "Eww," rubbing his cheek vigorously as the two dissolved into a fit of giggles.

He didn't mention the Gone People again.

"*Sometimes when I feel bad and t'ings look blue,*" Jack sang in a squeaky voice when they were four. He walked laps around Ophelia in the swing, twisting the chains up.

"More!" Ophelia encouraged.

"*I wish a pal I had, say one like you.*" Jack grunted as the chains kinked up and he couldn't twist her any longer. "Ready?"

"Yes," Ophelia giggled.

Jack let go and the little girl was sent spinning, her hair fanning out around her. They both cheered as her swing started to wind up in the opposite direction, and then slowly came undone. Ophelia groaned then slid off the seat, stumbling about, making Jack laugh.

"Now it's my turn," he cackled, reaching out to steady her shoulders.

Ophelia lost her balance and took him down with her, and the two were a laughing mess on the bark at the edge of the playground.

"Jack?" a man with a deep, odd voice called. The two children looked up to spy a tall, fair-haired adult smiling with a wave.

"Oh," Jack said, climbing to his feet. "That's Ambrose. He's my parents' fwiend."

3

"I'm here to walk you home," Ambrose said.

Even from her distance, Ophelia could see the sunlight glinting in the man's pale eyes. The way his grin didn't shift or fade as he tracked Jack's movements made her cold inside.

"Jack..." she began.

"I'll see you tomorrow, Opeelia," he called over his shoulder as he scampered to Ambrose.

The adult rested his hand on the child's shoulder, and Ophelia thought he looked rather like a grinning wolf talking to a little bird.

"Come along then," Ambrose urged in his peculiar voice with a chuckle. He ruffled Jack's hair and the boy threw her a happy wave then skipped ahead down the sidewalk.

Ophelia watched him go and wished Ambrose's voice would stop bouncing around in her head.

Jack didn't come to school the next day, or the day after. While walking home with her mother, Ophelia spotted a police car outside her house. She hid behind her mother's legs until the men gave her high fives and pretended she was so strong that she stung their hands.

"I'm Officer Morales," one said. "I have a son about your age."

Once her mother had welcomed them inside and they had settled on the couch, they asked the girl questions about Ambrose. Ophelia's father brought over a plate of Oreos.

"And what hair color did he have?"

"Yellow. He talked funny," Ophelia replied, hugging her mother's arm on the couch.

"Like he had an accent?"

"An... ac-cent?" she said quietly, testing out the word. Morales smiled as he took notes.

"Did he talk like Jack?" her mother asked. Ophelia shrugged and the woman turned to the police. "You know his parents are here on green cards?"

The officers nodded. "How old do you think this man was?"

"Old," Ophelia whispered.

"As old as me?" her father asked as he scooted the plate of cookies towards their guests.

4

Ophelia shook her head then lunged for an Oreo. "Much, *much* older. One of the oldest men in the world."

"So he had wrinkles, then," the second officer ventured, "like a grandpa?"

"Of course not," she replied, trying to take apart a cookie and breaking it. "He's older inside than out."

"Lia," her father hissed, resting a hand on her arm. "Please, pay attention. This is not a story."

"Here, watch this," Morales said, then grabbed an Oreo and twisted it, unlocking the two halves with a smile. "You try."

Ophelia did so and grinned when it worked.

"Here's a current photo." Her mother rested a picture of Ophelia and Jack on the table. The two children were eating cherries. Ophelia peered down at the photo, remembering the stickiness that clung to her fingers from the red juice.

"Jack is lost," Morales said. "We need you to help us find him."

She wanted to leave the house to look for her friend, but her mother wouldn't let her go to the playground anymore after that day.

Weeks passed, and the Gone People stopped showing her things. Her parents told her that she would never see Jack again, but Ophelia knew that wasn't true. He was only lost, and as the grownups forgot about him, she knew that it was up to her to find him.

1

Ophelia was in graduate school and hunting for a tome of poetry when she rediscovered the photo of her and Jack. The picture had been stuffed in a stack of old awards and certificates at the end of the bookcase in her bedroom.

Jack's languid curls were a black mess on his head, his shining eyes mere slits from his wide grin as the two children brandished their cherry-covered lips to the camera. Though her memories of her play-mate had faded, the sight of his impish face made her feel like she was missing something vital, like an organ. Or maybe it was just her child-hood confidence that had been taken with Jack's life.

"Who's that?" Alex asked, flopping onto her bed.

Together, they had been renting the old Victorian house in the Californian coastal city of Santa Cruz for over a year, though they had been friends for more than a decade. Alex was on the tail end of a Goth phase and was letting the black dye in his hair fade into the natural brown, his dark nail polish flaking away. They had met in middle school, and growing to be the same height at five foot eight inches had all-but convinced them that they were secretly twins who looked nothing alike.

Ophelia sucked in a breath then handed the photo over to him.

"Oh, look at you," Alex cooed. "You get so brown in the summer."

She smirked. "So do you."

"Greek isn't Trinidad... Trini... what do you call what your grandma was?"

"Trinidadian."

Alex narrowed his eyes, toying with the ring in his lip with the tip of his tongue. "Is that a cousin?"

"No." She looked up at the photo from her spot on the floor. "He was kidnapped when we were small."

"Jesus," Alex said, stiffening, the overhead light bouncing off the glossy photo. "That's horrible."

"Yeah," she sighed.

Alex's deep set eyes slid to hers in shock. "And you knew him?"

Ophelia nodded and carefully took the photo from Alex. She didn't want to tell him how she was there when Jack was wooed from her side, or how he was the one child who had made sense of her discordant imagination. Then again, that last part might just have been from the golden shimmer of memory.

"I didn't know your neighborhood was so dangerous."

"It's not." She returned the photo to the book. "I only found out the truth of what happened to him from other kids. My parents told me he moved."

Alex grunted. "On a happier note, my car was fixed just in time to go out tonight," he announced, rolling over onto his back.

"Another Philosophy Club meeting, huh?"

"How do you know I don't have a date?"

Ophelia cocked her head. "Because you haven't showered yet."

Alex flopped back over onto his stomach and gazed down at her, his broad brow bone hooding his pale eyes. "We're called The Eternalists and tonight's Descartes' Desserts. You should come," he added, prodding her shoulder. "There'll be brownies."

"I can't."

"Boooooring," he drawled.

Ophelia yanked out her laptop. "I'm supposed to be working on my thesis."

"Booooooring," Alex drawled again, leaning in to her ear.

Ophelia caught his chin then pinched his lips into a fish-face, making Alex cut off the sound with a squeak. "Adam's coming over later," she cooed. "And if you're going to be out, then..."

Alex's face twisted repugnantly as he yanked out of her hands and sat up. "*Really?*"

"You smell. Go shower."

Alex hauled himself off her bed and trudged into his room, muttering, "I smell like sunshine and unicorn kittens."

Ophelia listened to the faucet squeak to life in the bathroom and hugged her laptop to her chest, staring at nothing on the opposite wall, wondering over how well she had managed to forget the little boy with the infectious laugh. Thinking of him reminded her of the visions from the Gone People, and how she was sitting in her ninth grade health class, listening to the description of Schizophrenia, when she vowed to never speak of them again.

Given that what she used to see always took place in a grand house with women in beautiful dresses, she often wondered if it all stemmed from a little girl's desire to be royalty. In fact, she so rarely thought about her former abnormality that she mostly forgot it ever existed until prompted. Like right now.

The shower turned off, shaking Ophelia out of her reverie. Opening up her laptop, she let out a deep breath and focused on her shadowed reflection in the dark screen. Her broad face was half-hidden, but she could make out the distinctive curve of her eyebrows that her mother always loved, for when combined with her brown eyes, they lent her features a very open, cheerful appearance. Or so she had learned after years of having strange people approach her out of the blue, telling her even stranger stories all on the premise that she "looked friendly."

Her straightened bangs swept across her forehead while her brown curls fell past her shoulders, and she sometimes wondered if their bounce contributed to Alex referring to her as "an effervescent elephant" on account of her strong memory. She figured the remembering part fit. Her full lips were dull and lined and thin crow's feet splintered at the corners of her eyes. She knew they were just lines from smiling but they made her feel old all the same.

Fifteen minutes later and Alex was out the door, leaving Ophelia alone in the old Victorian. She moved into the living room, warming by the fire in the woodstove atop a fluffy white faux-fur rug, knuckles deep in her argument that the poet John Keats was undervalued in his time when there was a knock at the door.

"Adam," she sighed, closing her eyes. He was early, as always. His habit of hyper-punctuality often left Ophelia with half-finished assignments, which was inexcusable for a student intending to graduate the following semester.

Rising, she set her laptop and volume of poetry on the rug and made her way to the door, irritation bubbling, evaporating the Romantic poet with windswept hair strolling around in her mind.

"Babe, I haven't even—" she complained as she yanked open the door, cutting herself off as she was greeted by the sight of a young man who was anything but Adam.

His limp, wet hair was half obscuring his face and the scent of damp leather suddenly permeated the doorway. It was only drizzling out, yet the lanky man before her had obviously been in it for some time. Judging by the duffle bag in his hand and the guitar case on his shoulder, he looked homeless.

Ophelia immediately swung the door shut to an inch. "Can I help you?"

"Alex Marinos lives here, yeah?" the man asked.

She peeked out at him as she registered his accent. "How do you know him?"

He set down his bag and swiped a hand through his hair, sweeping it off his face. Ophelia felt her suspicion ease as she noticed how pleasantly his haggard features were thrown together, and then just as quickly discarded the thought. He looked like he hadn't had a close shave in his life.

"We're in European History together."

Ophelia pursed her lips and eased the door shut without latching it. "He isn't *in* History."

"Were," the man corrected himself.

"Were what?"

"Christ, we *were* in class together, now can ya please let me in? It's feckin' freezing out here."

She blinked. "It's *what?*"

"Bloody cold!"

Ophelia inched the door open again and narrowed her eyes at him. "I don't even know who you are."

"Brennan. Didn't he tell ya I was coming?"

"No, he didn't."

Brennan sighed and leaned against the wall, running a hand over his face. "Do I really *look* like a murderer?"

"No. But if murderers looked like murderers they'd never get away with anything. Hang on." She shut the door and latched it before texting Alex, asking if he knew anyone named "Brennan."

She peered out the bay window by the entryway while she waited for his response, hidden behind a curtain as she eyed the young man outside, his image slightly distorted by the drooping, aged glass in the pane. He tugged out a pouch of tobacco and had made and lit a cigarette before she fully registered what he had been doing with the white square of rolling paper in his fingers. Brennan leaned against the peeling paint on the side of the house, gazing out at the darkening street with a casual sort of nonchalance as he smoked. When coupled with his tight black jeans and boots, it made her wonder where his motorcycle was hidden.

Alex texted back before Brennan finished his smoke, saying, *Crap, sorry, yeah he's good people. He's gonna crash with us for a few nights.*

Ophelia crooked her jaw in irritation over just now being told they were expecting a guest, and then strode back to the door, unlatching the lock and swinging it open. "Looks like you're in the clear."

Brennan smirked as he stubbed out his cigarette on the wall and shouldered his bag. "You decide that while ya were gawking at me from the curtains?"

She let out an indignant guffaw from which she tried to distract

11

herself by tugging her cream knit cardigan down over her leggings. "I
— I wasn't—"

"Sure, it's grand, love." He winked as he hauled his sodden self into
the house, peering around curiously. The living room was on the left
and the kitchen on the right with a set of stairs leading up to the
second story directly in front of the entryway. Ophelia shut the door
behind him, wrinkling her nose at the scent of mildew and tobacco
clinging to his clothes.

"So, are you an exchange student or something?"

"Or somet'ing." He glanced at the stairs. "Alex's room up there?"

"Or something," she replied.

She caught the barest hint of a grin before he jogged up the steep
steps with his gear, looking far too tall for such an old house. Ophelia
cleared her throat softly, looking down at her laptop and book, aban-
doned on the white rug beside the woodstove.

So much for getting work done.

Brennan's scent trailed after him through the house, prompting
her to tug her sweater up over her nose.

Darting to a window, she opened it and started wafting the fresh
air in, only to realize that Brennan wasn't exaggerating. It really was
unseasonably cold outside. Shutting the window, she figured lighting
a candle would be more polite than asking her guest to bathe after she
had already accused him of being a murderer.

Heavy footfalls echoed down the stairs and Ophelia greeted him
with a tight-lipped smile. "Can I get you anything? Water?"

He strode past her and started yanking off his boots in front of the
wood burning stove.

"Tea?"

He squirmed out of his jacket and tugged a large vase full of deco-
rative branches over to the heat. Hanging the wet leather on them, he
accidentally snapped off some of the twigs.

"Just... make yourself at home." She arched a brow and stared as he
destroyed the arrangement.

"A beer would be lovely."

"Right," she said, her lips forming a thin line as he huddled around the fire like a vagrant. "Beer it is."

"Cheers."

"Um, yeah, about that," she called over her shoulder as she padded into the adjoining kitchen. "Where are you from?"

"I figured you'd be curious," he called to her. "Most people are."

Ophelia snagged a Lagunitas stout and popped off the top before carrying it back into the other room where she found Brennan lounging on his elbows, his socks facing the flames, his white V-neck stained down the middle from rainwater.

"You see," he began importantly, raising his eyebrows, which were arched over his almond-shaped eyes like the wings of a raven. "Once upon a time, my mam fell in love with this fella, and they—"

"You know what I meant," Ophelia snipped around her amused smile.

His eyes danced with delight as he gazed up at her, and when she handed him his beer, she wondered if they were brown or green. "T'anks," he said quietly.

"You left out the *H*."

Brennan studied her with confusion as he took a swig.

"In *thanks*," she explained. "You're Irish."

"Is that really my biggest tell? Not the *'mam'* or the beer?"

Ophelia shook her head then eased down on the couch seat farthest from him, scooting the apple-cinnamon scented candle even closer to ward off the assault on her senses. Picking up her laptop, she tapped the keyboard to wake it up.

"You are just hilarious," she drawled.

He shrugged and took another swig of the dark liquid. "Whatever ya say, Girl."

Ophelia narrowed her eyes at the paragraphs of twelve point, Times New Roman on her screen, realizing that it all may as well be gibberish with him around. "So how long are you staying?"

"Haven't figured that one out yet."

"But you live here? In Santa Cruz?"

He leaned his head back to look at her upside-down, his nearly

13

neck-length hair brushing against the rug. From the look of it, his black locks were just as determined to kink up when wet as her brown ones. "Isn't that the dream?" he asked. "Sunny California? What a load of shite. It's like winter every night."

"Sorry to disappoint," she said, "but I like it. Sun, sun, sun gets boring. The further into summer we get, the foggier the nights. I'll miss the rain."

He collapsed onto his back with a sigh. "Still a fair sight warmer than home. Is this real fur?" Brennan trailed the backs of his hands and bare arms on the rug.

"No, why?"

"Well, I was gonna say that I'm probably ruining it."

Ophelia wrinkled her nose slightly, not wanting to imagine the scent of more wet dead animal joining the fray. She looked about for another candle.

"How'd ya manage a place like this, if ya don't mind me asking?"

Ophelia didn't answer right away as she lunged towards the end table, her fingertips brushing the jar of colored wax just out of reach.

"Girl?" he pressed.

"My parents help with the rent," she grunted, then gave up, shut off her laptop and set it aside.

Brennan rolled over onto his stomach and peered up at her. His eyes were large but not in the buggy way that she associated with the British Isles. There was something distinctly foreign about his look, yet she couldn't place what felt off.

"So you're wealthy then?" he asked.

"I wouldn't... I mean, my parents have worked really hard for what they have."

"There's no shame in having help. There is some luck, though."

"I guess."

Her eyes narrowed slightly but her irritation was swept aside as her skin warmed and tingled from the way he was studying her face. Then something bright surged to the tip of her tongue, about to make a connection. Right as she parted her lips and sucked in air to voice it, the bright thing flew away, like a vanished sneeze.

14

"What is it?" he asked, his face tightening slightly, and she realized she must look rather stupid and tucked her chin in to her neck, making her look like a giraffe, or so Alex liked to say.

"I—nothing. I just... are you sure we've never—"

Headlights beamed in through the window, distracting her as they slid across the wall.

"My boyfriend's here," Ophelia announced, rising. She strode towards the door before she could observe Brennan's reaction to what she had been about to say. "He always comes over on Wednesdays. We watch *Survivor* together. It's the one night he doesn't have class." She winced inwardly at her babbling and yanked open the door, spotting Adam climbing out of his red truck and plastering a grin on her face. "Hey, babe."

"Hey." He locked his doors then trotted over. His wide-set, narrow eyes nearly disappeared above his smile, his straight blonde hair sticking out under a beanie. She stood on her tip toes to kiss the angel bow of his upper lip in greeting while he hugged her, his hands sliding south onto her backside.

"Oh, um," she cleared her throat at the contact. "We've got company."

"Huh?" he breathed against her mouth.

Tugging the large blonde inside, Ophelia rested her hand on the back of his baggy blue O'Neill sweatshirt then gestured to the Irishman who had gotten to his feet. "Brennan, this is Adam. Adam, this is Brennan. He's Alex's friend."

Adam nodded at the other man. "How's it going?"

"Grand."

"I see you're starting the night off well," Adam teased, gesturing to the bottle in Brennan's hand.

Brennan saluted him with his beer and a smile, but there was no hiding the stiffness that suddenly settled in the Irishman's spine as he straightened to his full height of about six foot, nor the intake of breath from Adam that broadened his chest. Ophelia resisted the urge to roll her eyes at the primitive, rooster instinct as Adam's back tensed beneath her hand.

"Want a beer?" she chirped, guiding Adam into the kitchen in an attempt to deflate him.

Adam followed her, a hand on her hip. "So, Alex's friend," he said quietly, using air quotes around the last word once they were alone. "Is he...?"

Ophelia looked over his shoulder to make sure Brennan was preoccupied. "I don't know. I don't think so."

She opened the fridge and snagged two beers, handing one to Adam before leading the way back into the living room.

Brennan was seated on the ground, watching the flames, his body more relaxed, and Ophelia wondered how he could be so comfortable in someone else's home. Then again, she always tried to be so unobtrusive when visiting others that Alex's mom once remarked that she would be dying of starvation on the floor before she asked for a bite to eat. Her family had distant English roots which she liked to blame for her occasional stiff upper lip.

Adam slumped onto the couch with a sigh, setting down his beer and rubbing his face with his hands.

"Rough afternoon?" she asked, sitting down beside him.

"I have two quizzes tomorrow. I've been studying all day."

"Oh yeah, *all day*, except for when you were surfing," Ophelia teased.

Adam peeked out from behind his long fingers. "That was for like, a half hour."

"Good. I hate it when you go out with sets that big."

"Probably one of the last we'll get all spring." He took a swig of his beer then eyed Brennan, who was shifting to face them with his back to the woodstove. "Do you surf?"

Brennan shook his head, seeming paler and smaller when she compared his lithe frame to Adam.

"He's not from around here," Ophelia whispered in Adam's ear.

"So I see."

Brennan leaned his hair back towards the heat and Ophelia was relieved that he was drying out nicely, even if his sodden jacket and boots weren't.

Adam shook his head ruefully, his eyes locked on the other man's. "You have no idea how many times I've tried to get her to come out with me. She refuses."

Ophelia squeezed his arm, realizing that he was trying to tease a reaction out of Brennan, who minutes ago Ophelia wouldn't have believed could go so quiet.

One of Brennan's dark brows quirked ever so slightly as he slid his gaze to hers, awaiting a response. A patch of hair was missing just behind the arch, as if it were once split open. Knowing she was the focus of his attention sprinkled warmth in Ophelia's chest, making her lips start to curl upwards, but she cut off the smile before it formed, looking away with a pathetic little half shrug. "There's just something about how big an ocean is that bothers me," she murmured.

"Man." Adam held the bottle out and studied it. "This stuff's dark."

Ophelia rolled her eyes and heard Brennan snort.

"I have no problem admitting I'm a Budweiser man," Adam said, setting the bottle down.

"That's horse piss," Ophelia countered. "Watered down horse piss."

"Well, listen to that," Brennan said softly, hopping to his feet. "And here I thought you were a lady." He clucked at her in disapproval as he strolled past, his damp pants hanging a bit too low. Were Adam not beside her, she would have let her eye linger on the lines of his hip bones peeking out from under his displaced shirt, but she instead tried to make up for her lapse by snuggling against the blonde's side.

Adam draped an arm around her shoulder and clicked on the TV, searching through to the recordings. *Survivor* had only just started when odd, scuffing sounds echoed from the kitchen. Scrunching up his face, Adam paused the show and fixed Ophelia with a curious expression. His broad cheekbones and the folds of skin under his brow bones gave his eyes an elongated look, as if they were as wide as his brows. "Is that a rat?"

Ophelia used his shoulder as leverage and peered over the back of the couch. For a while she couldn't see anything, then Brennan started whistling and she heard the sound of cereal being poured into a bowl,

17

followed by the unnecessary slamming of cupboards. As he put the cereal away, he gazed in her general direction and shut the cupboard door as loud as he could.

Sliding back down into her seat, she met Adam's baffled gaze with her own.

"Who is this guy?" he mouthed.

Ophelia shrugged, her eyes wide as she shook her head. "Just play it."

Adam resumed the TV show and, one minute later, there was a shout from the kitchen. "Hey, Girl, is the dishwasher clean or dirty?"

"*Girl?*" Adam asked her.

"Dirty," Ophelia called back.

"Cheers!"

Adam snorted softly, covering his mouth as he slumped down lower in his seat at the rattling of silverware that followed, as if the kitchen was being ransacked. Ophelia swatted at him but couldn't hide her own amusement.

"He's foreign."

"More than that," Adam drawled, playing the show again.

Brennan sauntered back into the room with a bowl of cereal and munched on it loudly at the blonde's side, prompting Adam to turn up the volume. Brennan narrowed his eyes at him, looking rather offended.

"Hard of hearing, are ya?"

Adam fixed him with a bemused half-smile before returning his attention to the screen.

A half hour later, the show was over and Adam was fighting to stay awake while Brennan strolled the small living room, pausing to peruse the books on the shelf. "You're in paramedic school, then?" he asked, his fingers halting on the spine of a medical text.

"He is." Ophelia gestured to Adam.

Brennan eyed the tired man skeptically then looked back to the books.

"Babe." She lightly shouldered the blonde. "You need sleep."

18

Groaning, Adam sat up straighter and rubbed his eyes. "I hate getting old."

"Are you ok to drive?"

"It's like, fifteen minutes away, why do you *always* ask that?"

Ophelia shrugged, feeling tight inside at his tone, wondering if he had forgotten that company was present. "I just want to make sure you get home safe."

Sighing, Adam rubbed her back before shoving himself to his feet. He glanced around blearily, grabbing their empty beer bottles and his full one and taking them to the recycling.

"I can do that," Ophelia insisted, rising, but Adam waved her off.

Sighing, she leaned her elbows on the armrest of the couch, noticing that Brennan had been careful to keep his back turned to them while examining the bookshelf.

"All right." Adam stepped up to her and gave her a kiss. "Seeya Friday. Brennan?"

The dark-haired man peered at him over a broad shoulder.

"Good to meet you."

"Cheers. *Slán.*"

Adam tugged out his keys then headed for the door.

"Text me when you get home," Ophelia called after him and he waved an affirmative before shutting the door behind him. Resting her cheek on her folded hands, she observed Brennan who offered her a shy smile before focusing on the books once more, making her wonder where the cocky lad who had burst through her door had gone.

"No word from Alex, huh?" she asked.

"I don't want to bother him."

Brennan's stiff shoulders made her tense, as if the air was thickening. She wondered if she should excuse herself and go to bed. That hardly seemed fair, however, considering she would be abandoning her guest in an unfamiliar house, even if that hadn't stopped him from settling in earlier. A muscle shifted under his sleeve as he tugged out a book, and she realized that she had been staring at his toned arms for some time now.

Blushing inwardly, she tucked her chin to her neck and straightened. "So, you play any sports?"

"A bit of hurling and football." He glanced at her over his shoulder. "Soccer to you."

"And what are you studying?"

He slid the book back then turned to face her with a sigh, resting his hands on his hips. "You have a lot of literature anthologies."

"I got my BA in English. I'm in the master's program at San Jose State."

"You must really like books."

She picked at her cardigan sleeve as she studied him. "What's wrong with books?"

"They're safe."

He missed her surprised expression as he headed over to the woodstove and busied himself adjusting his jacket on the vase, snapping off more twigs as he did so.

"I just... I'm good at it."

"At what?"

"At writing papers and analyzing. Applying literary criticism. It's like a playground."

Brennan chuckled softly. "I'll bet ya get top marks, too."

Ophelia narrowed her eyes, once again fixed on his back and ignoring the alluring way his torso tapered slightly at the waist.

"*Grades*," she amended. "And what's wrong with that?"

"Not'ing." He faced her, his expression softening, as if she had just become more foreign in his mind. "Not'ing at all. Your parents are proud, I'm sure."

"The least I can do is work hard while they're helping support me."

He nodded slowly, his voice soft. "Seems like you've got it all sorted out."

"I'm twenty-six, so I hope so."

"You're twenty-six?" he repeated, his brows shooting up so high that they were comical. "Ya don't look a day over eighteen."

"Is that supposed to be a compliment?" she laughed.

"Well, I mean..." he fumbled.

She rose to cut off his explanation and blew out the candle. "I should work on my thesis before I go to bed. You're welcome to the couch."

"T'anks."

Picking up her laptop, she set her volume of Keats' poetry on top, only to have it slide right off as soon as she turned around. Brennan caught the book before it hit the floor and placed it back on top for her. His face was only inches from hers, and at this nearness she could discern that his eyes were actually hazel and that his striking coloring hid somewhat goofy features. His ears were a little too big and his lower teeth weren't all that straight.

Ophelia's heart started thudding and a flush of embarrassment washed over her at the reaction. The corner of Brennan's lips quirked in an awkward smile, as if wondering why she was staring. Her pulse grew louder in her head until she realized the beating wasn't her heart at all, but was the pounding of drums. Hide drums. Brennan recoiled his arm, brushing it against her wrist. She could smell brine and wood smoke and suddenly felt that someone was on the other side of flames that she couldn't really see, studying her with such wildness that she forgot what it was to be tame.

"Are ya well?" Brennan's voice rumbled at her side, reminding her that she was in the living room, that the fire was contained behind iron and glass, and that the sea was a ways off yet.

"Yes," she somehow replied without the breath to do so.

Where the hell did that come from?

Ophelia forced a smile, hoping Brennan couldn't see the tremble that coursed through her. "Goodnight."

She brushed past him and his reply of "goodnight" was almost drowned out by the pounding of her feet on the stairs. Once in her room, Ophelia shut the door and set her laptop and book down on the bed, her arms trembling, for what she had just felt was the brush of a Gone Person.

2

In an effort to ease the shaking, Ophelia sat down on her bed, attempting to make sense of the impressions just imparted on her. The images were gone seemingly as they arrived, but the scents and sounds lingered confusingly and were strong enough for her to know that this was no case of an overactive imagination. Her childhood ailment was back.

Turning her computer on in an attempt to calm herself, she wound up reading the same paragraph of her paper over and over until the words slid out of focus and all she could feel was her chest tightening from the thought that she was ill. Or maybe thinking of Jack and how she used to be had just triggered a flare up. Lost in her thoughts, she didn't know how much time slipped past before there was a soft knock on her door.

"Girl?"

"Yes?" she called, stiffening as Brennan creaked the door open.

"I, um..." He cautiously stepped in with one leg, hugging the door to his torso. The way he wouldn't look at her made goose bumps spread over the back of her neck. "I lied to ya earlier. I only said I was Alex's classmate so that you'd let me in." He chanced a glance at her once he finished.

"Why?"

"It's a long story but… I'm a mechanic," he said tightly. "We knew each other from this… t'ing last month and he didn't have enough to cover the bill and I'm in a bit of a tight spot. Anyway, we got to talking and wound up bartering."

"Is that even legal?"

He shrugged. "Who's telling?"

"All right," she sighed, looking back to her screen.

He lingered in her doorway a few seconds longer, as if he wanted to say something more, but all that came out was a quiet, "Well, night then, Girl."

She looked up at his shuffle as he slipped out. "Wait."

Brennan peeked his head back in.

"I have a name, you know."

"So I assumed. But ya never gave it to me."

Ophelia smirked, realizing she had been so caught up in her paranoia over the man at her door and her attempt at propriety afterwards that she hadn't actually been proper at all.

"Ophelia Brighton."

Brennan's eyes danced a little, tilting his head back as he appraised her, batting the door back and forth with his hands as he played with it. "Ophelia," he tested. "Nah. I like *Girl* better."

With that, he slipped out and shut the door before she had a chance to respond. She sat on her bed in silence for several seconds before realizing the tightness in her chest had fled. Snorting and shaking her head, she looked back at her paper, but try as she might, the Romantic poet strolling the meadows of her mind kept vanishing like smoke.

By the time she noticed that Adam had forgotten to text her, she was sure he was already asleep but sent him an **All ok?** anyway.

Ophelia headed downstairs the following morning to find Alex's hair sticking out like floppy sprigs of grass as he cooked what smelled like batter and peanut butter.

"Hey you."

"Vegan pancake?" he offered.

23

"Sure," she replied with a smile, putting on the kettle. "How were the brownies?"

Alex curled a nostril in distaste, holding his spatula at the ready to flip the pancake at a moment's notice. "I know you think we're just a bunch of pretentious, entitled yuppies—"

"I never said that."

"But sometimes new people show up. I thought maybe I could meet someone, you know?"

Ophelia grabbed her favorite mug from its spot by the sink. The goddess Artemis was painted on the side, running beneath the full moon with her bow and quiver, chasing a buck with a wolf on her heels. Her parents had brought it back for her as a gift after a cruise in the Mediterranean. "Did you?"

"No. They were a bunch of pretentious, entitled yuppies."

Ophelia laughed, taking in his refined nose and distinctive lips, trying to look at her friend's fine-boned features as a stranger. Alex was elegant in his own way, and in fact, could pull off regal if not for his nose and lip piercings and the black gauges in his ears.

"You could always just have your car fixed again," Ophelia offered teasingly.

"Oh, God, sorry about that," Alex groaned, flipping the pancake. "I had no idea he was going to show up *the night* I made the offer."

"Don't worry about it."

"I don't know what I was thinking—I should've checked with you first. But I happened to glance in the back room at the shop and saw that he was sleeping there. That place stinks like gasoline and grease."

Ophelia grabbed two plates from the cupboard and set them on the counter. "So you decided to pay it forward and give him a place to stay?"

Alex's head wobbled back and forth, as if he had to force the next words out. "We met at a protest."

Ophelia arched a brow as she placed an Earl Grey teabag in her mug. "*The* protest? As in when you spent the night in jail?"

Alex winced, picking up a plate and setting the pancake on it. "We shouldn't have trespassed, but yeah. We had a lot of time to talk."

"He wears a lot of leather for someone campaigning for animal rights," Ophelia observed, filling the mug with steaming water.

"It was linked with an environmental thing. And for the record, several people tried to kick him out when they noticed his jacket."

The two chuckled and Alex hunted for the maple syrup. As Ophelia watched him, she remembered the brush of a Gone Person she had felt the night before and wondered how he would take it if she told him about what had happened. Once, years ago, she had mentioned the people she had seen as a child. He had reacted by telling her that he had spent half his childhood pretending he was a seahorse and she knew he didn't get it. Gauging his current exhausted appearance, she decided to wait and pretended not to notice when he left his dishes in the sink.

There was no sign of their Irish guest all day and Alex mentioned that he worked a lot. Brennan's guitar case, decorated in stickers of the Irish flag, harps and Celtic knots, rested against the wall in the corner of the room. She mused over what kind of person would stay at the house of someone he had only recently met, then wondered if the duffle bag was everything he owned.

Ophelia finished several pages of her thesis before heading over the Santa Cruz Mountains to her university by bus. The afternoon sunlight filtered through the redwood trees on either side of the highway. She had a habit of gazing out the window during the twisting ascent until she passed a gap in the trunks where she was greeted by a magnificent view of the rugged green ridges that always stirred something deep within her. It was only ever a glimpse, but it was enough for her to feel happy that she was safely inside a vehicle and yet longing to launch from it all at once.

Once past the summit, she spent the rest of the hour-long ride on the phone with Adam since she wouldn't see him until the following day. The sound of his deep voice and the satisfaction over getting work done on her paper had all but chased the arrival of the Irishman out of her head. The weather on the other side of the range was often different to that of the coast, but she did her best to cover all bases by wearing purple skinny jeans and a charcoal V-neck under her favorite cream knit cardigan, all finished off with her yellow and pink floral galoshes, even though there was no rain in the forecast. Her somewhat eccentric wardrobe often prompted Alex to claim she dressed like a colorful granny.

"Oh," she said with a little squawk. "You forgot to text me last night."

"Well guess what? I didn't crash and die," Adam teased.

"You could've," she insisted.

"You are so paranoid," he chuckled. "When has anything like that ever actually happened to you? Never, right?"

Ophelia shrugged even though he couldn't see her, picking at a ball of thread on her sweater. "You read about it all the time. Most car accidents happen within ten miles from home."

Adam sighed on the other side. "Well, in that case, I will be extra vigilant."

"Thank you," she said.

"Anything for you, babe."

Ophelia was smiling when she got off the bus, and as she strolled past the lawns and old Spanish buildings of San Jose State University in the setting sun, she mused over how lucky she was to be studying what she adored and to have Adam's arms to snuggle under at the end of a hard day. Whenever she was around him, she felt a weight lifted, as if she didn't have to make any decisions. She could just relax. Safe. Even if having a visit from a Gone Person last night for the first time in two decades had left her feeling like something, or someone, was missing.

Her two classes were back-to-back, and while in the midst of a seminar discussion on post-Great War Modernism and women in Hemingway's writing, Ophelia was once again amused by the differences between her beach town and the more conservative nearby Silicon Valley. An average afternoon in Santa Cruz could be spent amid women who didn't shave, men who screamed angry poetry, and people who told her she looked "exotic" and tried to place her race. Their guesses often amused her, for they always focused on her island blood rather than her predominant British heritage, and were nearly always wrong.

At the end of the day, she was happy to return to the fog and the gulls, even if it meant a commute. Boarding the bus at ten that night, she found a seat by a window and popped in her headphones, eager to let her tensing mind relax from the stress of only having a month to finish her thesis before she could graduate the following semester.

Closing her eyes, she rested her forehead against the window and the humming vibrations in the glass lulled her as the bus wound through the city streets and onto the twisting roads of the mountainous Highway 17. The ukulele song she was listening to finished, switching to a stringed, Classical tune. By the time she realized that she didn't recognize the music, it echoed around her, as if coming from speakers in the vehicle, and the chitchat of other passengers faded away.

"Now?" Ophelia whispered, startling herself and cutting off the music. Blinking, she glanced around the aisle, realizing that no one could hear her over the roar of the engine. Not that she would be the first person to talk to herself on a bus.

"Ladies and gentlemen," a male voice with a posh English accent echoed to her. The stringed tune returned with his voice, along with the scuff and shuffle of shoes sliding over a wood floor. She was filled with the sensation of movement, and before her waking eyes, the bus faded away and she was standing on a dais in a grand ballroom, her gloved hand linked around a man's arm. Heat radiated from his body, making her more uncomfortable as she gazed out at the couples waltzing and chatting. A corset hugged her torso, keeping her rigid and poised in her heavy, full-skirted gown. Her hair was all up on her head in a style that pinched her scalp and her shoes were anything but comfortable, yet still, she smiled.

Why am I smiling?

It was the last conscious thought Ophelia had before being fully consumed by this other woman.

The black suits of the musicians beside her stood out in contrast to the mint green of the walls, accented by gold filigree crown moulding. Her bare arm was scratched by the red wool of her escort's red military tunic and the sensation reminded her of her riding coat. She suddenly longed for her thighs to be wet from shrubs after a rain, her hair damp and cool as the wind tugged wisps free, the steady rhythm of a horse's withers beneath her, its hooves galloping with the pace of her heart.

How long has it been since I last rode?

Her mother had forbidden such excursions on the grounds of them being unladylike, however Amelia suspected that it had more to do with keeping her out of the sunlight. The richness of her complexion was darkened by time out of doors. Through the various powders purchased, her mother had made it very clear that she was to represent the epitome of an English rose and shun all thoughts of exertion or adventure.

"Ladies and gentlemen," the man at her side repeated, louder. The musicians stopped playing. Suddenly faces were peering up at her with pleasant smiles. So many faces. She clung tighter to the man at her side, her knees feeling like they had disappeared under the glisten of so many eyes. "I have an announcement."

She was shaken out of her momentary stupor when he shifted her left hand to his and raised it, the ring on her finger catching in the light of the massive chandelier overhead.

"Lady Amelia Grey Hollingberry and I are to be wed."

A chorus of approving coos and applause followed, during which Amelia chuckled softly, more out of the stress of so many minds thinking of her than from any genuine amusement. There was a blur of red at her side and the gold embroidery of her fiancé's collar and shoulder boards shimmered as he bowed. Amelia was left gazing at the top of his head. It was so slicked and darkened with pomade that she realized she didn't even know his natural hair color.

A chorus of congratulatory remarks filled the air as the applause died down. The waltz began again, to her immense relief, and the dark hues of the ladies' gowns became drifting dots of color in her peripheral. Her heart thudded as she was escorted off the dais, watching her feet, careful not to step on the inseam of her salmon gown.

"Amelia," a husky female voice greeted, and Amelia looked up to spot her sister Lucy with her arm twined around that of a soldier. It was a military dance, after all. "This is Mr. Richard Meyer, second-lieutenant. Mr. Meyer, this is my sister and Captain Charles—"

"Captain Kent and I are already well acquainted," the young man said softly, cutting her off. "Him being my superior."

"Yes," Lucy replied, her blue eyes sparkling in the bright lamplight, her chestnut curls twisted elegantly on her head with a few framing her bright face. "How remiss of me. Of course."

"Not to worry," Kent assured.

"Only Mr. Meyer and I were just talking," Lucy continued, and Amelia couldn't help but smile over the excited energy beaming from her sister, "and it seems he knows the Clarkes."

"Well, they are practically family," Amelia said, relief surging through her over being back amongst the other revelers. The warmth in Mr. Meyer's brown eyes when he looked at her younger sister made Amelia pay him more heed. "We shall have to have you all over for dinner some evening."

"Excellent," Kent said from her side. "Now, if you'll excuse us?"

"Of course," Mr. Meyer replied with a bow.

Amelia shot her grinning sister a covert wink as her fiancé led her onto the dance floor.

Fiancé. I am to be wed.

Though she had agreed to the marriage some time ago, it felt more real now that it was in the public eye. Most of the men present were either neighbors or soldiers from the nearby barracks, nearly all of whom were under her future husband's command. Being seen with such a respectable man gave her a glow of pride, power even, though she knew such thinking wasn't very befitting a woman in her situation.

Linking her right hand with his, she placed her left on his shoulder while his settled on her lower back, though she could barely feel it beneath the whale bone stays. The perfume of the other ladies couldn't quite cover the scent of sweating feet in slippers. Flushed, she hoped that she didn't smell, for Kent's sake. Over his shoulder, she spotted a set of black tails as a footman wandered the perimeter of the room, offering the guests refreshments from a silver tray. The sight of his livery and dark hair made her heart stutter with the memory of the scent of horse sweat and the creak of the stable door when he first caught her sneaking back to the stalls with her mount.

Leander. He had said he wouldn't tell.

Amelia forced herself to look away as she and her partner joined in the waltz. She leaned back into Kent's hand and bent her knees as they danced, and while she spun, she glimpsed Leander inclining his head to guests. His shoulders angled as he began to turn towards the dancers, and suddenly the music surged up, like a great wave, pressing against her ears.

Ophelia gasped, coming back into herself with a start as her ears popped and the bus slowed jerkily in sudden traffic. She looked about her with unblinking eyes, her heart hammering as she adjusted to her surroundings. The music piping into her ears was Bluegrass. Hastily clicking the back button, she listened to the intros of a few more songs, searching for the waltz tune that wasn't there.

Sighing, she leaned against her seat and closed her eyes. Sweat cooled on her forehead and she tugged her ear buds out and turned off her music. The sights and sounds of the ball that had felt so vivid only moments before were already starting to fade, like a week old memory. Though Ophelia knew what she had seen was much older than a week or month or a year.

Amelia had showed Ophelia a piece of her life, just as the Gone People had when she was small, and with a start, Ophelia realized that Lucy was the girl she had often seen as a child. Maybe too much time had passed for her to accurately remember the glimpses she'd had as a little girl, but she never remembered feeling someone else's emotions, or hearing thoughts.

What's wrong with me? Pressure bloomed behind her eyes and she rubbed them as a headache settled in her skull. *Who the hell are Lady Amelia and Leander? Captain Kent?* She searched her repertoire of historical figures and came up short. Or maybe the pain in her head just forced her to stop thinking.

When she entered the house a half hour later, she found Brennan's chest rising and falling languidly on the couch, apparently having been watching a marathon of documentaries on the Atlantic's wildlife. Biting the inside of her lower lip, she tiptoed around the front to see if he was asleep. His lips were parted and air was whistling through his nose, the tips of his slightly crooked teeth glinting in the light from the screen. Picking up the remote from the floor, she turned off the TV.

Though she had thought him to be sound asleep, the sudden silence startled Brennan so violently that he flailed as he woke, and fell off the couch. Ophelia had to leap back to avoid him landing on her boots.

"Brennan!"

"Jaysus Christ," he gasped before going limp on the rug. "What's *wrong* with ya?"

"I'm sorry!"

"Did someone die?" Alex shouted, peering downstairs with a scrunched up face.

"No," Ophelia called, even as Brennan answered with a, "Yes."

Alex's expression was stiff while he lingered on the stair for a moment then shook his head and retreated back to his room.

Ophelia winced and held out a hand to the Irishman. "Are you all right?"

Brennan groaned before taking her hand and tugging on it as he rose. He rubbed his chin moodily then plopped down on the couch. Ophelia stood beside him awkwardly, still holding the remote, taking in his tank top and the Celtic knot tattoo with a sword in the center on his bicep before offering the device to him. He looked at it then let out a funny giggle. "I just fell off the couch," he announced as if she weren't the one who made him do it, and she was thrown off by the twinge of pride in his voice.

"Did you hit your head?"

"No bother if I did. I'm already touched."

31

When he didn't take the offered remote, she pressed her lips together and set it on the coffee table by Alex's video game controllers. "I really didn't mean to startle you."

"I'd hate to see what you do when ya *mean* to." He somehow managed a wink while he continued to rub his jaw as he gazed up at her. "And ya thought *I* was the murderer. I'll have to sleep with one eye open from now on. What're you doing getting in so late, anyway, Girl?"

"Class."

"At this hour?"

"It gets out at nine-thirty but I have to wait a half hour for the bus."

He lowered his dark brows and glanced out the bay window. "You walked here from the bus stop? By yourself?"

"It's only a few blocks."

"It's dangerous. You ought to have a fella with ya."

"Well, thank you, gender police," she said, adjusting her messenger bag. "But I pack pepper spray. I'm fine."

Heading upstairs, she heard his answering, "Everyone's fine until they aren't," as her feet echoed on the wood.

Once in her room, she set aside her bag, yanked off her boots and flopped down face first on her pillow, her head pounding. She could hear Alex shuffling about across the hall and shoved herself up before padding in. She found him listening to his favorite Icelandic band and folding laundry. He shot her a conspiratorial look before eyeing the door, silently asking her to shut it. Ophelia did so then curled up on the dark duvet of his bed beside a pile of washed socks.

"What was that earthquake about?" he asked.

She shrugged. "Must be a light sleeper."

Alex snorted. "Ya think? How was school?"

"Fine..." She watched him fold a black and white striped shirt. "How was work?"

"Slow. Which is surprising because we usually have gobs of people buying coffee on cold nights like this. I got off early, though, and the antique store was having a sale. Check it out."

He pointed at a cameo brooch pinned onto his messenger bag,

amidst various buttons from nature conservancies and human rights organizations, offset with a rainbow peace sign and a neon kitten. The silhouetted white woman on the brooch was slightly yellowed with age, but other than a small chip out of the top left, the cameo was in surprisingly good shape.

"I love wondering who could've owned it before me. What she might have been like."

Tension knotted Ophelia's guts at the mention of the past and she realized that she wouldn't be able to sleep if she didn't tell someone what she had seen.

"Alex," she began, her voice soft and tight. "You know how some people are mediums and stuff?"

He nodded, setting a folded shirt aside and grabbing a pair of jeans.

"I think I might be one of them." She rolled over onto her back to gauge his full reaction. "No, I'm *scared* that I might be one of them."

Alex slowed in his folding. "Since when?"

"Since forever."

"What do you mean?" He eased down onto the edge of the bed, the half-folded jeans curled up around his arms as his shoulders stiffened.

"It hasn't happened in a long time but… today I… saw something. From someone else's life."

"Like a premonition?"

"No, it was like a moment from…. I used to call them Gone People," she said softly.

Alex pursed his lips, his grey eyes tracing the irises of her brown as he absorbed her words. "And you're… seeing them?"

"More than seeing them. It's like I *am* one of them. Today on the bus I must've dozed off or something because all the sudden I was in this other woman's body, in another time."

Alex's fine features were unreadable for the span of several breaths. "For real?" he asked, as if waiting for a punch line.

She pursed her lips as her stomach tensed, joining the ache in her head. "You really think I'd make this up?"

Alex looked away and when he spoke, his voice was quiet. "What was it like? This... this other time?"

"They were calling her Amelia. She had just gotten engaged... and was at a dance with officers of some sort. She spotted a servant named Leander and seemed worried that he would blab that he once caught her sneaking back to the house after going for a horseback ride." She was afraid to offer more details after Alex's eyes narrowed in thought.

"Leander..." he mused. "I think that's Greek."

Ophelia tested her lungs with several breaths as the tension inside lessened at his calmness. "Her fiancé was an officer named Captain Kent."

Alex's voice was surprised. "From *Star Wars?*"

"It's Captain Kirk from *Star Trek*, actually," she corrected, rising up to hug her knees. "Not Kent."

"Okay, this wasn't a space dream, then."

She picked up a sock and bopped him with it. "It was in the *past.*"

"*Long ago*, in a galaxy far, far away," he taunted.

"Alex, I'm trying to tell you something serious here."

He grinned crookedly and she knew that it was his version of being earnest. "Is that what mediums see?" he asked softly.

"I have no idea. I haven't had anything like this happen in over twenty years."

"And you're sure it's not just a dream? Something you possibly saw or read about? Like one of those period British soap operas?"

She licked her lips, her eyes shying away from his. "I wouldn't believe it if you told me the same thing, either. I don't know what it means. Maybe I have a brain tumor or something. All I know is that I'm getting glimpses into the life of a woman who's dead now, just like when I was small."

Alex took a deep breath before letting it out slowly. "It's not a brain tumor. People see lights and auras from those... not whole scenes."

"Then what is it?" she hesitantly whispered, dragging her eyes back up to his. Their pale grey sparkled from beneath the shadows of his brows.

34

"I don't know, but I don't think..." He shook his head. "You can be kind of obsessive about stuff, but that's not really an illness."

"I was *in* her head," she croaked. "I could hear her thoughts as if they were my own."

Alex looked over to his stack of books and studied them in silence for a full minute. In the quiet, she felt her tense thoughts begin to relax.

"You know," he began, "I've read so many philosophers. Each one has a different say on what a life is, and what a death is. I don't know who's right. But even science..." He twisted to face her again. "I always try to counterpoint whatever new theory I'm studying with empirical evidence, if there is any. You can't prove that a soul exists."

"But you can't prove it doesn't, either."

Alex nodded. "Exactly. And for a while I was so angry at my parents and the church that I figured it was all just bull. That when we die, we cease to exist, and that's that. But then I think of grief, and how crippling it is. When my grandpa died, I didn't eat for days. I could hardly get out of bed."

Ophelia studied his profile, knowing that he was downplaying his reaction, her eyes lingering on the bump in his nose bridge where a line formed when he was in the sun too much. They had been sophomores in high school when his grandfather's death had triggered a bout of depression. Now that she was an adult, she understood his grief had been much more complicated than mourning. His parents had sought him professional help after they caught him trying to overdose on his grandfather's Vicodin prescription. The memory soured her stomach and she had never been able to let go of the thought that Alex was once going to leave this world without so much as a goodbye.

Alex shook his head, his voice soft. "What would be the evolutionary advantage of feeling such pain? If we were in the wild—if I was living in a cave or something—I'd be so weak that I'd be easy pickings. So why did we evolve to feel so deeply?"

Ophelia shrugged. "To ensure that we help each other in life? For survival?"

"Yeah, but you'd think we'd have developed some sort of chemical off switch so that when someone dies, we recover quickly and aren't left so vulnerable. The fact that we haven't, biologically, makes me think that we don't end the bond because we still need it."

She chewed her lower lip, struggling to wrap her aching mind around his words. "For what?"

Alex smiled a little, his eyes warm. "Maybe death doesn't end anything and our emotions aren't cut off at the grave because a part of that person has never died. And it's that immortal part that we can still sense—that immortal part that we still love. The only reason for a bond like that to continue is if we will encounter that person again in some way. Just like..." He momentarily toyed with his lip piercing in thought. "Just like when someone you love moves far away. You miss them like hell but there's the possibility of seeing them again, so your bond isn't broken. Death could be the same."

It took a moment for his argument to unfold itself in Ophelia's aching head, but when it did, the pain subsided a little and her eyes danced with admiration. "And there it is. Alexandros Marinos' proof of a soul."

He shrugged, his hair jiggling a bit as he shook his head. "A soul, a spirit, a ghost, an immortal identity... energy... whatever you want to call it. I'm not trying to be all airy fairy but it just makes sense."

Ophelia nodded. "It does."

"So there must be a reason," he said, meeting her gaze. "A reason these entities can touch your mind. A reason one of them was showing you all of this."

"It was in England," Ophelia said quietly. "Why would I be contacted by a ghost from England?"

"Your dad's family was from there, right? Maybe it's a relative. Your grandma?"

"Longer ago than that."

He furrowed his forehead. "Great-grandma?"

"Keep going."

"Like... Jane Austen style?"

"It all looked fairly Victorian. Like the late 1800's."

He nodded, his eyes growing distant before a corner of his mouth quirked. "That's incredible.

Maybe you have some deep, dark family secret that needs to come to light."

Ophelia curled back up on the bed, relieved that the pain behind her eyes continued to ebb. "If that's the case, then I wish I could control it. From what I remember, it just sort of… happens. I have no say in how or why."

"Maybe a real medium could help you learn to harness it."

"Maybe," she said with a yawn. "Or maybe I'm just insane and you're insane for believing me."

"Well, that's been true for years," he reasoned, refolding the jeans. "Why would it suddenly matter now?"

Ophelia smiled at him. "I love you."

"Turd-nugget."

She lightly smashed her foot against his butt before sobering. "Thank you for listening."

"Of course, Elephant. You have to tell me if it happens again."

"I will."

He chuckled softly, shaking his head and glancing at the door in a habit that Ophelia knew was from not wanting others to overhear whatever he was about to say. A habit formed growing up hiding who he was. "I really thought someone had been killed earlier. Like, I literally felt the house shake."

Ophelia laughed louder than she meant to. "He was like a fish out of water."

"How does that even *happen*?"

"Ask *him*."

Alex shook his head before going back to folding his clothes. Ophelia watched him with slightly narrowed eyes, wondering why talking about Brennan's mishap made him feel secretive. Unless the Irishman himself made him feel something. "Do you think he's gay?"

"Who?"

"Brennan."

Alex set his folded jeans aside. "Nah."

37

Ophelia grabbed a shirt and began to fold, and Alex bumped her knee with his in thanks.

"I mean..." Alex began softly, his tension giving away that he had been gathering courage in the quietness. "He is kind of cute, though, in a lost-puppy-former-drug-addict kind of way."

"He wears tight pants. Like, really tight pants."

"I know," Alex said, a soft laugh in his voice.

She laughed, glad that she wasn't the only one who noticed, for looking at other boys made her uncomfortable, as if she were harming Adam in some way. "You're joking about the drugs, right?"

Alex pressed his lips together and looked away, as if worried he had said too much.

Ophelia shoved at his arm. "Alexandros."

"It was heroin and he's been clean for almost six months now," he hissed in a rush. "He's not dangerous or anything."

She shook her head, feeling vindicated for having thought Brennan looked shady the moment she saw him. "Thanks for telling me this *after* he's been living here."

"Shh, he might hear you."

"If he did, we would know, because there would have been another earthquake downstairs."

"You didn't care when you found out he'd spent the night in jail."

"Because he was with *you*," she hissed. "This is different. This isn't weed or—" She cut herself off, cricking her jaw as she shook her head. "Adam's gonna be pissed."

"So don't tell him."

Ophelia moodily shoved the pants she was folding into a pile, realizing that Alex was right. Softening, she observed her friend and waited until he met her eyes before she spoke. "Thank you."

"For what?"

"For believing me."

Alex smiled and stopped folding to wrap an arm around her in a hug, kissing the top of her head, and she realized that her headache was gone.

The following afternoon, Adam screwed one eye shut in thought while Ophelia watched him from behind a flashcard.

"I know this one… it's like, right on the temple." His brows nearly touched as he hunted for the word. "Pterion?"

She smiled and nodded. "And it's an important part of the skull because…?"

"It's the smallest bone?"

Ophelia scrunched up her face at his wrong answer. "The weakest."

"Dammit," he hissed, slapping his thigh. "I swore I *knew* that one. Patients with a trauma there can bleed out in minutes."

"You were close, babe."

"Close doesn't count," he groaned. "I'm gonna get someone killed if I don't get this right."

Ophelia sighed and set the cards down. "Why don't we take a break?" He moodily snatched the cards from her and she held her hands up defensively. "Oookay, never mind, then."

"Pterion. *Pterion*," he chanted to himself.

Rising, Ophelia headed into the kitchen and pulled out a loaf of Alex's vegan bread to make a sandwich. Adam's mood often depended on his hunger and he seemed like he needed to eat. "Want a PB&J?"

When Adam didn't answer, she shook her head and started making two anyway, knowing there was no reasoning with him when he had that determined tone. Glancing at the clock, she felt an anxious tug in her stomach. It was nearly four and she hadn't done any work on her thesis yet. She was halfway through spreading jam over one side of the bread when there was a knock at the door.

Ophelia answered it to find Brennan, whose eyes immediately darted to the jam-stained butter knife in her hand as if it were a bloodied weapon, and then back to her face with a screwy look. She hastily relaxed her posture.

"Oh, come *on*."

He shook his head and raised his brows, looking comically innocent. "I didn't say anyt'ing."

"I'm making sandwiches," she explained as she stepped aside to let him in. He was carrying his jumpsuit in a plastic bag, bringing with it the scent of oil and grease. He slowed his pace when he noticed Adam on the couch. Squaring his shoulders, he eyed the other man as he passed.

"Heya, Adam," he chirped.

Ophelia was relieved when the blonde glanced up with a smile, for sometimes he could get so distracted as to appear rude. Brennan disappeared into the cramped laundry room down the hall beneath the stairs so Ophelia went back to making their late lunch. She had only just set two sandwiches down on their plates when Alex came home and sprinted upstairs for the bathroom with a shouted, "I'm about to pop!"

Adam gritted his teeth and stared all the harder at his flashcards.

Brennan strolled out of the laundry room and into the kitchen, swiping a sandwich off a plate and taking a bite with such ease that Ophelia could hit him. "T'anks, love."

She blinked in surprise, leaning her head towards him. "What are you *doing*? That's mine."

"Itish?" he asked around a mouthful, his eyes widening. "I thought youwere—"

She held up a hand. "No, just… wait until you've swallowed."

"Whoo, I feel better," Alex announced as he hopped back downstairs then spotted the second sandwich. "Oh, sweet. You're awesome." He snatched it up and took a massive bite.

Ophelia looked between them, at a loss for words at the travesty. Brennan swallowed his mouthful dryly and fixed her with a guilty expression before offering her back the sandwich, jam dripping.

She shoved it at his chest. "Trust me, I don't want it."

"Oh, shit, were these…?" Alex asked, his wide eyes darting between the two.

She glared at him. "Do you honestly think I was sitting around all day, just pining for the moment two of my boys would get home so that I could make them sandwiches?"

Her lecture seemed to have only made Brennan hungrier. "*Your* boys?" he asked as he ate, his eyes dancing with amusement.

Ophelia's eyes flashed, daring him to speak with his mouth full again.

"I saw Brennan take one so I assumed they were extras."

"Dude, did he just eat my sandwich?" Adam called from the other room.

"Yes," Ophelia shouted back.

"*Dude!*"

"Tell him to make his own feckin' sandwich next time," Brennan mumbled after swallowing the last bite and grabbing more bread.

Ophelia watched him in shock as she realized that he not only finished a whole sandwich in less than two minutes, but was going back for another. "Same to you. And isn't the Famine over in Ireland?"

"Not at the shop."

Alex chewed slowly, each movement of the jaw ridden with shame as Ophelia narrowed her eyes at him.

"Girl," Brennan said, drawing her attention as he smeared crushed peanuts on the bread. His snug undershirt hugged the thin muscles of his chest and she hated herself for softening her anger towards him as she noticed. "I'm sorry," he said, locking eyes with her. "I thought you meant you were making loads of them."

"*Apparently.*"

"It's really good," Alex offered, saluting her with his sandwich.

"Quit talking about it," Adam whined from the other room.

"You poor baby," Ophelia chuckled, padding over to him and leaning across the sofa to slide her hands down his thick biceps. She eyed his flashcard with a picture of a wrist bone while he hugged her arm. "Life's unfair, isn't it?"

He smiled begrudgingly then tugged her down onto his lap, making Ophelia squawk with laughter as she clumsily landed on him.

"You know you're my secret weapon," he said quietly, wrapping an arm around her waist as she relaxed against his broad chest.

"Funny. Earlier I got the impression that I was annoying you."

He smiled then gently tugged on a shoulder-length curl. "Never."

Ophelia kissed him, playing with the tip of his tongue, and as he rubbed her back, she lost track of time until something scuffed on the coffee table. Breaking away from each other, the pair shifted to look at the two sandwiches Brennan had just set down.

"Hey, thanks, man," Adam said, lunging to reach the plate.

Brennan merely flitted them an apologetic look before darting back into the kitchen, making Ophelia feel awkward for having been kissing in front of company. She watched him go, knowing she ought to thank him, as well, but somehow the words wouldn't leave her mouth. Something about knowing he was a recovering addict made her worry that the sandwiches were just the start and that he would take all he could from her and Alex.

She helped Adam study for another half hour before he had to leave for class while Alex and Brennan talked quietly in the kitchen as they tidied up. After smooching Adam goodbye, she caught sight of Brennan heading upstairs to shower as she made her way back into the kitchen.

Alex greeted her with a wistful expression before peering up the stairs to make sure they wouldn't be overheard.

"Have you had any...?" he quietly asked, eyeing her intently.

She shook her head. "Thank God. The last thing I need today is another distraction. I'm so close to being done with my thesis that I just want to finish it early."

"Then get crackin', girl!"

"Please, don't you start calling me that, too."

Alex chuckled softly and tousled her hair before entering the other room to fetch his laptop.

Ophelia was halfway up the stairs when she heard the washer buzz below her as it finished. Reminding herself that she needed to do laundry, she fought down a flare of irritation over her own procrastination as she lugged her hamper into the small room. Opening the washer, she tugged out Brennan's jumpsuit and was about to place it in the dryer when she noticed that most of the stains were still there. Running a finger over a dark streak, she felt the bump of stitching and flipped over the collar, revealing a nametag that said *John*.

Her hackles rose at the incongruity. *Why would his jumpsuit have another man's name on it unless he is posing as someone else?*

*W*adding up the material, Ophelia tossed it into the dryer and turned the machine on before starting her laundry and heading back upstairs. Brennan was singing softly in the shower.

"Not'ing else would matter in the world today..." his meandering voice drifted as she passed on the way to her room, prickling at the sound. Alex may have chatted with the guy all night once, but that didn't mean he was deserving of either of their trust.

Her housemate had a habit of careless kindness and she adored him for it, but more than once it had left her cleaning up after him. Like the time last year when he had brought home a stray cat. Ophelia had never been fond of the species, and where others saw big-eyed, fluffy friends, she saw cunning, half-domesticated villains. Her theory was proven when the stray ended up shredding one of the arms of the couch, chewing through one of Alex's Xbox cables, and peeing on her bed, all before dropping flea eggs that hatched all over the house.

Alex had apologized profusely but in the end, it was Ophelia who took the cat to the animal shelter and had to flea bomb the house. Facing the facts wasn't one of Alex's strong suits, and the more she learned about Brennan, the more she feared he was just another stray waiting to drop fleas.

Powering up her laptop, she dragged over her stack of books on Keats' works and settled down on her bed. Music started playing softly downstairs and as she once again stared at her paper, she found herself jealous of Alex and the fact that once he finished his homework, he was done for the day. He didn't have to fret over completing a thesis, even if he also had to juggle work as a barista.

The Irishman whistled as he passed her room and Ophelia called, "Hey, Brennan," before she could think twice.

"Girrrl?" he crooned, easing open her door to look in. His wavy hair was damp and a casual swipe of his hand left it looking so messily elegant that she was actually envious she couldn't achieve the same look. Her musings were ruptured when he asked her what sounded like "Where's the crack?"

Ophelia's eyes widened slightly, darting from his hair to his face. "You *liar*. You said you were clean."

Brennan sniffed his armpit in confusion. "Do ya demand every guest shower before crossing the threshold?"

"I never said you smelled."

"That's sure what it sounded like from where I'm standing."

"Then it must be harder to hear in the doorway because I'm talking about *drugs*."

His lips parted while the upper one sneered, his expression enhanced by the fact that he appeared to have shaved for the first time since she had met him. "You're fockin' off your nut, Girl."

Ophelia leaned forward slightly, her own scowl settling in despite her bafflement at the way he pronounced the obscenity. "Did you just *curse* at me?"

"Must be hard to hear over there, too."

"I have every right to ask you. This is my house—"

"That your mammy and da are paying for—"

"That's none of your goddamned business."

Brennan stiffened, a taunting light in his eyes. "Did you just curse at me?" he asked, imitating her American voice.

"That's not a curse."

"Then why is it banned from your feckin' telly programs?"

She cast her eyes about as if there were someone else in the room who could pop over and help her. "I don't know. Because our country was founded by Puritans?"

"So ya admit it then?" he pressed.

"Admit *what?*"

"That you've got a stick up your arse?"

She rose to her knees at that and hunted for something to throw at him. Brennan tensed until she grabbed a small pillow.

He eyed it skeptically then snorted, and it was all the excuse she needed to peg him with it. He spun around to shield himself and Alex chose that very moment to step inside, inadvertently taking a pillow to the face for the Irishman.

"Crap," Ophelia hissed. "Sorry."

Alex blinked in surprise while Brennan laughed as he peeked out from behind his friend. "You call that a throw, do ya?"

Ophelia lunged for another pillow but Alex had recovered and held up his hands. "What the hell are you guys arguing about?" he snapped.

"He's a liar, that's what," Ophelia crowed, her weapon still aimed high, even as she glanced at it and realized it was a stuffed bear. "Brennan isn't even his real name."

Alex turned his gaze to the other man who shrugged, his eyes wide as he shook his head. "I've no feckin' idea, mate."

"Don't give him *that*," she scolded. "You waltzed right in here and demanded to know where the crack was."

"I don't waltz anywhere!"

"Actually," Alex started to correct, looking at him over his shoulder, but the defiant look Brennan gave him was so intense that he submissively looked away.

"And I didn't ask where the crack was, eejit. I asked what's the *craic?* It's an Irish word. Gaelic, ya know? Good times and fun. Like asking what're you up to?"

Ophelia slowly lowered the stuffed bear.

Brennan arched a brow, appraising her as if she had just lost her chance at something. "Not that I give a shite anymore."

Alex looked between them as Ophelia puffed out her chest. "Why wasn't your name on your jumpsuit?"

"How would you know, ya snoop?"

"I switched it into the dryer for you, dickhead. That's what I was going to tell you."

Brennan tried to take a step forward but Alex rested a hand on his chest. "And I'll bet you went through my bag while I was in the shower, didn't ya?"

Ophelia scowled and hunkered back down. "No."

"So, let me get this straight," Alex attempted, his hand still splayed on the Irishman's chest while the other pointed at Ophelia. "You think Brennan's lying about who he is?"

"It said *John*," she replied quietly, realizing just how petty she now sounded.

"Oh *wow*," Brennan mock-enthused. "Call in the God damned guards! I've my own feckin' name on it."

Alex dropped his hand as he gazed up at the taller man, surprise making his voice slightly higher than usual. "John?"

"Johnathan Brennan. What, did ya think Brennan was a given name?"

"Well, given that you *go* by it," Ophelia scoffed.

"Because my cousin was also named John but that's about as much your business as your parents are mine."

"What do your parents have to do with this?" Alex asked.

"Just drop it," Ophelia muttered, dragging a finger over her mouse pad to wake her laptop up.

"Jaysus," Brennan whined before stalking out of the room, leaving Alex in the doorway.

Ophelia sheepishly looked up at him, fighting off a blush. "I thought he said 'crack.'"

"You know, sometimes I think you *need* something to stress over so you make crap up." He slipped out of the room and Ophelia got up and shut the door behind him.

"It's called having a *brain*," she muttered.

She settled back down in front of her laptop but if her focus was

46

difficult to find earlier, it was even harder now. A good hour or so passed by without her accomplishing much of anything other than reading through her notes, and by the time she did get to writing, she was hungry again.

Slipping downstairs, Ophelia paused and leaned over the railing, peering about for any sign of the enemy.

"He's gone out," Alex said, startling her, and she was surprised to find him leaning back on the couch to look up at the stairs.

"I wasn't looking for him," she lied before heading into the kitchen.

"Uh-huh," Alex replied, unconvinced.

"*May* I speak freely, my lady?" the young maid Liza asked, chancing a glance at Amelia as she escorted her down the hall to her bedroom.

"Of course," Amelia said with an encouraging smile before her eyes slid back to the ring on her gloved hand as she twisted it about, thinking of the announcement at the dance earlier in the evening, her head aching from her hair being twisted up for so long.

"You see, some of the other maids and I were wondering..." Liza faltered and sighed, pausing in her step.

"Yes?" Amelia asked, the pain in her scalp overridden by the tense look on her maid's face. Liza twisted her small mouth before glancing up and down the hall with her large brown eyes, as if to ensure they were alone, her dark hair shining beneath her white hat in the light of the lamp she held.

"It really isn't my place," Liza continued quietly. "And I feel like such a busybody to even mention it to your ladyship, but it's about Mr. O'Dowd, the footman."

Leander O'Dowd. Amelia stiffened, a chill darting through her chest. Servants gossiped downstairs and with so many eyes in the house, it was difficult to hide anything. Thus far, however, she had thought her sneaking to have been successful. What if Leander wasn't the only one who had seen her stealing out to the stables?

Feign ignorance, she told herself, and smiled with a little shake of her head. "What about him, Liza?"

Liza's thin lips all but disappeared as she pressed them together, as if the situation was causing her pain. Amelia wished she wouldn't make that horrible expression, for it transformed her maid's heart-shaped face into something pinched and sour.

"Liza?"

"There is a rumor that when the Clarkes dined last week, they made inquiries about him, having lost one of their footmen to Influenza." Liza twisted her hands so fretfully that Amelia almost snatched them up just to stop her. "We're very fond of Mr. O'Dowd, my lady, and would be saddened by his departure."

Amelia was thankful for her corset, or else she would have sagged in relief. Liza was worried Leander was taking a position in another house. Her secret was safe.

"I see," she breathed.

"Myself, especially," Liza added quietly.

She has her eye on him, that is all, Amelia assured herself. *That is all.*

"Rest assured that they did not," Amelia replied. "It would do you well to listen to less gossip."

Liza nodded with vigor, her cheeks flushing even as she smiled sheepishly. "Of course, my lady."

She opened the door to the bedroom, and as Amelia stepped in, the pain in her scalp returned as her relief faded. She closed her eyes... and Ophelia opened them.

Ophelia was staring at her ceiling, her room filled with the pale light of a foggy morning. Lying still for several minutes as the blood rushing past her ears slowed, she absorbed the familiar noises of her surroundings: the cars on the street, a small yapping dog in the distance, the chortling of gulls, and the creak of the house. She took a deep breath and let it out shakily. The last thing she remembered was waking up enough to roll over onto her back for a few more minutes of sleep.

Amelia. Liza the maid. Leander. They had all been so familiar just moments ago, but even now, their imprints and emotions were fading, morphing them back into Gone People.

"Why me?" she whispered in the stillness. "What's your secret?"

Rolling back over onto her side, she listened to the house and determined that she was home alone. She had plenty of peace and quiet to work on her thesis. If only the memory of a long ago waltz and gossip with a maid would leave room in her head for her paper's argument. Whatever was going on with the stately country house and her possible ancestor was certainly an intrigue. Sitting up slowly, she tested her head, relieved to feel only slight pressure in her sinuses rather than the sharp pain that had followed her last vision.

Rising, she headed downstairs and ate a bowl of cereal, encouraging the scenes from her dream to waft away like smoke. As she chewed, she noticed Brennan's guitar resting against the wall by the vase with the branch arrangement that he had all but destroyed as soon as he had walked in the door. A spark of irritation flared up at the memory of their argument the night before, but she reminded herself that it had been her in the wrong, not him. Even if he had eaten her sandwich.

Her parents once offered to pay for her to study for a semester in Dublin, Ireland, but in the end, she had refused. Her rationale was that the classes offered were repeats of ones she had already taken, which was true, but in reality, it was the thought of being so far from what was familiar to her that frightened her into staying. As such, she couldn't even imagine the pluck it must take to move to another country indefinitely as Brennan had done. And by the sound of it, his time in America so far had been less than perfect. The last thing she wanted to be was that annoying Californian girl who jumped down his throat over a cultural misunderstanding.

It was early yet, or so she told herself, since it was before noon, and she rationalized that she would have plenty of time to write later in the day. In the meantime, she got dressed and headed out in her knitted cardigan over her favorite long lavender tank top that was soft with age, her jeans tucked into her floral galoshes as she strode through the fog and down the streets of Santa Cruz.

49

As she approached downtown, the amount of people out and about on Pacific Avenue served to remind her that it was Saturday. The main portion of the city center was a two-lane street, lined on either side by an eclectic mix of buildings, none of which being over four stories tall. Cars crept along so slowly amidst all the foot traffic of locals and students from the nearby university that she often wondered why people bothered to drive downtown at all. Small trees lined the sidewalk, providing shade and greenery to the benches below them that were mostly occupied by scruffy street musicians and resting homeless who flocked to the city from across the nation for its temperate climate.

The scent of Indian food wafted out of one restaurant, followed by that of vanilla from a bakery selling custom cookies beside it. Surfboards, wetsuits, and apparel were advertised at O'Neill's, and exotic lamps, statues, and incense from the East in a shop across the street. A fiddle player had set up beside the Organic Fast Food kiosk, his case open to accept tips. Ophelia offered him a smile as she passed, intentionally ignoring Bookshop Santa Cruz on her right, for sometimes all it took was one glance at the covers on display to entice her in and nearly bankrupt her. When visiting the city as a child, her mother often tried to walk through the independent bookstore as a shortcut from the parking garage to Pacific Avenue. When Ophelia was in tow, however, there was never anything short about the route and the girl would often wander off without even having the presence of mind to warn her mother that a book had caught her eye.

Ophelia ducked into the cafe Chocolate and ordered a coffee and a tea to go. The famous luxury drinks were a splurge she usually didn't indulge in, but she had an apology to make. Stepping aside to wait until her name was called, she studied the Aztec art decorating the walls.

A young man with well-kempt dreads and an unkempt goatee strolled in. His flip-flops were fraying, as were his khaki jeans, but his flannel shirt, orange-framed sunglasses, and Rasta beanie gave him away as a local university student rather than a vagrant. He placed his order then shuffled over to wait beside Ophelia. His head down, he made a sound somewhere between a whistle and a hum. After riding the bus for years and encountering many colorful people there, Ophelia was so used to such bizarre noises that she didn't take much notice anymore.

"Have you ever had the Frída?" he asked her, lifting his head but not quite angling towards her.

"Which one is that?" she asked with a forced smile.

"Oh, it's this gnarly Mexican hot chocolate," Mr. Bathroom Dreads enthused, but given his shades, she couldn't tell if he was looking her in the eye or not. "They put like, spices and stuff in it. It's an experience, I'm telling you."

"Sounds good."

"An experience, man," he repeated, his goatee drifting elsewhere before darting back to her as he feigned a sudden thought. "Hey, do you go to University Santa Cruz?"

"Nope," she said, wondering if he was attempting to hit on her. "But I live here."

"I thought so." He chuckled. "From the moment I walked in here, I was like, whoa, that chick looks familiar."

Instead of replying, she shifted her gaze to the barista, for the Rasta's breath smelled like stale weed and while his flannel may have fit comfortably at one time, he seemed to be in denial about gaining weight. The buttons looked about to burst.

"Hey."

Cringing inwardly, she looked back to find him holding a tan hand out to her, and she realized she couldn't place his heritage.

"I'm Trea. It's like Tea, but with an R." He offered her a lopsided smirk with surprisingly white, straight teeth, and she took his hand, giving it a shake.

"Nice to meet you. I'm Lia."

"Liiiaaa," he drawled, as if tasting her name. "Nice."

"Ophelia?" the barista called and she stepped up.

"Ophelia?" Trea repeated. "Even better. Isn't that from Shake-speare?" he asked as he followed her to the counter.

"*Hamlet*," she replied, accepting her drink with a "Thanks."

"Didn't she, like, drown herself from unrequited love or something?"

"Yeah." Ophelia smiled genuinely for the first time, for it had been ages since anyone had made that connection. "Crappy name to give to your kid, huh?"

"Heh. No kidding."

Ophelia offered him a smile over her shoulder. "Have a nice day."

"You, too, Lia."

She headed out and made her way back down Pacific Avenue, musing over how many hidden treasures, like Trea, were scattered about her little city, bringing color to daily life. Santa Cruz was known as the sister city to Portland, Oregon, so she could only imagine how many more oddities their larger counterpart must have. Turning onto a side street, she hoped she had the right auto repair shop in mind. Having never gotten her driver's license, she wasn't all that good at remembering such businesses.

Many families were out and about, heading to the movies or grocery stores. The occasional group of tourists strolled past, turning their heads to look at rainbow flags or great white shark postcards on display. As much as she was looking forward to the end of the semester, Ophelia was always thrown off by just how overrun Santa Cruz was by tourists in the summer.

The shop was within view and when she neared, her spine tensed as she realized that there would most likely be other people there to overhear what she had to say. She had never been one for airing dirty laundry in public.

A woman exiting held the door open for her with a smile and Ophelia thanked her as she stepped inside.

"Good morning," an employee at the desk greeted from behind his white handlebar mustache. "How can I help you?"

"I'm actually looking for one of your mechanics," she said. "John Brennan?"

The older man barely nodded before leaning back towards the door behind him and bellowing, "Brennan!" Ophelia winced a little, and when the Irishman didn't show up within ten seconds, the other man headed over to the back. "Just a minute."

"Of course," she replied, even if it was just to the swinging door.

Clearing her throat slightly, she adjusted the strap of her purse on her shoulder and glanced about at the fake fern in the corner and the framed photographs of the local kids' soccer and little league teams the shop had sponsored. One of the teams seemed to have done quite well, for the team was holding a tournament trophy and the teenaged boys had all autographed the photo. She was just deciphering a neat cursive spelling of the name *Ramiro* when the man returned.

He made a beeline for his computer with Brennan in tow. The Irishman dried his blackened hands on a stained rag, eyeing her with surprise. "Well, look who it is. The bigot."

Ophelia's jaw tensed at the jibe but she tried to keep her expression calm. "Good morning to you, too."

Brennan's almond-shaped eyes flickered to the clock. "It's 12:03."

"Twelve o' tree?" she asked, mimicking his accent before silently reminding herself that she was there to apologize.

He smiled smugly, even if there was a touch of exhaustion in his eyes. "You've once again proved my point for me."

Ophelia glanced at the man clicking away on the computer then back to Brennan. "I'm..." She stepped forward, as if being closer would keep them from being overheard. "I'm paranoid."

Brennan gave her a funny look before his eyes darted to the handlebar mustache and he nodded knowingly before holding the door to the back open for her. Ophelia hesitantly entered, for the workspace of the shop wasn't deserted and loud power tools revved and whirled as a handful of mechanics worked.

"I'm paranoid about him, too," Brennan muttered as he followed her in. "I mean, who does he think he is, on that computer all day? Probably trying to hack into a governmental database to steal proof that Muppets are actually alive." He sighed, shaking his head, his hands sliding into his jumpsuit pockets.

When it took Ophelia a moment to determine if he was serious or joking, he cracked a crooked smile, his eyes on the van his fellows were repairing.

"You are so annoying," she scolded, even if a laugh was in her voice.

"So you're here to insult me, are ya?"

"It's not an insult if it's true."

He pressed his lips together, nodding slightly as she cringed over what just came out of her mouth. "Right, well, I've got work to do."

Brennan tossed his rag onto a tool cart then sauntered over to the van.

Waltzer, she thought.

"I'm trying to apologize," Ophelia called out after him.

"For what?" He climbed up a step stool to peer into the raised vehicle's innards. The other two mechanics cast her curious glances but didn't seem to want to bother asking who she was amid the racket of their tools.

"For being my paranoid self and accusing you of being a liar."

Brennan shrugged and glanced at her before leaning down under the hood. The seam of his jumpsuit rode up and she pretended she didn't have a perfect view of his tight backside.

"There's no need," he said loudly so that she could hear him. "I *am* a liar. I've already told ya that."

She circled around towards his head and held up the coffee. "In that case, then have this without an *I'm sorry*."

He glanced at the cup, a line of grease already on his forehead. "Now, why would I go and do that?"

"It's really good."

Brennan's only response was to duck back inside and start twisting at something. Giving up, she set the cup down on the lip of the hood and took a few steps away.

"Where're you going?" Brennan called without lifting his head, and she wondered how he could see her. "I said ya didn't have to apologize for calling me a liar. But that doesn't make up for the way ya banjaxed everyt'ing just now."

"Banjaxed?" she asked, liking the way her tongue twisted around the word.

"You're so *annoying*, Brennan," he whined in his best California girl accent, which was disturbingly convincing. "Like, ohmigawd. This is me apologizing."

Ophelia snorted. "I so don't sound like that."

"Oh you *so* do, love."

"Okay, you know what? I take back my apology."

His chuckle echoed from inside the engine. "You can't take it back."

"Why not?"

"Because ya never even *gave* one to begin with."

"I—" she began imperiously, only to realize that he was right. Again. "Whatever."

Ophelia had taken a few steps towards the door when she decided that rescinding her apology gift would be a bolder statement and marched back over to grab the cup.

"Girl, why do ya always have to be so—" he snipped, rising out of the engine and turning swiftly to look at her, inadvertently causing a little disaster. His forearm whacked the cup of coffee that he didn't know was there, sending it flying into her chest and dousing her with hot liquid.

The power tools all stopped when Ophelia gasped and let out an indignant snarl as the painful heat soaked into her skin.

4

"*S*hite," Brennan hissed, scrambling down from the step ladder so quickly that he nearly fell. He snatched up the rag from the nearby tool cart and started wiping at the stomach of Ophelia's tank top, leaving greasy stains.

"You know what?" She shoved his hands away as the liquid cooled. "Just stop."

Spinning on her heels, she strode out as quickly as she could, heading into the front room, heat flooding her temples.

"Girl!" Brennan called after her but she didn't slow.

"Have a good day," the handlebar mustache said without looking up as she passed.

"You, too," she quipped, shoving the door open and marching out. She didn't slow her pace until she reached the old Victorian and let herself inside.

Alex was heating up a bowl of soup and fixed her with a curious stare. "What happened to you?"

"Brennan."

With that, she marched upstairs and yanked off her soiled clothing. Looking at the stains on her comfortable, ribbed top made her whine in mourning before changing into a clean shirt. Heading back downstairs, she filled a bucket with cold water then stuck her tank top in to soak before heading to Alex in the kitchen. "I thought you had class this morning."

"We got out early."

She grunted as she slid into an empty seat at the table while he pulled his soup out of the microwave.

"You okay?"

Ophelia took a deep breath and let it out slowly. "I had another dream thing last night."

"Did you?" Alex's pale, deep set eyes lit up as he sat down beside her. "What happened?"

"Amelia thought her maid discovered this secret of hers," she said, sniffing her shoulder and a curl, as the coffee scent lingered on her skin. "But she hadn't. If this woman wants my help, then she sure isn't making it easy."

Alex nodded as he blew on his soup. "Maybe showing you parts of her life is all she can do."

"Maybe." Ophelia studied the vegetable contents of his bowl before rising and opening the fridge, searching for something edible.

"Hey, I was thinking," he said to her back. "Have you told Adam about any of this yet?"

She pulled out a tub of hummus and snagged a bag of taco chips with a shrug. "Do I need to?"

"You told me."

"I've known you way longer." She dipped a chip in the spread and popped it in her mouth.

"But if it's happening again… I mean, you guys have been dating a year right? Or over?"

Ophelia nodded.

"That's a while. I've never even had a relationship that long."

She swallowed before replying. "Being stuck in an Orthodox school studying Engineering and hating every minute of it probably didn't help. You were a lot angrier back then."

Alex shrugged one shoulder but didn't argue. "If I were him, I'd want to know is all."

"Maybe," she mused, looking out the window at the street as the sun broke through the fog. She busied herself cleaning up both of their dishes after lunch, trying to map out how to approach Adam with the subject.

Using her writing as a distraction from the possibility of telling Adam about the Gone People, Ophelia found herself very productive. She had ten pages written before breaking for dinner, and another seven done by the time Alex said goodnight. Days with such accomplishments helped her feel like she had a justified purpose for all her free time, for she only had class on Thursday nights.

There was a knock and Ophelia peered out of the bay window to spot Brennan stomping out a hand rolled cigarette. She let him in without a word, even if he was fixing her with the same look he had when he had accidentally eaten her sandwich.

"Listen, Girl," he started, but cut himself off when she waved a hand in front of her nose to waft away the stench of tobacco and alcohol on his breath. Grunting with irritation, he yanked off his leather jacket and tossed it onto the couch before stalking into the kitchen.

"There's leftover vegan lasagna," she said tightly, following him in just to the doorway. "You're welcome to it."

"Cheers." He instead dove into a cupboard and pulled out a box of cereal.

She rested her shoulder on the doorframe and pointed to the stairs. "I'm gonna go, but it sounded like you were saying something..."

He set down the box with a sigh and fixed her with an earnest expression. "Are ya burned? I didn't mean to leave ya driving to distraction."

"I'm gonna assume that means something in English?"

Brennan smiled a little. "Angry, actually," he explained, opening up the cereal.

"You're just as good at apologizing as I am."

"What a pair we make, huh?" he asked with a soft chuckle and a wink, a wayward curl falling in his face as he poured the cereal.

Ophelia tried to keep a smile from her lips and told herself that she was lingering in the kitchen to fix a cup of tea and not because she liked the way the lock of hair splintered off a quadrant of his face, isolating a hazel eye. Or because the light in his expression when he just caught her attention sent a thrill through her. She put the kettle on the stove as he poured milk in his bowl then settled down to eat.

Plopping a decaffeinated green tea bag into her Artemis mug, she observed him over her shoulder. "I don't really think you're a crack dealer or anything, by the way."

"Good," he said around a mouthful, slurping to keep milk from dribbling down his chin. "'Cause I only deal meth."

"Nice try," she chuckled. "But you're not hick enough. Y'all gotta come from so deep in the redwoods that no one would ever find your mountain lab."

He grunted in agreement, shoveling in another bite.

"Where were you tonight?" she asked as she got another whiff of alcohol.

"At a pub—bar—with one of the lads from the band. There was a game on. Man U. vs Chelsea."

Soccer. Of course. And did he just say band?

"Have a good time?"

"It was great *craic*." He quirked a scarred brow and studied her from under his wayward curl. "Meaning *fun*."

"Good," she chirped before switching off the stove and pouring the hot water into her mug. She carried it to the table where she took a seat beside him as he read the back of the cereal box, milk dribbling from his spoon onto the tabletop as he held it absently.

Biting an inside corner of her lip, she plucked a napkin from the center of the table and slid it under his spoon, soaking up the milk. He eyed her as if she had just tied his shoes for him without his permission. "Are ya gonna put a bib on me, too?"

"Only if you start dripping onto your shirt."

"Christ, and ya have a fella." He shook his head incredulously.

"What is that supposed to mean?"

"Most lads want a girl, not a mam."

"Not in my experience, Judgmental Judy."

Brennan snorted. "Do ya wipe Adam's arse, too?"

Ophelia scrunched up her face. "Why do you always have to be so coarse?"

"That's not being coarse, it's a feckin' honest question."

"It's *belittling*," she insisted, hugging the warm mug with her hands as the scent of the tea wafted to her.

He let his spoon clatter in his empty bowl as he held up a hand, ticking off his points. "You hold his hand while he studies, you make him lunch, you have him let ya know he's home all right. I'll bet ya tuck him in at night."

"It's called *affection*. Just because you have no means of expressing yourself other than to make unnecessary comments—"

"I do, too."

"Yeah?"

"When I get all wound up I'm liable to bust a cranium," he boasted with a little squeak in his voice.

She nodded in mock contemplation. "And that translates to, what? Beat the crap out of someone?" He shrugged noncommittally. "What were you, raised in a pub?"

"*That* was an unnecessary comment," he scolded with glee over catching her at her own game.

"Oh, wow," she said sarcastically, "so I'm not perfect. Shock of the century."

"No one's perfect, darlin', but *you* are a hypocrite."

"Said the pot to the kettle," she snipped.

His grin was so full that it disarmed her completely, and as her irritation fled, she realized that she had lingered in the kitchen because she enjoyed their banter. Several heartbeats passed before she realized that his smile had infected her face and given her one of her own.

Ophelia looked away with a shake of her head, feigning indignation. "You must've given your parents a terrible time. You should be a lawyer."

Brennan's smile dimmed slightly as the light in his eyes flickered then went out completely. He looked down to the tabletop and used the napkin to sluggishly wipe up any sprinkles of spilled milk.

"I did," he said softly.

She cleared her throat as she realized she must've hit a soft spot for the first time. "You must miss them. Do you ever visit?"

"Not as much as I should." His shoulders lifted with a deep breath before he fixed her with a sad smile, suddenly looking much older than twenty-something. "They're gone."

"They... died?" she stuttered, wincing inwardly at her insensitive reaction.

Brennan nodded then rose and started washing his bowl in the sink. "Car accident."

"Oh my God, I'm so sorry," she said, turning to face him. "I had no idea."

"It was six years ago," he said with his back to her. "This truck just came flying around the corner in the wrong lane. We never stood a chance."

"Wait..." She set her mug on the table as she studied the back of his head. "You were *there?*"

Brennan placed the bowl and spoon down on the counter to dry, his movements stiff and delicate, his back tense. He lifted up some of his hair as he turned to face her, revealing a thin scar that ran down his forehead and ended in the naked patch on his eyebrow. Ophelia clutched her hands in her lap as he braced his palms on the counter behind him.

"I was in the back seat."

"That's so horrible."

Brennan's shoulders twitched. "We'd been out visiting the Wicklow Mountains, near Dublin, hiking until dark, which in January isn't all that late. I lost consciousness for a while there. I don't remember much." His gaze was distant, fixed on something over her shoulder, as if he could see Ireland in the distance. "The guards said it was an American or Canadian, though they never did catch the fockin' cunt." He winced, his eyes sharpening with focus again as he raked a hand through his hair, sweeping it back. "Sorry—arsehole."

Ophelia shook her head helplessly. "No... call him whatever you like. My God."

"I always wish... I mean it took a while for them to die." His voice dipped as he met her gaze and she forgot to breathe. "The bastard just up and left us on the side of the road. The car was covered with frost by the time help arrived."

"I'm sure you couldn't have saved them, Brennan," she whispered, remembering she had lungs. "Not if the doctors couldn't."

His shoulders twitched again and he looked at a chipped piece of tile on the counter as he ran his thumb over the broken edge. "Doesn't stop me from wondering, though."

Ophelia's mind wandered to her own parents: her father's grey eyes, her mother's soft, brown hands. Though it was only a week ago, the last dinner she had with them suddenly felt so painfully distant that she had the urge to call, even if it was past midnight.

"Here I am blathering on," he said with forced cheer as he straightened. "You've got that thesis to finish."

She shook her head, though what for, she wasn't sure, and despite wanting to hug him, she let Brennan slip out of the room without another word.

The next day, Ophelia wrapped her arm around Adam's as they strolled down the sidewalk towards her grandmother's house as the sun set.

"I hope she's making that roast again," he said, running a hand through his straight blonde locks to try to look nice in his collared shirt and jeans. "So good."

She smirked and squeezed his arm. While she never could understand why her grandma's bland cooking always got Adam excited for their occasional Sunday dinners, she was glad it made him happy. With his bulk, he needed to eat. A lot.

Adam guided her to the side of the street as a group of teen surfers scurried past, their wetsuits and damp hair speckled with sand, clearly unaware of just how much their boards were sticking out behind them as they padded past on bare feet. "Isn't this your cue to whine over not having gone out today?"

"Tomorrow," he announced gleefully. "Class is cancelled. You should come."

"I wish. I'm meeting my new thesis advisor."

"Sounds fun," he said sarcastically.

"Immensely. Though actually, I'm pretty lucky. He's one of the only Romantic scholars in the Bay Area and he just happens to have transferred to SJSU."

"Wait, I know you've told me before, but you're writing about Romance?"

Ophelia tugged her arm out of his and stopped walking. "Are you joking?"

"Uh," he drawled, blue eyes widening. "...Yes?"

"Damn straight. I've only told you about it a dozen times."

"Yeah, but babe, I have so much other stuff in my head that I can't pay attention."

Ophelia groaned and resumed walking.

"Wait, tell me about it again. I wanna know."

She could hear his flip flops scuffing as he jogged to catch up with her and allowed him to link their arms up again as they approached her grandma's house.

"Great, now you're mad at me."

"I'm not mad," she quipped.

"Oh yeah?"

The door opened and they were greeted by Nana, a waif of a woman whose white hair had been twisted into an elegant chignon and whose bony arms were full of hugs. She greeted them both with a soft chuckle and an embrace before shuffling further into the townhouse, leading them into the dining room.

"Something smells delicious," Adam announced. "Is that a pot roast?"

"You bet your britches," Nana said. "Come have a seat."

"You look beautiful, Nana," Ophelia said as she followed her grandmother into the kitchen while Adam sat down. "Let me help you."

"If I needed help, I'll ask for it."

K. M. RICE

"Yeah, right."

"Go. Sit. Relax. You're guests," Nana insisted, and Ophelia relented after deciding that she would be up and at her grandmother's side at the first sign that anything was too heavy for her.

The angel bow of Adam's upper lip twisted in a tentative smile as Ophelia sat down across from him.

"The Romantic Era was a period of literature," she explained.

"That's right," he hissed before rubbing his face. "I know you've told me that before."

"Well, you know what," she sighed. "I can hardly keep straight the difference between an EMT and a Paramedic so I guess I can forgive you."

Adam smirked, and he looked so relieved that she couldn't help but smile back. Tugging her arms out of her jacket, she twisted around to hang it on the back of the chair.

"Oh man," Adam said, leaning across the table. "There's like, black stuff on your shirt."

"What?" She craned her neck to examine a streak above her hip.

"Looks like… grease."

Ophelia groaned. "Brennan washed his jumpsuit at the house."

Adam shook his head. "Is he helping pay rent?"

"Not that I know of."

"He's totally left a stain. Tell him to use a damn laundromat."

Ophelia widened her eyes at him in warning and Adam hunched his shoulders, cowering slightly at her reminder to not curse in front of Nana.

"Here we are," Nana announced, shuffling in with a crock held between two oven mitts.

"Here, let me," Adam offered, reaching up to help at the same time as Ophelia. He got there first and Nana smiled at him as he took the crock from her and set it on the center of the table.

"Isn't that nice?" the old woman asked, crinkling her eyes at him. "You weren't a dummy who fell for a boy who was only fun at a party. You picked a keeper."

64

Ophelia slunk back into her seat, pressing her lips together since she had tried to help, as well.

"I'll pretend we didn't meet at a party," Adam chuckled.

"They don't make boys like this anymore," Nana insisted, patting Adam on the back and making him chuckle. "He's a real man's man."

Ophelia forced a smile and reminded herself that her grandmother was from an era where men and women had very separate roles.

"I appreciate the compliment, Nana," Adam replied.

"You better," she teased before easing into her seat. She opened the crock and started serving them plates without asking how much they wanted, and Ophelia wound up with one of the biggest steaming pieces of cow she had ever seen.

Alex would be mortified.

"Nana," she began hesitantly as the old woman handed Adam his plate with a smaller portion and he fixed Ophelia with a look, silently asking if they could swap. "Your mom was from England, wasn't she?"

"Indeed she was," Nana replied, settling down with her own plate. "From Harrow. That's about an hour outside of London."

"Is that the neighbor's cat again?" Adam asked, leaning back to peer at the screen door.

Nana twisted in her chair to look. "It better not be. He keeps spraying my door."

Adam gestured wildly to Ophelia and they switched their plates as quickly as they could while Nana wasn't looking.

"He must've just been cruising past," Adam said, drawing the old woman's attention back to them.

"Devious little... that's the problem with people these days," she said, pontificating with her fork. "No sense of decency. That cat ought to be neutered."

"Nana," Ophelia continued, "are there any stories about our ancestors in England?"

"Oh, plenty."

Ophelia waited for her grandma to continue but the old woman seemed preoccupied with cutting up her boiled carrots with the edge of her fork. Ophelia cast Adam an amused look over her grandma's habit of losing her train of thought and his broad chin seemed to grow as he smirked while he chewed.

"What kind of stories?" he prompted after swallowing.

"Well, now, let's see." Nana set down her fork and gazed up at the ceiling. "There's the one about the motorcar. And another about a bird nest that kept getting built right in the living room." She chuckled. "Apparently the ceilings were so high that they couldn't ever shoo it out."

Adam had a bemused smile. "Wouldn't it have to go in and out of the house to eat?"

Nana nodded her head in thought. "That's a good point. I suppose they must've had holes somewhere."

"Sounds like it," Adam agreed, shooting Ophelia an entertained smile.

"What's the story about the car?" Ophelia asked.

"That's a good one. Your great, great aunt Ida… would that be right? No matter. She was as big as a man. Now in those days, cars didn't have seatbelts. One of her children fell out and she leaned right over and hauled him back in. Just like that!"

"She was that strong, huh?" Ophelia asked with a smile.

"You heard her," Adam urged. "The women in your family are as big as men. Guess that's why you're tall."

Nana chuckled as Ophelia responded with, "No complaints here."

They ate in silence for a bit longer before Ophelia tried again. "So nothing juicy like family secrets?"

Nana shook her head then narrowed her eyes, once more staring at the ceiling in thought. "Now, wait. There was something my mother would hardly ever speak of, even when she was old."

Ophelia's spine went rigid. "What was it?"

"In those days it could've been anything. Reputations were so important. They were upper echelon, you see, so they paid great care to how they behaved and were perceived by others. It would do young folks well to try some of that. I got the impression that it was some sort of blackmail, but to be honest, I read so many books back then that I could just be confused. Just hearing what I wanted to hear. I have no one to ask," she finished with a hint of sadness.

Ophelia patted Nana's veiny hand, forcing a smile before returning to the food on her plate that she had hardly had a chance to touch while Adam helped himself to seconds. Prodding her grandmother much further would spark the blonde's interest, which she didn't want to do unless she was ready to tell him about the Gone People.

After the two bade Nana a good night and headed back to the old Victorian, Ophelia contemplated her grandmother's words. Whatever Amelia's secret, it must have been serious for her to be reaching across time and space to tell it.

Early the following afternoon, the Romantic professor Dr. Douglass sat hunched in his swivel chair, looking over the last page of Ophelia's thesis that she had brought in. "Is this everything?" he asked, peering up at her over his glasses.

She nodded, her lips tight.

"I had expected more substance this far into the semester."

"So did I. I've just been... distracted, lately. But now that I'm into the meat of the argument, it'll be a lot more detailed."

Dr. Douglass pulled off his glasses and straightened as he shuffled the stack of papers back into order. "That's just it. You don't really have an argument."

Ophelia tensed, an ember of irritation flaring in her chest. "What do you mean?"

"Keats *was* undervalued in his time. There's no question. Where's the argument in that?"

The bottom fell out of her stomach, extinguishing the ember, as she met the professor's blue eyes. "Well, Shelley claimed that the negative reviews were what killed Keats, which could—"

"You have an opportunity here to say something. To really *say* something and get your name out there. What you have isn't bad, but it's boring. It's safe. It may be new to you, but the rest of us have read it a dozen times before. I'd say you need to do more research."

"I've read Keats' collected works and I've read—"

"What draws you to him?"

Ophelia parted her lips to reply, only to have her mind go blank.

Dr. Douglass handed her the stack of papers. "Find out what it is, and start there. Don't throw any of this out. It's a good start. But don't be afraid to brush aside the Victorian sanitation of his image and go for the viscera. Reviews didn't kill him. Tuberculosis did."

Nodding numbly, Ophelia accepted the stack of papers and hugged them to her chest. She forced a smile to her lips in an effort to hide her rising panic over having less than a month to essentially start from scratch.

5

*B*y the time Ophelia got home, the sun was out in full force and her thoughts had all been poisoned by her failure. Standing alone in the living room, the air in her lungs grew humid and the clenching voice of doubt crept into her mind.

What am I doing? Am I wasting my life on this damn paper? What will I do after school? I should have kids by now. Lots of other women have kids by now. But I'm not lots of other women. I'm me. And I'm trying to do my best.

Closing her eyes, she willed the strange voice away. It usually crept up on her late at night, coiling around her stomach as it tossed sparks onto her flaws, trying to start fires, and its appearance in the daylight was even more unwelcomed.

Deciding that she couldn't face the creaking of the empty house, she swept her curls back with a bandana and donned a pair of board shorts and T-shirt before heading to Adam's favorite surfing spot, Steamer's Lane, in purple flip-flops. Peering down at the bobbing, black bodies in the waves, she couldn't tell which wet-suited form was Adam, but watched all the same as they tried to make the best out of the less than ideal swells.

After picking out the red and yellow of his board, she took the stairs down to the sand and waved to catch his attention. Adam waved back but showed no sign of paddling in, so Ophelia slipped off her flip-flops and wandered the surf, the chilly water of the Pacific lapping at her toes and ankles. The first rush of seawater was always the worst and made her hiss, but then her thermostat adjusted to the cold that was only half of her body temperature. Soon, the gentle coming and going of the waves grew soothing.

She lost herself for some time meandering in the surf, scanning the sand for seashells, focusing on the hunt for the pearly objects instead of the frantic poet in the back of her mind who kept pacing about, chucking papers into the air with cries of frustration. There was always something so calming, so natural about wandering the shore, knowing Adam wasn't far. At length, the fog returned with the tide, and the chill in the air gave her skin goose bumps. She found a warm patch of sand and nestled down against it as Adam paddled in.

"Were you watching?" Adam asked as he trudged up to her, his blonde hair nearly looking brown and flattened this way and that by the water.

"Sort of."

"Good."

"You did a lot of sitting," she teased, rising.

"I know. It was boring." He gave her a swift smooch so that he didn't drip on her. "But you still have your worried face."

"What's my worried face?"

Adam pressed his lips together and set his firm jaw, a line forming between his brows.

Ophelia couldn't help but smirk. "Let's get something to eat."

She followed him back to his truck and waited on the tailgate as he stripped out of his suit and toweled off before donning shorts and shirt.

"Mexican?" he asked.

"Yes, please. I love Alex but sometimes I need more dairy."

Adam chuckled and ruffled her hair. He kissed her before helping her off the tailgate and she grinned as she noticed the light smattering of freckles was back across his nose and cheeks from the spring sun.

An hour later, the two were finishing their enchiladas and tortilla chips at El Toro Bravo and Ophelia had aired her woes. "I mean, I hardly have any time and I don't even know what to write."

"Can you ask for an extension?"

"Only if I have special circumstances, which I don't. I'm just a slacker."

"So, what's the worst that can happen?" he asked, taking a sip of his iced tea. "You graduate a semester later?"

"Yes," she moaned, digging her fingers into the hair at her temples and displacing her bandana.

"Then you get to walk in the spring with everyone else. What's so bad about that?"

"It's another full semester of tuition fees."

"And your parents won't pay?"

She sighed and swirled a chip aimlessly in the chili verde. "I'm sure they would but... I'd feel like a failure."

"Lia." He rested a hand on hers and waited until she looked him in the eye. "You will never be a failure. Ever."

"But I—"

"Am a perfectionist?" he finished, arching a brow, making one of his narrow eyes look even thinner.

Ophelia smiled despite herself and didn't argue.

"If it makes you feel any better, I aced that skull test."

"Awesome."

Adam grinned. "Didn't I say that you were my secret weapon?"

She chuckled then kissed his cheek, her lips salty from the dried seawater on his skin.

By the time he pulled up to an empty patch of curb by the old Victorian, night had settled in. He leaned over the steering wheel to peer at the house and saw that a light was on in the bay window behind the curtains.

"Alex is home," he rumbled.

"There're two of them now," she said pitifully, resting her head against the back of the seat. "I'm almost never alone when you're free."

He rubbed her thigh. "No one's home at my place."

71

She smiled wistfully. "I wish. I just have to get started on this beast or I'll go insane."

"Then at least let me say goodnight."

He tugged her to his side and kissed her, parting her lips with his tongue. She mimicked him and felt tingles as one of his hands slid to her backside, gently kneading the muscle. While she never understood his obsession with her behind, she couldn't deny him his turn on, nor the fact that it made her more accepting of her butt and thighs that she had always thought were too big. One of her hands tangled in his fine, sticky hair. She could feel his grip tightening and knew he was about to pull her onto his lap, which she really shouldn't do if she wanted to get any writing done.

Ophelia let him anyway, and once she was seated, the pucker in his shorts zipper and the firmness underneath pressed against her center, flushing her body with warmth. She angled her pelvis to dig into the fabric and he gripped her backside with both hands in response. When she pulled away to catch her breath, Adam ground against her, making them both whimper. She rested her forehead against his neck, rationalizing that her paper could wait as a trill of anticipation coursed through her.

"Do you have anything?" she whispered.

"In the glove compartment," he muttered before grinding again, making her gasp. With fumbling hands, she reached behind her and found the box of condoms before pulling one out and pressing it into his palm.

"This is so ridiculous," he laughed against her lips before kissing her.

"We should move to the back seat."

"Why?" he asked, unbuttoning her pants.

"Someone might see us."

"No one's going to see us," he whined, unbuttoning his shorts.

"What if someone walks their dog or gets home from work or—"

He slipped his hand to the crotch of her shorts and gave it a squeeze, making her grunt. He chuckled at the sound. "I love it when you do that."

"Do what?" she whispered, rocking into his hand against the seam of her pants, her nipples hardening. She had always wanted him to touch them when they were playing around like this, but had felt awkward voicing such a request. Especially when grinding into his hand, his thumb pinching and pushing against her opening, was already making her crave him.

"Take them off," he panted, tugging at her shorts. "You're always so tight when you're stressed."

Ophelia struggled out of her bottoms as he tore open the condom. She peered out at the street again as she settled against his naked thighs. No one was around and the houses beside them were dark.

"Can't we move to the back—"

Adam tugged her underwear to the side and pressed into her, cutting off her response. She gasped at the itching pain as she was stretched around him, and then shifted her weight on his lap to be more comfortable.

"You all right?" he asked.

"I'm fine," she whispered, reaching down a hand to hold her panties aside as he started rocking his hips. The elastic kept snapping back and excitement coursed through her as she realized that she would have to keep her hand there. She could rub it against herself as she rocked into him without him noticing. The last thing she wanted to do was embarrass him like she did the first few times they had sex and she didn't climax.

Ophelia pressed her torso as close to him as she could, hoping they would just look like one person to any passersby. In an effort to pull back farther each time he pumped into her, Adam scooted her hips towards the steering wheel, which she wanted to protest but he was already gaining rhythm and it was difficult enough just to keep her seat. She rubbed her hand against herself with each thrust, and after a few moments she completely forgot about neighbors, even when her back made the horn chirp a few times.

"Oh God," Adam gasped above the squeaking of the bouncing truck cab. "Lia, you're so fucking incredible."

She gasped, rutting against him and her hand, gripping the fabric of his shirt with the other. Her breath came in wheezes as their rocking reached a crescendo, and she moaned as she tightened around him in climax, shaking her hips to get as much as she could out of the sensation. Adam grunted as her vibrations sent him over the edge, gripping her buttocks so tightly with his last few, frenzied thrusts that she had to resist the urge to squirm away.

"Adam," she hissed when his fingernails started to pierce her flesh, but just then he jerked and moaned, twitching in release.

Ophelia bit her lip to keep from making a sound as his grip tightened even more before he let her go with a gasp, his chest heaving as the truck stopped creaking.

"Jesus," he panted, resting his forehead against her collarbone while he reached down to secure the latex to him as she slid off and shifted onto the seat beside him. The coolness of the fabric momentarily distracted her from the throbbing in her backside as she tugged her underwear back in place. "Good, right?" he asked, lolling his head to take her in with a satiated smile.

"Very good," she panted, leaning over to give him a kiss as she snatched up her shorts.

"God, I needed that," Adam said, and she gave him some privacy as he disposed of the condom in a wad of tissues while she struggled into her clothing. "Feel better?"

Ophelia slumped back into the seat as he pulled his boxers and shorts on, the pain in her backside ebbing with a tingling sense of satisfaction. Her paper no longer seemed impossible and that slithering voice of doubt was silenced.

"I needed it, too," she giggled.

He kissed her cheek, jaw and neck before leaning across her to open the door. "I'll text you when I get home," he said with a smirk.

Ophelia wiped the sweat off her forehead then kissed him on the lips before hopping out and readjusting her shirt. "Love you, babe."

"You, too."

She shut the door and as she started down the sidewalk, she smiled to herself, knowing that he was waiting until he was sure she had gotten inside safe and sound before leaving. Ophelia gave him a wave as she opened the door then heard the truck engine start. Taking a deep breath and deciding to make a beeline for her room in case she looked a mess, she stepped inside.

Alex was frying something with beans that smelled how she imagined a market in Morocco might.

"Hey, Alex," she called as she darted past the kitchen. "I'm home! Just gonna pop in the shower."

"Okay," he called back.

Her pounding feet drowned the rest of what he said out as she legged it up the stairs, wincing as the muscles of her backside complained. She knew Adam never meant to be rough. It was just an unfortunate side effect of his strength to her size.

Snatching up her pajamas and a new pair of undies, she pinned up her hair and darted into the bathroom. Ironically, she noticed the hot and steamy air only after she registered the nearly-naked man shaving at the mirror.

Ophelia and Brennan squawked in surprise at the same time and his hands flew to his towel, ensuring that it was secure against his waistline.

"God, sorry," she gasped.

"You scared the shite out of me," Brennan replied, deflating as his adrenaline faded.

"I didn't know you were in here," she explained as he washed off the remaining shaving cream. His ribs rippled the light olive skin at his side when he bent over, and as her eyes glided along the defined muscles of his biceps and glimpsed the dark dusting of hair on his chest, she was surprised to feel blood once again pooling in her loins.

"You're grand," he replied. "It's your house. Besides, I try to do somet'ing that scares me every day. You just fulfilled today's quota."

Brennan straightened with a wink then dried off his face with a towel, and she was glad he had his eyes shut as he did so, for hers had gone straight to the patch of his abdomen to which the dangling towel seemed to be pointing. She wondered how a mechanic could get visible abs like that. Then again, the man was so thin that just about any muscle would show. And show it did, right down to the vein trailing away under the waistline of the towel, feeding blood to...

Ophelia's knuckles were white around her pajamas as she snapped her head back up to his face just as he hung the towel up.

What the hell is wrong with me?

"Cheers," he said quietly before resting his fingertips on her arm as he side-stepped out. Ophelia stood there, stiff and hunching over her ball of pajamas for several seconds, her arm tingling where he touched it. Scolding her body, she shut the door.

Once in the shower, she closed her eyes and reminded herself that she was an animal and that she was only so excited by the sight of Brennan because she was still aroused. As if one climax wasn't enough.

"Damn biological clock," she hissed, her voice blending with the rush of water. *I'm perfectly happy without a baby in the near future, thank you very much.*

When she got out of the shower and was back in her room, she had a text from Adam that read, **Hey babe, I'm home safe and sound. :)**

Ophelia smiled and thanked him before powering up her laptop with a sigh, closing her eyes and trying to lure her own reasons for being drawn to Keats out of hiding.

Alex popped his head in and knocked on the doorframe. "I have an extra veggie burger patty if you want it."

"Thanks, but Adam and I already ate."

Alex nodded. "Then I shall offer it to our resident Dubliner."

He slipped out and about five minutes later, Ophelia snorted as Brennan's voice carried upstairs. "What in the name of God is that?" He squeaked. "Are ya trying to kill me, pal?"

She got nothing accomplished that night, despite poring through her copies of Keats' poetry. Her mind kept wandering back to earlier in the evening, fretting over a neighbor having seen or heard her and Adam, and realizing that the thrill of possibly being discovered only added to Adam's lust. Ophelia hadn't lied when she had agreed that it was good, even if somewhat painful, which made the tantalizing memory of Brennan in nothing but a towel all the more unwelcomed.

She already had knots in her head from Amelia, but now it felt as if the two men had tied their own in her mind, as well.

The following morning, she rose and decided to go for a walk to help clear her head, hoping it would also work out the tenderness of her backside, since sitting hurt. As she stepped outside in a baggy tank top and shorts, she was surprised to find Brennan on the stoop, smoking.

"Aren't you supposed to be at work?" she asked, squinting down at him in the bright sunlight.

"Heaven forbid I have a day off. Where're ya off to?"

"A walk in the redwoods," she said before stepping past him to the street.

"*Slán.*"

Ophelia glanced back at him over her shoulder, intending to ask him what that phrase meant, when the state of him stole her words. Brennan had stomped out his cigarette and was staring at the brickwork below his boots, looking small and forlorn, huddled up as he was despite the warmth of the day. As if he was sheltering a raw, hollow place in his chest, and she couldn't shake the thought that he had no family in the world.

"Brennan?"

He squinted over at her, looking rather birdlike with his curved spine, as if ruffling his feathers.

"Come with me?"

Brennan straightened, hugging his torso. "Me?"

"No, Bob behind you."

To her surprise, he actually glanced over his shoulder, making her grin. When he looked back at her, his irritation was tempered by amusement. "Aren't ya afraid I'm going to murder ya once we're alone?"

"I never really thought you were a murderer," she insisted.

Brennan remained where he was sat on the stoop and the hesitation in his eyes, bordering on anxiety, gave her the wayward thought that someone was missing. Shaking off the feeling, she started walking and only made it half a block before she heard his running

77

footsteps as he caught up with her. Warmth bloomed on her skin when his arm brushed against hers as he slowed down to walk beside her.

"I've never even killed an insect, ya know," he said. "Least, not on purpose."

"Not even spiders?"

Brennan shook his head. "I love spiders."

She cocked her head as she listened to him. "You expect me to believe you've never once killed a spider?"

He shrugged. "I let them go outside."

"Why?" she asked with a chuckle.

"Why not? They're alive. It's their world, too."

His voice was somber so she didn't reply as they reached polished rail tracks rising out of the pavement. The railroad was once the means of transporting freight and lumber from the mountains to ships in the harbor, but had long since become nothing more than a fun way for tourists to travel from the redwoods to the beach. A popular route ended at Santa Cruz's main attraction, the Beach Boardwalk, which housed carnival rides and arcades along the shore.

Brennan rolled up the sleeves of his dark green plaid shirt until they were to his elbows, though she could see that a tank top was underneath and immediately redirected her attention from the chest hair peeking out.

"You can follow these tracks for miles up the coast," she offered as they fell into step along the metal road.

He studied the rails curiously. The two strolled in silence, letting the street noise fill the air as they crossed a few intersections and followed the rails to the edge of town where the pavement beneath the metal gave way to ballast drainage rock. Brennan peered at street signs and shops with keen eyes, and she realized that he had never headed this way before.

The shadows of the redwoods loomed in the distance, and when Brennan spoke, he didn't look at her. "You're walking funny."

Ophelia's galoshes nearly tripped on a timber crosstie. "What?"

He shrugged and made eye contact, his expression somewhat fragile. "Ya seem stiff."

She grimaced inwardly, having thought that she was moving normally. "I'm fine."

"Fair play."

They continued in relative silence for a few minutes as Ophelia tried to even out her gait. Though she had opened her mind to invite in the Romantic poet, images from Amelia's plight kept invading her head. She was startled out of her musings on the mystery of her possible ancestors when the cries of stellar jays rang out nearby. The pair spotted one of the blue birds dive-bombing a retreating crow overhead.

Brennan smirked and saluted the birds as he spoke. "My da used to say that if you see a lone magpie, it's a sign of bad luck, maybe even death, so ya salute him and say, 'Good morning, Mr. Magpie,' to try to appease him." He nodded his head towards the wedge tail of the retreating crow. "I'd say that fella's close enough." He paused before raising his voice to a shout, "Good morning, Mr. Crow!"

"That's a little superstitious."

"That was my da." He shrugged. "He was a bit old school."

She laughed at the American expression in his lilt.

"What?" he asked.

Ophelia shook her head. "You've been in California too long."

"What?" repeated with a laugh in his voice. "I'm not allowed to talk like your lot?"

"Please don't."

"Why not?" he squeaked. "I thought that was right."

"You're just..." She shook her head as she felt the temperature cool once they were beneath the boughs of the redwoods. "You're better as a walking stereotype."

Brennan guffawed. "*I'm* a stereotype? Then what do ya call your boyfriend the blonde, buff surfer?"

"Hey, we grew here, you flew here."

"Did ya just make that up?" he asked, glee making his voice an octave higher than normal.

Ophelia bit her lower lip as she looked away. "I heard it on a Hawaiian soap opera…"

Brennan's laughter was a borderline cackle at her admission.

"Shut up," she teased, lightly shoving at him. Brennan gently shouldered her back, and the press of his muscle against hers made her want him to do it again.

"So let me get this straight," he announced, his voice sobering even if he was still swaying on his feet with amusement. "You're a scholar, yet ya drench your mind in rubbish telly in your free time?"

"What, is that like, a crime or something?" she asked.

"No, it just makes ya…" He leaned his face tauntingly close to hers, a patch of the sunlight catching in the greens and browns of his eyes, and whispered the next word, *"normal."*

With that, he scampered a few feet ahead to gaze down through the trees at the San Lorenzo River at the bottom of their slope.

Ophelia slowly smiled, coming to a stop as she accepted what was as close to a compliment as she knew she would get from the Irishman. She watched as he crouched to pick up a fallen redwood stick, his dark pants tugging down as he moved, revealing more than he seemed aware.

"Your ass is about to fall out."

"Will ya catch it for me?" he replied, snatching up the branch and straightening, swinging it through the air, making it hiss. He grinned at the sound, his hair somewhat disheveled, and she kept her feet rooted to the spot when her fingers longed to touch his wavy locks as several fell in his face.

The redwoods that surrounded them were young by the standards of their kind, yet their trunks, covered in irregular reddish clumps of hair-like bark, still stretched so high that she couldn't see the tops. Ophelia paused to crane her neck backwards, trying to spy the uppermost canopy all the same. A squirrel flicked its tail on a bough off to her side then leapt onto the branch of a nearby tree, making the dark green leaves sway. The forest floor was a carpet of the warm orange hues of the fallen redwood stems covered in needles. Interspersed among the arboreal behemoths were bays and firs. Sword and bracken ferns thrived among the clover-like sour grasses that grew in patches. She had half a mind to pick one and dare Brennan to chew on the lemony stem but her companion seemed absorbed in his own little world.

"Having fun?" she asked, her voice tight.

"No," Brennan lied, swishing his stick again.

"Why?"

"Because ya won't swordfight with me."

"Why do I have to swordfight with you?"

He sighed in exasperation then headed back onto the tracks. "If ya have to ask, then there's really no point, is there?"

Branch still in hand, he tried to balance as he walked down the rail, placing one boot in front of the other.

"Yeah, I kinda killed it," she admitted, walking over to him.

"What happened to that tree?" he asked, using his stick to point out one that had been hollowed by fire.

"People used to do that to them on purpose," she explained. "They'd find a big redwood and gut them out to make a little house."

"Like the Good People?"

The expression pricked her ears for it was so near to Gone People. "The what?"

"Ya know, the folk who live in mounds and underground forts and such. From the Otherworld."

"The afterlife?"

"No, it's just the realm of the fay. Where the faeries live. You're thinking of the Afterworld. That's a place human spirits can go when they die before coming back. Sort of in-between the two."

Brennan shot her an impish smile as he balanced, as if to say *I'm doing this better than you.*

That did it. She had spent years walking down these tracks and wasn't about to let an outlander usurp her. As she hopped onto the rail opposite his, she felt lighter, and her galoshes and shorts reminded her of simpler days when all that mattered was how long she could play outside before dinner. With expert balance, she walked down the railing, easily passing him.

Brennan watched her pass then giggled, his eyes nearly disappearing from the breadth of his grin.

"What?" she asked, watching him over her shoulder.

He shrugged. "I like your smile is all."

She hadn't even noticed that her lips were curled until that moment and a blush crept up the back of her neck. The impulse to leap across the tracks and latch onto him was so strong that she almost did it. Before she could feel any guilt, she spotted a redwood switch that was bigger than his. Snatching it up, she crept up behind him then poked the tip into the small of his back, making him freeze on the tracks.

"Gotcha," she whispered.

Hopping off the rail, Brennan whirled around to face her, switch leveled at her collarbone, quirking a scarred brow.

"Now that's just plain dirty," he rumbled. "Sneaking up behind a lad."

Ophelia's only response was to swish her stick in silent challenge. Brennan held her gaze for a moment longer before lunging with a swipe. She stumbled backwards a step but easily parried the blow and then delivered one of her own. Their redwood sticks clacked together fiercely and the tip of hers broke off, making her laugh. She had to remind herself that the point of a fake sword fight wasn't just to cross sticks, but to get under the other person's defenses and poke them.

A jogger passed by them with an amused expression, but Ophelia followed Brennan's lead and ignored him, as if they were children lost in their own world. The momentary distraction was all the opening the Irishman needed, however, to go in for the kill. He lunged and swatted her thigh before hopping away like a bird, perching on a metal rail just out of reach.

The swat actually stung, so she spun about, her redwood switch whistling through the air as she rained blows down on him in punishment. Brennan could barely keep up with parrying them all, and started to giggle as he shuffled backwards on the rail in retreat. To her surprise, he lost his footing and stumbled onto the seat of his pants, sliding a few yards down the hill.

She gasped and dashed over, only to find him on his back and laughing.

"Are you all right?"

"I would make the worst pirate ever," he said between chuckles before climbing to his feet.

"I don't know about that. You *did* land the first blow."

Ophelia grinned, catching her breath as he dusted himself off. Several small cones and orange redwood twigs stuck to him, the needles clinging to his hair. Dusting off his shoulder, she silently set to work plucking the debris out of his locks, allowing herself the simple pleasure of letting the strands slide through her fingers.

When she pulled away, he was studying her with a light dancing in his eyes, and she remembered the sensation of being twisted up in a swing then let go to wildly unfurl. She hadn't felt like that little girl in a long time. Too long.

Brennan parted his lips and said something she couldn't hear over the rush of blood past her ears. She was about to ask him to repeat himself when the shadows of the redwoods spread, enveloping her until...

Amelia was walking down a dark hallway, holding a chamberstick candle for light, her body tense as she took each step carefully so as to avoid being heard. The walls around her were white and the candlelight played tricks with her eyes, making it look like the brass handles of the doors on either side were turning. At any moment, Amelia expected one to swing open, exposing her.

A breath startled her by coursing over her shoulder, puffing out the light. She jolted as she was suddenly thrust into darkness. She almost dropped the chamberstick as she spilled hot wax on her hand. Her hiss of pain morphed into a gasp as she was yanked against someone, then silenced by a hand on her mouth. Her heart raced as she was pulled backwards until her body was flush against a man's. He stopped, loosening his grip, and Amelia realized he had shifted her to a corner beside the stairs.

Footsteps echoed in the distance, further down the hall, and she calmed her breathing to listen. At length, they faded and a door creaked as it was quietly shut.

The man behind her relaxed, releasing her as soon as he was certain they were alone, and she didn't need a light to know it was Leander.

"Girl?" he said.

She blinked. *That's not right. This is...*

"Girl?" a voice called again, and she opened her eyes to find Brennan hunched over her, his thick brows lowered in worry.

Ophelia took several breaths as she tried to orient herself, feeling like she was floating until Brennan shifted and she realized that he was cradling her. She was on the ground, in the redwoods by the train tracks in Santa Cruz.

"Huh?" she grunted dumbly.

Brennan's face split into a grin, scrunching his eyes into slits. "Jaysus Christ, love, ya sure shook me."

Ophelia winced at the pressure blooming behind her eyes then shifted to sit up on her own. His hands guided her and didn't let go, as if he was afraid she would topple over.

"What happened?" she asked.

"I was halfway into my 'See? You're a Mam' lecture when all of a sudden it was like you'd walked into Joe Joyce."

She twisted her head to look at him. "I what?"

"Ya fell on your arse," he clarified, and for the first time, she noticed his voice was warbling. "Are ya hurt?"

"No, I don't..." She patted the back of her head, searching for a tender spot, but the only thing that was sore was her backside now that she was sitting on it. "I don't think so."

She shifted to get up, only to have Brennan rest a hand on her shoulder.

"Just sort yourself for a bit. There's no rush."

Ophelia nodded, closing her eyes as Brennan released her. When she opened them again, he was seated beside her.

"Do you think I fainted?"

He shook his head, his eyes dark and sharp. "I thought ya had a stroke. You just sort of... gasped and collapsed, then laid there twitching and moaning, as if you were trying to speak but couldn't."

"Oh." She rubbed her temples and when she looked over at him, he was frozen, holding his breath as if he thought she might explode. Ophelia offered him a reassuring smile. "I didn't have a stroke."

"Stick out your tongue."

"What?"

"Just do it."

Ophelia eyed him oddly before complying and his shoulders slumped in relief.

"It's straight. If you'd had a stroke it'd be sticking out sideways."

Sighing, she shoved off the ground and rose.

So much for solving my thesis problem.

Now all she could ponder was why Amelia was sneaking down that hallway to begin with, and what Leander wanted from her.

She started back down the tracks and Brennan stayed close to her side, his hazel eyes darting to her whenever she made a sudden movement. Ophelia smirked. "Now who's motherly?"

"Ya ought to go to hospital," he said, ignoring her attempt to lighten his tension.

"I'm fine, Brennan. Really."

While he didn't necessarily look convinced, he also didn't protest and seemed relieved when he got her back to the house and through the door without incident. To her surprise, however, Adam was waiting in the living room, watching Alex play a fantasy video game.

"Hey, babe," she greeted. "What're you doing here?"

Adam patted a small pink box on the end table. "Thought I'd surprise you before I had to go to class." His eyes slid from her to Brennan as the Dubliner closed the door. "I figured you'd be holed up, working on that paper."

"I just... needed a walk to help me focus," she said.

Brennan offered the other male a tight smile then headed over to Alex. Adam tracked his movement before approaching Ophelia.

"I brought donuts," he quietly said as he hugged her. She hugged him back, resting her head on his chest until she felt a tug on her hair as he plucked something out of it then held it up to her. It was a shriveled bay leaf.

"How weird," she said, trying to redirect him from any questions as to how it got there before she even knew what she was doing, because explaining to him that she collapsed would mean telling him about the Gone People, and she wasn't ready for that yet. Not when it might drive him away.

"Enjoy," he said, handing the donuts to her with a kiss before heading for the door.

"Where are you going?"

"Class!"

He popped out before she could say goodbye, and she gazed down at the pastries in the box, feeling bad for not having been home. "Anyone want one?"

"Do they have egg in them?" Alex asked, his eyes never leaving the TV as his elf alter ego ran through a forest in the game.

"I'm sure."

"Then no thanks."

"I'll have his," Brennan offered.

Ophelia wrapped one in a napkin then handed it to Brennan before making a cup of tea to have with hers. She sat down at the kitchen table and nibbled on her snack, her mind wandering to the servant's hallway and footman's hand on her mouth.

What had he done to Amelia after that?

She did a double-take when she noticed Brennan peering at her from the living room, keeping tabs on her. She narrowed her eyes at him in response and his expression shifted to one of such innocence that she thought she just glimpsed him at five years old.

The idea of Brennan as a child was scarier than she cared to imagine, for she could just picture him cackling gleefully as he set fire to whatever caught his fancy. Then again, if the playful side of him she had glimpsed that afternoon was anything to go by, he wasn't nearly as devious. A faint glow started up inside at the memory of how fully they had both smiled on the tracks.

Just then, her musings were interrupted by a fart from the other room. The backs of both boys' heads immediately swiveled to eye each other suspiciously. Alex hastily looked back to the screen as a dragon attacked his elf. "Recycling can!"

Brennan's eyes wandered the room in confusion. "What?"

"That's what you have to reach."

The other man shook his head. "What're you—"

Alex hit pause and tossed his controller aside so fast that Brennan never saw him coming as he launched onto the Irishman.

"Jaysus Christ!"

Alex bowled him over and sat on his legs, snatching up a couch cushion and beating him repeatedly with it.

"He doesn't know the rules," Ophelia called from the kitchen, finishing her donut. Brennan had his arms up, shielding his face and shouting.

"If you fart and don't say 'wizard,'" Alex explained as he bopped him, "then anyone else in the room names an object and we get to beat you until you reach it."

"Stop," Brennan barked but his laugh said otherwise.

"You have to make it to the recycling can," Ophelia shouted from the kitchen as she loaded their dishes then strolled into the living room.

Brennan fixed her with an indignant expression in-between bops, his hair sticking out every which way. "But that's *outside*."

She shrugged. "Rules are rules."

"She made them up," Alex said in a voice higher than normal as he meted out punishment. "Which isn't fair because she *never* farts."

"Ha," she crowed, climbing up the stairs. "As if."

Alex growled and slammed the cushion down on Brennan's face before climbing on top of it, muffling the other man's cries. Ophelia paused halfway up the stairs to look down at the rough-housing.

"Gnaw your way through, Brennan!"

Brennan was trying to speak so Alex shifted and lifted a corner of the cushion, revealing his red face with hair plastered all over.

"I'm sorry, were you saying something?"

"What if," Brennan started then dissolved into laughter. "What if they're silent but violent?"

Ophelia laughed as Alex shoved the cushion back in place with a triumphant roar and smashed it into his friend's face. Once upstairs, she tried to will her mind into focusing as she perused her bookshelf for a tome of Keats' early works. A loud thump echoed from below, followed by Alex's shout and Brennan's screams as feet pounded across the floor, then the back door slammed.

She chuckled softly, realizing how nice it was to hear so much laughter from Alex. Brennan was nothing if not a natural instigator, and the thought of not having him around while he was at work all week dampened her spirits. Both her and Alex had a habit of losing themselves in their studies, becoming far too introspective and serious. It was good to have someone more playful to remind them that games weren't just for children. Children...

"Ready?" a little boy with a lisp asked in her memory. He had sent her spinning on her swing. She was going to twist him up in turn when he instead scampered off with a man who was a stranger to her, never to be seen again. Never to be seen.

Jack. Jack was short for Johnathan.

Biting her lower lip, Ophelia pulled her phone out of her pocket, realizing that she had accidentally turned it off in her fall.

"I don't know where the recycling can even *is*," Brennan yelped below her window, then shrieked as Alex, who was a natural born sprinter, tore after him. She was surprised the Irishman could outpace him.

Powering her phone back on, she received two texts from Adam from an hour ago, letting her know that he was at the house and waiting. Deciding to make it up to him later, she called her mother.

"Hi, sweetheart," her mother greeted with warmth in her scratchy voice.

"Hi, Momma," Ophelia replied with a smile.

Ophelia wound up telling her about her new thesis director's request and filled her in on their houseguest while her mother complained that she couldn't sleep in the same bed as her father anymore because of his snoring.

After an hour, Ophelia realized that she had almost forgotten the reason that she had called.

"Anyways, I should finish what I started in the garden," her mom said.

"Wait, do you remember that friend I had in pre-school? Jack?"

"The boy who was kidnapped?"

"Was he from Ireland?"

"It's been so long now... I just remember they had accents. Could've been Ireland. Maybe Scotland?"

Ophelia tugged out the photo of her and her old playmate. "Did you stay friends with his parents?"

"They moved back home after that. Can't say that I blame them."

"Neither can I," Ophelia replied, distracting herself with the boy's wide grin and dark, shining eyes.

"What made you think of him?"

"Oh, I found this old picture of us. Just got me remembering, I guess."

"It was a terrible time for the whole school."

"I'll bet."

Her mother sighed on the other line. "Well, I love you, sweetheart."

Ophelia smiled. "I love you, too."

Once off the phone, she held the photo closer. The longer she looked at the picture, the more she became convinced that the child's features were the same as Brennan's.

6

*O*phelia's confidence increased as she realized that because Jack was a minor at the time of his disappearance, the media wouldn't have released all of the details of his plight. Jack could have survived, and his parents could have whisked their wounded child away to Ireland. Brennan being Jack would explain the sense of familiarity he had stirred in her from the moment she found him on her doorstep. It felt as if one of the knots in her head had come undone, releasing some of the tension in her mind.

But why didn't Brennan remember her?

Maybe the trauma made him block his childhood from his mind.

Ophelia waited until Alex had gone to bed before slipping downstairs and finding Brennan lying on the couch, huddled under a blanket, watching a documentary on the First World War in color. Plopping into the armchair, she peered at him as he sleepily held out the remote in silent invitation.

She arched a brow. "I watch junk TV but the mechanic watches obscure documentaries?"

Brennan smiled. "Because fock the world."

She laughed softly then sobered as she drank in his languid features, her guilt over bothering him at such a late hour pointing out that he looked on the verge of sleep. This was essentially his room, after all. When his gaze shifted to hers in question, the glow she felt from that afternoon tickled in her chest.

"Can we talk?" she asked.

"Are ya gonna tell me what happened today?" he asked huskily.

Ophelia pressed her lips together and sighed before shaking her head no. It wouldn't be right. Not when Adam didn't know yet.

Brennan's eyes lingered, giving her the sensation of unfolding before he muted the TV. "Then what's the *craic*?"

"Where did you grow up?" she asked, studying her hands, worrying that if she saw his eyes again she wouldn't be able to look away.

"Drumcondra."

"In Ireland?"

"Dublin," he explained with a yawn before shifting onto his back to better observe her.

"You were born there?" she asked, chancing a glance at his face, entranced when the flickering light of the screen danced in his eyes with images of men in khaki crawling under coils of barbed wire. He nodded. "You never lived anywhere else?"

"I've lived lots of places," he said softly. "That's what happens when your parents die young."

Ophelia stumbled on her own math. "But you would have been twenty-one then."

He let out a soft laugh and the amusement on his face made him look so much like her old playmate that she was certain she was right. "I was fifteen."

"No, because that would make you..." Her eyes widened and she leaned towards him a little. "You're twenty-one *now*?"

"Twenty-two. My birthday was..." Brennan's eyes shied away from hers. "It was the day I came here."

Ophelia studied the stubble on his jaw and the thin line between his brows and realized that she had only assumed he was her and Alex's age all along. Now that she knew he was younger, she found herself softening towards his immature behavior, as if he were a little brother.

No. She closed her eyes. *I don't want him to be a brother.*

"It's grand, love, I don't celebrate it," he offered, misreading her reaction.

"I just..." Ophelia shook her head before meeting his gaze again, and when she did, the little patch of warmth inside had gone cold. "I thought you were..."

"I get that a lot." Brennan put on a strained smile. "Means I don't get carded."

"I'll bet." She looked back down to her hands, realizing that despite how sure she had felt, he hadn't even been born when Jack was kidnapped.

"Ya can't sleep?" he asked, and she realized he was wondering why she was down there prying into his past.

Ophelia took a long breath and let it out as she rose. "Yeah. I'll try tea instead of bothering you." She shot him an apologetic smile before heading for the kitchen.

"Girl?" he called after her.

She paused and stared down at him on the couch. He was watching her with an unsettling look in his eyes that made her feel naked. "You're really not going to tell me what happened today?"

"There's nothing to tell," she whispered before striding into the kitchen, eager to be out from under his gaze. The knot she had thought to be untied was now twisted in an even more intricate, impossible pattern.

As she put the kettle on and pulled out a packet of chamomile, she felt a tingling sensation fading on her skin and realized pitifully that somewhere, in the back of her mind, she had been making up excuses for the way Brennan made her feel. As if being her old friend would make the warmth he gave her okay.

Now she had nothing to hide behind.

By the next day, Adam hadn't answered any of her good morning texts and Ophelia was starting to worry that he was either upset with her or dead. Her answer arrived when he came over that evening for their weekly *Survivor* viewing.

"Hey," Alex greeted as he answered the door and let Adam in. "How are you?"

"Ready for the semester to be done. You?"

"Same."

Alex tugged a blazer on over his V-neck and jeans before grabbing a pair of nice shoes as Ophelia stepped in from the kitchen.

"Hey, babe," she greeted with a smile, relieved when Adam hugged her, even if there was tension in his muscles.

Both stared at Alex who, even with the black gauges in his ears and piercing in his lip and nose, looked rather suave as he combed his hair back.

"Where are you off to, Don Juan?"

"The Poet and the Patriot," he replied with a bashful smile.

"That Irish bar?" Adam asked, plopping onto the couch, propping his flip-flopped feet on the coffee table.

"Brennan's band is playing at nine," Alex said, eyeing them with surprise. "You guys didn't know?"

Ophelia rubbed her arm, somewhat stung that Brennan hadn't told her about the gig when they had spent the afternoon together the day before. Then again, they had only known each other for a week and she had a boyfriend. Maybe he thought inviting her would sound flirtatious.

"You guys should come," Alex continued. "It's ethnic."

"I didn't know white people were allowed to be ethnic," Adam snorted.

"Oh, please," Ophelia scolded. "You look like you walked straight out of Scandinavia."

Adam's eyes sparkled with curiosity as he peered up at her.

Alex sighed and patted his pockets, making sure he had his wallet and phone. "It's Celtic Rock."

"Of course," Adam grunted.

Alex darted to the door. "See you guys there?"

"Sure," Adam replied.

Ophelia gazed down at him as Alex left. "You don't want to stay in?"

Adam shrugged and she hoped that if he didn't want to address the unanswered texts, he must be feeling fine. He was in a polo which she knew was about as fancy as he would get for going out on a weeknight, yet she felt the urge to make an effort.

"Then I'll go get ready."

"You should wear that black dress," he offered with a quirk of his lips that softened his strong jaw. "You look really hot in it."

Ophelia laughed and headed upstairs, tugging the ruched tank top dress out of her closet. She liked it, as well, but it was so tight that she had to wear a padded bra with it so that she still had a chest. Squirming into the dress, she dabbed on some makeup, flattened her bangs and combed damp fingers through her shoulder blade length curls to encourage them to tidily maintain their shape. Slipping into a pair of heels and her moss green jacket, she headed downstairs. Adam whistled at the sight of her.

"Damn, maybe we should stay in."

She winked at him and headed over to give him a kiss, hoping he was only teasing, for just the thought of having sex with him again right now made her recovering backside hurt.

"I worked on my thesis today," she said in an attempt to divert him.

"How'd it go?"

"*Pleah,*" she replied, sticking out her tongue.

"That's about how my studying went, too."

Ophelia tugged on his hand and he rose, slipping out onto the street with her. They linked their arms as they headed towards the bar several blocks away. As night fell, young people spilled out onto the streets. One of the benefits for the local economy of having a university nearby meant no shortage of college-aged bar-goers.

They passed another Victorian that had been converted into a coffee house, its rickety deck shaded by a small stand of trees. Ophelia recognized Trea on the porch, vaping and appearing to be in a deep debate with the guy across from him, still wearing his orange-framed shades though the sun had set.

94

He must be perpetually high to always be hiding his eyes.

As they passed by, she noticed that they were holding copies of Dante's *Divine Comedy.* She tried not to laugh, because he was in the same exact clothing as when he met her, only without the Rasta scarf, revealing his bathroom dreads.

"Do you know that guy?" Adam muttered in her ear before tugging her closer to his side.

"We met the other day," she said. "Classic Santa Cruz."

"He looks weird." Adam glanced over his shoulder at the man as they readied to cross the street. "I don't want you hanging out with him."

"I'm *not*," she insisted. "I hardly know him."

"Good."

"How is that your business, anyway?" Ophelia asked as they crossed the street.

"I'm just looking out for you, babe." He rested his hand on her lower back. "You know that."

Ophelia wrapped an arm around his waist for the rest of their walk, reminding herself of how lucky she felt when they had first started dating, for she couldn't believe someone as handsome and athletic as Adam would be attracted to a bookworm like her.

The exterior of the Poet and the Patriot had been painted in a colorful mural depicting a Celtic warrior, standing stones, and scenes from the old country. On either side of the main entrance were portraits of two men, one being Padraig Pearse, labeled the poet, and the other James Connelly, named the patriot. Ophelia ran Pearse's name through her repertoire of writers and didn't recognize him among Ireland's famous scribes. As she crossed the threshold, she felt somewhat awkward with the realization that she knew very little Irish history in general.

Ophelia spotted Brennan in his leather jacket and a dark green button-up with two other guys setting up in the corner, but the Irishman was so distracted by his gear as he plugged in his guitar that he didn't notice her. A Celtic tapestry had been hung up behind the instruments, depicting a tree with roots that extended as vast and abundantly as its foliage, and she recognized it as the Tree of Life. The image reminded her of what Brennan had said about the fay who lived underground and the Afterworld, and wondered if the Gone People existed in such an in-between state.

Alex waved at them from a table he had snagged. Adam tugged Ophelia over and they took their seats.

"All right," Alex said, "I'm buying. Who wants what?"

"You don't have to do that," Ophelia said.

"When else do we all go out together?" Alex replied, hopping to his feet. "Lia? Guinness?"

"Sure."

Adam made a disgusted face at her choice. "Tequila for me, bro."

"You can probably get that at every bar in town except for this one," Alex reminded.

"Fine. Then two of whatever lager's on tap."

Alex nodded and headed to the bar.

"Guinness," the blonde said, shaking his head. "I can't believe you can drink that stuff."

Ophelia cocked her head. "Dude, we're in a *pub*."

"Guinness is like, a meal in a can."

"Did you learn that in Nutrition?"

"Just look at the label."

"You are like, over two-hundred pounds of muscle, babe. I don't think you have anything to worry about."

Adam shrugged then tapped his hands on the tabletop, peering around, and she wondered if he had been talking about her body. Her dress was rather tight. *Tighter than it used to be?* She hunched down a little, realizing that she couldn't remember the last time she went for a run or even stepped on a scale.

"Ladies and gentlemen, lads and lasses," the tweed flat cap-wearing bartender said into the microphone, making the room quiet. "The Poet and the Patriot is happy to present to you Rover's Revenge."

The audience applauded as Brennan and the other two older men in the band smiled out at the small crowd, and Ophelia wondered if they were all friends, for Brennan rarely mentioned them.

"Here you are," Alex said, sliding the Guinness over to her. "And for you." He handed Adam his beers then sat down beside Ophelia, his lip piercing glinting in the muted light.

"Thanks, bro," Adam said before taking a gulp as the band started playing.

Ophelia winced as the bass electric played by the lead rang out over the speakers. *Why are performances always so loud?* It often made her wonder if she was the only one with proper hearing and wished she had brought earplugs.

The scruffy, red-headed lead singer, who had introduced himself as Brian, launched into a rock rendition of "Whiskey in the Jar" with a gravelly voice that made the song sound anything but traditional. Brennan accompanied him on his amplified acoustic guitar while a third man played drums.

Ophelia exchanged a look with Alex, who appeared impressed, then another with Adam, who looked like he was also wishing they weren't sitting so close to the speakers. Catching his eye, she wrinkled up her nose, making him smile and wrap an arm around her waist, resting his hand on her hip.

By the time the second song finished, she worried she was getting a headache from the racket. In an effort to distract herself, she eyed the other people in the bar over the next few songs, noting that many of them were middle-aged men and women, and judging by the overall whiteness of the room, mostly of Irish descent.

A small part of her was envious that they had such an accessible link to their heritage. Her mother had talked about a family trip to Trinidad for years, but they had yet to find the time or money to take it.

Though come to think of it, I can't complain, for I doubt anyone else in the room is connected to their ancestors enough to receive messages from them.

A large-chested young woman with spiky black hair and smoky eyes entered, smiling at the band before heading to the bar, and Ophelia found herself smiling as well, happy to see so many people enjoying themselves, even if the music wasn't exactly her cup of tea.

The dark-haired girl got a drink then stood a few yards from the band, bobbing to the music, holding her beer in an inked hand. Something prickled inside when Ophelia noticed that the girl's eyes and smile were latched onto Brennan.

Idiot, she scolded herself, commanding the quills rising on her skin to flatten. *It's none of your business who looks at him.*

Adam squeezed her thigh, drawing her attention back to him. "I'll be right back," he said in her ear before heading for the bathroom.

The song ended and the crowd applauded.

"We're gonna bring it down just for a minute, all right?" Brian announced, panting after the fifth song, his cheeks as pink as his hair. "And straight from Dublin herself, may I introduce John Brennan on acoustic!"

The audience cheered and applauded. Brennan looked afraid to meet anyone's eye as he offered a tight-lipped smile until Alex wolf whistled, making him laugh. Ophelia laughed, as well, and as she and Alex exchanged amused, conspiratorial smiles, she was happy Adam wasn't there to see.

Brennan started up a lively tune and the softer sound of his guitar soothed Ophelia's ears before he sang.

"Who are you, my pretty fair maid, Who are you, me honey? And who are you, my pretty fair maid, And who are you, me honey? She answered me quite modestly, 'I am me mother's darlin'.'

With me Too-ry-ay Fol-de-diddle-day Di-re fol-de-diddle Dai-rie oh."

"He's good," Alex said in her ear, and Ophelia nodded.

Brennan's voice was untrained but there was something about the rawness of it that cut through the air and frayed at the edges with electricity. The crowd around her started clapping in time to the tune and she and Alex joined in.

"And will you come to me mother's house, When the
    moon is shining clearly? And will you come to me
    mother's house When the moon is shining clearly? I'll
    open the door and I'll let you in
And divil 'o one will hear us With me Too-ry-ay Fol-de-
    diddle-day Di-re fol-de-diddle Dai-rie oh.

So I went to her house in the middle of the night When
    the moon was shining clearly So I went to her house
    in the middle of the night When the moon was
    shining clearly She opened the door and she let me in
    and divil the one did hear us."

Adam slid back into the seat beside Ophelia, looking around. "This
place sure woke up."

Ophelia smirked at him and kept clapping. She had forgotten how
fun interactive live music could be.

"Then I got up and I made the bed I made it nice
    and aisy..."

There was a hand on her arm, gripping her, but when she looked
down, there was nothing there. Until the walls of the pub morphed
into those of the darkened servant's hallway and she was once again
Amelia, trying to find Leander's face in the darkness. Rover's Revenge
continued to play, Brennan's voice echoing over the glimpses from
another time.

"Then I got up and I made the bed I made it nice
    and aisy."

Amelia's breath hitched as she reached a hand out into the darkness, her fingertips brushing against the layers of fabric covering
Leander's chest. She took a step towards him, flattening her palm
against the heat and the steady thud of his racing heart. His hand

shifted from her arm to her waist and she closed her eyes as she leaned in, her nose bumping against his before their lips met. Warmth surged from her chest as she kissed him in the darkness, sighing softly as he brought his other hand up to her hip, toying with her lower lip enough to send darting pleasure from the spot.

"Then I got up and I laid her down Saying 'Lassie, are
  you able?' With me Too-ry-ay Fol-de-diddle-day Di-
  re fol-de-diddle Dai-rie oh."

Several in the crowd roared and laughed at the lyrics and Ophelia was snapped back into the present. Blinking and sucking in a surprised breath, she realized that her clapping had fallen out of rhythm and tried to reorient herself in her century.

They were lovers. She felt as if she might quake from the weight of the discovery. *He wasn't blackmailing her at all. They were lovers. That was her secret.*

Brennan strummed and turned his back on the crowd, allowing the audience their fun before returning to the microphone, his voice and guitar far quieter.

"And there we lay till the break of day Divil the one did
  hear us And there we lay till the break of day And
  divil the one did hear us Then I arose and put on me
  clothes Saying 'Lassie, I must leave you' With me
  Too-ry-ay Fol-de-diddle-day Di-re fol-de-diddle
  Dai-rie oh."

His hushed singing made her jolt inside, as if she were in a dream and only just realized that someone was missing. Someone vitally important. The sensation was more powerful than it had ever been and she looked over at Alex and Adam, reassuring herself that they were there.

"And when will you return again When will we get

married? And when will you return again When will
we get married? When broken shells make Christmas
bells We might then get married With me Too-ry-ay
Fol-de-diddle-day Di-re fol-de-diddle Dai-rie oh."

Brennan finished the song with a wild strum and the audience
applauded. Ophelia sluggishly clapped with the rest of them before
excusing herself. She wove through the crowd seated at their tables
and the bar, through the darts room at the back and then ducked into
the one stall of the bathroom, closing her eyes. The pressure that
usually accompanied her visions hadn't shown up yet, for which she
was grateful, but this new twist had both knotted up and untied
everything she had ever seen.

Leander hadn't been holding anything over Lady Amelia's head,
after all. Her stolen rides seemed to have given birth to stolen
moments in the stables, away from prying eyes. Ophelia had to talk
to Alex.

Waiting until she felt more stable, Ophelia exited and returned to
the table, realizing that the band was taking a break. The musicians
were drinking and chatting with pub goers and Ophelia noted that
Brennan had been cornered by the girl with the smoky eyes and arm
covered in ink.

"You okay?" Adam asked as she sat down.

"Yeah." She smiled and squeezed his hand, noting that he had a
fresh lager in front of him.

"This is so awesome," Alex gushed, gazing at Brennan as the inked
girl was forced to step aside to allow him to chat with others. "It's like
we know someone famous."

"They're not bad," Adam called over to him.

"They're great," Alex enthused.

"Someone's in love," the blonde whispered into Ophelia's ear and
she lightly shoved at his shoulder, hoping Alex couldn't hear.

Rover's Revenge played a few more sets before finishing for the
night, and Ophelia was so distracted by her musings of the past that
she hardly heard the lyrics. Adam got them another round of drinks,

except for Ophelia who had hardly touched hers. Every time she took a sip, she thought of the calories that she didn't need.

The band was finishing up so Alex thanked Adam for the beer then made his way over to Brennan. The Irishman grinned and laughed as they chatted.

"In *looove*," Adam teased again, and Ophelia realized that she was smiling at the sight of her two happy housemates.

"Leave him alone," Ophelia reprimanded. "He's confused enough already."

"I don't see how. You either like chicks or you don't." Adam took a swig of his fourth drink.

"It's not that simple."

"Of course it is."

"Love never is," she muttered, surprising herself.

Adam leaned his ear closer to her. "Huh?"

"Nothing, dear," she teased, patting his cheek. "You better not have surfer's ear."

He shook his head no before polishing off his beer. "Hey—I'm getting another one. Keep drinking."

"Adam, you have class in the morning."

"You only live once, right?" he called to her as he made his way towards the bar, laughing a little too enthusiastically at his own joke.

Ophelia sipped her beer and scanned the room again, knowing he would regret it if he had a hangover tomorrow. Alex was now talking to a very clean-looking young man with short-cropped, black hair and a kind, full-lipped smile. Ophelia tried to keep her expression lax as she noticed that the two kept looking away during lulls in their conversation, their eyes dancing as they clearly hunted for excuses to keep their dialogue going.

Brennan was at the bar, leaning over to order a drink, and Ophelia felt like she ate something sour at the sight of the inked girl's arm around his waist as she clung to him. Brennan shot the young woman a look of affection that Ophelia had never seen on his face before, and she tensed at the sight.

Good. He ought to have someone. It's not like we—

"Babe?"

Ophelia looked up to see Adam peering down at her with concern and realized that he must've been trying to get her attention for a few seconds.

"You okay?" he asked before darting his eyes over to the bar.

"Can we go after you finish that?" she asked, because the girl was now hugging Brennan and the room seemed to have gone cold.

Adam nodded then chugged his drink, making her flinch.

"That's not what I meant!"

He burped then kissed her on the cheek and held out his hand. Taking it, Ophelia rose and tugged her dress in place before waving goodbye to Alex. As they headed towards the coolness of the open door, she thought she saw Brennan wrench his neck to look at her, but she didn't turn around.

Once outside, she leaned against Adam and he hugged her to him as they walked home. With a wave of envy tinged with guilt, she tried to focus on the man beside her rather than the one she had just left behind. Back in the old Victorian, she slipped out of her heels, her feet aching from having walked in them for so long. She was startled by Adam's hands on her hips, caressing her rump and thighs.

"Looks like we're home alone," he whispered in her ear with the smell of beer on his breath.

"I'm too tired," she lied, tensing as his hand slid over a bruise.

"No one can ever be too tired to have sex."

"Try being a grad student."

He settled for kissing her neck and wrapping his arms around her from behind. Ophelia closed her eyes and leaned back into his chest, but her relaxation was ruined by his quiet words. "What were you and Brennan doing yesterday?"

Ophelia opened her eyes and inadvertently tensed her spine. "We went for a walk. He'd never been on the tracks."

"You had leaves in your hair."

"Is it shocking that there are leaves in a forest?"

He pulled away and moved to lean against the back of the couch, and she knew for certain that he had ignored her texts on purpose.

"What's this about?"

Adam shrugged. "You tell me."

"What, you think we ran off and did it in the woods or something?"

There was no amusement in his eyes. "Looked like you'd been lying on the ground. You had dirt in your hair, too."

The muscles of her chest flared up, as if smoldering at the accusation. She stared at him with wide brown eyes. "Baby, that *isn't* what—"

"Maybe you don't want to have sex with me because you're doing it with someone else."

Ophelia pulled her shoulders back as the smoldering sensation morphed into irritation. "Are you *serious*?"

Adam studied her for a few moments before rubbing his face, his eyes drooping a bit at the corners with tiredness. "I don't know. Not really. But I keep worrying...."

"Why?" She tentatively stepped up to him, feeling like he had reverted to that confusing, unknown quantity who she had first fallen for. "When have I ever given you a reason to doubt me?"

"You haven't," he sighed, dropping his hands.

"Then why are you—"

"Why are *you* always convinced that I'm going to crash and die on my drive home?" he quipped back. "Sometimes people just... worry."

Ophelia's expression softened and she rested a hand on his shoulder, the tension inside her lessening.

Adam shook his head. "And you seemed upset that he was talking to that chick."

"I wasn't upset," she snipped, pulling her hand away. "I was spying."

Adam slowly smirked. "Spying?"

"Adam," she said, grabbing his hand. "I love you."

"It's just weird, though. Having another dude in your house who isn't gay. I don't like it."

"What am I supposed to do, kick him out?"

"Yeah... or, I dunno," Adam said as he toyed with her hand, "move in with me."

Ophelia sighed and tugged her hand out of his. They'd had this conversation before and it always made her feel claustrophobic. "Your place is tiny."

"Then I'll move in here," he suggested hopefully.

She shook her head. "If you're here twenty-four seven, I'll *never* get any work done."

Adam studied her, hurt flashing in his blue eyes, lowering his brows, before being replaced by something hard and unreadable that made his expression sharp. She parted her lips to explain when he hissed and shook his head dismissively, jerking away and heading for the door.

"Where are you going?"

"This is bull."

"Adam," she scolded, following him. "What're you doing? You're being ridiculous."

"Whatever." He yanked out his keys and opened the door.

Ophelia scurried over to follow him out only to have the wood slammed in her face. She froze, blinking from the echo in the old house and the eerie silence that followed.

7

"*S*hit." Digging her fingers into her bangs, Ophelia sucked in a tight breath, feeling as if her insides were morphing into concrete.

What the hell just happened?

She groaned and sank down onto the floor, tugging her phone out of her jacket, tempted to call Adam but hearing the rumble of his truck and seeing the flash of his headlights as he drove away halted her. He was only just out of the house.

What am I doing? She stared at his name on the screen. *I've done nothing wrong. Since when am I a pitiful little girl chasing after a boy?* Stuffing the phone back into her pocket, she rose and ignored the way her legs felt like jelly as she crawled onto the couch.

Resting her cheek on the cushion, she caught a whiff of an unfamiliar aftershave. The fabric smelled like Brennan. Something slid onto her cheek and she realized she was crying. Remaining motionless, she allowed the room to dissolve into a blurry mess as her eyes teared up.

Ophelia repeated their argument again and again in her mind, comforting herself with the fact that she hadn't said anything intentionally hurtful. If it stung that she wasn't ready for him to move in with her yet, then he would have to deal with it. She couldn't change the fact that she needed alone time every day for the sake of her sanity, which she felt like she was losing, as that alone time was currently being invaded by drama from the late 1800s.

By the time Alex came home, her eyes were dry, but he immediately did a double-take when he looked at her. "What happened?"

Ophelia forced a pained smile. "Adam and I got in a fight."

"A fight?" he asked, coming over to the couch. "Was it bad?"

She shrugged. "I don't think so. But we've never really had one before. Just arguments."

Alex nodded then sat down beside her, pulling her into a hug. "I'm sorry, Elephant."

Ophelia sniffled and nestled against him. The thought of telling Alex any of the details felt too tiring. "I saw you talking to that guy."

"Ramiro?"

She shifted to study him. "In the suit?"

"Yeah." Alex smiled. "He was cool. He's a teacher."

"Did you get his number?"

Alex tugged a business card out of his pocket and handed it to her. Ophelia flipped it over to find handwritten digits and allowed her delight over her friend's first steps to fill her, shoving out the darkness of her worry.

"That's great."

"I have no idea what to do."

"No one ever does," she sighed. "You just... wing it."

Alex groaned. "I can't. I'm too old. I'm supposed to have it all figured out by now."

"I didn't realize there was an expiration date."

"You know what I mean. You've had boyfriends and—"

"*Two*," Ophelia clarified. "Adam and... Ethan." She said the last name as if it was a disease.

"Ethan was a dick."

"To say the least," she agreed, preferring not to think of the boy she dated in high school who dumped her after she said she wouldn't be in an open relationship.

"The point is, you have experience. I don't. I'll just make a fool of myself. Which I really don't wanna do with this guy."

Ophelia pulled back to study him. "You can have as much experience as possible but it's different with everyone. You'll always have to find your way with each new person. So don't ever waste your time worrying about it."

"I guess."

"Besides, if he's worth anything, he'll find your inexperience endearing."

"Or head for the hills."

She poked his side. "You're beautiful."

"I don't feel it," he said quietly, his hooded eyes distant.

"Yeah," Ophelia agreed. "Neither do I."

Silence settled over the two for a few moments before she remembered the press of Leander's lips against hers when she was Amelia.

"It happened again," she whispered.

"The Gone People?'

"Twice, actually." Ophelia shifted to face him, her legs tucked under her as she filled him in on the details.

Alex ran a hand through his hair, disheveling several strands, his obsidian nasal piercing glinting in the dim light. "Lovers?"

Ophelia nodded. "Nana said that whatever happened caused such a scandal that the family hardly ever spoke of it."

"That would fit," he mused. "Could be why they moved to America. How salacious," Alex added with a grin. "You have rebel blood."

Ophelia returned his smile but didn't voice that right now, she was too tired inside to care who her ancestors were or what they had done to bring her into existence.

"We should get to bed." He patted her leg then got up and locked the door.

"Does Brennan have a key?"

Alex shrugged. "We'll be up when he gets back. He went home with that girl he was making out with. She had a gnarly Celtic cross tattoo."

Ophelia looked down to her nails as her breathing hitched. "Guess I missed that part."

"Groupies have their benefits." Alex headed for the stairs. "Sweet dreams, Elephant."

"Sweet dreams."

As she checked her phone for messages and saw that there were none, Ophelia strengthened her resolve not to give in and contact Adam. Heading upstairs, she showered then crawled into bed. Remembering her looming thesis work, she cursed Keats and the trouble he had caused her already stressed mind. Snuggling under her blankets, she thought of Amelia and Leander, wondering why it was so important that she knew of their affair, even if she was their descendant. There was a piece to the lovers' puzzle that she still didn't have.

It was a while before she realized her mind had shifted to Brennan, covering her thoughts with barbs as she imagined another woman writhing in rhythm with his body. Startled by her wandering mind in the wake of Adam's accusation, she forced herself to pluck off the barbs one by one.

I'm not jealous, she told herself, *just surprised that he's the kind of guy who would screw a groupie.*

Ophelia fell asleep knowing that was only half of the truth.

Thursday was spent reading and re-reading her favorite Keats poems before hopping onto the bus to San Jose State. Though she hated herself for it, she had checked her phone at least once every hour, but so far hadn't heard a word from Adam.

She tried not to let it bother her, but worry over his silence nibbled away at her in class until she reminded herself that she was being just as silent. It wasn't until her seminar was halfway over and they finished their discussion on Hemingway that she realized she had completely forgotten to start reading the next assigned book. Keeping her mouth shut throughout the analysis of James Joyce, she hoped she wouldn't get found out, and thankfully escaped without incident.

As Ophelia was walking to the bus stop after her second class, her phone vibrated as she received a text from Adam. Relief flooded through her as she opened it.

How was class?

Ophelia smiled and wrote back, *Good, how are you?*

I'm ok.

Me, too.

He didn't reply but the brief interaction put her at ease. She hated the thought of him being angry at her, but even more so, the knowledge that she had caused him pain. Once home, she found Alex with his laptop open. He peered up at her behind his black-framed glasses.

"Hey, you."

Ophelia headed for the stairs. "If I go into the bathroom, I'm not going to find a naked Irishman in there again, am I?"

"No, he hasn't come back yet. Wait, what?" Alex twisted to face her as she climbed the stairs. "When did *that* happen?"

Ophelia chuckled as she made her way to her room. By the time she had bathed and headed downstairs for a snack, Alex had gone to bed. She grabbed a tub of ice cream but then, remembering Adam's comment about calories, put it back. The front door swung open, startling her, followed by what sounded like someone kicking a soccer ball against everything in the room. She stuck her head out into the living room to find Brennan righting himself before shutting the door and stumbling a few feet into the house.

"Are you *drunk?*"

"No way in hell," he announced, grabbing onto the back of the couch for support. "It's only Wednesday."

"Friday," she corrected after seeing that it was after midnight.

"No shite?" He straightened and glanced around, and Ophelia noted that he was in the same green button-up and black pants he wore to perform.

She could smell the alcohol even from several yards away in the kitchen. "Brennan," she scolded.

"I'm not drunk," he insisted, then lowered his voice when she held a finger to her lips. "I'm as full as a Catholic school."

Ophelia started towards him, worried that his legs were about to give out from the way he was swaying. "A Catholic school, huh?"

"I'm not a focking Catholic," he hissed, looking offended.

"I didn't say you—"

"Catholics don't have sex. It's no fun if ya can't get your hole."

Ophelia shook her head, scrunching up her face. "Okay, I may not know exactly what you just said, but it sounded gross."

"'Cause you're hammered, love."

She raised her brows. "*I'm* the drunk one, now?"

"Sure, why else would there be two of you?" Brennan squinted, as if trying to make out which one of them was the real one.

Ophelia froze in shock. "Oh my God, this is really happening. You really are this wasted."

Brennan just stared at her with wide eyes and shook his head, as if she just asked him if he were responsible for a bombing.

Marching back into the kitchen, she filled a large glass with water and carried it into the living room only to find Brennan slumped on the floor, leaning against the back of the couch. "Here," she held out the water.

"I'm not thirsty, Girl."

"You need to drink."

Brennan winced and hissed. "That's what I'm *saying*. I can't drink anymore."

As she watched him fumble with his boot, she realized that this would be funny if it wasn't her caught in the middle of it. "It's water."

"I'm allergic," he muttered. When he couldn't get his boot off, he whined in frustration and banged his heel on the floor. Ophelia clamped a hand over his mouth, shushing him. She shoved the glass into his hand then squatted by his feet to yank off his boot for him. Brennan licked his lips, looking disgusted.

"Is your hand always that salty?"

"Probably." She gave the boot a yank and it came off. Peering at him, she saw that he was watching with half-lidded eyes. "Drink. The whole glass."

He pressed it to his lips and got down three quarters of it before spilling the rest on his jacket. Once again faced with Brennan and the scent of wet leather, Ophelia sighed. He struggled with the zipper and she helped him yank an arm out of his sleeve, pressing her lips tight together at the effort. "You know, I wouldn't have to act like a mother if you weren't such an overgrown child."

"I'm not a focking *child*," he protested.

"Aren't you foul when you're drunk?"

Tugging on one of his arms, she hauled him to his feet and over to the other side of the couch where he plopped down, one arm still stuck in his jacket. She yanked it off and he was startled as he noticed what she had done for the first time.

"Jaysus, you're taking my clothes off?"

"Shh," she hissed. "Just your wet jacket."

Ophelia hung the jacket up on the cold woodstove to let it air dry.

"If ya wanted to have your way with me, ya could've just asked," he slurred, curling up on his side and burrowing his forehead into the cushions of the back of the couch.

"Somehow I don't doubt that's all it takes," she muttered.

"No need to be a Mrs. Butler."

"What's a Mrs. Butler?" she asked, adjusting the heavy leather so that it wouldn't fall.

"My first foster mother," he said with a yawn, making Ophelia pause given the context.

She looked at his back over her shoulder. "And what did she do?"

"Everyt'ing," he grunted. "Crawled into my bed the nights her husband was away. Businessman or somet'ing."

Ophelia was thankful she didn't eat after all, for not only was her appetite gone, but any food in her stomach was curdling.

"Brennan, that's..." Somehow, she couldn't find the right word to express the violation she felt on his behalf and realized it didn't exist. "Illegal," was all that came out instead.

"Well, I know that *now*," he explained, as if they were talking about an assignment. "At the time I thought it was either that or the streets, ya know?" He yawned again and after several moments of silence, she forced herself to move and grabbed the blanket from the arm of the couch.

"That's horrible."

Brennan's side rose and fell evenly but he didn't reply, and she thought he had fallen asleep until his eyelashes moved as he blinked. "Had a face like a bulldog chewing a wasp," he said so quietly that she could hardly make out his words amid his slurring and accent. "It was all right. But she had these toys and…"

Ophelia didn't move as he trailed off, waiting to see if he would continue a confession she didn't want him to finish.

"And here I thought it was all passion and poetry," he said a little louder, twisting to observe her with a mirthless smirk, his eyes hollow.

She stiffly crossed over to him and held out the blanket. "You can still get her in trouble."

"Like anyone in their right mind would believe a sixteen-year old didn't want to poke a housewife?" he asked, taking the blanket from her with one hand before hugging it like a stuffy.

Ophelia shook her head. "No, screw that."

He shrugged. "It's over and done with, isn't it?"

She sighed and realized that though the water seemed to have helped straighten out his thoughts, his eyes were still unfocused and heavy-lidded with drink and he probably wouldn't be breathing a word of this to anyone were he sober. She ought to spare him the embarrassment and leave him alone.

"That's why they call it the past?" he pressed tiredly.

"Yeah." Ophelia rested a hand on his shoulder and gave it a gentle squeeze. "You need to sleep."

She hardly made it around the couch before his whispered words made her stop.

"Then why do I keep seeing it?"

"Seeing what?" she asked, looking down at him.

"The past," he whispered, craning his neck to look up at her. "A time before I was born."

8

A chill darted up Ophelia's spine and bloomed on the back of her neck, tensing her jaw. She gazed into his upside down face while her own blanched and she forgot to breathe.

"Why would you say that?" she whispered.

Something twisted behind Brennan's eyes and in the softening light of the dim room he looked much younger than his twenty-two years, despite his stubble.

"Somet'ing's missing," he whispered back.

She crept around to his front to look at him properly, and as his hazel eyes tracked her, she felt more than naked. It was like there was a night sky inside her and he could pick out the places stars were meant to be, even if she couldn't.

"What's missing?" she asked, her voice stiff.

Brennan's eyes slid away from hers and drifted over her shoulders and hands, pinched by something buried deep behind them. Turning up his palm, he weakly extended his arm towards her.

Hesitating, Ophelia eyed the lines of his hand before taking a step near him then slipping her fingers against his. The edges of his skin were rough and cracking from working without gloves, but as her fingers slid from the tips of his to the base of his palm, she heard the faint, agitated chanting of a crowd that wasn't there. When he gently closed his hand around hers, the crowd faded, and his arm shook with every beat of his heart.

"The world," he rasped.

Brennan's pale hand felt like a cradle to her brown, as if she was weightless and dear. Forcing her eyes away from their touching skin and to his face, the tug of longing in the bottom of her stomach was like the surging of the sea, enveloping the night sky inside.

The old house creaked loudly, startling her into yanking her hand out of his. Taking a step backwards, Ophelia fought off the pull of the tide inside and reminded herself of school, her fight with Adam, and Alex's smile. Of what was real.

"I'm going to bed," she muttered before hurrying upstairs.

Ophelia didn't look back as she all-but ran up the steps and into her room.

He's drunk, she told herself. *He doesn't know what he's saying. Unless...*

Her phone went off, startling her yet again, and she answered it as soon as she saw that it was Adam calling. "Hey."

"Did I wake you?" he asked.

"No, I was just..." She winced, realizing that she sounded as out of breath as she felt. "Startled."

"Sorry." Adam sighed on the other side. "I just wanted to apologize for last night. I was a real dick."

Ophelia sank onto her bed, forcing her body to relax and shake Brennan's words out of her head while listening to what she had longed to hear all day. "Yeah, you were."

"I know you're not the kind of girl to sneak around. I just get so... I don't know."

"Did someone cheat on you in the past?"

He sighed. "You could say that."

"Well, I'm not her."

Adam was quiet and the silence made her mind wander again and she wondered if she should tell him about the Gone People.

"Adam?"

"Yeah?"

"We can have our own place one day. After I'm done with school."

"Deal."

Ophelia smiled as he yawned on the other end. "Go to bed."

"Only if you're in it."

"Don't push your luck, mister."

Adam chuckled softly. "I'll see you soon. I love you."

"Goodnight."

Ophelia listened for several seconds to make sure he really had hung up before setting down her phone and letting out a breath she didn't even realize she was holding. Their fight was over. Everyone was safe. All was well.

Then why do I still feel such longing for something I can't even understand?

While she wanted to continue her conversation with Brennan, he looked like he hadn't gotten any sleep in at least a day and would be of no real use to her until he was sober. She would have to wait. Closing her eyes, she replayed Amelia's memories in her mind until she could no longer hold onto them and sleep claimed her.

Ophelia scolded herself when she woke up and it was past eleven. Hurrying downstairs, she leaned over the railing and peered at the couch. The blanket was neatly folded and draped on the arm. Her eyes darted to the woodstove but the leather jacket was gone.

"Dammit."

Heading back upstairs, she paced, considering going down to the shop to find Brennan and speak with him, only to realize how obsessive that would be. She opted instead for changing into a charcoal sweater dress, leggings, and her floral galoshes before taking her laptop to a coffee shop downtown, thinking that a change of scenery might help her write better.

The commotion and noise was distracting, however, and as she jotted down notes from peer-reviewed papers, she kept accidentally including snippets of other people's conversations. After a few hours of reading literary analyses of Keats' poems, her head was growing tight and she came across an article about how the poet's tragic life mirrored his writing. He had died at age twenty-five, never able to wed the love of his life, Fanny Brawne. Ophelia already knew about their romance but, deciding she wanted to learn more, tracked down a book that included their collected letters and placed an order for it on the library website.

The walk home in the failing light was pleasant for a spring afternoon. The trees lining Pacific Avenue glowed with little white lights wound around their trunks, lending the main street a festive atmosphere. As she approached the old Victorian, however, she could hear raised voices. Slowly climbing the steps, she was surprised that one belonged to a woman.

"You are so fucking selfish," the woman shouted.

"This has not'ing to do with—" Brennan started, and Ophelia unconsciously held her breath as she stopped outside the window, eavesdropping beside the glass that was thickening with age at the bottom of the bay window pane.

"I don't know his number," she barked. "So just give it to me and—"

"Dammit, woman, I said *no.*"

"Then I'll take your fucking phone," she shrieked, seemingly unaffected by Brennan's calm tone.

"Jaysus, will ya listen to yourself?"

"Don't give me that."

"You're off your nut, Charlie."

"You're so fucking superior now, aren't you?" Charlie snarled, and guilt gnawed at Ophelia's stomach for continuing to listen. "As if you aren't just as fucked up as I—"

"I'm *clean* now, dammit, and trying to keep you straight, love."

"Oh, you're clean?" Charlie replied with mock-agreement. "That's why you were so blackout drunk that you probably don't even remember screwing me?"

"We didn't—"

"Yeah, we did, you fuck up. But you know what? *Fuck you.*"

Ophelia winced and took a step away from the window. She wouldn't want someone listening if this was her argument.

"Charlie," Brennan began, his voice shaking with forced calm. "I'm sorry, but ya have to go now."

"You're such a God damned whore."

"This isn't even my *house*. How did ya find me?"

There was a pause before Charlie spoke again. "I'm not leaving without his fucking number."

The floorboards creaked as the gap between the two of them closed. "What're you gonna pay him with? Huh?" Brennan hissed. "Do ya have any idea what he'll do if he doesn't get what he's asking?"

"Not everyone wants money, Brennan, but you already know that. We've worked out other arrangements."

"Oh, Jaysus Christ."

Ophelia's throat soured and she had never felt more pampered and sheltered in her life.

This shouldn't be happening. This belongs to a world I've never even glimpsed.

Brennan's boots echoed and the two inside were quiet until Charlie spoke, sounding sane for the first time. "Thank you."

Footsteps headed for the exit and Ophelia grimaced, searching for a corner to hide behind.

"Wait," Brennan called as Charlie opened the door.

Ophelia backed up to the sidewalk, deciding to pretend that she had only just arrived. Brennan stepped out in black skinny jeans and an equally dark button-up, making him look pale as he yanked open his wallet. He handed the young woman, who Ophelia now recognized as the buxom, inked girl from the pub, everything he had.

"Just give him that and he'll leave ya alone, yeah?"

Charlie smiled and stuffed the money into the pocket of her ratty coat. "Yeah."

She headed down the stoop, only to freeze when she spotted Ophelia so near to the house. Something about Charlie's angular, heart-shaped face tugged on a thought that Ophelia couldn't identify before the other young woman spoke.

"Who the hell is this bitch?"

Ophelia's lips parted in shock, all guilt over having eavesdropped evaporating. "*Excuse* me?"

"She *lives* here," Brennan said, hastily shutting the door and coming down the steps to stand between the two women, as if worried they would fight.

"You didn't say you lived with another chick."

"He doesn't live *with* me, I have a boyfriend," Ophelia corrected.

Charlie eyed her skeptically.

"Charlie was just leaving," Brennan explained, his tense eyes darting to the black-haired woman.

She didn't say so much as a goodbye as she brushed past the two to scurry down the street, pulling out her phone. Brennan watched her go with raven-like eyes, and Ophelia caught his jaw quiver before he whipped his head away and marched back towards the house with a curt, "Sorry about that."

Ophelia followed him in and shut the door as Brennan darted around the living room, righting knocked over furniture. One of the end tables' legs had snapped and he grimaced at it before looking at her with a pitiful expression.

"I can fix it, no bother."

Ophelia's eyes shifted from the broken end table to the scattered books and candles that Brennan hadn't had a chance to put back yet. "What the *hell* happened in here?"

"She's... a brick shy of the load," he offered tensely.

"To say the least." Ophelia set down her bag and stepped past him, gathering up the jar candles and books.

"Do you have any wood glue?"

"Probably not."

"I'll snag some, then, and it'll be grand."

Ophelia eyed a crack in the glass of one of the candles and realized it had hit the edge of the woodstove. "Did she do all this?"

Brennan hunched by the table, trying to lodge the wood back together in a temporary fix, a wedge of his lower back peeking out between his shirt and pants, and she wondered how he never seemed to notice how close he always was to mooning people.

"She had to have somet'ing to throw at me, didn't she?"

Ophelia stiffened and peered around, thankful the addict didn't go for one of the lamps her parents had bought from an antiques store. "I hope she missed."

"She did... mostly. I'm good at dodging by now." Brennan straightened and tugged up his jeans, eyeing the rickety table before looking at Ophelia over his shoulder. "I'm class at banjaxing everyt'ing, huh? I had no idea she even knew where I was."

Ophelia set the books back down on the coffee table and glanced around the room, realizing that Brennan was the only thing worse for wear. His eyes were puffy and his hair was unkempt with wavy locks popping this way and that.

"She's, um..." he started before fidgeting with his sleeve. "We used to..."

"I got that part. I think the whole street did."

"Jaysus." He locked eyes with her. "I'm *so* sorry, Ophelia."

A spark lit in her chest at the sound of her name on his tongue for the first time and she couldn't keep the amusement from her face.

"What?" Brennan asked, his posture stiffening somewhat in concern.

"You just inadvertently revealed that you *do* know my name, after all."

Brennan looked hesitant to indulge in her good humor for a moment but a corner of his mouth quirked as he looked away.

"It's fine," she soothed. "No harm done."

He slid a candle onto the end table, his back to her. "She didn't used to be like this. She had this loud laugh that would make you laugh just to hear it." Brennan's shoulders were tense, even if his voice was soft. "We hadn't done heroin before and were at this party together and... then we were both looking for a good time all the time. Somehow it just... got out of control."

Ophelia stepped up to his side and noticed that his hand was shaking the candle as he stared at it.

"Her mam kicked her out," he croaked. "I guess she's staying with some friends, but... she thinks it's all just part of growing up. Like it's no big deal. Like it might not ruin her. Control her. Define her."

Ophelia rested her hand on his and the shaking stopped. "I wish I could give you advice," she said quietly. "But I've never even smoked pot, much less seen heroin."

"I know ya haven't," he replied with the faintest smile as he looked at her. "You're too refined for all that." Tugging his hand out of hers, he slipped upstairs and quietly closed the door to Alex's room.

She sighed, looking up at the stairs and telling herself that he needed space. There was nothing she could do to get him out of the mess he had made, anyway. Heading into the kitchen, Ophelia focused her energy on something she could control: dinner.

By the time Adam accepted her invite to eat with them, Alex was home and she could hear him and Brennan talking upstairs.

"Hello?" Adam called, sticking his head in through the front door. The blue of his eyes seemed to match the hue of his O'Neill hoodie as he looked into the kitchen.

Ophelia smiled and hurried over, wrapping her arms around him in a long hug as he hoisted her off her feet with the tightness of his grip. "I've missed you."

"Me, too."

He swayed with her in his arms for several seconds before letting her go and following her back into the kitchen.

"Spaghetti?"

"With homemade sauce."

Adam helped her set the table as she finished the meal. The buzzer went off as the pasta finished boiling and Ophelia looked at him over her shoulder as she drained it. "Could you tell the boys that it's time to eat, please?"

He nodded, took two steps towards the bottom of the stairs, and then bellowed, "Get your asses down here for some food!"

Ophelia set the pot of pasta down with an annoyed expression as he chuckled. Footsteps echoed on the stairs as she tossed the noodles with olive oil, but only Alex appeared.

"Where's the leprechaun?" Adam asked.

Alex flicked his eyes over the tall blonde before looking at Ophelia, silently assessing if they were still in a fight and relaxing at her calm demeanor. "He's not hungry."

"Then do I get to eat his?"

"Really, Adam?" Ophelia asked over her shoulder while serving herself. "It's all carbs. And you complain about *my* calories."

"When have I ever said a word about what you eat?" he asked incredulously.

Ophelia shook her head but didn't want to risk getting into another argument and dropped it. A quiet part of her mind wondered if Brennan wasn't coming downstairs because Adam was there.

"Are there eggs in the noodles?" Alex asked, picking the box off the counter and reading the label.

"An egg isn't gonna hurt you, man," Adam said.

"They treat those chickens horribly," Alex muttered before spotting the word *vegan* on the package.

Once they were all served up with spaghetti and salad, they dug in, and Ophelia pretended the discussion Adam was having with Alex over the treatment of hens on industrial chicken farms wasn't irritating her. Her thoughts kept drifting upstairs, wanting to ask Brennan more about what he had said the night before.

"This is delicious, babe," Adam said, squeezing her leg and forcing her mind back into the present.

Ophelia smiled in thanks. Alex cleared the table and, to her surprise, started washing the dishes, so the couple headed over to the couch to finally have their weekly viewing of *Survivor*. She kept her ear trained on the stairs, hoping Brennan would come down to eat, for he was skinny enough as it was, yet the evening continued without any sign of him.

"Hey," Adam huskily said, squeezing her shoulder as she lay there on his stomach, rising and falling with each breath. "We're good, right?"

She smiled and kissed him in response. He left an hour later with a promise to text her when he was home safe and sound.

Alex watched her from the kitchen table where he was finishing his paper. Though the laptop screen reflecting on his glasses blocked out his eyes, she knew they were tracking her as she put the kettle on.

"What?" she asked.

"Nothing." He looked back down to his keyboard and started typing.

"Alexandros?"

He sighed and pulled off his glasses to look up at her. "You just seem like something's bothering you."

"I'm fine," she replied with a soft chuckle. "Adam and I aren't fighting, I have a whole thesis to rewrite, and a crazy woman tried to destroy our living room and failed—what's not to be happy about?"

Alex smirked, even if he didn't look completely convinced. "Just checking in."

Ophelia considered telling him that Brennan claimed he had been seeing the past, as well, but given that the secret so closely followed an admission of something far more painful, it didn't feel like it was hers to share. Instead, she crossed over and hugged Alex from behind before kissing the top of his head.

"What're you working on?"

"Voltaire," he replied. "He didn't fit well into the Enlightenment and I'm pointing it out whether my professor likes it or not. He was totally a proto-Romantic."

"That sounds like fun. I wish my thesis was so straightforward," she pouted.

"You'll get there," he quietly soothed. "Just stop worrying about it and it will come to you."

Ophelia patted his shoulder in thanks and he sighed, closing his laptop.

"I have to go in at five in the morning tomorrow."

"That's inhumane."

"Time to kick the Dubliner out of my room," Alex groaned as he rose. He gave her a one-armed hug goodnight, his laptop tucked under the other. "Sweet dreams, my effervescent elephant."

"You, too, my darling poo-face."

Alex headed upstairs and Ophelia glanced at the kettle, willing the water to boil faster. Looking down at her hands, she picked at her nails, realizing that as happy as she was to see Adam again, there was still that patch of longing inside. Maybe they needed to talk more about their fight. Or maybe she just needed time to adjust to the fact that they would undoubtedly fight again.

"What's the story, Girl?" a voice came from behind her, and Ophelia jumped and squawked, startling Brennan in turn. "Christ."

"I didn't hear you come in," she gasped, twisting to face him and noting that he was barefoot.

"Looked like you were with the faeries."

"Yeah," she sighed then cleared her throat. "There's still some pasta left."

"Cheers," he replied, even as he ducked into the cupboard and pulled out a box of granola cereal. "Guess I fell asleep."

Brennan's eyes were less puffy than they had been that afternoon and he looked like he felt better after what must've been a massive hangover. The teakettle whistled and she poured the hot water into her Artemis mug before dunking in a bag of Bengal Spice and taking a seat. Brennan added milk to his cereal and forced some bravado into her voice.

"I make really good sauce."

He glanced at her as he put the milk back into the refrigerator. "I'm sure. I love spaghetti."

"Then why are you eating cereal?" she asked. "Again?"

"What's with you and the tea?" he countered, sliding into his seat beside her. "I thought Americans didn't like it."

"Don't change the subject."

"Your lot once threw a fair bit of it into the Boston Harbor." He was about to take a bite when he shot her a significant look before making a show of placing a napkin below his bowl. "It's an honest question."

Ophelia shrugged. "I just always have."

"Then maybe I've just always liked cereal," Brennan said around the spoon.

"It's hardly filling."

He shrugged. "And it's hardly expensive."

She cocked her head, peering at his dark features through the distorting steam rising from her mug, making her feel like he was looking at her from somewhere else. "That better not be why you're eating it."

"I already stole your sandwich," Brennan garbled before swallowing. "And I won't have anyt'ing to my name till Tuesday next."

"Because Charlie took it all?"

Brennan's eyes darkened and he looked down at his bowl. "She didn't *take* anyt'ing. I offered it to her. And I know that was wrong when youse are putting me up, but I—"

"It wasn't wrong," Ophelia cut him off. "I... overheard the end of your argument."

He winced.

"You were trying to protect her," Ophelia continued. "You must really care about her."

Brennan's chest rose with a deep breath that he didn't release, his eyes downcast. "Well, that's the funny t'ing, isn't it?" He studied her. "The people we hurt the most are the ones we care about."

Ophelia shook her head. "That's not true."

"Of course it is," he replied, lowering his head and scooping up another bite. "You can hide behind your four walls and your mam's milk all you like, but in the end, it's God's honest truth. When you love someone, ya tether yourself to them, and tethered people spend their time tripping and falling and stepping all over each other."

"Or helping each other walk straight," Ophelia countered, surprised by the indignation in her voice.

Brennan took a bite and didn't reply. Ophelia wrapped her hands around her warm mug and shifted in her seat, the cinnamon and spices of the tea tickling her nose. Telling him that he was being negative didn't exactly seem fair given what she knew of his past.

"It's complicated," he quietly said, though if he were referring to Charlie or relationships in general, she didn't know.

"It sounded to me like she was manipulating you."

Brennan arched a scarred brow at her. "Trying to help her avoid prostitution *isn't* manipulation."

"But it got her what she wanted."

He shook his head. "Ya don't know her."

"You're right." Ophelia sighed. "I don't. And people who greet each other with 'who the hell is this bitch?' are usually wonderful."

Brennan released his spoon with a clatter and leaned back in his chair, his expression tight. "Are ya finished now?"

Ophelia cringed inside, realizing just how far she had strayed from casual conversation, but her next words were defensive all the same. "You can do better than her."

He dropped his head in his hands.

"You've helped her all you can."

"I used to *be* her. Jaysus, don't you get it?" Brennan tilted his head to peer at her with a dark look. "I told ya it wasn't safe at night because *I* was the kind of lad you had to worry about. I know what it's like to be willing to do anyt'ing, *anyt'ing* for a fix. I even screwed a fella once—it was that... dealer we were talking about. That's when I knew enough was enough. I couldn't do that again. And I have no focking idea why I'm telling ya all this and I should just shut my gob and get my arse out of your house." Brennan rose only to plop back down. "Jaysus, did I really blather all that to ya last night about the lady and the riding crop?"

Ophelia blinked in shock, trying not to lean back in her chair over how much wrong just spewed out of his mouth. "You... left out that part."

"Well, there was one," he added pitifully before thumping his head on his folded arms.

She carefully set her tea down, studying him as if he were a wounded, diseased animal, her pity mingling with trepidation over never having encountered so ill a creature. She wanted to touch him, to offer him some form of comfort, but she worried that he would shatter under her hand.

"I'm focking disgusting," Brennan said as he slowly raised his head, his face red with shame as his voice squeaked. "And I don't belong here."

"Why not?" she whispered.

"Because you're decent," he croaked, and when his eyes latched onto hers, they were shimmering. "And I'm not a good person."

Ophelia tensed but shook her head in disagreement.

"I'm *not*."

"You're trying," she said quietly, feeling as if growing up with a warm bed full of stuffed animals and having pancakes for dinner was sucking all of the air out of the room. "You've been given a shittier hand than the rest of us, but you're still fucking trying. And that matters. A lot."

Brennan's spine tensed as if it was made of metal coils. "I *chose* to shoot up that shite, I *chose* to bring Charlie to that party. Christ, I helped her—"

"You didn't *choose* for your parents to die," Ophelia said, cutting him off, and he flinched away at her firm voice. "And you damned well didn't choose to be raped by a forty-something woma—"

"It wasn't—"

"The moment you said no, it was. Even if you were too scared to voice it."

He stared down at the milk in his bowl, his skin flushed and his breathing tight, as if he might crack.

Ophelia let her words settle in his mind, even if all they had done was tighten her throat and chest with the need to do something. Because wrecks didn't look like the living, breathing man before her. Wrecks were faceless, contorted bodies in alleyways and clinics and morgues. Not at her kitchen table with a consciousness so battered and bruised that up and down no longer existed. That the line between safe and afraid had vanished, and love and abuse were one and the same.

"I'm sorry for darkening ya," he whispered, his shoulders and spine quivering as he remained transfixed on his cereal bowl. "I don't know what's wrong with me. When I'm around ya the words just... They vomit out."

Ophelia's eyes traced the tremor in his lower lip and the way the unshed tears had clumped his dark lashes together. Her throat was dry and taut as she spoke. "You haven't told anyone this before?"

Tendons shifted in the pocket below his temple as he clenched his jaw then hesitantly dragged his eyes across the table towards

. M. RICE

her. He looked on the verge of weeping and the strength it was taking to rein in his emotions showed in the hitching of his breathing as his gaze settled on her hands. When his hazel finally locked onto her brown, the longing inside seemed to grow and fill Ophelia with loneliness, like an empty night sky. She had never seen such core-deep anguish grappling with trust in another living being's eyes.

Raising her hand, she slid it across the table with slow, deliberate motion, afraid of startling the broken-winged bird across from her. Brennan's eyes didn't leave hers until she curled her fingers over the back of his palm, prompting his gaze to drift down to her skin against his. The touch warmed the vastness of the sky inside as she gave his hand a gentle squeeze, even if it was cold and limp in her grip.

"I'm right here," Ophelia whispered, nearly flinching as her voice cut through the quietness. "Whenever you need me."

Brennan's mouth drew in, as if he was about to be sick, and he tried to tug his hand away only to have her grip it tighter.

"I mean it."

"How could ya?" he squeaked.

"Because of who you are."

His eyes darted to hers in surprise and she squeezed his hand again as he parted his lips to contradict her.

"You make Alex laugh. Really laugh," Ophelia said, her voice gaining strength. "He doesn't have to pretend anything around you. He can just be himself. And you had the strength to make the choice to stop using." Her lips twisted in a smile. "You *chose* that. No matter what else you also chose, you chose that."

His gaze softened as her words seemed to soothe something burning inside, his eyes clearing. At length he drew in a deep breath and let it out, his shoulders slumping as he did so. She could tell by the despondent way he glanced at the cereal remaining in his bowl that he wasn't hungry anymore. She pressed the warm tea towards him then wrapped his limp hand around the mug.

A small, bashful smile transformed his face from forlorn to beautiful as he hugged the ceramic in both hands, and Ophelia didn't feel any shame or guilt for noticing as much. He pulled the warm tea towards him as if it were a treasure.

"You can stay here, you know," she said softly. "You're sleeping on the couch—don't worry about rent."

He shook his head. "I couldn't—"

"There's no shame in having help," Ophelia said, reminding him of his own words on the night they met. "But there is some luck. And by the sounds of it, you're overdue for some."

Brennan's smile made his eyes shine, and for a moment she wondered if there was something wrong with her face given the intent way he was gazing at her.

"Does it ever get old?" he huskily asked.

A line formed between her brows and something tickled in her chest. "What?"

"Being a hero?"

Ophelia let out a soft laugh and looked away. "No, I'm... If I were you, I'd hope someone would give me a chance. It's nothing heroic."

"If murderers don't always look like murderers, then heroes don't always look like heroes."

She smirked and parted her lips, hunting for a means to dismiss the compliment but was distracted by the warm glow inside at the way he was watching her while he sipped the tea, and she wondered if he felt it, as well.

A quiet calm settled over the room, as if they had both had a good cry even though neither had shed a tear. Brennan drank the warm liquid and it seemed to restore the stability to his breathing.

"There are a lot of repair shops," he said, running his thumb over the stag on the mug. "Alex had never been to ours before. I'd almost forgotten I'd met him."

His eyes were sharp as they found hers, as if he expected her to glean his meaning.

"Must've been cheaper," she offered.

Brennan grunted. "The old man overcharges for everyt'ing. Especially oil changes."

"Mr. Muppet Conspiracy?"

129

He chuckled softly and nodded before biting his lower lip. "The t'ing is, if Alex had never come in and recognized me..." Brennan let out a shaking breath and the earnestness of his gaze made her wonder how he could ever tell a lie. "Then I..."

"You wouldn't be here," she finished for him.

"I'd be a fair sight worse off, that's for sure."

Ophelia nodded, feeling at peace with the quiet, composed way he was looking at her after baring such wounds.

"What if it wasn't random?" he whispered, and the hairs on the back of her neck rose one by one with tickling tugs. "What if sometimes people are meant to meet each other?"

"What do you mean?"

"Ever since the car accident, my life has felt like..." He sighed. "During the Famine, men got work as laborers, only the food they were paid wasn't enough to keep them going. The western countryside is littered with these roads to nowhere that just end where all the workers died. Famine roads. I feel like I've been on a famine road ever since that night. And then you..." He winced inwardly and swallowed with effort, as if worried the words would cut his mouth. "When I'm around ya, it's not a dead end anymore."

Ophelia's eyes stung from not blinking and her chest felt tight, as if she couldn't take full breaths. *Someone's missing*, her mind whispered, and she tried to dismiss his words to ignore the voice. "You just need stability for a while."

Though his features didn't change, something wilted in his eyes and he looked away. "Maybe."

"We all need a hearth and warm meals," she continued, and the more she distanced herself from his honesty, the duller her longing became. "I always had that. I was privileged in that way. So I'm happy to give it to someone else."

Brennan nodded mutely and as she rose, she built a wall inside in an attempt to pretend she wouldn't stay up all night talking if he asked her to.

"It's late."

He looked up at her as she stepped past him towards the stairs. "Hey, Girl?"

Ophelia looked at him over her shoulder, one foot on the stairs.

"I'm here, too, if ya ever need me."

She offered him a thankful smile before heading up the stairs, his words unintentionally leaving behind the sting of what she was missing.

Adam had let her know that he got home safe but she was too tired inside to respond. When she lay down on her bed, she felt a hand tangled in her hair and lips pressed against hers. The dim, white walls of the servant's hallway bloomed out of the shadows and her chest was so full that she felt like she could burst.

Amelia jerked her face to the side, pulling her mouth away from Leander's to catch her breath.

"It's Liza," she whispered. "I thought she knew, but she was only worried—"

"I see her watching me," he panted against her moist lips in his lilt. "I should tell her that her hope is for naught."

"Don't." She rested her forehead against his, closing her eyes and running her fingers through his wavy hair, somewhat crusted with pomade. "You must pretend. You must pretend that you've never met me or someone might notice that—"

"I can't. I could never, *mo chroí*."

"Leander," she whispered, but he cut her off.

"The moment ya first smiled at me, I was free. All expectations and stiff collars suddenly faded, and you were my one splotch of color." His hand rested against her cheek, his thumb running along the soft skin. "My colors."

Amelia smiled, for while she had never had a gift for words, Leander had just opened her chest and scooped them out for her, like vibrant butterflies that he blew into the air and sent fluttering about them in the darkness.

"Someone might come," she whispered, and the butterflies' wings singed as they fell to ash at the knowledge that she didn't know when she would next be able to see him like this. "I should go."

His sigh stirred her curls and he released her. Reaching out, she felt the side of the staircase and was about to pat her way to the first step when his soft voice stopped her.

"Amelia?"

Turning towards the sound, she heard the striking of a match. The hallway was suddenly illuminated as Leander stepped forward to light her candle. She smiled in thanks, anxious to leave now that someone could identify the pair of them.

When Leander met her gaze with whimsy in his eyes, Brennan's dark features flickered in the dancing, golden light.

9

Ophelia stared at the page beginning a letter from John Keats to his brother and sister, dated Sunday 14 Feb.—Monday 3 May 1819, but the antiquated words kept shifting about on the page, switching order and rippling with sighs.

It must've been a dream, she told herself.

Brennan had filled her head with so many disturbing thoughts the night before that it wouldn't be weird for her mind to have sifted through them in her sleep, making him appear in her dreams. Except that her glimpses of the Gone People weren't dreams.

The memory of how impassioned she had felt as Amelia left her with more than a hint of jealousy. What she was doing with Leander broke all social rules and expectations. Even the Victorian publication of Keats and Fanny Brawne's letters fifty years after his death was cause for scandal, and the two had been engaged.

How could Amelia have been so sure of herself, so trusting of the fire in her breast as to risk everything she had?

"Focus," Ophelia scolded herself, rubbing her eyes before fixing them onto the page again. The most she had accomplished all day was to pick up the collection of Keats' letters from the library, even if she had been attempting to read them for an hour, a post-it at the ready for note-taking on the back of the book.

This is the world—thus we cannot expect to give way many hours to pleasure—Circumstances are like Clouds continually gathering and bursting, Ophelia read. *While we are laughing the seed Of some trouble is put into the wide arable land of events—while we are laughing it sprouts [for it] grows and suddenly bears a poison fruit which we must pluck—Even so we have leisure to reason on the misfortunes of our friends; our own touch us too nearly for words.*

"Too nearly for words," she whispered, re-reading the last sentence. The passage redirected her thoughts as she realized that she had indeed had the lack of misfortune and leisure to worry over the plights of her friends. It was that luxury that prompted her to offer Brennan a place to stay indefinitely, even if she knew the act would upset Adam.

But why did Leander look like Brennan?

He had told her when he was drunk that he kept glimpsing a time before he was born. Maybe he showed up in her vision because he shared the same ability as her. Maybe that was why they met, as he seemed to be hinting when he said that some things were meant to be. Any other significance of those words shoved her into thoughts too new and dangerous to even look at.

"Boo," a voice shouted in her doorway, and Ophelia leaped a few inches off her bed, gasping. Adam laughed and stepped in. "Gotcha."

"You psychopath," she shouted, resting a hand over her racing heart.

Adam smirked and reached out to hug her, only to have her slink away. "You really didn't hear the door downstairs?"

"No," she snipped, glaring at him. "You are so evil."

He pouted and looked up at her as he took a seat on the floor, the childish expression odd on his angular face. As always, he was wearing his uniform of shorts, T-shirt and flip-flops no matter the weather.

Ophelia slowly smiled as her heart calmed and she shoved at his blonde head.

"You must've really been focusing. Is that what you were doing last night?"

"What do you mean?"

"You didn't text me back," he replied, his eyes flickering up to hers with a tightness that he thought was casual but she knew was reconnaissance.

"I fell asleep," she offered with a dismissive smile, the realization that she just lied to him for the second time in a week sneaking up and kicking her from behind.

"Well, I don't have anything to do today." Adam leaned up and she met him halfway and kissed him. "Let's go out."

"I can't. You know I have to keep working."

"Lia," he said with a sigh. His golden skin was taking on the pink hue it did when he had been in the sun a lot, darkening the band of freckles over his wide cheekbones. "We both know you're not actually going to finish it in time. Not when you have to start all over again."

"Adam," she scolded.

"I'm not trying to be mean, I'm just saying..." He shrugged. "I know you. You're a slow writer."

"You didn't even know what my thesis was about until last week."

"It doesn't matter what it's about. I mean, what's one more semester?"

Ophelia bit the inside of her lower lip, realizing that there was no point in arguing with him over graduation dates when he still had so much schooling left. "And here I thought you'd be pushing me to finish so that we could start hunting for a place."

"Oh, shit. That's right. Get to work!" He slapped her hip then climbed up onto the bed with her.

"As if I don't have enough distractions," she began before she was even aware of what she was saying.

Adam's narrow eyes flinched at the concerned look that darted across her face. "Is Alex bringing people home?"

"No," she squawked. "Nothing like that."

He looked down at her lavender bedspread and picked at a piece of loose stitching. "The leprechaun, then?"

135

"Brennan is not a leprechaun," she muttered, marking her page and closing the book. "That's like calling you a Viking."

"Why not? Vikings are hot."

Ophelia turned to face him. "You think I want you to call me Islander?"

"The UK and Trinidad *are* all islands."

She shook her head. "Sometimes I wonder about you, Adam."

He smirked and kissed her again before picking up her book and leafing through the pages. "I can't believe you can read this stuff. It's so dense. And there's like, no white space on the pages."

"And what's in your medical texts? Stick figures?"

Adam's smile faded as he studied her. "Seriously—what's distracting you?"

Ophelia gazed into his clear blue eyes for the span of several heartbeats, so many words surging to the surface. She wanted to tell him the truth. "Do you think people sometimes meet for a reason?" she asked instead.

He shrugged a little. "Like us?"

"Sure."

"I doubt it. I'm not a big believer in fate, you know? I think we make our own futures."

"So... it wasn't fate when I brought you a towel after you drunkenly dove into the pool at that frat party?"

The angel-bow of his upper lip quirked. "Not at all. That was carefully calculated."

"Oh, yeah?" she countered with a smile.

"I'd been trying to get your attention all night."

"So your best idea was to strip down to your boxers and leap into a pool?" She had never told him that she actually had noticed him long before that, since a guy as tall and fit as him was hard to miss. But at the time, she had passed hasty judgment because he had been talking quietly with a boy she knew from high school who was in and out of prison.

"It worked, didn't it?"

Ophelia chuckled. "Only because it got me to talk to you."

"That's all I needed," Adam said, his voice quieting as he sobered. "For you to give me a chance for once."

She cocked her head slightly. "You say that as if you knew me before that night."

Adam shrugged. "I felt like I did."

Ophelia smiled and hugged his arm. "I felt like I did, too."

Adam gave her a squeeze then pulled back to look at her face. "So, no trouble from the Irish guy?"

She could tell him about Brennan coming home completely wasted, or about Charlie's destruction and the terrible things Brennan had confessed the previous night, but Adam was already looking for an excuse to turn on the younger man just because he was male and in her house. Ophelia smirked and shook her head. "You know me—I'm always finding something to worry about."

Adam kissed her forehead. "Go ahead and work, then. I'm gonna go mess with Alex's stuff before he gets home."

He hopped out the door before she could ask what that meant, but she got her answer a few minutes later when she heard a video game rev up, followed by artificial gunshots.

Returning her attention to the book, she opened back up to Keats' letter and started reading once more.

Call the world if you Please "The vale of Soul-making". Then you will find out the use of the world (I am speaking now in the highest terms for human nature admitting it to be immortal which I will here take for granted for the purpose of showing a thought which had struck me concerning it) I say 'Soul making' Soul as distinguished from an Intelligence—There may be intelligences or sparks of the divinity in millions—but they are not Souls till they acquire identities, till each one is personally itself.

The words on the page caused her sense of longing, which was now familiar, to ache. Alex's argument over the existence of a soul came back to her, and when accompanied with the memory of Amelia's confidence, she knew without a doubt that the woman's soul was unique and intelligent enough on its own to stir envy in a girl over one hundred years later.

I can scarcely express what I but dimly perceive—and yet I think I perceive it—that you may judge the more clearly I will put it in the most homely form possible—I will call the world a School instituted for the purpose of teaching little children to read—I will call the human heart the horn Book used in that School—and I will call the Child able to read, the Soul made from that School and its hornbook. Do you not see how necessary a World of Pains and troubles is to school an Intelligence and make it a Soul? A Place where the heart must feel and suffer in a thousand diverse ways! Not merely is the Heart a Hornbook, It is the Minds Bible, it is the Minds experience, it is the teat from which the Mind or intelligence sucks its identity. As various as the Lives of Men are—so various become their Souls, and thus does God make individual beings, Souls...

A particularly loud explosion from the speakers downstairs bounced against the walls of Ophelia's mind, but she didn't let it in. The heart was an educator of the soul, and life was but a playground wherein some souls were made and others vanished for lack of experience. Like her and Jack at the park. He didn't know any better than to leave with that man, and his life was snuffed out.

But was his soul?

Whispers started pouring out of the thrumming night sky in her chest. Scrunching her eyes shut, she pinched the bridge of her nose as her sinuses began to ache. *Go away*, she hissed at the voices and pain as the chiming of cutlery and laughter echoed to her. *Not now. Not when I feel so close to...*

"You seem fidgety, my darling Lia," a refined English voice stated, and Ophelia looked to her side to see Kent's face clearly for the first time. Adam's broad features fixed her with a concerned smile as they dined at a lavish table, the curve of his upper lip exaggerated by a thin mustache. The yellow light from the gas lamps bounced off pearly teeth, garish earrings, golden cufflinks, and a crystalline chandelier overhead. The fading scent of lobster lingered in the stagnant air.

Amelia watched as Kent's narrow blue eyes flickered over her family and neighbors, who were all in gowns and suits with tails, every hair on their heads as controlled as their smiles. As if they were at a wedding with weapons drawn and not a social dinner. When he was sure that no one was looking, the young man at her side, once again in his red uniform, rested his gloved hand on her thigh. Amelia glanced down at his touch, startled by his boldness, but met his gaze with a placid expression.

"I had a devil of a time today," Amelia said as Ophelia's surprise at the military man's identity was overridden by the society girl's restraint. Her mind was racing with images of lace and roses, Leander's eyelashes and the scent of horse sweat. "I had to send all of the lace back."

"Oh?" Kent asked, dabbing at the corner of his mouth with a cloth napkin. "What was the issue?"

"Just a miscommunication, darling," Amelia said coolly. "Nothing to trouble yourself with."

"All the same, I would like to be of assistance wherever necessary."

Amelia offered him a smile, fighting to control the dozens of minute muscles in her face as Leander entered in his black and white livery with a tray, bearing dessert.

"After all," Kent continued, "It was my idea to push up the date. The papers are already speculating over what your gown will look like." His blue eyes sparkled as he fixed her with a playful look.

She shook her head and plastered on an innocent expression. "If this is your attempt to coax me into revealing details then you will be sadly disappointed, Charles."

Kent chuckled softly. "You can't blame a chap for trying. I'll be the envy of the entire Court when I show up with you on my arm."

"You flatter me," she said softly, looking away from him but anywhere other than Leander, who was making his way around the table, offering tarts to each guest by handing them a pair of silver tongs so that they could serve themselves. Eyeing the lap of her jade gown, Amelia noticed a small stain and reminded herself to have Liza launder it later. Returning her attention to the people around her, she spotted her sister Lucy, whose blue gaze was unfocused as she adjusted the sleeve of her scoop neck dress that showed off her elegant collarbone and matched the hue of her eyes. Her bosom pillowed with a bored sigh, and Amelia reminded herself not to do the same.

"It's a shame this business in South Africa has called upon you," Amelia's father said from the other end of the table. "I rather hoped the Boers could be rational about all of this."

"Indeed, Lord Hollingberry," Kent replied. "Then again, if their idea of negotiating is offering an ultimatum, I am happy to give them a taste of English diplomacy at the tip of my sword."

Amelia's mother shifted uncomfortably and offered a reassuring smile to Lucy, as if the mention of violence had frightened her debutante rather than awoken her from a stupor.

"I could have told you back in '81 that we would have trouble again," the aging Lord Clarke offered.

"I don't see why they can't just leave everything but the diamond mines to the negroes," Mrs. Clarke offered. "I hear some of them speak English."

"Imagine that," Lucy piped up, startling their mother with her husky voice. "A negro with a brain? What a positively revolutionary idea."

"Don't be sardonic, dear, it doesn't suit you," their mother quietly scolded.

Lucy raised her head defiantly. "What will happen when all of the jewels have been dug out of the ground? Those poor black fellows will be left with nothing to even build a life upon."

Lord Hollingberry forced a chuckle, sharing a glance with the other gentlemen present. "A woman's view on politics is always so refreshing. Discussing the blacks as men with prospects at all."

"Don't scold her because she cares, Papa," Amelia defended before she realized what she was saying.

"Sounds like you have an uprising on your hands, Lord Hollingberry," one of the other men said with in a taunting voice.

"Indeed," Lord Hollingberry agreed with forced humor.

"Really, that's enough now, girls," their mother snipped with lips so tight that they had lost their creases.

"Next thing you know, they'll be campaigning for Irish Home Rule," Lord Clarke said, causing a chorus of hearty chuckles.

"Worry not. The Dutch population in Africa is small compared to the English these days," Kent offered with a smile that diffused any tension, and Amelia utilized his distraction to glance at Leander as he served, but the footman hadn't reacted to the jibe at his homeland. Not a soul in the room probably even remembered that he was Irish, if they had ever known in the first place. "We are already setting up refugee camps for the Boer women and children," Kent continued. "It's all quite civilized for the Dark Continent. I've never known a Dutchman to outwit or outmaneuver an Englishman. Taking control of the colonies will be a relatively simple matter."

"So say all men on the brink of war," Lord Hollingberry commented before cutting off a bite of his tart.

"This shall be the last war Queen and Country shall see for decades, I am certain. In two short years, a new century is upon us, after all. 1900 will bring about great prosperity, mark my words."

Lord Hollingberry offered Kent a smile that didn't reach his eyes. "May that be true."

"I quite agree," Amelia's mother enthused, raising her glass of wine. "To the future."

Lord Hollingberry nodded and held up his glass, as well. "The future."

Amelia and her fiancé followed suit, along with Lucy and their neighbors. "To the future," they all chorused, glasses raised high.

Leander watched with a small, forced smile before making his way past Lucy and over to the captain.

"To *our* future," Kent said quietly, locking eyes with Amelia. "In two weeks' time, you will never want for anything, my darling."

She smiled, hoping she had managed to keep the sourness of guilt from her eyes as she saluted her fiancé with her glass and took a sip of the wine. His hand once again discreetly slid onto her leg under the table as he gazed into her eyes.

Metal clanged beside their heads and both started in their seats before glancing up at Leander, whose white-gloved hand was scrambling to grab the tongs once more.

"Leander," Amelia gasped in relief, only to hitch her breathing as she realized how familiar she may have just sounded.

"Are you quite all right?" Lord Hollingberry asked from across the table.

Leander offered them all a reassuring smile. "New gloves, my lord."

"Ah." Lord Hollingberry nodded in understanding before taking another bite of his dessert.

"My dear chap," Kent said, peering up at him. "You look flushed."

Amelia stared at her empty plate before deciding that ignoring the comment might look more suspect than showing concern. She glanced at Leander and her heart stuttered when his pale olive skin only darkened more at the attention.

"Are you ill?" Kent asked.

"No, Captain," Leander assured as he offered the other man the tongs. "But I t'ank you for your concern."

"You must tell the cook not to leave the oven door open so," Amelia offered, forcing steadiness into her voice as Kent served himself a tart. "It must make it terribly uncomfortable downstairs."

"We manage, my lady. Not to worry at all," Leander replied quietly, moving to serve her.

She leaned away from his hunching torso as she placed the tart on her plate. Leander moved on to serve Lucy before heading stiffly for the buffet to set down the tray. Amelia's eyes darted to her fiancé's and she was startled to find him studying her. Unbidden heat rushed to her breast but she fought to keep it from her cheeks.

Something darted behind Kent's eyes but it was replaced with a doting smile before he turned his attention to the tart and the discussion her father and Lord Clarke were having about Arthur Conan Doyle's latest. Lucy's gaze was fixed on her sister, her composure slipping just long enough for a spark of mischief to enter her eyes.

Their mother may have banned the detective books from their household, but Amelia had borrowed copies from Liza and lent them to Lucy. The younger girl had devoured them with a frenzy, staying up all night to read. And now the pair of them were forced to sit straight and pretend that they had no interest in the discussion around them. The twinkle in Lucy's eyes was more than enough to distract Amelia from Leander's presence and she had to fight back a laugh as Lord Clarke repeatedly fumbled around the name of the principle character, Sherlock Holmes.

Amelia delicately cut a fork through the strawberries and crust on her plate, but even as she brought the bite to her parting lips, the view of the dining room vanished, replaced by a closet.

With a deep breath, Ophelia glanced around at her bedroom as the clank of cutlery faded. Digital gunshots echoed from downstairs.

Adam. Keats.

"I'm not engaged," she whispered, closing her eyes in relief, her hand waywardly feeling her ribs for her corset that was thankfully gone.

In an impulsive effort to run away from herself, Ophelia hopped to her feet and hurried out the door. She almost ran into Brennan as he stalked down the hall, his expression as broody as if someone had just tripped him then blamed him for it. He looked at her as he passed, his eyes shadowed by glowering raven brows, and his teal Henley and jeans flickered in and out of a footman's black and white livery until he ducked into the bathroom. She only glimpsed a strong, bare back streaked with blue paint before he closed the door on her, after which she wasn't even sure she saw the anachronistic image after all. She tried to swallow but her throat had gone dry.

"Leander?" she gasped.

Adam laughed downstairs and Ophelia descended. A hand gripping the rail, she peered down at his thick, T-shirt clad shoulders.

"Adam?" she whispered.

He pried his eyes away from the TV screen, craning his neck to look up at her, and as he did so, the white fabric of his shirt morphed into a red wool tunic decorated with golden shoulder boards while a thin mustache divided his face and pomade slicked his hair.

"Yeah?" he asked, though his voice was still Californian even if he looked like Kent.

Ophelia's features pinched as she shook her head, her eyes darting to the kitchen as Alex walked out, sipping an herbal iced tea. Relief flooded her when his image remained the same and she realized that she had frozen halfway down the stairs. She was about to continue her descent when Alex's face morphed into something much softer and delicate as he became Lucy with a lingering nasal and lip piercing, dressed in the elegant blue evening gown the Victorian girl had just worn in Ophelia's vision.

The embroidered fabric swished in motion as the bustle slid past the end table that was no longer broken. In fact, it was not their end table at all, but rather was something far grander that looked to be made of cherry wood. The satin of the dress shimmered in the light cast by a massive candelabrum mounted to the ceiling, and the furry white rug on the ground was replaced by a tapestry from a market in the East. The glass of the window was clear and roses bloomed outside in the light of the setting sun while the scent of fresh paint lingered in the air.

Lucy glanced up at her and offered a smile in greeting before taking a seat beside Adam, causing the dress to waft away like smoke, leaving Alex looking like a modern young man with gauges in his ears. Adam groaned as his character on the screen was killed, taking with it the youth of the house as the furniture vanished.

"Lame," Adam whined before craning his neck to look up at Ophelia, once more entirely himself. "How's it going?"

Ophelia parted her lips to reply but for the life of her, couldn't find the air to fill her lungs. Hurrying down the stairs, she looked out the curtain and spotted the familiar sidewalk and street outside bathed in the light of the setting sun with no sign of rosebushes.

"I didn't hear a knock," Alex offered, thinking she was spying on the stoop.

She looked at the two of them over her shoulder and found Alex watching her expectantly while Adam loaded a new game.

"Must've been the wind," she choked out around her dry throat.

Alex narrowed his eyes slightly at her odd behavior and Ophelia slipped into the kitchen, eager to be out from under any scrutiny while her head was spinning dizzily. Once alone, she poured herself a glass of water and downed it, closing her eyes.

"Your name is Ophelia," she whispered to herself. "You live in Santa Cruz in two-thousand—"

"Do you wanna go out to eat, Lia?" Adam called from the other room as the boom of gunfire once again erupted.

"Sure," she called, though if he had asked her to repeat her answer she wouldn't be able to tell him if she had said yes or no.

"Wanna come, Alex?"

"If Brennan can."

"Guess that means we have to go somewhere that serves potatoes."

Ophelia slammed the glass down on the counter, her mind slowing in its spinning.

"Elephant?" Alex called at the sound.

"There was a fly," she weakly replied, her eyelids heavy. Sinking into a seat at the table, she rubbed her temples and took long, steady breaths. At length, the dizziness faded and she comforted herself with the familiar lemon scent of the dishwashing soap and the fake radio chatter of the video game.

Come to think of it, what is Adam playing, anyway?

Rising, she headed to the living room and gazed across the dark and fair head to the screen, finding a soldier running through a destroyed city. A soldier. Like Kent who didn't know that the entire world could go to war. Twice. Slinking over to the couch, she peered at Adam's profile as he screwed his face up in concentration, slightly flushed with the effort of killing the enemy on the screen.

The stairs creaked behind her and the longing in Ophelia's chest thrummed with each footstep. She looked over her shoulder to spot Brennan strolling past, casting the screen and the man in front of it a distasteful look before catching her eyes on him and softening his gaze. He stopped halfway to the kitchen, as if he were going to speak or thought she would. Neither did.

"Brennan?" Alex called. "Wanna come eat with us?"

His eyes didn't so much as flicker to his friend's but rather stayed locked onto Ophelia's. "I will."

She didn't blink, and her longing throbbed with her heart as his shoulders rose and fell with each breath, as if he knew they were lovers in a past life. Then the throbbing vanished with a jolt.

No one is missing. I've found them all. We are the Gone People.

"*D*ammit," Adam hissed, chucking his controller, and Ophelia looked over to see that his soldier had died again. "Okay, let's go."

When she turned back, Brennan was gone.

"Babe?" Adam asked, rising. "You look tired."

Ophelia forced a smile for him, fighting off the lingering nausea after having her world spin backwards in time. "I didn't sleep much last night."

"I can tell."

He pulled her into a hug and Ophelia closed her eyes, breathing in the scent of sunscreen on his skin, reminding herself that he was a paramedic student who loved to surf and eat her grandmother's roast. The memory of him as Kent had placed a filter between them, the same as when a loved one did something upsetting in a dream and the lingering emotions tainted reality against all logic.

The walk to the restaurant and the hunt for their seats was a blur to Ophelia as she sifted through everything she had seen. A part of her feared for her sanity and health, but the other part repeated Alex's words of comfort. *People see lights and auras from brain tumors... not whole scenes.* Not whole scenes. And they certainly didn't live them.

So I have existed before, she mused as she slid into a seat beside Adam. *And so have my friends. Reincarnation is real.* The thought made her lips quirk in an amused smile. *Wars have been fought over which religion of the book is right, and they're all wrong. At least about this.* Straightening, she gazed up at the ceiling fan whirling above their heads, sending down a subtle breeze. *Unless, of course, the book in question is a collection of letters by a poet who died at twenty-five.*

Ophelia's gaze settled on the boys around her as she became aware of her surroundings for seemingly the first time. Sweet and sour sauce tinted the air and the fan was blowing away the faint nutty scent of raw fish.

"I am absolute rubbish at this," Brennan said with a grimace, angling his menu to Alex as he looked over. "What the hell is a...*negi?*"

Alex laughed softly. "That's a G, not a K."

"That's how I said it."

"No, you said it like how *Rugrats* say naked."

Brennan blinked at the other man.

"Nakey."

"What the hell is a Rugrat?"

"You had the worst childhood ever," Adam said with a chuckle. "They were these awesome babies."

Brennan merely curled his upper lip at the blond, and Ophelia knew he was thinking they were a brick shy of the load, as he would say.

"Just get the Guido," Alex said, redirecting him. "Avocado, cream cheese, garlic, basil, macadamia nuts. It sounds totally random but it's so good."

"Yeah, if you've got something against protein," Adam said, studying his own menu.

Ophelia picked up hers. They were at her favorite sushi place, Mobo.

Clearing her throat, she looked over the list of food, breathing a sigh of relief as she finally felt anchored to the here and now and her own emotions once more.

Adam laughed, pointing at something on the menu. "They have a roll called the Pineapple Express. Classic."

"Well, I'm getting the Death Star," Ophelia replied.

"Good thinking."

A server came over to take their orders and Alex helped Brennan pick out something tame while the rest of them handed over their menus. Ophelia studied the Japanese American's face, wondering if he lived a past life, too.

Was he in Japan then? For their nationalities seemed to be linked to their eternal beings in some way. Three out of four of them had blood ties to the islands of the North Atlantic. But then there was Alex, who was nearly fully Greek while Lucy had been an English rose, so maybe their souls weren't as simple as all that.

A more rational person would be wondering why they could remember events from a past life, Ophelia mused. But instead, she was filled with gratitude, for the atmospheric lighting of the restaurant reminded her of the yellow gas lamps, and the chatter of other patrons was really the rumbling of so many souls.

Life isn't a series of random occurrences acted out by bumbling bodies. Life is a vast sea of immortality.

Ophelia rested a hand on her chest as understanding spread throughout her, soothing her veins with wonder. Her introspection was interrupted by the server setting down a steaming kettle.

"Tea," Ophelia mused with a smirk as she touched the warm, earthen pot. "That's where I get it from."

"Huh?" Adam asked, glancing at her.

"Nothing," she replied, shaking her head with a smile that only grew when her eyes settled on Brennan seated across from her. They may all be playing different parts in her current life, but he was the final piece. Everyone was together again. He caught her happy look and hesitantly returned it, as if wondering why he was being awarded such a smile.

"The shop busy lately, Brennan?" Adam asked.

"Enough," he replied softly before shifting his dark gaze to meet Adam's.

"So do you, like, get free repair work done on your car and stuff?"

Brennan sucked in his lower lip and shook his head.

"That's lame."

"I don't have a car."

"They drive on the other side of the road," Alex explained.

"Cars are overrated," Ophelia said, realizing how distant her voice sounded as she wondered if her distaste for driving was also an artifact from her Victorian life. She couldn't blame Brennan for not wanting to get behind a wheel after what happened to his parents.

"You bunch of hippies," Adam teased. He rested his hand on Ophelia's thigh and gave it a squeeze, reminding her of his turn of the century English counterpart. "I'm surprised you're letting him order something with cream cheese, Alex."

Brennan's gaze flicked between Adam and the pierced young man before asking, "What's wrong with it?"

"It isn't vegan," Alex explained. "Adam likes to think I'm a dictator about these things."

"We can't eat a bite without him checking every label," the blonde defended.

"Then eat at your own damn house," Alex countered with a chuckle. "I don't barge in there all the time and start criticizing your diet."

Adam furrowed his brow. "I don't criticize."

"What do you call it then?" Alex deadpanned.

"I voice my opinion," Adam said with false snootiness.

"Loudly," Alex agreed. "I'll eat egg and dairy if I know where it comes from. That hatchery in *our* city was grinding up live chicks that were males. Just chucking them into the machinery."

"Jaysus," Brennan gasped.

"It's a *chicken*," Adam replied, leaning in towards Alex. "My mom used to raise them. They have no brains."

"It's animal cruelty."

"It's not cruel if it doesn't know it's alive."

Alex shook his head. "You can't prove that."

"Didn't you guys already have this argument?" Ophelia asked.

149

Both ignored her.

"Death is death," Alex pressed. "You can't justify unnecessary killing."

"What do you think war is?" Adam asked with an incredulous laugh.

"An abomination."

"One that's keeping your ass safe."

Ophelia sighed and looked away from Adam, wondering if his frustration over the video game had his blood so close to the surface, or if a part of him remembered being a soldier.

"From what?" Alex asked. "Afghani peasants?"

Adam just shook his head, making an effort to bite his tongue.

For his part, Brennan seemed to be paying them little heed, looking as out of place as Leander while his mind wandered. Though given what Ophelia knew of Brennan's life, she doubted there was much of the cultured footman left in him. Lucy's reformative spirit seemed to have kept its fire burning in Alex, and Adam likewise shared Kent's confidence in his own views. Just as she began to wonder what ever became of Leander and Amelia, Alex spoke again with a pleasant chirp in his voice while he played with his chopsticks.

"The weirdest guy came in today."

"That describes this whole feckin' city, pal," Brennan said.

There was a basketball game on TV and Adam used the Warriors as an excuse to distract himself. Ophelia knew him well enough to tell when his irritation was simmering just below his self-control, but she was thankful he had managed to shove it down that far for the sake of not ruining their outing.

Alex chuckled as he continued his story. "He like, had these dreads and reeked, I mean reeked of weed. I was expecting him to order some intense chai or something, but instead he waited in line, then was all 'Hey bro, where's the mic at?'"

Ophelia's mind sharpened when the stoner voice her friend was imitating rang a bell. "Was his name Trea. 'Like Tea, but with an R'?"

"Yes," Alex gasped, slapping the table with a laugh.

Brennan scrunched his nose. "Wouldn't that be...Trey?"

"Do you know him?" Alex asked, and Adam poured himself a cup of the tea as he drew his attention back to the table.

"I met him at Chocolate, downtown."

Alex chuckled again. "That's hilarious."

"Why did he want a mic?" Brennan asked.

"Sometimes we do readings," Alex explained, "but that's usually at night and we didn't have anything planned. But it was slow so I was like, alright, I'll give you the mic." He leaned in, amusement dancing in his light eyes, and Ophelia grinned, realizing that his having been her sister could be why they had always understood each other so well. "So he took the mic and was like 'Testing, testing...' then started reciting all of this slam poetry and like, no one could understand half of what he said. It was really bizarre. I should've filmed it."

Ophelia and Brennan chuckled while Adam smirked.

"What was it about?" she asked.

Alex rubbed his face. "It was like... all New Age or something. Like, really bizarre. There was something about how he didn't give the queen the key, fighting for the goddess and killing ravens and fucking a deer which made the sun implode."

"Jaysus."

"Sounds like an awesome party," Adam offered.

Their food arrived and while the rest of them dug in, Brennan looked rather skeptical of his seaweed-wrapped roll, once again seeming out of place.

"Dude, if you don't eat that, I'm going to plug your nose and Alex is going to sit on you, and we're gonna stuff it in your mouth," Adam threatened.

Brennan stiffened, as if he'd just caught a whiff of something nasty, and then took a tentative bite. A look of surprise crossed his face and he popped in the rest of the roll.

It was dark out once the four left the restaurant to make their way back to the old Victorian. A homeless man sidled up to them out of the shadows as they passed. Ophelia knew better than to make eye-contact as she registered his layers of clothing and stained skin and didn't break her purposeful stride.

"Can you spare any change?"

Ophelia pretended she didn't hear him and stepped closer to Adam.

"Sorry," Alex offered with a placating smile.

"At least you're nice," the homeless man replied. "Unlike that bitch."

Ophelia wrenched her head around with a glare, assuming he must've meant someone else, when she was met with his stormy eyes.

"Yeah, you," he called out.

Adam wrapped an arm around her, silently urging her forward while shouting "Fuck off" over his shoulder.

The homeless man launched into a string of obscenities that was only cut off by Brennan rolling and lighting up a cigarette then handing it to him. "Sure, fock Cromwell, the Queen, and the Black and Tans."

"Thanks, man."

Brennan nodded then made one for himself. "*Slán*."

Ophelia's pulse surged as she recalled the angry glint in the man's eyes and she leaned into Adam's side with a rush of gratitude for his sheltering presence. He rubbed her arm and gave her a squeeze, kissing the top of her head. The comfort his touch sent surging through her made her fret over him one day not being there, though where the wayward thought came from, she didn't know.

"What a bollix. He was some prick, huh?" she could hear Brennan remark behind them as he split off from the group, lighting his cigarette.

"Where're you going?" Alex called.

"The lads wanna rehearse, I'll see youse later!"

Brennan lifted a hand in farewell, his eyes darting across each face, settling on Ophelia's last and lingering a heartbeat longer before trotting off. She felt a tug as she watched him go and reminded herself of who she was holding onto.

Once back at the old Victorian, they piled onto the couch and channel surfed. Alex seemed preoccupied texting someone whom she suspected was the guy from the Poet and the Patriot. As Ophelia basked in Adam's body heat, she had trouble focusing on much else. Her mind was tired and thin.

Later in the night, she tried to stay awake for Adam's *I'm home safe* text, but fell asleep anyway.

Ophelia woke up around three in the morning in a cold sweat, panting. Her room was dark, illuminated only by the distant glow of a streetlamp outside her window. Alex's door wrenched open and his feet pounded on the stairs, making her sit up.

What woke us up? An earthquake? Her answer came in the form of a chilling scream from downstairs, as if someone was being burned.

Brennan.

Ophelia kicked off her lavender comforter and scrambled to her feet before hurrying down the hall. Peering from the top of the stairs, her heart rattled in her chest as she expected to see an attacker but instead spotted Brennan on the couch. No one else was in the room, other than Alex, who bent over and shook him.

A nightmare, she realized with a rush of relief before hurrying down the stairs.

"Brennan," Alex hissed. "Brennan!"

The young man woke up with a gasp, surging upright, the whites of his eyes glinting in the dimness. Ophelia rounded the corner of the couch just in time to see Brennan yank himself away from Alex with a yowl.

"It was a dream," Alex soothed, keeping a hand on his friend's shoulder, but Brennan didn't seem to have heard him, or fully woken up yet.

"Get away from me," he snarled.

"Bren—"

"Get away!" He lashed out and landed a punch to Alex's lip before breaking free and scrambling towards the corner of the room.

"Alex," Ophelia gasped as her friend's hand hovered over his chin when his lip started to bleed around his piercing.

"I'll be fine," he said tightly, delicately adjusting the ring around the wound, watching Brennan as he pressed his face against the wall, as if trying to hide.

The blood rushing past her ears thudded after seeing the red on Alex's lip, but the way Brennan was shaking and rocking, repeatedly knocking his forehead against the wall, tempered her anger.

"What the hell is wrong with him?" Alex whispered.

She shook her head, her mind racing through all of the terrible things he had told her, not knowing which one had surfaced to bare its canine grin. Swallowing past the stickiness of her throat, she slowly shuffled towards him.

"Brennan?"

He didn't break his rocking and as she neared, she realized he was crying. Her chest clenched in response, even as her body remained tense, and she cautiously kneeled a few feet from him.

"It's all right," she offered. "You're safe."

"I want Mam," he croaked, his fingertips yellowing against his undershirt as he tightened his arms around his chest.

"I'm sure you do," she whispered, reaching a trembling hand towards him.

"Elephant?" Alex cautioned from a few feet behind her.

"It's all right," she repeated, so softly that her words were almost inaudible. Her fingers brushed the bare skin of Brennan's right shoulder above the Celtic knot and sword tattoo and he flinched. "You're safe."

Alex's unease crackled behind her as Brennan stopped rocking and tensed. She rubbed her thumb along his bicep and he curled in tighter, as if he were a coiled snake ready to strike. Ophelia stiffened, ready to jerk away in case he lashed out, but just then, he let out a pitiful gasp and deflated. She slid her hand to his face and rested it against his cheek as lightly as if she were holding a hatchling.

"Look at me."

A tremor shot up his spine but after several shaking breaths, he complied. His face was shadowed in the dim light and his shimmering eyes appeared black as they timidly trailed up to hers. Her heart stuttered, for in that moment, the years were stripped away, and she was left facing a frightened, confused boy.

"Op'elia?" he rasped, his eyes sharpening with recognition before

OPHELIA

relaxing with such trust that her own apprehension dissipated. Ophelia smiled and nodded, allowing her hand to rest properly against the flushed, moistened stubble of his cheek.

His breathing hitched as he studied her face then he cast his eyes about the room, lips parting in surprise as he seemed to trickle back into himself, his frame shaking from every heartbeat. Once assured of his surroundings, his spine sagged in relief and he sank to the seat of his sweatpants.

"You okay now?" Alex whispered.

Brennan seemed to have just noticed his tears and frantically wiped at his cheeks, as if the wetness there was something disgusting. The wall thumped as he leaned back against it, sniffling and nodding stiffly.

"What happened?" Ophelia asked, drawing her hand back to her side.

He shook his head, his eyes fixed on the shaggy white rug, his forehead red from bumping against the wall.

"You don't want to tell us?" Alex asked.

"I just want it to stop," Brennan croaked, curling in an arm and cradling it as if it were broken. The despondent look that flickered over his features made Ophelia worry that she should have taken him to receive professional help days ago. After all, as a literature student, she wasn't exactly equipped to help someone so damaged.

"You want what to stop?" Alex asked gently, taking a step towards the pair.

Brennan swallowed hard and clenched his jaw, his gaze never leaving the rug, and Ophelia instinctively knew they just hit a roadblock. Looking over her shoulder at Alex, she eyed his bleeding lip. "You should put some ice on that."

Alex shifted, hesitant to leave her alone with Brennan after his explosion of violence, but complied anyway. Ophelia shot him a thankful expression, even if the adrenaline dissipating in her limbs made her feel as tense as Brennan had been moments ago.

"Brennan?" she started softly.

His chest hitched as he folded his legs in close, his eyes hidden beneath shadows.

"It's just us now."

He ran his fingers along his cradled arm, inspecting the bone.

"Are you hurt?"

Brennan shook his head no then let out a deep breath, thumping his skull back against the wall, his eyes glittering as he took her in. "I was... I was in a room," he began hoarsely.

Ophelia settled down to sit cross-legged and both could hear Alex shuffling about in the kitchen.

"I'm always in a room." Brennan dug a palm into an eye socket with a wince. "Every time."

"You were frightened."

"I can't get out. There's a window but it's up too high for me to reach. I can only... I can only see the car parked by the curb, so I must be in a basement."

She nodded, gripping her hands in her lap as she steadied her own breathing.

"I'm mostly alone, trying to escape, when..." He swallowed hard and dug his fingers into the scalp on either side of his head. "I don't even have anywhere to hide," he groaned.

"Hide from what?"

"The man," he croaked. "Ambrose."

Ophelia could swear the air was sucked out of the room, leaving her in a noiseless vacuum with nothing but the thudding of her own heart. "Ambrose?"

Brennan nodded miserably.

"H—How do you know that's his name?"

Brennan shrugged. "I just know it when I'm there. Like I know who he is."

Ophelia cocked her head, willing the air back into the room, the synapses in her brain firing too quickly to keep up with.

"Jack?" she whispered.

He peered across at her, his hands stiffly drifting away from his head. "That's what he calls me."

Ophelia's jaw trembled and she rose to her knees, braced on her palms as a surge of excitement and vindication rushed through her with a little boy's laughter. She wanted to tell him that she never gave up on him, that she always knew he would one day be found. That she had already thought she had found him once before, but his age threw her off. His age that must be a lie. Instead, all that came out was, "You were the puppy."

Brennan's raven brows twitched together. "What?"

"When we played house, remember? You were the puppy and I was the mommy."

He eyed her up and down and sounded far steadier when he spoke. "I think I'd remember playing house with ya, Girl."

"When we were young," she added with a shake of the head. "In pre-school."

"I didn't know ya then."

"Of course you did. You were called Jack and you talked funny and you… you made me feel…"

"What?"

Ophelia leaned back on her haunches. "I remembered things back then. Things I wasn't supposed to. And you always understood, like you remembered, too. Stuff from before we were born—just like you said the other night."

Brennan hunched his shoulders a little, and she realized that he must be cold with nothing but a tank top on his torso.

"It's the car," he said. "I heard him talking to a neighbor about how new it was. Right off the assembly line. Made the same year I was born."

She parted her lips to reply, only to realize that the math once again didn't add up, no matter how much it ought to. "But you weren't a baby when you were kidnapped. You were four."

His shadowed frame froze as he stopped breathing.

"Wha—" she began.

"I didn't say anyt'ing about being kidnapped."

"That's what I'm telling you," Ophelia enthused. "I was there when it happened. I remember."

Brennan whined and pounded his palms against his temples, screwing his eyes shut, and she realized that no matter how many knots she had untangled in her mind, there were still plenty more, and Brennan's head was tight with them.

"It's okay," she whispered.

"Am I still dreaming?" he whined.

Ophelia pursed her lips and scooted over, wedging against him with her back to the wall, feeling a tickling warmth as her side pressed against his.

"I can't be," he answered himself. "My focking head hurts too much."

Headaches. The past. The bright thing that flew to the tip of her tongue when they first met. Leander. Not Jack. But still Jack.

Just like that, a large knot untangled and flapped proudly in her mind.

"You're remembering a past life," she whispered breathlessly.

Brennan fixed her with a screwy look from behind a scarred brow. "What?"

"You're too young to be Jack. But you *were* Jack, once. You were killed by Ambrose and came back... you came back as you are now. As John Brennan."

He looked as if he had just had dog poo wafted under his nose as he listened to her, and she worried that she was only tightening the knots in his head.

"I can remember, too," she explained. "At first I had no idea what was going on. I thought they were visions from Gone People—dead people. But they weren't at all. They were—*are*—memories of a life I lived before this one. And you were there, and Alex and Adam."

"And Toto?" he asked.

She was about to ask who when she realized he just accused her of being Dorothy from *The Wizard of Oz*. "Don't be an ass."

"You're off your nut," he replied with a soft chuckle.

"And you must be perfectly sane since you punched Alex."

Brennan's eyes widened. "I didn't."

"Actually, um, hi," Alex said as he stepped out of the kitchen, holding an ice cube wrapped in a paper towel to his lip. "It was more of a..." He mimed a flailing arm coming awkwardly towards his face.

"Christ, I'm so sorry, Alex, I never—"

The other young man waved him off, an eager glint in his pale gaze as he transfixed on Ophelia, as if he had been eavesdropping the whole time.

"I was gonna tell you," she offered.

"So who was I in your past life? Kent?" Alex asked with a smirk that made him wince a moment later.

"Actually... you were my sister."

Brennan grunted in a half-laugh. "He was a girl?"

"You were a servant," she countered.

Brennan sobered. "I'd rather be a girl."

"Just wait till you feel a corset."

"Wait a minute," Alex said, his hooded eyes darting between the two before he pointed at Brennan. "*He* was the servant?"

"Leander," Ophelia bashfully replied, a flush building in her chest as Alex latched onto the implication that she and Brennan were once lovers.

Brennan looked between the two of them. "Who's Leander?"

"Adam was Captain Kent," Ophelia continued quietly then sighed, meeting Alex's gaze.

He nodded knowingly, keeping the ice to his lip.

"Didn't he make cereal?" Brennan asked.

"Captain *Crunch*," Ophelia corrected. "God, what is it with you people?"

Brennan fixed Alex with a questioning look, silently asking if the other male believed her.

"*You're* the one who told me that I make you feel grounded, Brennan," Ophelia said. "It must be because we were best friends when we were little. When *I* was little."

"Plus, you guys were—" Alex cut himself off at the fierce look Ophelia shot him.

Brennan shook his head, his eyes mere slits, his moist lashes glistening. "Even if it's true, why would I be remembering *any* of this?"

159

"There must be something in your past that you need to know now," she offered. "At least... that's as far as I've gotten."

The Irishman studied her at length and the warmth his gaze spread to her skin wherever he looked reminded her of the heat of a distant bonfire. She didn't want it to stop.

No, she scolded herself. *He isn't Leander anymore. Adam. Think of Adam who you betrayed as Amelia.*

"What do you see?" Brennan quietly asked.

Ophelia took a deep breath. "An estate. It's 1898."

"Like a plantation?" he asked.

"It's a country house England. Apparently that's why I like tea." She smirked and his smile slowly mirrored hers.

"And I was the help?"

She shrugged with a grimace.

"Christ, no wonder you're always trying to better everyone's etiquette."

"I do *not*," she scolded.

Alex giggled, locking eyes with Brennan. "She *so* does."

"There are just certain ways things should be done," she defended, but the statement only made Alex snort.

"So why have I always been shite at entertaining?" Brennan asked. "Shouldn't I be totally deadly at serving?"

Ophelia shrugged. "The life you lived before this one was as Jack, which is probably why you remember it. I see more of my old friend in you than..." She hesitated but the way he was looking at her wouldn't let her trail off. "Than Leander," she finished, ignoring the heat of Alex's gaze boring into her.

Brennan took a deep breath and let it out slowly, looking down to his hands. "Jaysus... I was murdered."

"Which is probably also why most people *don't* remember their past lives," Alex added before blinking, as if to shake himself awake. "I kind of can't believe we're actually having this conversation."

"Alexandros," Ophelia scolded.

"I mean, I believed you, Elephant, I did, but..." He shrugged. "That was just an idea. This is different. There are two of you now. I can't chalk this up to you having an overactive imagination."

She leaned towards him. "*Overactive?*"

"It's just a lot of existential concepts to accept, is all."

"I thought you were a philosophy major," Brennan said.

Alex shrugged. "This is meaning of the universe stuff, not old dead white guys."

Ophelia smirked at that last part.

"So you think we're mad?" Brennan asked. "Because I *feel* mad."

Alex shook his head. "I think you two are making each other remember. I mean, what are the chances that you would find Brennan in two lifetimes?" He half-closed one eye in thought. "Three?"

"Three," Ophelia quietly agreed, feeling Brennan's heart starting to race beside her.

"Maybe it's this," Brennan offered, his eyes darting between them. "You two."

She offered him an encouraging smile, remembering how thankful he was when she told him he could stay. Which would fit. As a servant he had nothing to his name, just as he had nothing now, and in both lives, she was in a position to help him. "Maybe."

"It's late," Alex offered after a contemplative silence. "We should get some sleep."

Brennan hesitantly nodded then rose, offering a hand to Ophelia to help her up. As she accepted, she studied what she could make out of his face, feeling a sense of accomplishment mixed with a strange sort of confusion over having been right. Jack was never really gone.

They whispered goodnights and Alex followed Ophelia up the stairs, pausing in her doorway as she stepped inside. "Lia?"

She turned to face her friend. "Everything's complicated enough as it is. If he doesn't remember his life as Leander, then it isn't important to the here and now."

Alex nodded pensively. "The whole thing is just so weird."

Her tension softened into a smile as she remembered the affection she felt for Lucy. "You're amazing."

Alex fixed her with an exasperated expression and opened his door. "Goodnight."

"Goodnight."

Sinking back onto her mattress with a sigh, she felt like a weight had been lifted from her chest now that so many of the wrinkles in her mind were smoothing out and straightening. For the first time in ages, she felt like she truly understood herself.

Which is why I love Keats, she realized with a jolt. *His words hold up a mirror, reflecting the nuanced, inaccessible parts of ourselves that we didn't know existed until we recognized them in his work. My thesis. I know what to write about now.*

*A*melia was studying a painting in the drawing room after coming through, when Lucy sidled up to her with a smile. She cast her eyes upon the portrait of their great grandfather depicted as a fit hunter.

"I wonder at the likeness," Lucy mused. "He was certainly rumored to be a large man."

The older girl glanced over her sister's shoulder at their mother who was busy entertaining Mrs. Clarke while their father and the rest of the men remained in the smoking room, including Kent, sharing glasses of brandy. After Leander had fumbled while serving that night, Amelia's mind had grown tight, as if she were trying to hold onto too many fleeting thoughts at once. It was difficult for any one to settle long enough to stir an emotion.

"You shouldn't fiddle with your hands so," Lucy quietly stated in her husky voice. "You'll worry your gloves right through."

Amelia took a deep breath and let it out shakily before she fixed her sister with a polite smile. "Of course."

Lucy shook her head, admiration shining in her blue eyes. "I would be frightened, too."

"It is just all happening so fast now that we've changed the date," she said quietly before darting a gaze towards their mother to ensure they weren't being overheard. "I can hardly keep up."

Her little sister nodded, pursing her full lips before whispering her next words. "I didn't mean the wedding."

Amelia smiled politely, eyeing her sister as she held her breath. "Oh?"

"I meant... I would be frightened to break his heart, as well." She met her gaze. "Though you're terribly brave for it."

Amelia parted her lips to ask whatever she was talking about, but just then, the door was opened as the men came through. She slid into her mask of contentment once more as Lucy wandered from her side.

Kent entered, smiling at his fiancée, but even as he strode towards her, the drawing room faded away and Ophelia was left staring at her laptop screen. Blinking, she peered around her living room, reminding herself of who and where she was, surprised by the lack of pressure behind her eyes and the ease with which she had once again slid into her current identity.

The transition was so fluid, in fact, that a surge of frustration coursed through her over the memory having stopped.

How could Lucy have known about her and Leander? Which man's heart was Amelia about to break?

Groaning, Ophelia studied her screen, satisfied at least by how many pages she managed to write in a few hours. If she could maintain her current pace, she would be able to finish her thesis on time. But it was little use trying to continue writing while her mind was so distracted by a conversation held over a hundred years ago. With Alex going out after work to hang out with Ramiro, and Adam spending the day training in the back of an ambulance, she decided not to cook.

The fog was already rolling in so she grabbed her moss green jacket and headed out into the world in a cream Henley and jeans tucked into her galoshes, thinking over her favorite restaurants from which to order takeout. As she wove down the backstreets to the main strip of Pacific Avenue, she thought of how much simpler her life had been just a few weeks ago. Like Amelia, the complications had all started when she encountered the Irishman.

"Whoa, hey," a deep voice drawled, and she looked up to see Trea jogging to her side after having crossed the street. "Ophelia, right?"

Santa Cruz was small enough to bump into people she knew, but usually large enough that chance encounters like the one with the UCSC student didn't occur like this.

"Trea, yeah?"

He grinned, flashing his surprisingly straight, white teeth beneath his orange-rimmed shades. "See, I knew it from the moment I saw you. I was like 'that chick's something special.' Memory must be your superpower."

Her response died with her smile as she realized that he was right.

Elephant, she heard Alex's voice tease in her head.

"So what brings you into town, man?"

Ophelia resumed walking and he fell into step beside her in more of a shuffle than a walk so that his flip-flops rarely left the ground.

"Dinner. You?"

"Oh, this is my place. Welcome to *mi casa*," he said, jerking his head out at the city surrounding them, his hands in his pockets. "Did you hear that they're actually putting an elevator into that thing?" He gestured to a building that was under construction. "It's like they think this is New York or some shit. Am I right?"

A chuckle escaped her, even though she knew he wasn't trying to be funny. He did have a point, however. Anything over four stories would look like a monstrosity in the cityscape.

"Hey, can I tell you something personal?" he asked, peering at her from behind his shades.

Ophelia tensed. In her experience, confessions like that from people like him were always things that made her feel like she needed to wash her hands afterwards. "Sure."

"I really dig your aura," he gushed. "It's like, so vibrant and, I dunno… womanly. You have a voluptuous aura." He let out a stupid laugh and Ophelia forced a smile, finding herself once again wondering if he thought he was being flirtatious. "You're like, a priestess or something, man."

"That's very kind of you," she replied quietly, avoiding looking at him as she picked up her pace, only to realize she had no idea to which restaurant she was headed.

"So have you found your Hamlet yet?" he asked.

She pursed her lips in polite apology. "I have a boyfriend, if that's what you mean. Sorry."

Trea pursed his lips and shook his head. "Don't be sorry. That's not what I mean at all."

"Then what did you mean?"

He shrugged, the already-taut fabric around his flannel button-holes tightening even more. "You've got this vibe about you. Like you're looking for a lost soul."

Ophelia didn't realize she had slowed her pace until she stopped completely outside of an herbal remedies shop. Trea shuffled to a halt beside her, raising his brows in question.

"I mean, we're all here to better ourselves, right?" he asked. "This is like, an experience, man. An *experience*. And then it's done and we start all over again and fill in all the blanks."

"Fill in the blanks?"

"Like, check this out." Trea shifted into a relaxed posture and started talking with his hands. "I was a squirrel in my past life. I saved up all my nuts for the winter but didn't live long enough to eat any of them. So you know how I was born?" She shook her head and he leaned in and whispered, "With three, man."

Ophelia observed him, studying his clear tan skin stained with the scent of marijuana, with amused surprise. "Three?"

"Life gave me back my nuts in a completely different way. See, it's all about edification, ya know? Learning all we can so we can find some kind of happiness."

"So you're a Buddhist?" she asked.

"Nah, man, I'm just a dude. I'm not selling anything. But when I see the truth, I've gotta share it, ya know?"

She nodded, a part of her wondering who was around to see her talking to him. "So you're not trying to reach Nirvana?"

Trea let out a disapproving sound. "Man, that became like, unreachable the moment Kurt Cobain—oh, you mean the state of supreme peace of mind! I was gonna say, 'What? This chick's too young for that.'"

Ophelia just blinked at him, too confused to reply.

"Anyway, I just thought I should let you know." He looked up, as if tracking a fly, then started to wander off.

"Let me know what?" she asked.

"Don't let your life repeat itself," he called, walking backwards. "Or you'll be back to ground zero."

A car honked and slammed on the breaks yet still bumped into Trea's thighs as he walked backwards onto the street.

"Whoa, man, you just totally threw off my mystic exit!" Trea scolded the driver.

Ophelia's chest had filled with an odd stillness as she turned away, her feet shuffling aimlessly.

Don't let your life repeat itself.

A relieved smile graced her lips as she realized why she had Amelia's memories.

Adam.

He worried that she was betraying him because she had, even if it wasn't in this life. Lucy's statement about heart-breaking lingered in her mind. While Ophelia didn't know how Amelia's story ended, enough events had already been set in motion to cause Kent great pain.

That's my purpose, she thought. *To right my wrong. To love him with all my heart.* The thought ought to comfort her, but instead, she felt intimidated. *For how can I love someone enough to make up for a whole lifetime?*

At length she realized that she had wandered all the way to the beach. The wharf was in the distance and a bread bowl of clam chowder suddenly sounded like a marvelous defense against the chill in the foggy air.

The Santa Cruz Beach Boardwalk sprawled to her left, its premiere roller coaster, the Giant Dipper, roaring down the wooden tracks while delighted screams echoed. Judging by the noise, the place was rather busy for a Sunday night in early May, and she wondered if some schools had already let out for the summer. Pockets of people walked on the sidewalk, headed to and from the attraction. A tall, lanky figure pulled apart from a crowd and stood off to the side, facing her.

Ophelia did a double-take when she recognized Brennan. His leather jacket was zipped up to the neck, his hands stuffed in his pockets as his wavy hair fluttered about in the breeze. Though he was just a man standing still as a stone in a stream of people, the way his narrowed gaze was fixed on hers made the cacophony of noise from the amusement rides nearby fade until all she was left with were his hazel eyes and the distant thunder of the sea. As if they belonged to a quieter world.

She wondered who he really was, because there was nothing subservient in his straight back, and nothing childlike in the way the brush of his skin warmed her. Ophelia smiled, tucking her hair behind her ear as it whipped across her face. Brennan sauntered over to her, arching a scarred brow.

Waltzer

"And here I thought ya didn't like the sea."

"Being in it and by it are very different things," she replied.

He smiled a little as he came to a halt beside her. "Where's your fella?"

My fella?

"Training," she replied. "What're you up to?"

Brennan shrugged, pulling his hands out of his pockets. "Helps me think."

"And here I thought you tried to avoid that," she prodded. It did the trick and teased out that infectious grin, even if she didn't realize that was what she wanted until she was already infected.

"I'm from an island," he defended.

"You must miss wandering Irish beaches."

He let out a soft chuckle. "Hardly. Clearly, you've never seen the Atlantic. There's a reason the Spanish called your coast *pacified*."

Ophelia's smile faded as she realized that his repertoire of knowledge didn't mesh well with her image of a drug addict. She somehow kept the man before her and the user separate in her mind, which was just fine, for she had only met the one and didn't want to meet the other.

"Where're ya headed?"

"Only one way to find out," she said before turning to walk towards the wharf. He followed her as if tethered by a leash, appraising her with a playful look in his eye, reminding her of Jack.

Come to think of it, how could he look physically the same as Jack when it was a separate life? And how could he and Adam look so similar to their Victorian counterparts? The thought made another knot form in her head.

"You sure seem happy."

"I started working on my thesis again," she chirped.

"Then this is cause for celebration. We ought to get a round."

"It's Sunday."

"A California girl who likes Guinness is reason enough to get bladdered on a Sunday."

"Oh, that conjures such a nice image of a full—wait a minute." She peered at him out of the corner of her eyes and shook her head. "How'd you know that?"

"You said ya like stout," he fumbled then relented. "Well, you were drinking it at the gig, weren't ya?"

And here I thought he hadn't even noticed me there. An amused smile settled on her lips as she wondered if he remembered the dress she was wearing. *You mean the dress Adam loves,* she scolded herself.

"What're you writing about, anyway?" he asked.

"Um... John Keats, and how his articulation of the creative process and the subconscious has inspired great minds. At least that's what I've started with, but it still needs a lot of tightening and—"

"Keats?" he asked with a soft laugh.

"He's a poet," she explained. "He wrote—"

"*I am certain of not'ing but the holiness of the heart's affections and the truth of imagination,*" Brennan quoted with a touch of whimsy in his voice.

Ophelia grinned. "How did you know that?"

He raised his brows. "What? Ya think uni students have the monopoly on poets—"

"That's from a letter, not a poem."

Brennan shrugged. "My mam was a big fan. I wanted to get it as a tattoo to honor her but it was too long."

"That is *so* sweet," she crooned, stopping.

"It's not sweet," he griped, looking disgusted as he angled his torso away from her.

"It *is*."

"I was gonna get it on my arse," he defended, talking over her.

Ophelia laughed again. "Keats on your ass?"

"Didn't quite have the right ring with me, either." He started walking again, a smile dancing in his eyes.

"Sounds hot to me."

"Really?" he asked, suddenly completely serious.

A pleasant flush darted over her skin at his reaction and she forced herself to change the subject. "You're eating clam chowder whether you want to or not."

Brennan sidled up to her with an overdramatic seductive look that she pretended was awful even as it made her breathing hitch. "Sounds hot to me," he said, his warm breath tickling the baby hairs on her forehead. He pulled away before she even registered his movement.

Tease. Ophelia followed him as he continued down the wharf.

"This t'ing's long," he commented.

"Yeah," she chirped, pretending that sentence didn't make her thoughts flicker to something else. "Haven't you been down here before?"

"Of course."

Brennan came to a stop by the railing, peering out at the slate grey sea in the distance before sweeping his head to the beach behind them as the roller coaster rumbled, the screams of the people on the ride echoing across the water.

"I love the Giant Dipper," she said, following his gaze.

"Never been."

"What?" she squawked. "I thought you said you'd lived here for—"

"It's too expensive," he complained with a wince before pulling away from the railing, the wind tousling his hair.

"You live a very sad life."

"You'd be off your head to get into one of those devious contraptions designed to—"

Ophelia laughed. "There is just no end to Irish quirk in you, is there?"

Brennan glanced her up and down, arching a scarred brow. "Wouldn't *you* like to know?"

"Ha-ha," she taunted mirthlessly, nearly stomping over to him as she grew careless of her legs. A distant part of her mind whispered that she was flirting, but she gave herself permission. After all, they were only words.

"So where're we going?" he asked, pretending to be focused on the walk ahead of them while delight danced in his eyes.

"Stagnaros," she replied.

"In that case..." He latched onto her shoulders and steered her in the opposite direction. She realized with a burn in her chest that she had been so distracted that they had walked right past it. "Ya see," he started, lowering his head beside hers with a hand on her shoulder as he pointed out the sign, "that's an S, and that there is what we English-speakers like to call a T."

"Is that right?" she asked, wishing she could stop admiring the rumble in his throat when he was this near.

"Dead on. Though if ya give it a bit more of a head it becomes a cross, which, ya know, really takes all of the fun out of it."

Ophelia twisted to examine his profile. "You really don't like religion, do you?"

He shrugged. "Not religion in general, but certain religions, yeah."

Brennan turned his face towards hers, and before she could even finish the thought that she had never been this close to his eyes, she glimpsed a forest in their green and brown, scattered like so many trees.

"Why?" she whispered.

"They're unnatural. Hell-bent on controlling people instead of protecting what they ought to."

"And what's that?"

"Dignity," he said quietly, letting his hand fall away from her shoulder, leaving her with a chill where it had been. "Freedom. The earth."

"The earth?"

He nodded, his eyes tracing her features, making her wonder what he saw when he looked at her. For though she had known him in two of his lifetimes, she couldn't help but only see him as the man in front of her right now.

"You said you were afraid of going into the sea?"

Ophelia parted her lips but couldn't find it in her to reply when his raven brows twitched the slightest bit, as if he were fighting some impulse, his eyes darting to her mouth.

"I can't imagine anyt'ing more worthy of respect, or divinity, than the sea," he continued huskily. "Mountains, storms…"

She smiled and rested a hand on his chest. "You really do fit in with us hippies."

Giving his jacket a pat, she thought she could feel a wild drumming under his flesh when she pulled her hand away and headed towards the restaurant.

"That's the worst crime of religion, isn't it?" he asked as he followed her. "It made us forget."

"Forget what?"

"My point exactly."

Ophelia shot him a questioning look as she opened the door, causing him to hastily latch onto it and hold it for her, playing the part of the gentleman.

Maybe there is some Leander in there, after all.

Once inside, they were greeted by a server and led to a table by one of the large windows. "This is perfect," Ophelia remarked.

Brennan wrinkled his nose and turned to the hostess. "Can we sit outside?"

Never mind.

The woman glanced between the pair of them with surprise. "Of course. It'll just be a bit chilly."

Brennan caught Ophelia's tight expression. "You're a fan of the Romantics, aren't ya?"

"What does that have to do with eating in the cold and wind?" she asked as they followed the hostess onto the narrow patio upstairs, overlooking the sea.

"How can you appreciate the sun if you're never cold?"

As if on cue, an icy gust kicked up as they took their seats. Their hostess offered them an amused smile as she handed out menus.

"Cheers."

"Actually, we already know what we're getting," Ophelia announced before placing their orders and handing the menus back to the woman.

"There's the mam I know," Brennan said with a jeering look, leaning his chair back on two legs once they were alone.

Ophelia tucked her chin in to her neck like a giraffe. "What happened to 'that's hot'?"

He shook his head innocuously. "I don't know what you're on about, Girl."

She rolled her eyes, causing his placid expression to shift into a smug smirk. "Do you enjoy taunting me?"

"I'm not taunting."

"Seriously, you're like a little boy with a stick, prodding me for attention."

"I'm not prodding."

"You're right—you're completely innocent."

He let his chair fall back on all fours. "I am *far* from innocent."

A dozen responses flew to the tip of her tongue but none came out, and she didn't know if it was the memory of Adam's smile or of the damaging hands that had touched Brennan that kept her quiet, even when he was inviting her to speak. Another gust cut across the patio, strong enough to fling even the curls that reached down to Ophelia's shoulder blades.

"Well, you certainly know how to show a girl a good time."

"Oh come on, this is the sublime," he enthused, throwing his arms out. "This is what it's all about."

"My nose is running." She looked about for a napkin.

"Use your sleeve."

Ophelia shot him a disgusted look. "What are we—five?"

Brennan leaned across the table to her. "Live a little."

She fixed him with a defiant stare before dragging her jacket sleeve across her nose with a sniffle, making him giggle.

"Was that so hard?"

"Oh, shut up."

"I told ya I wasn't innocent."

"I can feel the corruption seeping into me already."

Their hostess returned with their clam chowder in bread bowls then set them down on the table. "Will that be all?"

Ophelia locked eyes with Brennan. "No. Two pints of Guinness, please."

"Of course. I'll be right back."

The Irishman slowly grinned, baring his slightly crooked teeth that suited him so well. "Well, call the guards."

"I know. I'm out of control."

"I have that effect on women."

"You know, humility isn't exactly your strong suit."

Brennan laughed and grabbed his spoon. "So I've heard. Not very fitting for a servant, is it?"

She studied him at length as he stirred his chowder, waiting for it to cool, wondering at his seemingly unperturbed manner. "You've sure accepted everything well."

He shrugged as he tore off a bite of bread. "People talk about it all the time—meeting someone ya swear you've already known. Someone you're just immediately comfortable around, against all logic. You're the first t'ing that's made sense in a long time."

She remembered Adam confessing that he had felt the same way. As she noticed just how much time had slipped through her fingers while walking on the wharf, she had the sensation of drifting without anchor. Until Brennan darted her a shy smile as he gauged her reaction to what he had just said, and she realized that she didn't need an anchor while he was near, filling her sails and making her forget to worry while she set her own course in unchartered territory.

"I know the feeling," she quietly replied, and the hope that flared in his eyes both tickled and terrified her.

A contented silence settled over the pair while they ate, and as Ophelia once again had the sensation of thawing at his side, her mind issued her a peculiar warning by reminding her of the smoky-eyed girl who had trashed her living room.

"So. How's Charlie?"

Brennan shook his head casually, and she only realized that she had just instinctively tried to throw distance between them when it failed. "Haven't seen her since you have."

"Hopefully that's a good thing."

"In my experience, it's usually bad. Means she's been off on a binge or somet'ing."

The mention of the other woman dimmed the mood the slightest bit, but the nonchalant way he talked about her made Ophelia wonder how much of a connection was left between them at all. Satisfaction calmed her nerves, and with a start she realized that a part of her had seen Charlie as a threat from the moment she touched Brennan.

Which is not a thought I should have in the least, especially when I'm supposed to be righting my wrongs by showering Adam with affection.

"You've gone pale," Brennan quietly observed, and Ophelia realized that she hadn't taken a bite for some time. "Here."

He unzipped his jacket and struggled out of it.

"Oh, no, I'm—"

But he had already taken it off and gotten to his feet. She offered him a thankful smile as he held it out to her and she slipped her arms into the warmed sleeves.

"This is a pleasant day in Ireland," he explained, tugging the thin dark green of his familiar plaid shirt down around his torso. "A heat wave there is 77° Fahrenheit."

He sat back down with a doting expression as she folded the leather over her chest, surprised by its weight. The simple act filled her with such longing in the bottom of her stomach, wishing they really were just a girl and a boy on the wharf.

Don't think about anything else, she scolded herself. *Just live in the moment as he's asking you. A moment is all you need to cure yourself.*

"What's it like?" he asked, cocking his head slightly. "Going to university?"

Ophelia parted her lips, but the earnestness of his childish question clenched her heart so strongly that she could hardly find the words to answer. "Better than high school," she said. "Most everyone who's there *wants* to be there, which makes it easier to learn."

He didn't blink as he drank in her words, as if hungry for them.

"My campus is really nice. Safe. It's easy to make friends."

Brennan's gaze drifted away as he absorbed her words and she realized that for all his bravado, he longed to be like her and Alex.

"Have you ever thought of applying?" she asked.

He pursed his lips and shook his head, forcing a wide smile that she recognized as a mask for the first time. "Barely got past my junior cycle."

She was going to ask what that meant when she realized that, given what he had said his home life was like at sixteen, she didn't need to.

Once they finished their meal, their moment ended, and maybe it was the beer, but she craved more.

"Look at ya," he appraised loftily, bouncing back from any dampened spirits as she drained her glass. "Unrecognizable."

She dragged her sleeve, which was actually his, across her lips in a show of wiping off the foam, making him chuckle. They paid for their meal then wound through the restaurant and back out onto the wharf. "This goes both ways, you know."

"I should hope so."

"If you get to push me, then I get to push you."

He shook his head haughtily. "I'm un-pushable."

Knowing that she never did get to give Jack his turn on the swing made her chest clench, but she shoved the dark memory aside by reminding herself that it was over and done with and that he was back anyhow. "We'll find out, won't we?"

Brennan shook his head as they sauntered down the paved pier. "If ya try to shove me into the water, I'll..." He trailed off, swallowing as he wracked his mind.

"You'll?"

"Take my coat back, for starters."

Ophelia shook her head in mock shock. "I have never been more afraid."

"There's more where that came from."

She chuckled and bumped her shoulder against his, the alcohol warming her belly. When he shoved back, his hip pressing hers, she forgot to think about anything other than the delight of this instant in time. He stuck to her side, his arms folded over his chest, and she knew that even if he was cold, he wouldn't admit it.

Brennan hummed softly as the waves crashed and hissed below them, and she found the rumble in his throat so soothing that she longed for more. "Why don't you ever play at home?" she asked.

"Don't want to bother anyone."

"You have a lovely voice."

Brennan chuckled, his tongue sticking between his teeth childishly. "Nah."

"*Yeah.*"

"Brian's the singer."

"He should give you more songs."

"You make us sound so official."

She watched the handful of people on the beach, bundled up and playing soccer or volleyball on the sand lined with the tire tracks of lifeguard trucks. The view was blocked by hotels as they stepped back onto sidewalk at the end of the wharf.

"Isn't that what you want to do? Make music?"

"You could say that."

"I mean, what did you want to be when you grew up?"

"Never really gave it much thought."

"Liar." She shoved her shoulder against his again, their thighs brushing teasingly.

He smiled bashfully at the sandy concrete below their feet. "There are these little dairies all over Éire. I always sort of fancied that life. But it's not really somet'ing you can get into after being raised in the city."

"Being a farmer?"

Brennan's gaze flickered to hers. "How about you?"

"Oh, I don't know," she said with a sigh. "I suppose I'll teach."

"You just can't get enough of those four walls, can ya?"

The shrill ringing and circus tunes of the games in the arcade bounced around in the air as they passed by, headed for the Boardwalk. Brennan's eyes darted around in surprise as he realized what she was up to.

"Oh no, you're not…"

Ophelia's response was a devious smirk which sent him spinning on his heels and striding in the other direction. She caught his hand and yanked him back over with a laugh. "I don't think so, lad."

Brennan went limp as he allowed himself to be yanked back over to her side while she got in line to buy tickets. "You're ridiculous, ya know that?" he accused around a crooked smile.

"And you're incorrigible."

"T'anks, love," he chirped, standing a little taller.

When he slipped his arm around hers, pressing to her side in the cold, it was so simple and pure that she wished they could wait in line for hours. A part of her whispered that this was only a moment, and that he would never be hers, but she opened a window in the back of her mind and ushered out the naysayer. When it was her turn, she bought enough tickets for the pair of them then tugged him towards the roller coaster.

"Think of this as my late birthday gift," she said as one of the cars came roaring down the big hill, making Brennan blanch as he watched it. "You'll thank me after."

"Why do ya think they're screaming?"

"They're having *fun*."

OPHELIA

"Or dying."

She tagged their ticket card at the entrance then they stepped through the turnstile inside the building. The crowds seemed to be thinning for the line moved quickly. As one of the cars thundered past over their heads, the building trembled and Brennan's eyes widened as he tensed. "Earthquake?" he gasped.

Ophelia laughed. "It's just the roller coaster."

"What if I puke?"

"You *won't*." She squeezed his arm in emphasis.

The action teased a whimsical smile out from behind his timid features, sending off fireflies in her chest.

One of the trains came to a halt as the ride ended and a little boy stepping off whimpered and wiped tears from his cheeks. Brennan watched him shakily climb out then fixed Ophelia with an accusatory look.

"You're cruel, ya know that?"

She slid her fingers down their linked arms and into his hand, giving it a supportive squeeze that didn't end even after it was their turn and they sat down at the front of the roller coaster. Brennan all but yanked her hand against his stomach with a death grip as the safety bar was lowered over their laps, making her laugh.

"I've changed my mind," he squawked, turning his waxy face towards her. "I want to get off."

"What happened to 'do somet'ing that scares ya every day'?"

He swallowed hard, unable to argue against his own logic, and it was too late anyway. The car shot into the darkness of the tunnel, twisting and turning before bursting into the grey dusk light as it climbed the big hill.

"Holy shite," Brennan barked.

"There could be kids behind us," she scolded above the clicking of the ride as the train climbed upwards.

"Then I'm only saying what they're all feeling," he squeaked, his voice cracking. He peered down and squeezed her hand painfully before fixing his impossibly wide eyes on her. "This is focking *high*."

She leaned in to his ear and whispered, "Get ready."

179

The anxiety fled at her nearness and he tracked her face with his nose, about to smile from the distraction when the clicking stopped. They only had a second to look ahead before the car barreled down the hill, tearing screams from both of their throats. They swooped into a tight turn and over another hill and Ophelia forced Brennan's hand into the air with hers. Apparently that was asking too much and he immediately fought with her to yank it back down.

Their tug of war distracted them and as they banked into another turn, she didn't brace herself and smashed against him with a squawk. By the time the last few, startling hills were over, Brennan was hugging their linked hands to his chest and laughing heartily, though from joy or hysteria, Ophelia couldn't tell.

"Are you okay?" she asked with a chuckle as they pulled to a stop.

He nodded, letting go of her hand to wipe at the tears forced from his eyes. The lap bar released and the two climbed out.

"Mother of God," he gasped, still laughing.

She climbed out then led him down the ramp to the counter where the other passengers were gathering, peering up at their photos taken by a camera on the side of the tracks.

"Lookit," he squealed, pointing out theirs before cackling.

"Best. Picture. Ever."

On the screen, Ophelia was laughing, hoisting their linked hands in the air, while Brennan was screaming for dear life, his eyes shut so tightly that they were two dark lines. She tugged out her phone and snapped a photo before zooming in and holding it up for Brennan, who was leaning over her shoulder to see.

The sight launched him into another peal of laughter. "You'd have thought I'd weed myself."

"I told you it was fun."

He tugged on her wrist until she was against his chest and he wrapped his arms around her in a swaying hug. "It was. T'ank you."

Ophelia basked in his warmth and the thud of his calming heart as she rested her cheek on his collarbone. He absently rubbed her back and she shifted her chin to gaze up at him. The forests of his eyes were so full of hope that it looked like faeries were having a dance amid the trees.

Someone bumped into the two, forcing Brennan to shuffle his feet and offer the teenager an apology as another crowd surged down the ramp to cluster around the monitors. He pulled away and rested a hand on her back to guide her to the side, out of the crowd.

As his warmth faded, Ophelia felt like her lungs were only half formed, for she just had a whole string of moments, and it wasn't enough. She wanted more.

12

"It's baltic," Brennan barked, hurrying up the steps to the old Victorian ahead of Ophelia, practically dancing as he waited to get inside while she tugged out her keys.

She unlocked the door and he darted into the living room then huddled in the corner of the couch. "I thought this was warm for Ireland."

"The sun was still out then."

She pointed at the woodstove as she headed into the kitchen, delight fluttering about in her breast when she realized they were home alone. "The wood's in the back."

As she filled the kettle with water, she could hear his booted footsteps followed by the slamming of the back door and smirked. By the time she had made two cups of blackberry tea, Brennan had a fire going and was as close to the stove as he dared without actually touching it.

Ophelia placed his mug on a coaster on the coffee table. "You can have your coat back."

Brennan shook his head, rubbing his arms. "I'm grand."

She spotted his guitar in the corner, outside of its case, and crossed over to it, plinking a few strings, trying to lure out the musician in the room. "I wish I could play. I've never been good at music."

He watched her, huddled by the fire like an urchin. "It just takes practice."

"It's more than practice. It's talent."

"*Heard melodies are sweet, but those unheard are sweeter.*"

Ophelia smiled. "More Keats?"

"Don't get used to it. I've about used my entire arsenal," he offered with a small laugh. "I remember that one because it used to confuse me when I was small."

She carried the guitar back to the couch, settling it on her lap as she absently plucked the strings.

"I think it's about adoring mystery," she said slowly as she thought. "Those moments that don't contain anything tangible, yet keep us yearning. Like the space between two events, where anything is possible."

He had shifted and relaxed a bit as the warmth spread across his back, and he watched her with dark eyes that reflected the flames, reminding her of something ancient that she couldn't hold on to. "Anticipation."

Ophelia nodded, running her thumb along one of the frets. "Music is everywhere, even if we can't always hear it." She accidentally plucked a high-pitched string, sending a discordant whine in the air, and she laughed at the timing.

Brennan smiled and crossed over to her, gently taking the guitar and raking his thumb across the strings above the soundhole before adjusting the tuning. She watched his hands with admiration. They were tough and often stained from work, but now they were nimble and delicate as they pressed on the neck above a fret and plucked a string or two at a time in a soft melody. She smiled, the room feeling warmer with each chord as the soothing tune chased the shadows from the corners of her heart.

After all, what is a life but a string of moments?

The tea heated her belly and her knee touched Brennan's as he played, making her feel drowsy.

"What's it called?" she whispered.

"'The Banks of Claudy.' It's a trad song. Better for a harp."

"Sing it," she asked.

"I'm useless at it," he said, scrunching up his face.

"Not to me."

He took a deep breath, his eyes still on his guitar, but even so, she thought she could see his cheeks pink up. He plucked the strings a few moments longer, finding the tune, before quietly singing.

> "'Twas on a pleasant morning all in the month of May
> Down by the Banks of Claudy I carelessly did stray I
> overheard a damsel most grievously complain 'It is
> on the Banks of Claudy where my darlin' does
> remain.'
> I boldly stepped up to her, I took her by surprise I know
> she did not know me, I being in disguise
> 'Where are you going my fair one, my joy and heart's
> delight Where are you going to wander this dark and
> stormy night?'"

His eyes and hands were focused on the guitar, though not for lack of practice. She was certain that if he looked at her as he sang, something between them would change. Every word tickled inside and she savored the feeling. With the fire crackling whenever Brennan's voice paused, it was not difficult for her to imagine that the pair of them were actually in an Irish cottage or pub by the sea.

> "It's on the way to Claudy's banks if you will please to
> show Take pity on a stranger, for there I want to go
> It's seven long years or better since Johnny had left
> this shore He's crossing the wide ocean where the
> foaming billows roar.
> He's crossing the wide ocean for honor and for fame His
> ship's been wrecked, so I've been told, down on the
> Spanish Main It's on the banks of Claudy, fair maid

whereon you stand Now don't you believe young
Johnny, for he's a false young man.
Now when she heard this dreadful news, she fell into
despair For the wringing of her tender hands and the
tearing of her hair 'If Johnny he be drowned, no man
alive I'll take Through lonesome shades and valleys,
I'll wander for his sake.'"

Ophelia's eyes drifted over his hands and lips and eyelashes and in that moment, she understood how the loss of one person could drive a woman to such desperate grief.

"Now when he saw her loyalty, no longer could he stand
He fell into her arms saying, 'Betsy, I'm your man."
Saying 'Betsy, I'm the young man that caused you all
your pain And since we've met on Claudy's banks,
we'll never part again.'"

Brennan finally looked up at her as he finished the song, and her drowsiness cracked and faded as she reminded herself that he was still there, warm and listening to her every breath.

"He tricked her," she whispered. "That's terrible."

"It's her fault for not recognizing him."

"But she was devastated."

He slid his guitar aside and sighed as he sank down against the couch beside her, his shoulder inching towards hers as the cushions shifted under his weight.

"But it ended up okay, didn't it?"

Ophelia leaned into his arm with hers, the snapping and flickering of the fire lulling her mind into a state of ease where she was content to just let things... be. Tightening her legs underneath her, she pressed closer and rested her cheek on his shoulder. Brennan tensed at first then seemed to give in with a soft sigh, twining his arm around hers and linking their hands as he rested his temple against her hair.

She watched the dancing flames behind the thick, dirty glass of the woodstove, knowing that the contented warmth filling her with such delight had nothing to do with the burning wood. All the same, she couldn't help but be enchanted by the dancing orange, yellows and blues, wondering over just how ancient the presence in her living room was, and how it had been at the fireside when she had first realized just how much she...

Just how much I what? she asked herself, her thought wafting away like smoke. She was about to chase after it when Brennan spoke.

"What if it wasn't a disguise?" he asked softly, and the rumble in his voice pressed against her crown. "What if he really did drown... but then came back?" He swallowed hard and she could feel his tension mounting as the drumming of his heart intensified. "For her?"

A tingle darted up her spine, the cold edges receding before she could even really notice them, leaving her with something more primeval. She shifted to take in his face, and the aching in his eyes was far too much for someone so young, even after all he had been through.

"You were just a boy," she whispered.

"What if that wasn't the only time we knew each other?" he asked.

Leander. Could he possibly remember?

"Because even if I had been your friend when I was four in this life, I'd hardly remember ya *now*. And certainly not enough to..." He trailed off, his eyes tracing a curl before reaching out and fingering the tip, sending a pleasant tingle into her scalp. Whatever war going on inside seemed to exhaust him and he wilted, resting his forehead against hers, their cold noses touching, and she was torn between pulling away and leaning in. "Is this wrong?" he whispered.

Yes. No. Yes. How could it be?

Nothing would be more effortless, and terrible, than to kiss him.

She tilted her chin and sank forward, but just as she was about to press her lips to his, Brennan sucked in a lungful and yanked his head away. The coldness of the air without him stung and she parted her lips to ask what happened when she heard what he already had: someone was stepping through the front door.

The panic that surged inside siphoned all the color from the room as the door shut.

Don't be Adam. Oh God, please don't be Adam.

"Oh," a surprised voice said. "Hello...?"

She didn't look up when the last word was drawn out as a question over the sight of them. It was Alex.

Brennan's face was still only inches from hers and he looked about to be sick, his stubble all the darker for his suddenly pale complexion. He closed his eyes and swallowed tensely, inching away from her as she breathed a sigh of relief, her heart hammering erratically after seeming to have done a somersault.

"Hi, Alex," she said quietly with a smile, her cheeks burning as she kept her head bowed for several seconds before facing him over the back of the couch.

Alex's expression was surprisingly unperturbed as he met her gaze before locking the door behind him. "Cold night, huh?"

"Yeah," she agreed.

Brennan was now sitting upright and only their knees were touching, but one look at the shame in his shoulders reminded her that they were seen.

Alex cautiously stepped into the room, careful not to look at either of them as he made his way to the fire and warmed his hands.

"How'd your date go?" she asked, her heart slowly returning to its normal pace.

"For once I think it actually was one," he said with a soft chuckle. "We ate and went to a movie then had drinks." His eyes danced as he shared with her. "Is that retro or what?"

She smiled, latching onto her friend's excitement rather than the heat and darkness radiating from the man at her side.

"We need more wood," Brennan mumbled before shoving off the couch and heading down the hall to the back door.

Neither Ophelia nor Alex corrected him that they didn't. She watched Alex track the younger man with his eyes until the back door shut, then his gaze darted to hers, arching a brown brow in question.

She hugged her knees to her chest, her throat growing sticky. "Please don't make me talk about it."

"Well," he whispered. "You two were once..."

"I know. But this has nothing to do with Leander. This is just... *him.*"

Alex nodded slowly, his expression grave. The fire crackled and they waited for Brennan to return. The house creaked, as if attempting to dissipate the rising tension.

"I want to hear more," she said, forcing cheer into her voice as the weight of what just almost happened settled deep inside. "What's he like?"

Alex studied his hands as he thought for a few seconds, and she realized that he had taken out his piercing as his injured lip healed. "Patient... and passionate. He's a high school teacher for special ed."

She widened her eyes. "That's impressive."

Alex nodded before studying her again, his hooded eyes nearly burning with curiosity. "I thought things were good again with Adam," he whispered.

"They are," she groaned.

"Then why are you—"

"I said I don't want to talk about it," she snapped before peering down the hall to make sure Brennan hadn't slipped back in. "I think that's why I'm remembering," she muttered. "To... treat Adam better."

"So, you start by kissing Brennan?"

"We didn't kiss," she hissed, leaning forward.

Alex shrugged. "I'm not judging, I'm just... confused."

"Welcome to the club."

Alex peered at the back door. "Want me to go talk to him?"

"No."

"Want me to talk to Adam?"

"*No.*"

He nodded, growing quiet as she snatched her mug back up and swirled around her teabag.

"Was kissing all you did?" he asked.

Ophelia hopped to her feet. "We *didn't* kiss."

Slamming down her mug hard enough to spill some of the tea, she strode down the hall and had to slow herself before opening the door.

Brennan twisted to look up at her from his spot huddled on the back porch, smoking. Her eyes settled on the small pile of firewood at his side.

"I was going to bring that in," he offered before blowing a column of smoke away from her and stubbing out his cigarette.

Sighing, she hugged his jacket around her in the cold and eased down next to him. "We can trust Alex."

"Right ya be."

Ophelia scooted closer so that their hips were touching. She wanted to rest her head on his shoulder again but was now restrained by a corset of reality. A flame seemed to be flickering in Brennan, burning down the weak fence he had put up around himself. She almost thought she could hear the shower of sparks as the defense failed and he wrapped an arm around her side, hugging her body to his. Neither spoke, for there weren't quite words to explain the shattering of the simplicity that they had been living in all evening.

So many moments.

It was only now, with the world catching up to her with the reminder that the sun would rise on another day of homework and laundry, that she acknowledged those moments as stolen.

"I feel Éire like an aching drum in my blood," Brennan whispered, though the distance in his voice made her doubt he was only speaking to her. "*Ireland. Ireland*, it pulses. Except for when I'm with you. For at least a little while, I don't miss home so terribly. In fact, tonight, it felt like I'd never left... or maybe that I'd returned."

When she looked up at him, he was gazing at her with such yearning that she understood for the first time that there already was no going back. No matter what happened, she would never forget John Brennan.

"I—" she began, but was interrupted when something vibrated in her pocket. She tugged out her phone to find Adam calling.

Brennan's eyes drifted to the screen mournfully. "You should get that."

She nodded stiffly as he coiled his arm back to his side.

"Hey," she greeted, answering the call.

"Hey, babe," Adam chirped on the other side. "I'm on my way home. What're you up to?"

"Nothing much."

Brennan rose and she tried to catch his eye as he headed back into the house, but he pointedly ignored her.

---

*A*melia walked into her room with her maid, tugging off her gloves and ready to be out of her evening gown, when Liza halted and fixed her with a tight expression.

"Liza?"

The dark-haired woman had a disapproving scowl and her eyes darted to something by the window. Amelia followed her gaze, surprised to find the silhouetted outline of a man in tails in her room, facing the moonscape beyond the panes.

"My lady?" Liza asked.

Amelia didn't take her eyes off the figure as she recognized Leander's broad shoulders. The thought that Liza should not know that he was there was only a buzzing in the back of her mind, for all she wanted to do was run to the man who reminded her of the scent of a late spring morning.

"Thank you, Liza. That will be all."

"But, my lady—"

"I will ring for you when I am ready."

Liza hesitated before obeying her mistress and slipping out the door, her cheeks burning. Once they were alone, Leander's breathing quickened and he turned to face Amelia, his features tight and coiled, dashing the smile from Amelia's face before it had the chance to fully form.

"Ya didn't tell me," he began, his voice quaking, "that you had changed the wedding date."

Amelia shook her head. "He was called up and suddenly there was no time."

Leander's eyes softened as his jaw quivered. "Whatever ya do, don't lie. Please, don't lie to me."

Her throat constricted at the softness of his voice and she shook her head. "I assure you—"

"Of not'ing. Other than my own foolishness." He took a step towards her then stopped himself, lowering his voice as his eyes shimmered in the moonlight. "I *believed* you."

"What would you have me do?" she hissed. "Sneak onto a ship to Italy tomorrow? Disappear amongst the beggars of Paris?"

"You think I would make ya beg?"

Amelia pressed her lips together, her own eyes beginning to sting. "Of course not. But my situation is far from simple, Leander. I have to be very cautious. For both our sakes."

He shook his head, shaking loose tears. "She warned me. She warned me that I was just a playt'ing to you. That I'd be cast aside when ya had your fill."

Amelia stiffened, her chest burning at the sight of his tears. "Who would say such a thing?"

"It doesn't matter now," he whispered, turning so that his shoulder was to her as he wiped his cheeks.

"Leander," she demanded, "*Who?*"

"I'm not a pet," he barked, narrowing his dark eyes at her. "Ya don't own me. And if you think for one second that I'll follow ya to his house and be some sort of consort, then—"

"Who on God's green earth do you think you are speaking to?" Amelia snapped, marching towards him. He dropped his head and she stopped inches away. "Your superior? The future Mrs. Charles Kent? A heartless mistress?"

"I'll go," he whispered so softly that she barely heard it.

"If you value your existence you will not move from this spot until I tell you."

Leander flinched but didn't dare lift his head, so she latched onto his chin and forced him to look at her. He tried to jerk his jaw free but she held fast and could feel his teeth grinding beneath her fingers.

"Stop," he growled.

"Who am I?" Amelia demanded.

"I asked ya to stop," he seethed.

"Answer my question."

"I don't want to be here."

"Who," she repeated, leaning in until their faces were almost touching, forcing Leander to close his eyes, "am I?"

For several moments, the only thing Amelia could hear above the rush of blood in her veins was Leander's labored breathing. Then he answered in a whisper. "A storm."

Amelia blinked in surprise, straightening.

"Your hair was tangled."

Amelia released the footman and lowered her voice. "My hair?"

Leander reluctantly met her gaze with his red-rimmed eyes. "Like the only comb that had ever touched it was the wind when ya galloped."

Stretching her fingers, Amelia studied her hand that had just gripped his jaw, her skin numbed as if she could still feel his stubble. She spoke without having enough air in her lungs to make her voice firm. "Your faith in me must be very weak if you could be so easily swayed by the gossip of a maid."

"It's been two months and sixteen days since you've looked like that. Since you've gone for a ride. Since ya walked in the woods and had color in your skin. Since ya—"

"Why would you keep record of such a thing?"

Leander's eyes were sad. "Ireland."

"What?" she gasped, for her chest ached, as if her corset was tightening.

"I would've taken ya to Ireland," he whispered. "Not the streets of France or the waterways of Italy, but to the green countryside where we'd wake to the dunnock's song and fall asleep to the wind against the pane and a peat fire in the hearth."

The whale bone stays were now grating against her ribs and she couldn't tell if her chest was expanding or if her garments were shrinking.

"But ya never leave the house anymore," he continued, gently catching her hand in his and pressing his thumb into her palm. "The horses can't even remember your touch."

"But you do?"

Leander smiled wistfully as he pressed her hand between both of his, warming it. "I'd sooner forget all the colors of the world."

Amelia was now sure something was wrong with her clothing, or maybe it was just the largeness of the night sky inside as it expanded into her lungs and legs and fingertips.

"I pity other women with brains," she whispered. "The happiest of girls are the simpletons who know nothing else but what is asked of them."

Giving her hand a squeeze, Leander released it with a soft sigh and took a step away from her. "It's not so different as a man. Goodnight, my lady."

Though she tried, she couldn't lift her head to watch him go. His light footfalls neared the door, taking the warmth of his nearness further and further from her until she was sure she was cooling inside. Cooling inside, because he had filled her and always would if she could only find the words to convince him to stay. But even as his hand fell onto the door handle, the words wouldn't come. So she moved instead.

Striding across the room, Amelia latched onto Leander's shoulders and shoved him against the wall. He let out a startled gasp that was cut off by her lips against his. His heart knocked on her palm from inside his chest when she pressed her hand to him. Moments later, he was massaging her lip with the gentle press of his tongue. The sensation teased tickling warmth out from the recesses of her being, pooling in places that made her pulse catch up with his.

"I am going home," he gasped. "I have to go home. I can't watch ya get fenced in by him. See you in a cage."

Amelia pulled away enough to study his face as she panted. The images his words conjured were on fire in her brain, for they were everything that made her want to scream with billows for lungs that had never been weakened by a corset. The claustrophobia of her expected nuptials made her soul howl and gnash its teeth when she allowed herself the quiet to actually ponder the prospect. But here before her... here before her were eyes that reflected the endless winding paths of the forest and a world without fences if she could only take the first step into their wilderness. She cupped Leander's cheek and ran her thumb along the soft skin by his ear as she smiled.

"Then show me Ireland."

The delighted grin that blossomed on Leander's face was enough to assure her that she was so full inside that she actually was about to suffocate in her dress. Because the happiness in his eyes made her want to adore every lash and freckle and curve of his body. Her need to be with him without the uniforms of their stations shook her left breast with her heart. Using her hand on his cheek, she guided Leander's head downwards in silent permission. She closed her eyes as he planted teasing, sucking kisses on her bosom. But it wasn't enough.

Turning around, she gestured to the hooks holding her dress in place. Leander's hand ran down her stiff back before finding the clasps and gently undoing them, tickling her back with his scratchy chin as he kissed it. Amelia kicked aside her pinching heels, her blood racing with anticipation as the dress around her became looser and looser until it fell away completely.

She tugged on her camisole, yanking it off over her head as she looked at Leander behind her. "Take off your jacket."

"So we're back to orders now, are we?" he admonished, even as he shed his outermost layer.

She pulled off her stockings then faced him in nothing but her corset and drawers. The sight seemed to render him speechless, but he didn't need to say a word. The desire in his eyes made her skin heat with knowing he wanted her. Amelia pressed her body to him, tangling her fingers in his hair as she dug her lips into his mouth, searching for a release, a means to press out the burning in her skin that was concentrating in her lips and loins as she guided him towards her bed.

Her other hand slid up his front, unbuttoning the vest of his livery, followed by his shirt, until she was able to rest her hand upon the warm hair and skin of his chest. Leander pulled his lips away from hers, panting, "Ya know we can't," even as he lay down on his back.

She crawled on top of his thigh, burrowing her crotch into the muscle as she bent over him to suck on his neck, momentarily wondering what had come over her but trusting it all the same.

"I didn't choose Kent," she murmured before toying with his earlobe, pressing her swelling breasts to his chest, delighting in the way being on her knees with thighs spread made her feel open and blooming. She wanted to take off her corset, but Leander's worry over her reputation caused a wayward streak of propriety to rear its head.

"*Mo chroí*," he whispered as he hardened against her knee, and the sensation would have startled her if she hadn't once plied Liza with questions over how coupling worked.

She knew men liked to be touched there, and in fact, had always been curious what one felt like, so she stopped kissing him to take in his face as she slid a hand to his crotch and cupped the stiff, buoyant flesh.

"What're ya doing, girl?" he gasped before raising his hips to press into her hand, and the wanton whimper in his voice was enough to forget she was a lady.

She gently squeezed the full ball of cloth, making him groan and prop himself up on his elbows, his shirt falling away to reveal the thin muscles of his chest. His lips were tantalizingly swollen and she kissed them while pushing the fabric off his shoulders with her free hand then leaning back to admire him. She caressed the bulge in his trousers with her thumb, making his chest rise and fall as he panted, closing his eyes and swallowing, wincing as if fighting for control.

"It's all right," she whispered as his pelvis quivered underneath her. "We won't. Will we?"

She gripped his length and remembered Liza's red-faced metaphor of milking a cow, so she tightened her hold and gave a gentle tug. Then another, making Leander's eyes snap open as his hips twitched in response. The primal reaction stirred something deep within, something she didn't have to think about to understand as she grew wetter against his leg, for her drawers didn't have a crotch.

Flexing her backside, she pressed against his thigh and rubbed, gasping and tightening her hold on him at the flush of hungry heat that bloomed in her loins. She had touched herself before, of course, sometimes while thinking of Leander, but this was different. She could hear his panting and smell the sweat starting to bead on his hairline, mixing with the pomade, as he arched his hips again, silently asking for more.

Amelia squeezed and pulled, shoving herself harder against him with a squeak. He sat more upright, as if to ask her to stop, or that she was pulling too hard, or to pull harder, but nothing came out and she knew it was everything at once. Grunting, she ground her pelvis against his warm muscle, falling into a rhythm of rubbing and tugging, heat making her skin burn and his body jerk. His hand rested on her hip for a moment, and she was aware of him taking in her flushed, sweating face as she rocked against him. He caught her hand in his, forcing her to release her hold on him. The pressure on her hip guided her and she moved her leg to straddle him, her center pressing against his length startling her back into herself for a moment.

This is how girls become with child.

But so long as he kept his lower half clothed, she could see no harm, and resisting the urge to grind against him as he started rocking his hips was too much. She dug into the firm flesh beneath her and the pant he let out at the contact stripped away everything but the blood rushing past her ears.

She may not have ridden for some time, but she would be damned if this wasn't like posting. The mattress dipped beneath her knees as she moved up and down in a rhythm, his hips bucking under hers in time. Though she tried to stay quiet, several gasps escaped as she rode harder and faster. Soon she was nothing but burning skin and pulsing, aching loins writhing against his with ferocity. Leander kept letting out muffled sounds, as if she was making him delirious with either pleasure or pain, his grip on her hips tightening.

He twitched and twisted about several times, as if yearning for something he was denying himself. She was swollen and sweating and wet, growing sore as she rubbed against him, spiraling towards a release that felt ever just out of reach. Then Leander started panting her name with desperation. She clamped a hand over his mouth to quiet him, even as she rationalized that there was no one to hear them. After all, her quarters were at the opposite end of the dining room.

Just when her hips started to ache from the effort and she worried they were doing something terribly wrong, he arched his spine and jerked up against her with startling strength. He bowled her onto her back, supporting her hips as he rutted against her crotch, a gasping moan escaping from deep within his chest. A new wave of heat coursed through her at the sound and the pace of his thrusting hips. Then he went stiff pressed against her, shuddering and gasping until he stilled, his body relaxing.

"Sorry," he whispered, and she could barely hear it above the racing of her blood and the aching of her own loins, begging for more.

"What happened?" she asked.

He pulled away, sweaty and panting and planted a few kisses to her lips and breast before sliding his hand along her inner thigh.

The touch sent a trill of excitement through her swollen center that made it pulse all the more with need. *Please touch me there*, her mind begged, her chest heaving as she locked eyes with him. *Please.*

His fingers tickled her hair, making her gasp and spread her knees apart. He kissed her jaw as he started to slowly massage her flesh, and she moaned when her wedge slipped between two of his fingers, sending a shudder deep into her core. She arched her hips against his hand, and he gave her small mounds of flesh there a gentle squeeze as he sucked on her neck.

"More," she gasped, leaning her knees out wider.

His massaging worked around her cleft, squeezing her flesh until it pressed against the wedge with the most delightful ache. She pressed up into his hand with each pulse, feeling the flush on her skin renewing even as Leander's sweat dried. But he was too gentle, and this was taking too long after their frenzied, bucking heat.

She slid her hand down his arm to rest on his and he stopped kissing to pay attention. Pushing on his wrist, she guided his hand until it rubbed against her, pressing down hard into her moistness. Leander complied, watching her face to make sure he didn't harm her. She rocked her hips in rhythm, encouraging him, and grunting in surprise when one of his fingertips pressed against her opening with one rock, then slid in with the next.

The sensation was new and curious and she tightened her grip on his wrist to ensure he didn't pull away as she pressed against him, panting as each stroke pressed a soft fingertip against her rim.

She rocked faster and wondered if this was what a bud felt like, for she was filling so rapidly that she was certain she would burst into colors. Leander started to say something but whatever it was, she didn't hear past her panting and the rubbing and the way his finger kept pressing, teasing her entrance until she arched and bucked. The digit slid inside with each thrust, her grip tight on her lover's hand as she guided it back and forth, in and out of her while rubbing against his palm.

The bud of her body cracked as it felt the sun, and she didn't care how unladylike it was to be gasping and jerking with something inside her until she contracted around his finger, arching her back and gasping desperately as she bridged against his arm, pinning it in place as she writhed and shook, riding out her climax until she felt like she was going to burst.

She didn't realize that she had shoved his finger nearly up to the hilt inside until she collapsed onto the mattress and felt it slip out. Panting, she craned her neck to study Leander, finding his face flushed and awed, his pupils wide with arousal. His expression sent another, calmer tremor through her loins and she gasped before letting her knees fall back together.

"God almighty," was all he could pant before brushing the hair off her face and kissing her.

Amelia smiled with satisfaction. "Did I hurt you?" she softly asked.

Leander twitched, as if he wanted to kiss her and start all over again, but restrained himself. "Only by filling my head with what being together properly will feel like."

"Then enough waiting," she said, rubbing her bare foot along his calf. "I want to hear the dunnock."

Leander's smile nearly split his face as he fell against her in a hug, kissing all over her cheeks before pulling away to gaze at her. "There's a full moon on Sunday. Darlin', we could leave without so much as a lantern to give us away."

Amelia's smile faded. "Sunday?"

Leander nodded. "Unless ya really did want to elope tomorrow."

"My mother has invited Kent and half the county over for a dinner."

"I know," he whispered. "So I doubt you'll be missed for some time."

Her smile returned and she kissed him again, wrapping a leg around his hips.

13

*I*t would be a lie to say that Ophelia didn't stay in bed half of the morning, replaying the most intensely erotic experience of her life that didn't even belong to her current lifetime. While Amelia's emotions had long since worn off, Ophelia's head was still full of the images and sensations of doing everything but with a man who looked and sounded exactly like Brennan. A part of her was envious that her Victorian counterpart was more sexually expressive than she could ever dream.

When she finally came downstairs past ten, she was relieved that she was alone in the house. It would be difficult enough to face the Irishman after last night without the added complication of just how much she had enjoyed her latest memory, to say nothing of having almost cheated on Adam.

She fixed herself some eggs, which had become a luxury she only ate when Alex wasn't around, and had her breakfast while wandering the house. Ashes sat in the cold woodstove, Brennan's blanket was folded neatly and placed at the foot of the couch, and the pile of firewood he collected was still sitting outside on the porch. The sight made her hope ache, and she resumed the same seat she had last night beside him. The sunlight warmed her skin and she closed her eyes, feeling the ghost of his presence at her side.

"I need a job," she murmured as she opened her eyes, longing for a meaningful distraction from the web of lives she was trapped in.

Once finished eating, she headed back upstairs and delved into her thesis with a fury. The simple task of putting words to paper, of taking ideas and stretching and shrinking them, flipping them from front to back in her mind, was soothing. She could control her work, unlike everything else around her.

A part of her wanted to tell Adam that something was wrong—that it shouldn't be so easy for her to hold hands with another boy—but that knowledge would only cause him pain. The thought of his wounded eyes sickened her inside. She had already betrayed him in one lifetime.

Had she considered flirting with someone other than her boyfriend two weeks ago, she would've been tainted with guilt. But as much as she didn't want to hurt Adam, she felt no remorse over the moments she had stolen with the raven-haired young man. Despite the darkness he had shared with her, he refused to be soured in her mind.

By the time Adam arrived that afternoon after class, she was surrounded by her copies of Keats' texts and piles of printed out pages.

"Babe?" he called up the stairs.

"In here," she shouted back before wincing. Not telling him felt like a lie.

How has fibbing become so easy lately?

Adam powered up the stairs in his flip-flops. "Wanna come to the gym?"

She offered him a smile that tugged on the bottom of her stomach. "No, thanks."

He strode in wearing a red O'Neill T-shirt and shorts and glanced about at her pile of books before reaching for her hand. She took it and rose to her knees, leaning over to kiss him in greeting, and the action was so familiar that it soothed her troubled heart.

"I've missed you," she whispered.

Adam pushed some of the books aside and sat down on the bed next to her, wrapping an arm around her and kissing the top of her hair. "What's wrong?"

She shook her head, pressing her temple into his neck and closing her eyes.

"Hey," Adam rasped, rubbing her back. "What happened?"

Ophelia took a deep breath, trying to fill her mind and body with his familiar scent of sunscreen and surf, wanting it to calm the rattling of her thoughts as it had so many times before. Instead, it was just a smell, which made her cling to him all the tighter, as if he were fading even while in her arms.

"Bad dream?" he asked quietly and Ophelia nodded.

Adam kissed the top of her head again and rubbed her back in soothing circles. Her tense shoulders began to sag as she relaxed against him. After a minute or so, he lightly plucked her bra strap to get her attention and she looked up at him to find a smile waiting for her. In that moment, she felt small and light, and the tightness in her mind faded away.

"Well, you're safe now," he said. "I won't let anything happen to you."

She leaned up and kissed his lips. "I love you, Adam."

His smile grew and she kissed him again, unable to keep Kent out of her mind and how, like Adam, he was so assured and prepared to play his part and do whatever was asked of him, despite the consequences. Cupping the sides of his face, she pressed her tongue against his, hoping he could feel the gratitude radiating from her heart.

"Damn," Adam chuckled when they parted for air. "All work and no play makes Lia—"

"Don't," she said, running a hand through his fine hair.

"Don't what?"

"Don't dumb this down. Not everything has to be dumbed down."

Adam kissed her before resting his hands on her hips. "I thought stupidity was my charm."

She smirked before sobering, tracing a finger down his strong jawline. "Your quiet strength is your charm."

Adam's bowed lips twitched in a funny smile, his blue eyes warm with adoration and she knew he was trying to come up with a way to dismiss her compliment and failing. Grinning, she kissed the tip of his nose then turned to face her laptop again. For several minutes, she read and wrote while he hugged her from behind, resting his chin on her shoulder, and she could see the contented expression on his face reflected in the screen.

When she hit save and pointed out the growing word count, he kissed the bare portion of her shoulder and murmured, "That's my secret weapon." With a sigh, he squeezed her sides and got up, stretching. "I can't wait until that paper is done."

"Me, too."

"I'm gonna go work out."

"Have fun."

He slipped out the door with a smile and called, "I'm tired of sharing you with old dead guys," over his shoulder as he headed into the hall.

Ophelia sighed. *If only you knew...*

Returning to her paper was more difficult than expected after his visit, but once she managed to get into the swing of things, she finished another few pages before dusk. Feeling very accomplished and calmer for having one less worry on her mind, she headed downstairs and heated up some of the spaghetti from a few nights back.

She was about to sit down and eat when Alex came home, smelling of chai. "How was work?" she chirped, hunting for another distraction as her mind began to wander through memories of what she was doing at this time last night.

"It sucked." Alex sighed as he yanked open the fridge. "One of the machines broke. Elena couldn't fix it so we didn't know what to do."

Ophelia winced in sympathy as she sat down, some of her hunger fading at his jerky movements. Alex's even-keeled temper was one of the reasons they got along so well, and it took a lot to push him over the edge of the patience and acceptance he had worked so hard to build after the depression he went through as a teenager.

Snagging a soy yogurt, Alex opened it and began to eat. She appraised him as he did so, noticing that the black dye from his recent Goth phase was finally blending nicely with his natural chestnut brown hair. His lip was healing but he hadn't replaced his ring, and now that she thought about it, he had taken out his nasal piercing, as well. She reminded herself for the thousandth time that just because he was upset didn't mean that he would lose his way again. Knowing she worried over him would twist his heart.

The memory of Lucy's compassionate smile skirted on the edges of her thoughts, but she couldn't bring herself to fill Alex in on all the Victorian details, for they were becoming increasingly private. Both ate in silence for several minutes and she could tell by the delicate way that he was chewing and studying the pink strawberry swirls of his yogurt that words were building.

"Look," he began quietly. "I know I'm like, the worst person to ever listen to for relationship advice, and I know I don't really understand this… remembering thing," he paused, looking up to meet her brown eyes with his grey. "And I know you'd never hurt anyone, but…"

"But what?"

"He's barely twenty-two. I know he acts a lot older, but he's like a little cousin or something, I don't know." He shook his head, his face twisting around what he was trying to say. "I guess I just… I don't want anything bad to happen to either of you."

Ophelia nodded stiffly, a chill settling inside at the seriousness of his tone. "I know," she said softly.

"I'm not saying you have to do something one way or the other, just… be careful. With him."

She swallowed past the sudden dryness in her mouth, irritation flaring up at the idea that she was being careless in some way, or that she had control. "Brennan can more than take care of himself."

Alex's next quiet words stripped away any indignation and left her as warm as she was frightened. "You don't see the look in his eyes when he talks about you, Elephant."

"He talks about me?" she whispered.

Alex smiled a little. "More like pretends he doesn't whip his head around every time he hears your name."

Her smile shined much brighter inside than out as she rinsed out her dish, wondering how she went from the girl who was taller than most of the boys she liked yet still couldn't get their attention, to suddenly having more attention than she knew what to do with. Instead of feeling flattered, she was torn and overwhelmed.

Heading back upstairs, she returned to writing and began a section on Keats' own sources of inspiration, namely Fanny Brawne, the upper-class girl a penniless poet ought never to have had. She tried to focus on their story, but the tragic romance had always upset her to the point of tears at the best of times, much less now when she felt stretched thin inside. As she read one of his letters to his love and muse, she felt an eerie sort of illness over seeing words that the private man had never meant to be made public. Knowing that her life as Lady Amelia had almost overlapped with Fanny Brawne's left Ophelia a little jealous that other literature students could research documents and see them just as artifacts from a bygone age, rather than leavings from passionate, breathing people she had nearly lived beside.

Guitar music echoed from downstairs and she smiled, realizing that Brennan must be home. Slipping out the door, she followed the lively tune until she could spot him on the couch, strumming with his eyes closed, playing by ear. Ophelia sat on the top stair, out of sight, and listened with her chin on her palms while he played the same song several times, as if practicing for a gig. Alex was on the opposite end of the couch, curled up with his phone, his refined features washed out by the light of the screen.

She studied the Dubliner's body language, hopeful that he wasn't upset over the previous night. It was difficult to tell when he was so focused on the music, but then he opened his eyes and peered at Alex, looking bored. When he bit his lower lip and slowly leaned towards him, her worry over their stolen moments fled.

Alex didn't seem to notice the movement at his side and Ophelia pursed her lips, fighting off the urge to warn him. Brennan rose up to his knees, inching his torso over the other man, his eyes sparkling as he bit the tip of his tongue. Alex smiled a little as his phone buzzed, reading a new text, Brennan perfectly still beside him. Then the dark-haired man strummed wildly, making Alex gasp and twitch his thumbs on the keypad before freezing, staring at Brennan as if he had just intentionally rammed into his car.

"Ha!" Brennan crowed before pointing and falling onto the seat of his black jeans with a cackle.

"That wasn't *funny*," Alex panted, resting a hand over his heart.

Ophelia couldn't hold in her laughter anymore and chuckled from her perch on the stairs, prompting Alex to dart her a surprised glance.

Brennan rolled onto his back with laughter as Alex's eyes remained wide, like a cat expecting another loud noise, waiting to bolt.

"It's *not* funny," he snapped louder as Ophelia headed downstairs.

"You," Brennan squeaked, his knuckles white around the neck of his guitar as he tried to breathe. "You about weed your pants."

"No, I think I *did*."

"Oh, God," Brennan barked, dissolving into another peal of laughter.

Cheeks flushing, Alex shifted his glare from Brennan to Ophelia as she headed over to the two and sat down on the coffee table. She toed Brennan's leg with her bare foot.

"Hi," he chuckled, lolling his head to look at her.

"Hi."

Brennan sobered as he studied her and she wrinkled her nose in playful response, warmth spreading on her skin wherever his eyes touched.

"Great," Alex whined, looking up from his phone. "You made me send him a gibberish text and now he's asking what it means."

Brennan arched his neck back against the cushion below him in exasperation. "Oh, for God's sake, man. Give it a rest, will ya? You've been texting him for *hours*. I thought teachers were busy."

"It has *so* not been hours," Alex muttered as he composed a reply.

Ophelia looked between the two before noting the way Brennan had narrowed his eyes to slits as he slid his guitar down to rest against the couch. "Seriously, Alex, ya have no balls."

Alex merely pinched his lips together and shook his head, ignoring the taunt as he typed.

"How many times have ya seen him now? I mean, *actually* seen him?"

"That's none of your business," Alex muttered.

Ophelia opted not to take a side, amused by where the two males were taking this, feeling like she was on some sort of reconnaissance mission to learn how the other half schemed.

"Once? It was once, wasn't it?" Brennan pressed, observing him over his folded knees, but Alex ignored him. "Texting all the time doesn't make up for for—" He cut himself off as the other man leveled a glare at him. Brennan let out a soft sigh. "If you want him to know ya like him this much, you need to make a gesture."

"I'm not sending flowers," Alex muttered.

"I'm sorry," Ophelia finally piped up. "But I'm curious what John Brennan would consider a romantic gesture given that you seem to think dining in the freezing cold and chugging beer is some form of bonding."

A blush grew in her chest the moment the words started spilling out at having almost slapped a label on their moments. She resisted the urge to look at her fidgeting hands instead of his eyes.

"Well, I'm sorry if I'm not posh enough for ya, Miss Victorian," he teased. "But I happened to have had a lovely time yesterday."

She tried to fight off her smile and failed so miserably that what came out instead was a tortured twist of the lips.

Brennan giggled. "Have ya got a fish in there?"

"You seriously think I need to *do* something?" Alex asked. "I mean, *obviously*, I like him. He knows that because we're talking."

The Irishman merely grunted, distracting himself with picking at the thread of a fraying buttonhole on his grey Henley, though Ophelia wasn't entirely convinced that he actually was distracted.

"How's the paper?" Alex asked, rising and stretching.

Brennan all-but commando rolled off the couch, landing on his feet and casually circling behind Alex as the shorter man chatted with her.

"Great," she replied, and while she filled him in on her progress, Brennan stealthily settled in on the couch in the seat Alex had vacated, quietly texting. A part of Ophelia wondered if he was talking to Charlie then reminded herself that it was none of her business.

Alex patted his pocket then glanced behind him, looking for his phone, when his eyes settled on Brennan and froze.

"That's not yours."

Brennan raised his dark brows innocently as he paused in composing a message. "It isn't?"

Alex didn't even make a sound as he lunged, latching onto Brennan's wrists and trying to wrestle the phone from him. "What did you *do?*"

"Not'ing! Help me, Girl!"

"Oh, no," she replied. "You got yourself into this all on your own."

Alex gave up on trying to pry the phone from Brennan's fingers and instead lowered his mouth to his exposed wrist and put his teeth on him.

"Jaysus," Brennan squawked, letting go of the device.

Flustered, Alex snatched up the phone then bounded away, hastily scrolling through the texts Ramiro had thought he was sending. Brennan rubbed off his wrist with his other sleeve, looking like he had smelled dog poo again.

"Ya *bit* me."

Ophelia took his hand in hers and studied his skin. "There's hardly a mark."

"You..." Alex snarled, stiff as he slowly turned about to face the dark-haired man, "invited him *over?*"

"For dinner. Tomorrow." Brennan shrugged. "Is that a problem?"

"You should have *asked* me!"

"You were doing it all arseways," Brennan squeaked.

Alex's eyes widened. "*What?*"

"If he'd asked you," Ophelia defended, "you would've obsessed about it so much that you'd psych yourself out and not do it."

Alex shook his head, looking like he wanted to snap back, but just then his phone buzzed. "Great," he whined. "He said he'd love to come."

"That's fierce," Brennan enthused.

"Don't worry about it," Ophelia said, settling down in the empty cushion beside Brennan. "I'll help you cook. It'll be fun."

Brennan gave her a smile that said he thought it would only be fun for the pair of them and torture for Alex. A light danced in his eyes, making her glow inside, but knowing that Alex was in the room, potentially observing them, reminded her of his warning earlier in the night. Thinking of Adam, she knew she ought to excuse herself and go back upstairs, or use her paper as a means to pry herself from the Irishman's side, but the words wafted away in her chest before ever reaching her lips. There was no more denying that the hope smoothing out lines on Brennan's face and making him bright was reflected on her own features.

The following morning, she awoke and headed downstairs to discover that she was once more home alone despite Tuesday being Brennan's day off.

"Right," she said to the emptiness. "No more distractions."

After breakfast, she wrote several pages, realizing with a jolt that she was nearing the end of her argument. Alex texted her to ask if she could pick up some bunches of basil for the pesto he was making that night. Tired of sitting so long and eager to walk off the ache in her back from hunching over her laptop, she pulled on her galoshes over grey leggings and a blue tunic and headed out, even if the weather was too warm for the boots.

She stopped in her tracks when she saw a large man hastily turn away from her house, as if having been eavesdropping, even though there was nothing to hear. Narrowing her eyes, she recognized the Rasta scarf tied around bathroom dreads like a bandana and knew it was Trea. A shiver coursed through her as she realized that she had left one of the curtains partially open and he could have been spying on her.

And here I'd thought you were just a harmless hippie.

Making sure that she wasn't being followed, Ophelia headed over to New Leaf Market and bought the basil and a few other groceries. When she returned to the house, she kept a careful eye out for anyone who may have been watching her, then approached the door. A braid of long, dried grass rested on her doorstep and she picked it up, its sweet scent wafting in the air. She looked over her shoulder for any sign of Trea, feeling slightly more at ease if leaving her a gift had been the reason he was hanging around, but still uncomfortable with the idea of him knowing where she lived.

Once back inside, she locked the door and set the grass on the rickety end table. It was nearly five, so she decided to try to ease the burn of Alex's torture last night by chopping up the basil to get a head start on dinner. Ophelia was nearly done when a knock sounded at the door and she stiffened.

What if it's Trea and he tries to force his way in?

Creeping over to the bay window, she peered out to spy and was surprised by her relief when she recognized Brennan's slim, familiar form. Darting to the door, she unlocked and opened it, the irony of having once been afraid to let him in and happy to do so now making her smile. "Where have you been?" she asked.

"On a hike."

His skin had a hint of umber in it, as if he had gotten some sun, and for a moment the two faced each other awkwardly, as if expecting the other to say something.

"Well, don't just stand there like a vampire," Ophelia teased, blushing and stepping aside. "Come in."

Brennan smirked and strode inside, and instead of his usual stench of tobacco, the scent of clay and coolness clung to his white shirt. When coupled with his blue jeans that were a much more relaxed fit than his regular snug garb, she was surprised by how classically American he looked.

"Needed to clear my head," he said with a sigh, flopping down on the couch.

"It's shockingly more difficult to do with memories of a past life kicking around, isn't it?"

He groaned and dug his fingers into his hair, his elbows propped on his knees. "Ain't that the truth?"

Ophelia crossed over to him, sitting down on the arm of the couch, far closer than she probably should have been.

"Did you have another dream?"

She bumped her knee against his with the question, prompting him to uncurl and lean his head back against the cushion, studying her with tired eyes.

"Yeah," he said quietly.

She let her gaze drift to her hands on her lap, feeling her heart clench with the memory of Jack's cherry-lipped smile. "I hope I'm not the reason you're having to go through this."

He shook his head in the peripheral of her vision. "Why would ya say that?"

"Because I was born this way," she explained, meeting his gaze again. "I've always remembered things I shouldn't. It was quiet for a while… until… until I met you."

A flare of anticipation suddenly breathed life into his frame as he straightened. "Really?"

"You never had it happen before you met me?"

He shook his head. "Though last night it was just… I had a dream about the accident again, only this time I was able to get out and save my parents. Then I woke up wondering about t'ings… and how strange it is that if we'd just left the park a minute earlier, literally a *minute* earlier, we'd have missed the truck."

Ophelia nodded, frosty inside over how tortured she would feel if such a thing had happened to her.

"I mean, I've thought about it loads of times, but sometimes at night, when I forget how the world works, I wonder why I can't just go back and fix it. They were waiting for me. I'd run back up the trail to take a picture of a fox that had darted past. If I'd just come when Da called..." He shrugged and sighed, then fixed her with a soft smile, as if apologizing for his tone. "But it is what it is, and there's no going back, no matter how much we wish we could."

Reaching out, she squeezed his knee, feeling woefully inadequate to even respond, for try as she might, she couldn't think of anything in her past that she would want to change as desperately.

Brennan's nose twitched and he twisted, looking into the kitchen. "What're ya making?"

"We."

"What?" he asked, returning his gaze to hers.

She grabbed his hand and gave it a tug. "*We* are making pesto and tortellini."

Brennan flashed a crooked smile as he allowed her to pull him up. "Oh, is that right?"

"You got him into this mess, so it's only fair that you help," she reminded as they entered the kitchen.

"I'd hardly call it a 'mess.' More of a... furthering t'ings along."

She finished up chopping the basil while she sent Brennan on a hunt for the food processor. As he plugged it in, she caught sight of his Celtic knot tattoo again. "You've never told me about that, you know."

He followed her gaze to his arm and pulled up his sleeve, revealing the sword in the middle. "I got it when I was a young one."

Her eyes traced the blue ink, realizing that the knots intersected, each forming a design that looked like a triangle made of overlapping leaves with a circle in the center. "What's it mean?"

"It's a symbol for the trinity," he replied as he scooped up several handfuls of chopped basil and placed them in the food processor.

"And you said you weren't Catholic."

"There are other trinities, ya know. Older ones."

"Well excuse me for listening to your 'I hate religion' tirade the other day," she said playfully, making him smile.

"You don't forget anyt'ing, do ya, Miss Elephant?"

"Not when you're the one saying it."

Her expression immediately sobered as she realized what she had just revealed and the softness in his gaze at her words prompted her to look away.

"It stands for the Maiden," he began quietly, granting them both a reprieve by ignoring the truth she just bared. "Mother, and Crone. The three stages of the moon and the female life cycle."

Ophelia studied the tattoo once more, appraising him in a new light. "Most men don't want anything remotely associated with *female* and *cycle* within a mile of them."

Brennan smiled a little then ran a trickle of water as he washed his hands, having filled the food processor.

"The colleen—the Maiden, makes a boy a man. She arms him for battle." He turned off the faucet and leaned against the counter as he dried off his hands, facing her. "The mother is like Maeve, and she makes a man into a superman, or a hero. The crone is like the Banshee, and gives the hero immortality through his death."

"Oh," Ophelia said softly, setting the cutting board and knife in the sink. "So in other words, it has nothing to do with woman in her own right, but rather what she can do for a man."

Brennan's expression was blank as he appraised her before a sly grin slid into place. "Two halves make a whole, darlin'."

"And let me guess, the sword is a phallic symbol?"

He glanced at his arm then let out a soft giggle, as if surprised at her brashness before meeting her gaze again, setting the dishrag aside. "Sure, if ya want it to be."

"So, you basically have sex tattooed on your arm."

He cracked a crooked grin. "Jaysus, listen to the state of ya. Wanting to do t'ings with my arm." He shook his head in mock disapproval and Ophelia couldn't help but blush at the memory of Leander's hand. His brows twitched together at the look on her face and he lightly kicked her calf, his voice high. "I'm just codding ya."

"You're what?" she asked, tucking her chin in to her neck until it disappeared, for "cod" made her think of codpiece which made her think of—

"You're simplifying it," he continued, folding his arms over his chest, unintentionally thickening the muscles of his biceps. "It's not just about a woman. The woman is a symbol for our universal mother: the earth, the land. Without her, we're not'ing, and we live and die at her whim."

The sunlight coming through the window was splayed across his face, making his eyes look more green than brown. The way they tapered at the outside corners turned them up the slightest bit. She couldn't' get enough of them and didn't realize she was staring until the kitchen clock ticked in the silence and she closed her parted lips.

"You're not a hippie at all. You're a pagan."

Brennan winked. "Heathen more like. And proud of it. I'm feckin' filthy."

"Oh?"

"Wouldn't *you* like to know?" he said huskily, and in that moment, she wouldn't mind playing the part of the maiden and making him a man. His eyes clouded a little, as if he knew what she was thinking, and she was suddenly aware of just how alone they were. His gaze trailed to her lips and she felt her skin tightening pleasantly in response. She had to not only remind herself of Adam, but that what Brennan had divulged of his past set him apart from other boys in her mind. As if he had been made fragile by damaging hands, despite the hint of wantonness in his eyes and the stiffness of his posture.

"We're not finished yet," she said softly.

"Damn right we're not."

"With the sauce," she amended with an admonishing smile, forcing herself to look away from the expression on his face that was piercing her.

"Of course. Whatever else did ya think I'd meant?" he asked, turning to wash the utensils in the sink. "You're the pervert here, not me."

Ophelia let out a guffaw. "*I'm* the pervert?"

"Right you be," Brennan enthused, washing the cutting board. "Trying to turn a sword into a twig and berries."

"For the record," Ophelia groaned, shaking her head, "I happen to know that a penis looks nothing like a sword."

Brennan's jaw gaped in a triumphant expression, as if he couldn't believe she had just taken the bait, but whatever he was about to say was cut off by Alex's voice.

"I totally walked in at the right moment."

Ophelia hastily turned so that her face was away from both men as she grabbed a flask of olive oil, the back of her neck burning.

"You see what I have to put up with the moment ya leave?" Brennan asked Alex. "It's just obscenity after obscenity with this one."

"Right?" Alex asked, though his voice was too stressed to be truly playful.

Ophelia shoved the olive oil into Brennan's chest then hunted for the walnuts.

"And now she's giving me oil."

"*John Brennan,*" Ophelia snapped, rising with the remainder of the ingredients and attempting to fix him with a stern expression that immediately melted at the amused look on his face. If she didn't know better, she would think he liked it when she yelled at him.

Alex bustled around the kitchen, pausing for a moment to grab at his head. "Have you started the water boiling?"

"It's not even six," Ophelia reminded him.

"I know, but I'd like to have everything ready in case he comes early."

"Don't ya hate it when that happens?" Brennan commiserated.

Ophelia whacked him with the bag of walnuts and Alex didn't even crack a smile.

"I'm serious, you guys. You have to knock it off. You're acting so immature."

"Oh, that is *so* not fair," Ophelia squawked.

Alex's eyes darted around the counters before patting his shirt, as if just noticing that he needed to change. "Shit—start the water."

"Alex," Brennan began but the smaller man cut him off by whirling around to face them on his way to the stairs.

"*Guys,*" he boomed. "Be normal. For once. Tonight. *Please.*"

Ophelia's expression sobered while Brennan merely shook his head, his face blank. "Sorry, pal, but not gonna happen."

"Brennan!"

"Normal's overrated. No one here even *is* normal. *You're* not normal."

"I'm trying to be serious," Alex whined from the stairs, and Ophelia had to turn away to hide her smile.

"I'm *being* serious," Brennan defended.

"No, you're not. You're being disrespectful. Just like you were last night when you stole my phone, and at the protest when you went off on that guy about how gingers like him should be rounded up and put into camps."

"I was being funny," Brennan drawled.

"He punched you in the face!"

"Jaysus, what's the point of being Irish if ya can't make a fockin' ginger joke? Lord knows there ain't any other benefits."

"I mean it," Alex cautioned, one foot on the bottom stair, a finger pointed at Brennan's chest. "Behave yourself."

"I *am* housebroken, you pompous arse!"

Alex's feet pounded as he headed upstairs. "You better be or you're eating outside like a dog!"

Brennan craned his neck to peer up after him, actually looking insulted. Alex's door slammed shut. Brennan turned to stare at Ophelia when she snorted, unable to keep her laughter in any longer. "Well someone's got their knickers in a twist."

"Just ignore him," Ophelia giggled, pulling out a pot and filling it with water.

Brennan crossed back over to her, pausing to lightly kick her calf, which she in turn retaliated without looking. He responded by bumping his hip into hers, so she hit his back harder. She caught his eye with a provocative look and he redirected his cocky expression elsewhere, pretending he didn't just accept her challenge.

Once the pot of water was heating on the stove and Ophelia was pouring the walnuts into the food processor, Brennan reached over her to grab the salt out of the cupboard, intentionally smashing into her backside.

"Excuse me."

Ophelia's head snapped up at the contact, but he snatched the salt and was gone before she could fully register what he had just done to her. Arching a brow, she watched him salt the water then marched by, brushing past him forcefully enough to jerk his hip with a, "Pardon me."

"Oh, pardon *you*, huh?" he asked, stepping into her path, his face inches from hers.

"Yeah, sorry, I didn't see you there," she replied with as much seriousness as she could muster then kept walking, forcing him to back up, her gaze over his shoulder. "Sorry, still don't see you."

He giggled as he nearly tripped. "Watch where you're going."

His backside hit the counter and she smashed her legs against his knees, maintaining her mock seriousness as she looked up, her nose nearly brushing his, and there was no ignoring how comfortable she felt pressed against him.

"Am I in your way?" she asked.

"Maniac," Brennan yelped, his hands held out to block her from coming any closer even as his eyes once again darted to her lips.

"Oh, my *God*," Alex shouted as he headed back downstairs. "I'm in a house full of teenagers!"

"Hey, that was only t'ree years ago for me," Brennan barked as Ophelia turned away from him.

"Oh, yes, remind us all of what a baby you are," Alex muttered as he scurried over to the stove and checked the water, having changed into a charcoal V-neck sweater over a white button up.

"I ain't no babby," Brennan scoffed, hopping up so that he was sitting on the counter. "And it's not my fault I was murdered when I was four."

"That's what I'm talking about," Alex hissed, whirling around to face the younger man who was swinging his legs as he plucked walnuts out of the food processor and ate them. "You guys have to keep that on the down low."

"I *do*," Ophelia snapped, narrowing her eyes slightly at Alex. "You think I walk around telling everyone that I'm an English noblewoman?"

Alex took a deep breath and closed his eyes, clasping his hands before him as if in prayer. "Of course not. I just... I really, really want tonight to go well."

"Then go have a wank in the shower, you're too uptight," Brennan suggested.

Alex slowly turned to face him, his cheeks tinged pink as he worked out what the Irishman had just said. Ophelia stayed quiet, her eyes drifting between the two. Brennan's swinging legs slowed as he registered Alex's expression. He furrowed his forehead, pulling his fingers away from his mouth after having stolen another nut. "What?"

Alex pointed to the second floor. "Out. Now."

"Fine," Brennan growled, sliding off the counter and stalking to the stairs. He paused with his hand on the railing. "But you're not my real father!"

With that, he stomped upstairs.

Ophelia found herself snorting again as she poured the tortellini into the boiling water and set the timer.

"Can we give him money and ask him to eat somewhere else?" Alex asked.

"Just be yourself," she assured, squeezing Alex's arm, but he didn't look convinced.

Realizing that she looked more like she was dressed for a yoga class than for company, Ophelia headed up to her room and changed her blue tunic for a long, rose-colored top with a lace exterior. She complimented the plunging neckline and cap sleeves with pearl earrings before adjusting the skirted hem of the long blouse that covered the back of her grey leggings. On her way down the hall, she had to avoid distraction by pretending that she didn't see Brennan lying upside-down half off Alex's bed, leafing through a philosophy text, his wavy hair nearly touching the floor.

"What's this?" Alex asked as she came back downstairs while he set the table. "Decided to stop competing in Granny Fashion Week?"

Ophelia stuck out her tongue then blended the ingredients to make the pesto. She drained the pasta and tossed it with the sauce, all the while feeling a lingering warm glow inside. Her housemate handed her several wineglasses, and as she set them on the table, something about the sight of them made her still.

Boisterous laughter echoed around the room, and as she peered about for its source, she caught Alex fixing her with a curious expression.

"Elephant?" he asked, but his voice morphed, becoming husky and feminine, his features softening until she was looking at Lucy.

The snug rigidity of a corset hugged her middle and she glanced down to note that she was in a sapphire evening gown, the beaded bib glittering in the gaslight. She was once again seated at the Hollingberry's grand dining table, surrounded by her parents and the Clarkes, along with several other families who had come to call. Kent dined beside her father. Mr. Meyer sat opposite her and Lucy, watching their exchange with curiosity brimming in his dark eyes. Returning her gaze to her sister, Amelia was surprised to note that the younger girl was standing beside her chair expectantly.

14

"*L*ucy, whatever is it?" Amelia asked.

"Only, I was wondering if you could help me to my room," Lucy said, sagging slightly against Amelia's chair. "I'm feeling out of sorts."

Nodding, Amelia hastily rose. "Of course, my dear." Entwining her arm with her sister's, she shot a forced smile to their surrounding guests.

She met her fiancé's curious gaze and offered him a reassuring glance. Any question darted out of Kent's eyes and he nodded his understanding. Mr. Meyer started to rise, as if to offer assistance, but Lucy waved him off with an apologetic smile.

Once out in the hall, Lucy fanned herself as a footman closed the door behind them.

"I suddenly am so flushed," she gasped.

A flutter of worry flapped in Amelia's chest. "Shall I send for the physician?"

"I don't think so. I just need some fresh air."

Amelia nodded and guided her sister towards the back of the manor. She picked at the cameo brooch on her chest, her gaze catching on the shadows cast by wall hangings and her own reflection as they neared the exit. Once outside, they were greeted by the crisp air of an autumn evening and the silver grey brightness of the full moon.

"Shall we sit?"

"No, I'd rather like to walk."

Complying, Amelia rubbed her sister's arm. "You don't feel overly warm. Perhaps it was the fish?"

Lucy shook her head, her expression tight with discomfort as they strolled, the gravel of the path crunching beneath their heels. Silence settled between them as Amelia felt her tension mounting, worrying Lucy could have been exposed to Influenza on one of her recent trips to London. Her worry was replaced by confusion when they passed behind a large shrub and her sister suddenly perked up, pausing in her step with a bright smile, healthy and hale as ever.

"Lucy," Amelia scolded, "what are you playing at?"

"I had to deceive you," the debutante gushed. "I had to or else it would have looked staged. You're a terrible actress, you know."

Amelia's lips parted in surprise as she struggled to make sense of her sister's meaning when a male voice spoke behind her.

"*Mo chroí.*"

Spinning on her heels, she spotted Leander in the shadows of the stables, looking more like a farmer in his dark tweed trousers, waist-coat and jacket, than a footman. Her grin made it difficult to speak when he led two saddled horses out of the shadows, her pack snug on the back of one. "You two—"

"Hush, now," Lucy whispered. "You've got an hour, maybe two before they notice we haven't sent word. Don't waste it."

"Oh, Lucy," Amelia gasped, falling on her sister in a tight embrace. "I can never repay you."

"Yes, you can," Lucy quietly replied. "By being happy together."

Amelia pulled away and cupped her sister's face in her gloved hands before kissing her forehead. "I'll let you know once we're settled."

Lucy nodded with a hint of sadness in her eyes. "Don't fret on it now. You know where to find me when the time comes. I'll think of some ruse so that I can visit. As often as I can."

"Please do, my lady," Leander said from the shadows.

"Again," she replied with an arched brown brow. "It's Lucy."

With one last hug, Lucy pulled herself away from her older sister and continued back towards the house, leaving Amelia alone with Leander.

"Amelia?" he whispered, sending a chill up her spine as she watched Lucy go, hoping that they would live near each other again once the scandal of her elopement blew over. *Elopement.* She faced Leander and the sight of her lover holding a horse for her, looking just as nervous as she felt, made her wonder if she was doing the right thing.

"There are some travelling clothes in the tack room," he said quietly. "But please, change quickly."

She nodded, noting the way his lower lip kept shaking. "I'll need your help with the dress."

Leander glanced around, his dark eyes sharp as flint before shutting the horses in a stall and following her into the tack room. The door closed loudly behind them, and almost sounded like wood on linoleum, complete with an odd clatter that shouldn't have been there. Until she realized it wasn't the door at all, but a chair she had knocked over on her way down.

A chair?

Peering around, Ophelia was surprised to find herself on the seat of her leggings on the floor in her kitchen, a chair warbling on the linoleum beside her.

"Can you hear me?" Lucy's voice asked before deepening into Alex's. "Elephant?"

Looking up, she spotted her housemate falling into a crouch beside her and felt his hand on her shoulder.

"Did I knock over the chair?" she asked.

"Are you okay?" His pale eyes darted over her in concern. "You caught yourself before you could hit your head."

"I fell?"

"At first I thought you tripped but then you went down hard with your eyes all... creepy."

Ophelia winced as she realized that she bruised her hip on the way down. "Creepy?"

"Like, *Exorcist* style."

Remembering the wine glasses and how the sight of them had sent her into a memory that had played out over several minutes, she was surprised that very little time seemed to have passed here. "I was having a... I think she—"

A knock sounded at the door, startling them both.

"Shit," Alex breathed. "He's early."

Ophelia attempted to wave him away. "I'm fine."

"You just almost fainted."

Climbing to her feet, she rested a hand on her bruised hip before righting the chair while Alex continued to study her fretfully. Another knock sounded on the door and she grabbed his shoulders, shoving him towards it.

"Go."

The hesitant, concerned look in his eyes reminded her of Lucy, so she fixed him with a warning glare. Quickening his step, Alex obeyed and headed for the door.

Ophelia waited until he was out of sight before pulling out the chair and sitting down, closing her eyes. Her sinuses were tight but she could easily bear the discomfort. What she didn't understand was why the memories surfaced when they did, and why they cut off at teasing moments, like a Victorian soap opera.

"It's great to see you," Alex greeted as his shoes scuffed on the stoop, and she wondered if he was giving Ramiro a hug. The two entered the kitchen and she rose, but if asked later, she wouldn't have been able to repeat a word she had said, for her mind still felt half left in the stables and 1898.

Ramiro was dark brows and a black buzz cut, smooth brown skin stretched over high cheekbones that still had some baby fat with warm, earthen eyes and a firm handshake. He smelled of something that had a hint of lime and kept his hands in his pockets while he told them about his day and jingled his keys while talking about a student who cussed him out in class. She spoke at some point and laughed at a joke about the needle dispensers in the public bathrooms downtown.

Then they were sitting and passing around the salad, and Brennan was standing on the stairs, his wet hair combed back off his face, which was hiding behind Alex's thick, dark-framed glasses. Alex tried to hide his cringe at the Irishman's modified appearance and Brennan didn't seem to be able to see properly, for he bumped into the table on his way over. Ophelia's world came into focus for the first time when he sat down beside her, near enough for her to try to count his lashes.

"Brennan," she gasped, feeling the wood of the chair beneath her and smelling the basil in the pesto. "What're you wearing?"

"I don't know what you're on about, love," he replied, a slight line forming between his brows. "I look perfectly *normal*."

Alex loudly cleared his throat and Ophelia realized with a pang of sympathy that Brennan was doing as much as he could to embarrass his housemate. If she didn't know better, she would have thought they were brothers in their past life.

"Brennan's in Rover's Revenge," Alex explained. "The band that was playing at the Poet and the Patriot when we met."

"That's right," Ramiro enthused. "I knew I knew you from somewhere. You didn't have your glasses on."

"I wouldn't have," Brennan said. "I wasn't normal then."

Ramiro's polite smile lingered the slightest bit, looking confused, so Ophelia redirected him to spare Alex. "You like Celtic music?"

Ramiro shrugged. "To be honest, I don't know why I went in that night. Guess I didn't have anything else going on and heard the music. It was just one of those things that was meant to happen. Because the moment I met him," he paused to jerk his head towards Alex, "I felt like we'd met before, you know?"

Brennan fumbled with his fork and adjusted the glasses on his face while Ophelia felt like the gravitational pull on her body just increased as she nodded.

"I was lucky," Ramiro continued. "I almost scrimmaged instead."

"Footba—soccer?" Brennan asked.

Ramiro nodded, stabbing some pasta with his fork. "I went to school on a scholarship and still like to play whenever I can."

"*Finally*," Brennan declared, leaning back in his chair. "A man who knows what a real sport is."

"Heck yeah." Ramiro high-fived the Irishman, making the tension leave Alex's face as he smiled.

Brennan's knee bumping against Ophelia's drew her attention to him and she caught a fleeting smirk on his lips before he took a bite of salad.

"We all ought to play sometime."

"That would be great. I could use the exercise. Some days I feel like I'm playing whack-a-mole." Ramiro pointed at the table, imitating talking to his students. "Sit down, be quiet, stop talking."

Brennan chuckled as he reached for the parmesan cheese, only to promptly swipe at thin air as he suffered from his depth perception being off thanks to the prescription glasses. Scrunching up his face, he focused and tried again, but still came up short. The other three watched him in confused silence until Ophelia took pity and inched the plastic tub towards him.

"T'anks, love."

She shook her head in amused disapproval and when he met her gaze through the corners of his eyes, she did a double take, for his lips were curling as if sharing a secret. Then the glasses faded, and a side parting formed in his hair, and she was looking at Leander.

He peered at her from the door he was guarding in the tack room. When she met his gaze, his eyes shifted from anxious to soft, as if he were wilting under her attention.

"What is it?" she asked, rubbing her bare arm against the chill, standing in her camisole.

"Not'ing," he whispered. "Just you."

In the past she would have felt shame over being seen in a state of partial undress, but instead, she felt strength.

"You'll want to hurry," he said softly, forcing his eyes away from her.

She nodded, bending over to snatch up the traveling dress that had been hidden in an empty burlap bag of feed. Leander stole another look at her, smiling as if he couldn't believe his luck. The same smile lingered on Brennan's newly bespectacled face as Ophelia returned to the present.

"Where did that braid of grass come from, Ophelia?" Alex asked, and Ophelia closed her eyes for a moment before focusing on him.

"What?"

"Ramiro was wondering."

"Sweet grass is used in a lot of Indigenous ceremonies," Ramiro explained. "To purify the air, chase away bad spirits, that sort of thing."

"Are you Native American?" Alex asked, wiping at his mouth with a napkin.

Ramiro blinked at the young man beside him. "Dude, don't tell me you just now noticed I'm Mexican."

"It, um," Ophelia cleared her throat, focusing on Alex's gages in an attempt to anchor herself. "It was a gift," she finished quietly.

"My grandma used to have it hanging in her house," Ramiro explained with a smile. "It's been a long time since I've smelled it."

"It's lovely," she added before rising to clear away her plate, only to have one of her knees try to give out. Brennan's hand was on her hip, steadying her even as she straightened. Looking at him over her shoulder, she offered him a dismissive smile, surprised to find him on his feet. "Too much wine."

Though the thick frames of the glasses hid his brows, she knew they were nearly touching with the way he was looking at her. Slipping away from his hands, she rinsed her plate off in the sink while Ramiro chuckled, "If I had a dollar for every time that's happened to me…"

She loaded her plate in the dishwasher then slipped into the other room when Alex and Ramiro began discussing different local vineyards while Brennan's footsteps sounded behind her. He stood in front of her when she sat down on the couch, feeling as if she had just had a hot flash. Looking up at him, she found the Irishman wincing and scrunching up his face as he tried to look at her, which made her laugh.

He slowly smiled then fell into the seat at her side, squeezing his eyes shut and rubbing them as he took off Alex's glasses. "I feel woozy."

"I'll bet."

Brennan looked sore when he turned to face her, as if waiting for her to speak. When she refused, he cocked his head. "Girl, ya didn't even *have* a drop of wine."

"You don't wear glasses."

"I wanted to look clever."

"I wanted to cover for...."

His voice was soft as his face relaxed, the torment from the lenses fading. "For what?"

Ophelia winced, smelling polished leather and dust. Her eyes darted to his torso to see if his leather jacket was the source, but he was still only wearing a white T-shirt... a white shirt that grew a collar and was hidden behind a dark tweed vest and jacket. His hair was still swept back off his face without the footman's side part, but she could no longer tell if she was looking at Brennan or Leander.

Alex and Ramiro laughed in unison in the other room, but the Irishman before her didn't react. Instead, his brows twitched together the slightest bit, as if hearing something in the distance. It was the baying of a hound.

Leander twisted to look over his shoulder, and when he spun back around to face her, his dark eyes were alight with panic.

"Someone's here," he gasped.

She shook her head, torn between responding that of course someone was there and remaining on her feet despite the cold bursting in her chest.

Feet?

Yes, she was standing in the tack room, and Leander was looking about, his wavy locks shaking loose as he hunted for an escape that didn't exist while the barking grew louder.

"Leander," Amelia whispered, reaching out a shaking arm.

The moment he saw the shimmer in her eyes, he darted over and took her hands, hugging them to his chest before kissing one of her knuckles.

"It'll be all right, *mo chroí*," he said in a shaky rush. "Just tell them I forced ya to run."

She shook her head, her lower jaw quivering as she tugged her hands out of his to latch onto the lapels of his jacket, unable to cut through the cacophony of her mind. She was alone. In her camisole. With a servant.

I'm ruined. Is this real? It must be a dream. A nightmare. This can't be happening.

The hound was just outside and its bay harped on her consciousness.

As the door kicked open, Leander bumped the tip of her cold nose with his, gripping her wrists, forcing clarity into her senses.

"I would fight," he whispered, his gaze boring into hers, and she realized he was asking for her permission. She shook her head the slightest bit.

Leander swallowed hard, his grip on her wrists relaxing.

"Back away," a voice behind him bellowed above the racket of the barking dog. Amelia recognized him as Buchanan, the Scottish groundskeeper, and he had his trusty shotgun tucked under one arm. "Don't ye touch her."

Closing his eyes, the footman did as he was told and released Amelia. His heels dragged on the floorboards when he took a shuffling step away from her, his gaze downcast submissively.

Buchanan came forward, shortening his hound's leash as it lunged at the pair, startling her. In that moment, the cold coursing through Amelia froze into a rigid blade and she brought herself up to her full height.

"That is quite enough, Mr. Buchanan," she scolded, surprised by the strength in her own voice.

"My lady," he protested, his bearded face ruddy as he reined in his dog. Leander cast him a sidelong look through the narrow corners of his eyes, his back to the man.

"Yes, I *am* your lady, and I am ordering you to call off that ridiculous creature and leave at once."

Buchanan's lips parted as he shook his head. "No can do, love."

"Mr. Buchanan," she growled, her voice low as she took a step towards him. "If you wish to keep your position, you will—"

"Keep my position?" he laughed. "Who do ye think would run this grubby place if it weren't for me?"

"That is hardly relevant."

"Oh, it's relevant when you think ye can order me about like a bloody servant." He sneered at Leander and punctuated his final word by spitting on the younger man's shoulder.

Leander jerked and squeezed his eyes shut, his face flushed and his fists clenched.

"I told Lord Hollingberry it was a bad idea to let that one be anything but a stable boy," Buchanan continued, jerking his head towards Leander. "Let them Irish take a bit and they run amok. Now look where it's led. He's turned Hollingberry's pride and joy into a whore."

Amelia sneered at the accusation and Leander's eyes blazed as they darted to hers, his jaw clenched with self-control.

"Does that make your blood boil, son?" Buchanan taunted, kicking his hound to the side and leveling his shotgun at Leander. "Does that make ye want to hit me?"

A tremor shot through Leander's shoulders, his breathing heavy.

"Look at me when I'm talking to ye, boy," Buchanan demanded.

Leander spun around to face him and Buchanan grinned at the redness in the younger man's face, chuckling softly.

"When my father—"Amelia began imperiously.

"Your father?" Buchanan asked. "It was him who threatened to fire Liza if she didn't speak."

Amelia's throat went dry.

Papa? Liza? It cannot be.

Leander shook his head, his voice warbling. "We don't want any trouble, Mr. Buchanan."

"Then ye won't mind going quietly." Buchanan pulled a pair of handcuffs out of his pocket and tossed them onto the floor.

The younger man looked between Buchanan and the metal links before turning his gaze to Amelia, who tilted her chin in acquiescence. His back stiff, Leander crouched and picked up the restraints. Buchanan watched him like a constable, the shotgun leveled at the Irishman's chest, before nodding at Amelia.

"Put them on him."

Fixing her lover with an apologetic look, she took the cold metal from Leander's limp fingers in her gloveless hands. Her arms shook as she placed the cuff onto one wrist then paused over the second, letting her fingers slide over the smooth skin exposed there. Meeting his eyes, she held his stalwart gaze as she fastened the second cuff.

"I'll see your colors. I'll find you," Leander said softly, his voice strained. "I'll come."

Amelia reached out to touch his face, her breath clouding, but Leander stepped away before her fingers could do much more than brush against his skin. Head bowed, he stiffly approached Buchanan, who roughly grabbed Leander's arm and jerked him to his side, his eyes latched onto hers.

"Go ahead and put that dress back on then head inside. Finish your supper. Then go upstairs to your room."

She willed the tears pooling in her eyes to vanish as she continued to stand tall. "And Leander?"

"Will stay out here with me for now. If he tries to run, I'll shoot him. If you try to run, I'll shoot him. Understood?"

"And then what?" she asked, cocking her head slightly as her eyes cleared. "You'll inform the authorities, I presume?"

"Prison is a messy business. No one wants a scandal. I'm sure we'll make other arrangements to deal with this whelp." He yanked on Leander's arm and Amelia nodded stiffly, rejuvenated by the knowledge that there was room to negotiate.

"There's one thing we can agree upon."

Buchanan looked at her in surprise at that, but she ignored him as she snatched up her lavender evening gown, stepping back into it and tugging the straps over her shoulders. After fastening the clasps she could reach in the back, she turned away from the two men and looked at Buchanan over her shoulder.

"If you would be so kind?"

Shooting a warning look at Leander, Buchanan tied his now quiet hound's leash to a tack hook then approached her. His thick fingers fumbled slightly and she caught him shooting Leander a haughty look as he finished.

Knowing that the sight of her lover's face might chip away at her determination, Amelia focused downwards as she gathered up her skirts. Her brooch was lying on the tack room floor and the groundskeeper had stepped on it, taking a sliver out of the upper left portion of the cameo. Leaving it behind, she strode past the two to the door without looking at either of them.

"You're to wait in your room," Buchanan reminded as she stepped onto the threshold. "Immediately after dinner. At the slightest sign of trouble upstairs, you'll be washing your bonny boy's brains off the saddles."

"Yes, Mr. Buchanan," Amelia replied, meeting his gaze with irritation in her voice. "You've made that abundantly clear."

Buchanan inclined his head and, against her better judgment, she stole a glance at Leander, whose contrite expression softened with hope under her eyes. The barest hint of a smile twitched on her lips as she readied herself to trudge out.

Laughter erupted behind them and Leander craned his neck around to spy at its source. The part in his hair and his tweed suit faded, leaving Brennan twisting to peer over the back of the couch and into the kitchen of the old Victorian.

When he turned back around to face Ophelia, his expression was slightly annoyed, as if the two men laughing in the other room just interrupted a confession. He parted his lips to ask her something when he noted the rigidity of her posture as Amelia's fear fled, leaving immense relief in its wake.

"You're here," Ophelia whispered, lunging to wrap her arms around him. "You're safe."

One of Brennan's arms was pinned to his side by her sudden affection so he hugged her back with the other.

"Sure, where else would I be?" he asked, bemused.

Ophelia pulled away and snatched up his hands, running her fingers over his wrists to check for cuffs.

Brennan laughed softly, if only out of confusion. "You can search all you like but ya won't find any more pervy pictures on me."

She grinned at that then fell against him in another hug, cradling his head, never having been so thankful to live in an era and country where class and propriety meant so little. Brennan wrapped both arms around her this time, his scratchy cheek pressed against hers as he relaxed in her embrace. He didn't say a word but the drumming of his heart and his quietness hummed through her like a balm, making her feel solid. For the first time, she knew deep inside that no matter what memories surfaced, they couldn't hurt her, for the same stalwart resolve that gripped Amelia resided in her soul.

Brennan's heart was steady and strong and she didn't care that the way she was holding him revealed just how dear to her he had become. He ought to know her feelings. His pulse intensified, as if she could hear each beat as an approaching footstep.

No, those are *footsteps. Not again.*

She clung tighter, her fingers digging into the thin fabric and muscle on his back, desperately latching onto the present. His arms tightened around her in response, his heart rate climbing until he grew stiff and weak in her arms.

A door opened and she waited to see if Mr. Buchanan or Lord Hollingberry would appear, or if the old Victorian house would turn into the family estate, yet nothing changed. The door quietly closed, and Brennan felt like dead weight in her arms, even as his heart hammered enough to shake the two of them. She was about to pull away to ask what was wrong when a soft grunt sounded behind her, followed by the shuffle of flip-flops.

Jerking around, she just had time to catch sight of a flash of yellow hair and a blue hoodie before Adam slammed the door shut behind him, hard enough to rattle the house.

15

Ophelia scrambled to her feet, not sparing Brennan a glance as she hurried for the door.

Adam was stalking down the steps then paused in the dusk, nearly doubling over, his hands in his sweatshirt pocket, and the sight shoved the air from her lungs.

"Adam," she gasped, hurrying down the stoop after him.

"Stop," he growled, twisting to keep his back to her.

"Baby—"

"Stop!" He whirled around to face her, his bronzed skin flushed and his narrow eyes glinting in the streetlamp light.

Ophelia shook her head, the most terrible sickness creeping up her back, as if her spine could get nauseas. She parted her lips to speak but needed air and her lungs were still refusing to work in the face of the tumult radiating off him.

"I mean..." Adam ground his teeth together, pulling his hands out of his hoodie to grab at his hair. "What the *hell?*"

She shook her head, feeling any of her confidence in Amelia's strength fleeing her.

His face reddened as he clenched his jaw then let his arms fall to his sides. "Are you sleeping with him?"

The accusation, following on the heels of their fight where she was blamed for the same thing, stung so much that tears pooled in her eyes.

"Are you?" Adam bellowed, taking a step towards her.

She shook her head no, her throat cramping.

Adam's lips pressed together in a thin line as he breathed noisily through his nose, his eyes latched onto hers with such intensity that she felt as if they were ripping out her bones one by one, leaving her nothing but a puddle on the sidewalk.

"I can't hear you," he ground out.

"Of course I'm not," she whispered.

"I can't hear you," he repeated, latching onto her upper arm and tugging her closer to him.

"No," she shouted back, causing her tears to break free.

Adam relaxed his grip, his own eyes shimmering as he searched her face, and when he spoke again, his voice cracked. "So what is it? Because you've been obsessed with him since the night you met."

"*You* have," she snapped, feeling her resolve return.

He lowered his head and took a step back but didn't release her arm. "Excuse me?"

"You have so little trust, that the moment I made a friend who happened to be male you were suspicious."

Adam shook his head. "That's not fair."

"Where are my girlfriends?" she seethed, even as she knew that he was right, no matter how much she wished he wasn't. "Where is my room-mate from last year? I haven't seen anyone in months because you—"

"Don't pin that on me."

"You only tolerate Alex because he's gay."

He released her then and smiled mirthlessly, shaking his head. "You are being *so* high school. I haven't seen *my* friends in ages, either."

"I told you to stop dumbing things down," she snapped. "There is nothing simple about this."

"So... what?" He flung out his arms, his tears fading. "Instead of talking to me you take it out by doing God knows what with—"

"*Nothing's happened*," she replied, and her growing anger erased any thought that she was not being entirely truthful.

He shook his head again, and she noticed his features anew since the first time they met, his raw emotion flushing out his freckles, making him look like a stranger.

"You know," he said, his quiet voice squeaking a little. "I thought we had a good thing here."

Ophelia let her shoulders relax as she deflated. "We did."

"What changed?"

She held a hand to her temple and closed her eyes, remembering the handcuffs and the scent of the saddles, wondering if telling him would have ever made any difference. "Nothing has changed," she said softly, opening her eyes.

"Baby," he whimpered, his eyes once again glistening. "You're not even giving me a chance."

"Of course I am."

"I love you and you love me and you're just…" He closed the gap between them. "You're infatuated with this guy, that's all." He reached a shaking hand up to the side of her face and when she held his gaze and didn't bat it away, he slid his fingers into her hair. "It'll pass. It's not worth losing this. Losing us."

Closing her eyes, Ophelia allowed his words to trickle into her, his touch filling her with the sensation of being shielded and safe. Familiar. Slowly nodding, she completely relaxed her body and let him pull her into a gentle hug.

"I can't lose you," he whispered into her hair and she wrapped her arms around him, breathing in the lingering aroma of sunscreen left on his heated skin.

Taking a deep breath, she sighed and wiped her tears while he tightened the hug.

"I can change," Adam continued. "I can be whatever you want me to be."

She shook her head. "You shouldn't have to change."

"I don't care," he replied with a hint of panic. "I *will*."

Remaining in his arms until her eyes dried, she pulled away with a quiet sniffle. "We have some work to do," she said softly. "Together."

"Yeah," he agreed, slipping his hands down to hers.

She gave them a squeeze and a pitiful smile. Kissing her hand, he walked her up the stairs to the house, pausing when he stepped on something. Ophelia followed his gaze and spotted another braid of sweet grass. Adam looked irritated when he kicked it away, as if it were a cockroach, and then met her gaze.

"You should probably go home," she said.

Adam nodded. "But we'll be okay? Nothing's going on?"

Her words were gnarled and thick and couldn't come out, so Ophelia rose onto her tip toes and kissed him in response.

He squeezed her hand to his chest before hesitantly shuffling down the steps and towards his truck. Ophelia watched him go, waiting until he was in the vehicle. A deep tiredness settled over her, as if her very soul was exhausted. She offered him a weak smile and a wave goodbye as he drove past. Slipping back inside, she worried that she would find Alex and Ramiro awkwardly milling about the kitchen.

Instead, they seemed to be upstairs, laughing and listening to Alex's Icelandic music in his room, apparently oblivious to her argument. Brennan was nowhere in sight, and she wondered if it would be more kind to hunt for him or to go to bed without a word.

"I think it would be best," an Irish voice said from the corner by the woodstove, and she realized with a start that she hadn't seen Brennan in the shadows, sitting with his back to the wall with the bay window. "If I just up and went."

Ophelia sighed, hunting for his face in the darkness, only able to faintly make out his features. A twinge of longing coursed through her exhaustion as she realized just how much she adored his voice.

"You don't have anywhere to go," she said softly.

"I'd rather be on the streets than somewhere I'm not wanted," he said, shoving off the wall and to his feet.

His words nicked the tired calm that had settled inside. "You shouldn't have listened."

"Of course I listened," he said softly, treading past her to grab his jacket off his guitar case in the corner. "He sounded ready to hit you."

She shook her head. "He wouldn't."

"Ya sure about that?" he asked, shrugging on his leather.

"Absolutely."

Brennan shook his head the slightest bit, his expression dark as he tugged his sleeves down.

Ophelia tried to swallow but it was as if all the moisture in her mouth had grown thick. "Don't do this," she whispered.

"I'll wait until his fella leaves," Brennan said. "No need to cause a scene."

"Brennan—"

"Listen, Girl," he said louder, his voice wavering. "I've brought ya not'ing but trouble since I darkened your door." He grabbed his case and slipped the guitar inside. "I'll always be sorry for that," he whispered before zipping it shut.

Something tightened inside and she felt sick with herself for wanting Brennan to stay even if it hurt Adam. "You're always at work," she tried. "We hardly see each other as it is."

Brennan met her gaze, his hazel eyes sharp, as a curl broke loose and fell in his face. He took a step towards her, his shoulders rising and falling with whatever it was he was about to say, and she realized with a start that she was looking at his lips and wondering, against all logic, if kissing him would change his mind.

Footsteps sounded on the stairs as Alex and Ramiro descended, and Brennan's raven-winged brows twitched together in consternation, as if he could tell what she was thinking.

"Don't," was all he whispered.

"I can't believe how late it is already," Ramiro was saying, and the moment he stepped into the living room, Brennan donned the most convincing happy face Ophelia had ever seen.

"Time flies when you're having fun, huh?" he replied, raking a hand through his hair and disheveling his dark locks.

"Let me walk you out," Alex said, stepping in front of Ramiro to lead the way to the door.

Brennan brushed past Ophelia and headed for the stairs, about to leg it up when Ramiro paused to wave. "It was great meeting you both."

Ophelia could only manage a tight-lipped smile while Brennan chirped "cheers" before jogging up the stairs. Alex's gaze lingered on Ophelia, as if trying to assess if something was wrong from his distance, before returning his attention to Ramiro and slipping outside.

Once alone, Ophelia sank down onto the arm of the couch, staring forlornly at the Irish flag stickers on the guitar case beside her. *Was it really just hours ago that we were laughing in the kitchen? And a few hours before that when Adam was warm and solid behind me as I wrote?* The strain of the moment and drama of Amelia had worn away her sense of reality and time. Brennan's footfalls echoed upstairs, and moments later, he descended with his duffel bag packed.

Heading back into the room, he scanned it for his possessions, never once letting his eyes settle on Ophelia. Assured that he hadn't left anything behind, he glanced at the door.

"They still chattin' away?"

"Yeah."

Brennan nodded and shouldered his guitar. "I'll chat to him later."

Still without looking at her, he headed for the back door, and his indifference stung, even if Ophelia knew it was forced. When she heard the hinges squeak, she hopped to her feet and followed, catching him just as he was stepping out.

"Wait."

"Jaysus, Girl," he groaned, ignoring her and heading into the small backyard that was overgrown with weeds.

"Brennan," she scolded.

"There's not'ing to wait *for*," he barked, spinning around to face her. She regretted having wanted him to look at her when his eyes flashed and he was once more the wounded animal she was so afraid to touch when she had gifted him her tea that night in the kitchen. "So just..." He gestured towards the upstairs. "Go back to your feckin' poet."

"I know I've disappointed you," she said, her voice far firmer than she felt. "And Adam. And it's not fair to anyone."

He appraised her for some time before the guitar case slumped a little on his shoulder and his expression softened. "You haven't disappointed me, love," he said quietly. "I've disappointed myself. I can't blame you just because you're not who I wish ya were to me. And you're doing what's right."

It was as if her insides cemented together, for she couldn't speak, even as she wanted to argue that she didn't know what was right anymore. Brennan hesitated a moment longer then took a step towards the side yard.

"Just," he began, his face twisting with the words. "Be more careful with your kindness from now on. Ya never know when it will actually stick inside someone else."

His hair curtained his face as he turned away, and Ophelia lingered on the back porch until she heard the gate click shut.

As she turned to head back inside, the toe of her shoe hit a small stack of firewood, and she sank onto the ground, her whole body contracting in a dry sob as she lost her shred of control. She wanted to cry. She needed to cry. But instead, all that came out were gasps as she tried to grab at the fraying strands of her mind that flapped in the wake of all that just happened.

The front door shut as Alex returned into the house after having bid Ramiro goodbye. She focused on his footsteps as he puttered about in the kitchen then headed upstairs, probably assuming that she was in her room. Curling to hug her legs, she rested her forehead on her knees and closed her eyes, forcing her breathing to even out, grasping at any measure of calm and letting it fill her. There was nothing to be done now. There was nothing to fix. She just had to give herself time to adjust to her new reality with Brennan gone and Adam...

Sighing, she heard Alex's feet hurrying down the stairs before stopping in the living room. "Elephant?"

She held herself tighter, not wanting to speak for fear it would shatter the quietness in her mind.

"Ophelia?" Alex called again as he wandered the house. Eventually, his footsteps sounded in the hall and the back door creaked open. "There you are," he said with relief. "Do you wanna tell me why Brennan left this note on my bed?"

She glanced up at him to find a piece of paper in his hand with short, messy scrawl. Alex's deep set eyes were hooded with his concern, but all Ophelia could muster inside was tiredness. Shoving to her feet, she dusted off her palms and backside, realizing dully that her arm ached where Adam grabbed it earlier and her hip where she had fallen.

"I'm really tired," she muttered. "We can talk about it later."

Alex blocked her way back into the house and scrutinized her for a moment, frowning before nodding and stepping aside.

"Did you have a good time tonight?" she asked, pausing in the doorway and forcing interest into her voice as she looked at him over her shoulder.

"Yeah," Alex softly replied. "I did. At first, I... but that lunatic in glasses kept me distracted from my nerves." He folded up the note from Brennan and she nodded with a half smile before bidding him goodnight.

Once upstairs, she showered and curled up in bed, not even bothering to straighten her bangs. Yet despite her exhaustion, sleep took its time in coming.

Nothing has changed, she chanted to herself. *My life is just like it was two weeks ago before I met Brennan, except I have a better thesis. Nothing has changed.*

Her fingers dug into her sheets, and it wasn't until she admitted that everything had changed that she managed to fall asleep.

She awoke to several texts from Adam, asking how she was doing and if it was ok for him to come over that night for *Survivor*. She replied that of course it was, and then felt a twinge of guilt over sounding so confident when she was anything but. Faith in her reality had been shaken, but this time it had nothing to do with her visions and everything to do with her current life.

Alex was downstairs eating breakfast before class when she

headed into the kitchen. He offered her a smile which she returned as she put the kettle on to boil then shuffled about, pulling out her Artemis mug and a sachet of Earl Grey. Alex read the stiffness in her movements and didn't ask a question. Instead, he rose and tugged her into a hug. Sighing, she rested her head on his shoulder, relaxing as he swayed back and forth, rocking her.

"Thank you," she whispered when she pulled away.

He brushed some of her bangs aside with a whimsical smile, and he didn't have to speak to let her know he loved her.

Once Alex had left for class, Ophelia headed upstairs and once again began work on her paper. A detachment settled inside when writing about Keats and Fanny Brawne, and she took comfort in the security of dusty pages and the rhythmic clicking of her fingers on the keyboard. Resting her fingertips on her lips, she leaned back and stared at the sentence she had just written before punching the period button.

Adam arrived early, bringing Chinese take-out. Ophelia latched onto him in such a tight hug that he didn't even have time to set down the food. He hugged her back as best he could, his biceps pressing against the bruise he had left on her arm.

"I finished my thesis," she said.

"No way. Baby, that's great."

She smiled because she knew she ought to be happy or satisfied or proud, but instead, it just felt like finishing a load of laundry or an assigned reading. He kissed her and she hated the numbness in her lips.

What the hell is wrong with me?

They unpacked the meal and settled onto the couch, eating while they watched their show, and the longer she was beside him, the meeker her mind felt.

"You've been quiet," he said softly.

Ophelia sighed. "I didn't get much sleep last night."

"Do you want to talk about it?"

She shook her head, knowing that the only thing they ought to talk about were her memories from another time.

"Look," he said, turning to face her. "These things happen, okay? It doesn't make you a bad person. It just makes you human."

"I never meant—"

"I know. And that doesn't matter now. All that matters is us. This." He tilted her chin towards him then kissed her, slowly, teasing her lower lip. A spark of heat darted through her, cutting the quietness inside, and she clung to the familiar bodily reaction to his touch. Bringing her hand up to cup his face, she slipped her tongue in his mouth and he immediately responded, his hands sliding to her backside with a happy groan.

This is good, she told herself. *This is who I am.*

One of his hands clenched on her rump and she shifted to sit on his lap, moving her lips to his neck, kissing her way down his collarbone while he ran his hands over her backside. Her fingers unbuttoned his shorts and gave them a tug. He laid her down and she spread her knees as much as she could on the couch.

"Turn off the lights," she whispered.

A perplexed expression crossed Adam's face as he pulled off his shirt. "Why?"

Her gaze lingered on the smooth, golden contours of his chest, tracing the thick muscles. "I just want to feel you."

He smiled crookedly then reached onto the end table to switch off the lamp before crawling on top of her. She arched up against him, focusing on the blood swelling her loins as she stripped off her shirt and shorts.

His kisses were slow and teasing but her mind was distracted by the scent of Brennan's aftershave on the cushions. She wondered where he went when he had left, and what it would be like to feel him pressing into her instead of Adam. Her cheeks flushed at the thought and she tried to shove it out of her mind until she realized that Adam was right, and her infatuation had gotten the better of her. She tried to blame Amelia and Leander, or even Jack, but instead all she heard was the strumming of Brennan's guitar and the rumble of his voice as his cheek scratched against hers.

An ache settled in her shoulder as her torso bumped against the arm of the couch, jerking her back into herself, and she realized that her hips were gyring, setting a faster pace. Adam happily obliged and she felt a wave of shuddering heat course through her as he panted. Latching onto his back, she angled her pelvis towards him and gripped his sides with her knees. He took the silent cue and rutted even faster, making her shoulder bang into the armrest over and over. It hurt but she didn't mind and dug her fingers into the muscles of his back, focusing on the sensation and sound of him slapping against the slick outside of her, reminding herself of what he was doing to her body and just how desperate he was for her.

In the past, such thoughts were enough to make her begin to tighten and gasp, but instead, all she felt was the ache in her shoulder and a building need for more. Tightening her thighs against him, she bucked her hips, throwing off their rhythm and making sweat trickle from her hairline. Adam rested his forehead in the crook of her neck, panting hard against her and grunting softly as he restrained himself, slowing. She let her entire body jerk with each measured thrust until moans escaped her throat.

Adam groaned in response then wrapped an arm around her back as he hauled her up and onto his lap. She bounced on his thighs in a frenzied rhythm. He gripped her hips and yanked her towards him with each thrust, and she wrapped her arms around his shoulders, her hands slipping on the sweat of his back as she begged her body for release.

"Lia?" he grunted.

"Say something," she gasped.

"We can do this every fucking night."

Closing her eyes and focusing on maintaining her seat, she shook her head, her voice high. "Something else."

He was quiet for a few moments, and she started to unwind an arm from his neck to touch herself when he caught her wrist in his hand and grunted, bowling her over again, holding her hips up off the couch as he pounded into her. She closed her eyes, shoving aside the renewed pain in her shoulder and focusing on his ragged breathing.

He whined her name, and knowing the power she had over him in this moment made her start to coil around him.

Adam continued to slap against her as she tightened more and more, yelping as she built towards her release.

"More," she moaned, even as she clenched.

He cried out, his fingers digging into her hips, and knowing that he was on the brink of his control was what finally sent her over the edge. Her entire lower half convulsed and she jerked forward with a cry, latching onto his back again as he pumped into her, moaning as he released in unison.

He spilled inside of her as she shuddered, gasping, slowing the rocking of her hips, her hair plastered to her sweaty neck. Adam collapsed, taking her down with him as he pulled out, panting. A deep satisfaction coursed through her and she clung to the memory of feeling his release, desperately wanting the rawness to make her feel the same way about him as she did a month ago, but her only thought was gratitude for her birth control implant.

"Jesus," he moaned into her shoulder.

An apology was on the tip of her tongue, but she didn't let it out.

"I deserve this," he gasped, the hint of anger in his voice making him sound like someone else, and she didn't tell him that the thought of him restraining himself in some form of penance was what she had needed to orgasm.

"Thank you," she whispered with a hint of guilt over the emotion in his voice.

He shifted to kiss her, heat still radiating from his body. They lay in each other's arms until their sweat dried, then she rose and led him to the bathroom. She had never showered with him and expected it to be some sort of enticing experience. Instead, as her physical satisfaction left, she was again filled with detachment.

Once clean, they curled up on the couch and channel surfed. Adam fell asleep within ten minutes, and Ophelia settled against him, feeling secure.

This is normal, she repeated to herself. *This is who I am.*

After an hour or so, she woke Adam up and walked him to the

door. They shared a long kiss goodnight and once he was gone, she took a painkiller for her sore body, wondering at her own desire when they had made love.

Then again, it wasn't desire, was it?

Feeling somewhat ashamed, she realized that their sex had far more to do with yearning to feel something that wasn't there than any genuine passion. Something that couldn't be replaced or grown by being an animal, no matter how much she wished it was that simple.

"So... Ramiro and I kissed last night," Alex said, leaning his temple on her doorway as she finished e-mailing her thesis advisor later that night.

Ophelia grinned. "That's adorable."

Alex smiled bashfully as he wandered in then sat beside her on the lavender comforter. "It was good."

"You deserve good."

"So do you," he replied, turning to face her then reading the message over her shoulder. "No way—you finished?"

"Weird, huh?" she replied. "I've yet to see if it's any good."

"Of course it is. You're brilliant. We have to celebrate."

She stared ahead at the screen, her pleasant expression fading.

"I need Adam," she said softly. Alex cocked his head and she met his gaze with her tired brown eyes. "I always have."

He smiled softly and rested his hand on hers. "He needs you, too."

She studied their hands in her lap then he ruffled her hair and rose, heading for the door.

"Is that love?" she asked so quietly that she was surprised he could hear her above his own footsteps.

Alex paused in the doorway, his pale eyes darkening with pity as he studied her. "I don't know."

Ophelia took in a deep breath and let it out shakily. "That's what I thought."

16

*O*phelia caught up on as much of her reading as she could the following afternoon before catching the bus to head across the redwood ridges to school. Her professors' voices were both difficult to focus on and soothing in their simplicity. She found herself delving into class discussions with a joy that she hadn't felt all semester. They could talk about a book and its set number of characters in a world that was limited from cover to cover. Contained. Except that every once in a while, an historical event would sneak into the text, and she would be reminded that, like her present life, the novel didn't really exist in a vacuum. Every book and outside event that had come before it influenced its birth, consciously or not, just like her life.

"I'd just like a break," she said into the phone after class on her way to the bus stop.

"What do you mean?" Adam responded, his voice tight.

"Nothing. It doesn't mean anything. Just that I'm super overwhelmed. I need some me time."

"Okay," he reluctantly replied, his voice even tighter.

Her throat constricted in response and remained painful the entire bus ride back to Santa Cruz. By the time she got off at the metro center, she knew she had done the right thing. It wasn't fair to Adam to give him false hope while she was so confused. As she stepped off the bus and wove through the cluster of people, she spotted Trea milling about in the distance, looking like he was lost in a foreign city.

Immediately angling away from him, she started her walk to the old Victorian, hoping he wouldn't see her. The last thing she wanted right now was to have to deal with a stranger's weirdness, to say nothing of her worry that he would follow her home.

"Hey, Ophelia!"

Closing her eyes, she quickened her pace, pretending she didn't hear him.

"Did you get my message?" he called to her across the street.

She merely offered him a polite smile and a little wave as she rounded a corner and power walked back to the house. Ophelia pondered how Trea thought leaving sweet grass accounted for a message, then realized it wasn't worth the brain cells she would expend wondering. After all, her city's motto was, "Keep Santa Cruz Weird."

Once inside, she heard Alex talking on the phone in his room. She smiled as she passed his door, for his voice was soft as he spoke about his day. Mundane details. Closeness.

The house was quiet as the following days slipped past without any visions or flirting and Ophelia felt more and more grounded. An ache had settled in her chest, dull and constant like a vacant organ.

Someone's missing.

The reality of finishing her thesis started to trickle into her consciousness with a glow of pride. She and Alex took to playing board games at night, and she laughed more than she figured she ought to for being separated from her boyfriend. Alex even gave her one of his controllers and taught her how to battle his elf as a dwarf in his favorite fantasy game.

Saturday night, Alex and Ramiro took her out to celebrate her achievement. After an Italian dinner, they wandered the streets as a trio, looking for a bar, when she guided them to the Poet and the

Patriot. Ramiro bought them all a round of Guinness, and Ophelia's eyes scanned the crowd as she sipped her drink.

"Hey," Ramiro said, raising his glass. "To graduation."

Ophelia smiled and wiped some of the foam off her upper lip with her sleeve before raising her glass with his and Alex's. "To graduation."

"And to my best friend," Alex added.

The three clanked their glasses together then drank, and Ophelia yanked Alex's head over and smooched him on the cheek, making him laugh. Ramiro's earthen eyes were warm as he reached out to rub Alex's back for a moment before turning his attention to the stage as a band set up their gear.

Ophelia's eyes darted over the musicians then to the door. Alex rested a hand on her arm.

"He's not here," he said softly.

She looked back at him, her brow furrowed in a pathetic attempt to play dumb.

Alex's expression was apologetic and she realized he had been keeping a secret. "I saw him at the shop the other day. Guess he's living in the Super 8 Motel."

Grabbing her glass, Ophelia pretended she was interested in her drink as she took a sip. "How is he?"

"Quiet."

She rotated her glass on the table, watching the condensation on the outside collect in droplets that slid down the side like tears past her fingerprints.

"Like you," he added softly.

Ophelia took a deep breath and let it out, feeling the ache inside sharpen until she realized that it was a want. A yearning, lonesome want.

The band started playing a Brazilian tune, and she willed the music to distract her from the memory of a cold night when the quiet thumping of a heart beside her and the soft lilt of an Irish song was all she needed. A stolen moment.

Anything worth having shouldn't be stolen.

"He's singing about how his love for a woman made him question his faith," Ramiro explained to Alex. "And everything he was before no longer mattered. Like he was obliterated and remade by his affection for her."

Alex nodded, though it was clear that he appreciated Ramiro's attention far more than the music.

"And something about an… armadillo?"

Alex did a double-take then laughed.

"Hey," Ramiro defended. "It's Portuguese, not Spanish. Give me a break."

Alex rubbed his shoulder then returned his attention to the band. Ophelia watched the two, a glow settling inside at the sight of Alex so at ease and enjoying himself.

She walked home several paces ahead of her friends, giving them some privacy as they linked hands and strolled at a leisurely pace. They paused at the street corner by the house and Ophelia went on ahead, slowing when she noticed someone smoking a cigarette on the stoop. Despite her distaste for the habit, her heart fluttered and she quickened her step, hoping it was Brennan.

When the figure rose, however, she saw that it was a woman with short black hair and a ratty coat. "Charlie?"

The girl stubbed out her cigarette with a long exhale, her smoky eye make-up smudged as if she had slept in it more than once. "You must think I'm a creeper."

Glancing over her shoulder to make sure Alex and Ramiro were still nearby, she stepped closer. "What's up?"

Charlie shrugged. "Guess he's not home, huh?"

Relaxing and feeling more than a little satisfied that the Dubliner didn't run back to Charlie's arms when he left, Ophelia shook her head. "He doesn't live here anymore."

"No shit?" Charlie screwed up her face and stomped a foot. "I've been waiting here like, an hour."

Ophelia studied the other woman's stubby nose and large eyes, feeling as if she had seen her more than twice before. It was only now that she knew Brennan wasn't with the other girl that Ophelia could admit she was pretty in her own, hard-edged way, and there was something she envied in her forcefulness.

"There's a women's shelter in town," Ophelia said quietly. "Just so you know."

"Fuck that noise," Charlie laughed, tugging out a cigarette pack.

Charming as ever.

"I have my own place."

"Good," Ophelia replied, readying her keys. "Brennan was worried for a while that you were homeless."

Charlie's dark brows twitched together and she shifted to place a hand on her hip, cocking her head at the taller woman. "I thought you had a boyfriend."

"What's it to you?"

"Why're you talking shit about me behind my back?"

"Oh my God," Ophelia whispered in exasperation, shaking her head and brushing past her. She headed up the stoop to unlock the door, refusing to be dragged into any more drama than necessary.

"Seriously," Charlie insisted, starting up the stairs. "What else did he say?"

Sighing, Ophelia turned to face her, words surging up in her breast so quickly that she couldn't stop them. "That, apparently, you have an incredible laugh," she snapped, making Charlie freeze in her tracks. "That he was worried you weren't being careful. That he had ruined your life."

Charlie blinked several times, pulling her head back. "Oh."

"Yeah," Ophelia snapped back.

"Well… do you know where he is?"

"No, I don't," she lied.

Charlie stepped backwards off the stoop. "I, um… I'm sorry," she muttered, seemingly afraid to look at Ophelia, sounding genuinely contrite.

Ophelia parted her lips to reply when Charlie's eye make-up faded, her dark hair grew and coiled into a bun, and her ragged jacket morphed into the black and white uniform of a maid. With a start, Ophelia realized that she was looking at Liza.

The maid's gaze was apologetic as she continued. "I truly am. Though I don't expect you to forgive me, my lady."

Amelia was stiff, standing outside her bedroom door after the dinner. Liza awaited a response she didn't receive then opened the door for her mistress, staring at the ground. A part of Amelia felt pity for her maid, but even that small emotion was too much to expend when she was focusing so hard on remaining composed and in control for Leander's sake.

Leander. Had Liza shared their secret out of spite because Leander didn't care for her?

Stepping into her bedroom, Amelia strode towards the window, hearing the soft click of the door as Liza closed it. From the third story, she could see the moonlit lawn and the distant stables where a dim light glowed in the tack room.

Now that she was certainly alone, she let her posture fail and dropped her face into a gloved hand with a gasp.

How has everything become so twisted and turned on its head? How can my lover be shackled and at gunpoint? More importantly, how can I spare him?

The heavy footfalls of a man sounded in the hall and Amelia straightened, preparing to face her father. She could do this. She could talk him out of sending Leander away.

"Really," Liza's voice returned, and suddenly her Victorian bedroom vanished and Ophelia was left on her doorstep, facing Charlie. "Other chicks don't like me." Charlie continued. "And you're obviously..." She flapped her hand at the taller girl helplessly. "Anyway, seeya."

With that, Charlie hopped off the stoop and started down the street, cupping her cigarette as she lit it.

Ophelia watched her go with a shuddering sigh, wondering if there really was such a thing as strangers anymore. And if Charlie was Liza, they were friends once... even if they had wound up just as strained as they were now.

"Wait."

Charlie paused, the tip of the cigarette glowing as she took a drag.

"He's at the Super 8," Ophelia replied, feeling her stomach coat itself with sick, though over jealousy or the worry that Charlie would once again cause a scene for Brennan, she didn't know.

The other woman smiled a little and jerked her head in a nod. "You're all right." With that, she continued down the street, pulling out her phone to undoubtedly look up directions.

Alex and Ramiro were still chatting under the streetlamp, and as Ramiro bumped Alex's shoulder with his, Ophelia finished unlocking the door and slipped inside, kicking something as she did so. Switching on the lights, she found yet another braid of sweet grass.

"Seriously, Trea?"

Heading upstairs, she showered and readied for bed, combing her fingers through her wet curls and straightening her bangs as her mind absorbed her latest memory, wondering for the hundredth time what became of Amelia and her love triangle. Checking her phone, she had no new messages, and was both happy and a little disappointed that Adam had been faithfully respecting her wishes by giving her space.

She heard from her thesis advisor the following day and scheduled to talk to him before class that Thursday. The grin wouldn't leave her face as she reread his words to her: *You have done a fine job and even brought to light some elements of Keats' psychological process that I hadn't previously considered. It was a pleasure to read.*

The natural high filled her throughout the day and into Monday, though even it couldn't soften the burning of wanting inside. By the time Tuesday arrived, she had already called her parents and Nana to gush about the praise and how she would be graduating on time after all. A knock sent her downstairs, two at a time, once again in her leggings and blue tunic. Forgetting to spy out the window, she opened the door and was surprised to find Brennan. Her wanting disappeared, but her initial smile faded when she took in his pink, puffy eyes and the miserable hunching of his tall frame.

"What happened?" she gasped.

His voice cracked when he spoke. "She's dead."

Ophelia stopped breathing and her feet became heavy as she wondered if she had heard him properly. "W—Who?"

Brennan swallowed hard, his eyes shimmering. "Charlie."

"No," she whispered. "I just saw her... a few nights ago."

He nodded, causing his tears to escape as he swallowed. "Yeah, Saturday. She came by and..."

His eyes drifted away dejectedly as he shook his head, unable to hold onto his own thoughts.

Ophelia's chest tightened as she remembered how Charlie had stood in that very spot three days ago. Stepping to the side, she motioned for Brennan to come in. He stiffly obliged and paused in the entryway, his eyes drifting to everything and nothing at the same time, looking like a stray.

"What happened?" she asked, easing the door shut behind him.

Brennan wiped at his cheeks with his palms, sniffling quietly. "Someone found her body by the levee."

"Oh my God," Ophelia breathed. "She seemed perfectly fine when she—"

"I guess she still had tubing tied to her arm," he croaked, hugging his chest, his eyes still drifting listlessly around the floor. "And she wasn't harmed."

Ophelia eased onto the back of the couch, her fingertips pressed to her lips. "So she overdosed."

Brennan lifted his head slightly, as if to agree, but his face flushed and scrunched up in pain as he shook his head. "Jaysus, I killed her."

Ophelia straightened, stiffening. "What are you talking about?"

"I shouldn't have..." he gasped, tears escaping once again. "She told me she was going to him again, so I gave her more cash. I should've just let her..." He shook his head helplessly. "I don't know. But now she's dead. And it's my fault." A sob wrenched from him and he hunched over, digging his hands into his hair before lowering to a crouch, and Ophelia knew that he was hardly aware of his own actions.

Settling down on her knees beside him, she rested a hand on his back as he gasped, falling onto the seat of his black pants with the force of his tears.

"Brennan..."

"I'm the reason she tried it," he wailed hoarsely. "And if I hadn't given her money the other night, she would still be alive."

"You don't know that."

"Yes, I *do*," he snapped. "She wasn't stupid. She was funny and beautiful and all we ever did was fight..." He took a shuddering breath. "But I already miss her."

Taking his warm, limp hand in hers, she gave it a squeeze.

His bleary hazel eyes met hers, looking all the more green for the red surrounding them. "She didn't deserve this," he whispered.

"I know," Ophelia replied, her own throat tightening, though admittedly more from the tattered man at her side than the girl she hardly knew. "She was lucky to have you."

"No," he croaked, shaking his head and pressing his lips together as he sucked a breath in through his nose. "I brought this on her. I may as well have pulled a trigger for what I've done."

She parted her lips to argue when a sick, heavy sensation tugged at her stomach. "I told her where you were," she whispered. All the warmth and color felt sucked from her skin as she realized that she was the one who had set things in motion. "If I hadn't sent her to you..."

Brennan took in several shuddering breaths, studying Ophelia's face before seeming to notice that his hand was in hers for the first time.

"She was resourceful," he said, his voice still croaking even as his eyes slowly dried. "She would've found me eventually."

Ophelia closed her eyes, pressing her free hand against one of her sockets. "I thought I was doing her a favor. I shouldn't have said anything."

He shook his head, his limp curls falling into his face. "Don't."

"But it's true," she insisted, her eyes misting over. "I should've kept my mouth shut."

"Christ, don't ya cry, too," he pleaded, his eyes tearing up again.

"I can't help it," she defended.

"But if you cry, *I'll* cry!"

"Don't yell at me," she snapped.

"I'm not," he barked around a sob.

Ophelia gasped when her throat constricted with tears as Brennan whimpered at her side for a moment before a bemused smile tugged at the corners of his lips. She narrowed her eyes at first then couldn't help but let out a small laugh at their ridiculousness. Her pleasant sounds trickled to him and he let out a soft chuckle, despite himself. After several long seconds of hiccoughing breathing, her tears faded and she was glad to see that his were on their way out, as well, even as any humor bled from his expression.

"Oh, Charlie," he croaked, bringing his knees up and leaning against the back of the couch as he dug his palms into his eyes. "Why'd ya have to do it, love?"

Ophelia sniffled and shifted so that her back was against the couch, as well, her side flush with his.

"She made her choices," she said hoarsely. "And really, that's all that matters. If she didn't get the money from you, she'd have gotten it elsewhere."

She waited for a response but Brennan remained in his pose and all she could see was his trembling lower lip as he tried to calm his breathing beneath his hidden eyes.

"Just like if she so easily tried heroin with you, she would've with someone else."

He groaned out a shuddering sob, pulling his palms away from his sockets and straightening his legs.

"You did the best you could by her."

He shook his head minutely. "Just wasn't enough."

She slipped her arms around one of his and hugged the limp appendage to her chest. "Nothing could have been enough. She had to want to change, like you did."

Brennan sucked in a ragged breath and let her words trickle into his mind before nodding a little. They sat in silence for some time, and she felt the tension leave his body as he relaxed beside her.

"We're going to Hell, ya know," he said quietly. "Laughter is disrespecting the dead."

"I was laughing at *you*," she said, giving his arm a little tug.

She was rewarded with a half smile. "I always manage to have women laughing at me. Charlie probably is right now. She'd make endless fun of me whenever I'd get hammered and start blubbering."

Ophelia pressed her lips together to keep from saying, "that doesn't seem very nice."

"Have any arrangements been made?" she asked instead.

"I don't know. Her mam didn't like me much. Christ." He dug his free hand into his wavy hair. "I'm sure she blames me, too."

Ophelia sighed. "Then maybe that's something you can be for Charlie."

"Be what?" he asked, looking at her.

"The person her mom blames instead of her daughter. Instead of herself."

The thought quieted him, but the anguish was gone from his face, even if just out of exhaustion, for he looked as if he had been crying for some time before he showed up. Biting his lower lip, he drifted away in thought and Ophelia guided his head to her shoulder. He relaxed against her and she shifted her hug on his arm to hold his hand, twining their fingers together.

"I'm so sorry that this happened to her," Ophelia said quietly. "But I'm sorrier that you have to grieve."

Brennan adjusted his cheek on her shoulder and was quiet for the span of several heartbeats before speaking. "When somet'ing like this happens, it just... brings up everyt'ing else, ya know?"

She nodded, remembering his parents, and kissed his forehead. He squeezed her hand in silent gratitude. They remained on the floor until she started to wonder if he had fallen asleep against her. Letting go of his hand, she felt him shift in response, so she gently peeled away as he straightened, leaning his head back against the couch as she rose.

Offering him an encouraging smile that he seemed too tired to return, she padded into the kitchen and put the kettle on. She was grabbing two mugs and packets of Bengal Spice when she noticed him slip in after her, delicately sliding into a seat at the table, the leather of his jacket creaking.

His cheeks were still tearstained and combined with the puffiness of his red eyes and the pink tip of his nose, she couldn't help but wish that he still had a mother to turn to. Grabbing a paper towel, she moistened it with warm water then wrung it out before pressing it to his cheek. He rested his hand on hers with a quiet, "T'anks, love," taking it from her to dab at his face.

She placed the bags of tea in their mugs then offered him a smile when he finished wiping at his eyes, even if the action hadn't much improved his appearance.

"Feel better?"

Brennan nodded solemnly and the sight of him still so wretched caused the wanting inside her to return with a fury.

"Here," she said, grabbing a box of cereal from one of the cupboards before setting it on the table before him. "Eat up. Your favorite food."

His eyes sparked to life a bit as he took in the maniacal leprechaun on the bright box. "Lucky Charms? *Really?*"

"What?" she asked. "Doesn't remind you of home?"

He smirked a little at that and she grinned in response before grabbing the kettle as it started to boil.

"I should never have left," he said softly.

Ophelia poured hot water into their mugs then set them down on the table, sliding one towards him as she took a seat.

"And then where would I be?" she asked.

"There's always Boston and New York," he said huskily, and she looked away as his ignoring of her question pricked the rest of his words. "If I could get there... flights home are cheaper."

She stared down at her mug, watching the steam rise and curl, realizing that she couldn't blame him if California hadn't turned out to be the golden state from the fables.

"So, you're moving back to Ireland?" she asked, unable to look at him.

"I've been dying to for ages now. I just... I never could save up enough. And it's not even as simple as all that, anyways." He sighed.

Ophelia nodded, forcing a smile onto her face as she looked up

K. M. RICE

from her tea and studied his profile. She wanted to ask him to stay, to see if being around her more would make him feel like he was home again. Or to ask if he thought about her as often as she thought about him. But instead, something else came out.

"I finished my thesis."

Brennan's expression lifted some. "That's deadly. I'm proud of ya."

Her smile shifted from forced to real at that and she slid her hands around her mug, toying with the warm ceramic.

"Can I read it?"

"What, on the plane?"

A flash of confusion alit in his gaze until he bowed his head, as if he had been chastised. "You..."

"It's fine," she replied with a little wave of a hand. "I was just—"

"You'd like Dublin," he said suddenly, meeting her gaze, his eyes much clearer.

"I'm sure I..." she trailed off as the timidity in his face gave his words a new meaning. "I..."

"I mean... You're almost done with school."

She nodded in agreement, and for the life of her couldn't fight through the rush of excitement and fear at the idea of pursuing such a wild scheme to actually say anything coherent, even as her jaw worked.

"Ophelia," he said softly, resting a hand on hers, as light as a bird. "I don't like him. Even if he wasn't your fella he... he's... off. You'd think butter wouldn't melt in his mouth."

She let out a short laugh. "Adam?"

"He's too perfect."

"He's anything but perfect," she defended, remembering how her arm had ached after their fight and the emptiness she felt after making love with him.

"He makes me uncomfortable," Brennan insisted.

"Because he feels threatened by you."

Brennan shook his head. "It's not that... it's... it's deeper than that."

She was about to argue when she wondered if he could possibly have leftover animosity from Leander.

258

"I… I hardly know you," she said.

He let go of her hand, recoiling his arm, looking stung. "Ya hardly know me," he repeated bitterly. He coughed out a short breath, looking down at the table. "Then I guess I made a mistake in coming here. I just… I needed to see someone."

"I didn't mean it like that," she pleaded.

"I just thought," he squeaked, "I've bared the darkest parts of my soul and ya don't think I'm horrible."

"Of course you're horrible," she said, raising her voice. "But in the most irritating, annoying, wonderful way."

Brennan's lips curled impishly and his eyes bore into hers, his back rigid, as if he was afraid that breathing would rupture the moment.

"Do ya mean that? Because… I feel beautiful when ya look at me."

"Because you *are*," she whispered, and was only able to hold his gaze for a few more seconds before slowly leaning in.

He brought a hand up and stiffly swiped back her hair, his wrist trembling slightly, and she closed her eyes at the touch of his fingertips on her temple. The tip of his nose brushed against hers with hesitation, so she tilted her chin and wrapped a hand around the back of his neck, the soft touch of his hair tickling her skin. Then the scratch of his stubble was on her chin and his lips against hers in a shy press.

17

*O*phelia kissed Brennan back with more pressure, encouraging him to respond in kind. His lips were dry from having shed so many tears, but thrill coursed through her at their touch, as if she was back on the Giant Dipper. His free hand rested on her hip and the wanting inside vanished into a teasing hum when he slipped the tip of his tongue against her lips, moistening the kiss. Mimicking him, she giggled when their tongues brushed first once, then twice. Brennan laughed softly, as well, pulling away to kiss her chin and the corner of her mouth.

She rested her hand over his on her cheek and kissed him again, even while he tried to speak. "I've wanted to do that for so focking long."

"I don't feel beautiful when you look at me," she murmured against his lower lip, and he started to pull away to study her so she caught his face in her hands and looked into his eyes, losing herself in their greens and browns. "I feel strength."

When he smiled, it was as if the forest in his eyes suddenly had a sun, and she grinned, laughing softly as he nuzzled his nose against hers before pulling her into a hug. She sagged against him as he did the same, and she lost track of time as they bore each other's weight and his heart sang against the walls of his chest. The empty space inside was gone, replaced by a bright light, like a star had settled next to hers in the night sky of her soul, warming and blending its light with her own.

"I'm supposed to be at the shop," he murmured, breaking into her thoughts.

"It's Tuesday. Tuesday is your day off."

"I don't have days off anymore."

She pulled away to drink in the happiness radiating from his skin. "Don't go. Please?"

His smile was soft as he leaned his forehead against hers. "Anyt'ing for you, darlin'." He chuckled softly, toying with one of her curls. "Besides, I already called in sick."

She nodded, her smile fading with his laugh as each remembered why. Ophelia smooched his cheek and had to resist the urge to adore his face with more kisses as she rose, tugging on his hand.

"I want to show you something."

Brennan trailed behind her, keeping his hand in hers as she led him up the stairs and into her room. He peered around and she realized he hadn't set foot over her threshold since she assaulted him with a pillow. She headed over to the bookcase while he unzipped his jacket, revealing a crumpled blue shirt underneath, but as he folded the black leather over his arm, she caught sight of something odd sticking out of his pocket.

"What is that?"

He followed her gaze. "Oh." He tugged a braid of sweet grass out and showed it to her. "I found it outside my door this morning."

"You..." she began, her mind reeling over the oddity. "You know Trea?"

"Who?" he asked, reading her B.A. diploma on the wall and eyeing the graduation photo with her parents.

Wondering if Trea had decided that he was now the friendly neighborhood shaman, she returned her attention to the bookshelf and tugged out the old photo of her and Jack.

"Here," she said softly, holding out the picture.

Brennan took it from her and grinned with recognition as his eyes settled on the smiling little girl. "God, you were a little toot! What a dote." He looked up at her with amusement. "Ya look nearly the same."

Watching him intently, she pointed to the boy at her side in the picture and Brennan's smile faded, replaced by a look of confusion.

"It's real," she said.

Brennan eased down onto the bed as if he were arthritic, his raven-winged brows coming together. "But that's..."

"Jack. You."

He shook his head then peered up at her with startled eyes. "But he *looks* like me."

"I know. I don't understand it, either."

Brennan shifted and opened up his coat, unzipping a hidden pocket and pulling out a tattered photo of what appeared to be the same bright-eyed boy with wild black hair, grinning in the lap of his mother on the hood of a truck, his father leaning against it, gazing at his family with adoration. He held his old family photo side-by-side with the picture of Ophelia and Jack, and there was no doubt that they depicted the same child.

His confusion was evident, but having had some time to get used to the idea, Ophelia was more interested in the fact that he carried around a photo of his parents, carefully tucked away in a breast pocket by his heart. Like a lost child trying to find them again, even if they couldn't be found. The thought made her throat constrict and she sat down beside him, laying a hand on his knee.

"Do ya really think anyone would notice if we were always reborn in the same body?" he mused.

"Probably not. Especially not before cameras." Ophelia rested her cheek on his shoulder as she studied the two photos. "I loved Jack."

They sat in quietness, studying the two pictures while cars drove by on the street and a seagull chortled outside.

"You and Jack... maybe you were supposed to grow up and fall in love and get married. But then it was ruined when he... when I..."

"You're here now," she said, wrapping her arms around him.

"But there's no such t'ing as 'supposed to,'" he argued with himself, even as he rested his ear on her head. "There is no God or power planning these t'ings. Because if there was, how could it get muddled by somet'ing like a human murder?"

"Welcome to my world," she said with a soft laugh, "where you ponder the meaning of life while washing dishes."

"Doesn't everybody?" he asked.

She snorted then picked up the photo of his family without letting him go. She studied his mother whose dark, curling hair was blowing across her face in the wind, her arms wrapped tightly around her son's Buddha belly. The idea of Brennan ever having been round made her smirk.

"You look like her."

"A little like my da, too," he said in a tone that told her he'd had this conversation with himself so many times that he was excited to share it with someone else. "He had funny ears like me."

"You don't have funny ears," she chuckled, even as she remembered thinking as much when they first met. In retrospect, she had immediately taken note of his flaws as a defense mechanism, when really she had been drinking in his familiarity and loveliness.

"Do too," he said with a squeak. "They're massive."

"You're right. You're the one who ought to be called Elephant."

"Don't wind me up, now," he warned, lightly pinching her side.

"Don't what?"

"You're asking for trouble."

"That started the moment I met you."

He smiled, kissing her crown. Ophelia shifted, releasing him enough to press her lips to his, delighting in the scratch of his chin against hers and tenderness of his mouth, as if each touch was treasured. Kissing someone had never felt like this before. This was using her body to say words of delight in a language that she didn't even know existed.

Then his lips hardened, like fingers, and the room was once again Amelia's. They *were* fingers—her fingers—pressed against her mouth as the heavy footsteps approached, stopping just outside her door.

Stand tall, she scolded herself, then pulled her shoulders back. *I will not let Papa intimidate me. I will—*

The door creaked open and the man who stepped in lacked her father's portly figure, but was instead Kent, his eyes broken with betrayal as they met hers. She had never seen the military captain look more fragile and she couldn't breathe.

Then the pressure on her lips was back, massaging tingling warmth into her mouth as she kissed Brennan.

Kent. Adam.

She was breaking his heart all over again. Her lips stopped moving and Brennan slowed, reluctantly pulling away as she stiffened.

"Love?" he asked, worry tightening his face when he noticed how she had blanched.

"Adam," she whispered.

He sighed softly and gently carded some of her hair back behind her ear before nodding with a tender smile.

"It's all right, darlin'. I'm happy just to hold your hand."

She started to shake her head, needing to tell him that she wanted to kiss him, to learn his body, to adore him, until she realized that this couldn't be easy for him, either. Instead, she smiled and squeezed his fingers, and the hopeful happiness on his face told her that he would stay, and that they had all the time in the world to find their way through their web of lives.

He took his old family photo and carefully tucked it back into his jacket before handing her the picture of Jack. She rose and set it down on the bookcase, facing out, no longer a painful reminder of something lost.

"Do ya still remember t'ings?" he asked. "From before you were born?"

Ophelia nodded. "Only you and Alex know."

"Not your family?"

"I talked about it when I was that age." She pointed to the little girl grinning out from the picture. "But they just thought it was all make-believe. And I'm glad. Because if they didn't, they would have had me in therapy, or worse."

"My parents would've thought I was off my nut, too." He toyed with the zipper on his jacket for a moment. "Why do ya think we remember? Brains rot and turn into jelly when we die and that's where memories are stored, right?"

"I guess there's more to it than that. An... individuality of the soul."

His eyes drifted away from her as he considered this, and they were still somewhat puffy. She realized just how tired he looked and suddenly doubted that he had slept all night.

"How, um..." She cleared her throat. "How did you find out? About Charlie?"

Brennan stopped toying with the zipper. "The police rang me," he said quietly. "Around eleven. Her last five calls before the dealer were to me. They wanted someone to help identify her."

"Oh, God," she breathed, stepping back over to him.

"We went down to the coroner..." He shrugged. "She looked like she was sleeping, more or less. Sleeping with her jaw gaping open, her skin pale... sort of yellowed."

"That must've been painful," she said, sinking back down onto the bed beside him.

He shook his head, his lips pursed in thought. "Maybe she's already back."

"What do you mean?"

"As a baby." He turned to face her. "I'm not'ing special, yet I came back. I'm sure she can too."

"Yeah," Ophelia replied, smiling, knowing he was right since she had already known Charlie as Liza. "Come here."

She lay down and patted the mattress beside her.

Brennan all too eagerly obliged, as if his whole body ached. "Would ya really come with me?" he asked, picking up her hand and toying with her fingers.

The tickling touch absorbed her and it took her a moment to answer. In the past, the thought of leaving her country and home had always frightened her, but feeling the warmth from his body and the hope in his dream brushed away the fear that had gathered for years, like dust, revealing her inner Amelia. Amelia who had so much more to lose, yet planned to elope to the emerald isle.

"Yeah." She slid her fingers against his, making him smile, his eyes half-lidded. "It would be a nice break."

"It'll take me a bit to put the money by."

"Don't worry about that now." She rested their joined hands on his chest. "You need some sleep."

Brennan groaned. "Not again with the mam t'ing."

"*Really?*"

"You started it."

"All right then, don't sleep. Just lie quietly."

He gave their linked hands a tug, twisting his neck to gaze at her. "I never sleep during the day."

"Why not?"

"It's obscene."

"It's not obscene," she replied with a quiet laugh, snaking an arm under his neck to comb her fingers through his hair, delighting in the tickle against her skin.

Brennan sighed, pressing closer to her at the touch before draping his ankle over hers. "*You're* obscene."

"I know. I've completely corrupted you."

He let out a squeaky chuckle then quieted, his breathing settling into a rhythm with hers.

She was tempted to take a video as proof when he fell asleep five minutes later. As she lay beside him, she mused over how comfortable and delighted she was with a man she had barely known for a month and wondered if he could be right about Jack. There may not have been any sort of plan, divine or otherwise, but his soul seemed determined to find hers, and vice versa.

I'll find you, Leander had said. *I'll come.*

Whether his grit and perseverance in his hunt for her came from Leander or Jack, she didn't care, for it was Brennan she wanted.

Which meant that she would have to talk to Adam, and soon. The thought of disappointing him made her ache. Knowing the pain she would cause, and the probable paranoia about future girlfriends cheating on him, made her feel sick to her stomach, and more than a little in the wrong. Yet she hadn't intended for any of this to happen and she certainly hadn't asked for it.

That's why I've remembered. To not sneak around behind his back like I did as Amelia.

Alex came home an hour or so later and Ophelia slipped off the bed, careful not to disturb the Irishman after remembering the time she had frightened him into flopping off the couch just by turning off the TV. Hearing her friend puttering about in the living room, she tiptoed down the stairs and paused halfway. She couldn't help but smile when he caught her eye and raised his brows. "You look happy."

"I *feel* happy," she quietly chirped.

"Why are we whispering?" he asked, lowering his voice to match hers.

"Brennan's asleep upstairs."

Alex pulled his head back, eyeing her at length. "That's new."

Her high spirits were tempered by the memory of why Brennan arrived in the first place, and her smile faded before leading Alex into the kitchen and filling him in on all that had happened.

"Without Adam I just always felt so... exposed," she said quietly. "Like I couldn't trust my own thoughts. But I do now. Brennan has helped with that, but mostly it has just been... me. I mean, I wrote a thesis in less than a month."

Admiration shone in Alex's eyes. "Because you kick major ass."

"I never realized how complacent I'd grown."

"And just like that... you know which path to take." He smiled weakly. "Whereas I can't even choose my socks in the morning."

Alex's phone buzzed and when she spied and saw that it was a call from Ramiro, she wondered why the teacher was using his phone during school hours, and then realized with shock that it was nearly four.

"Talk to him. He's more important than me," she said with a wink.

"Yeah right, turd-nugget," Alex replied, even as he brought his phone to his ear.

Heading back upstairs, she walked into her room to wake Brennan up, knowing he would feel offended over having been out for so long. Upon seeing him sleeping, she stilled, for his face was reposed and unmarked save the thin scar winding from his eyebrow into his shock of black hair. Without the distraction of his wit or accent, she was free to gaze upon him as just a man. The sight of him made her brim as she filled up to the very top.

Keats' poetry fluttered about in her breast and she latched onto it, letting it warm her as she settled on the mattress and smoothed out a waving lock of his hair. *"A thing of beauty is a joy forever,"* she quoted the opening of *Endymion,* and Brennan stirred under her voice and touch. *"It's loveliness increases; it will never pass into nothingness."*

Brennan snorted and jerked, waking up with a slight start and leaving behind a drool stain, shattering her poetic moment with the welcome imperfection of reality. Blinking, he propped himself up on his elbows and peered around blearily, the side of his cheek lined from the wrinkles of her comforter. "Huh?"

"I thought you didn't sleep during the day," she teased, prodding his side.

"Only on Wednesdays and Jewish holidays," he mumbled, sitting up and rubbing his face before glancing at the time. "Jaysus, the day is gone."

"Did you have somewhere to be?"

"Is it still Tuesday?" he asked as he held one eye shut while he yawned. "The lads wanted to rehearse for a new gig."

Disappointment pooled in her stomach but she tried to keep it from her face as he raked a hand through his hair. Sitting down beside him, she rested her shoulder against his, feeling gentle pressure as he leaned back. She studied his profile as he stared ahead, his eyes unfocused, and she realized that wanting him to stay was selfish. Grieving for his former lover and welcoming a new one was too much for one day.

"Go," she prompted.

He nodded solemnly, his eyes drifting to his knees as he tried to gather his wits about him.

"You can come by tomorrow," she said. "Or... Friday. Whenever you have time."

Brennan's eyes twinkled even as he looked at her shyly. "It's weird... you wanting me here."

"You don't have to," she said, her pulse quickening as she realized she might sound pushy. "But it would be nice to see you again soon."

"Nice?" he asked, raising his brows.

"It'd be feckin' fabulous," she enthused, making him grin.

Brennan donned his jacket then followed her downstairs, greeting Alex with a "Heya."

"Staying for dinner?" Alex asked, angling the phone away from his ear as he paused in conversation.

"Don't wait up for me," Brennan replied, ruffling the other man's hair before heading for the door with Ophelia on his heels. He sighed when he stepped out into the evening as the coolness of the fog crept in.

"Have fun," Ophelia offered, suddenly awkward, for kissing him goodbye would be both the most natural thing in the world and the oddest.

"C'mere, Girl," he said, holding out an arm and folding her into a hug when she obliged. She could feel his lips first on the top of her head then on her temple before he stilled, holding her for several more seconds before letting her go. Trotting down the steps, he tugged out a pack of rolling paper and tobacco.

Ophelia wrinkled her nose. "You know, you drop from a ten to a two the moment you stick one of those in your mouth."

Brennan peered up at her from the sidewalk beneath a wayward curl as he rolled the pinch of loose leaves in a paper. "So American."

She shook her head with a dismissive smile, deciding that conversations about health hazards could wait. "Be safe."

"I will." He smiled up at her, zipping his jacket shut. "*Slán.*"

She blew him a kiss on her fingertips with a wave as he walked away, and then rolled her eyes when he lit up the cigarette. Once back inside, she grabbed her phone and sank onto her bed, her stomach heavy as she composed a message to Adam.

Hey, she wrote. ***Can we meet tomorrow? We need to talk.***

Of course. The swiftness of his reply clenched her heart, for she knew he had been sitting by his phone, waiting to hear from her all week. *I'll come by.*

Thank you.

Knots formed in her stomach, twisting with ugliness. The easy thing would be to put everything she wanted to say to him into a message so that she didn't have to see the look on his face. Easy wasn't always right, however, and at the very least, she owed him the decency of talking to him face to face.

A few minutes later, she received a picture from Brennan. It was his band mate, the singer Brian, bending over and adjusting something, his butt crack exposed. The sight made her smirk, but even the humor couldn't cut through her worry.

Her tension mounted as the day ended and the following began, enhancing her nagging sensation of nausea. A late spring rain storm was on its way up the coast from Mexico, bringing with it charged, humid air. Comfortable in a pair of pink leggings decorated with roses and her knit, long cream cardigan, Ophelia tried to distract herself by catching up on her assigned readings on the couch while she waited to hear from Adam.

"You haven't eaten," Alex scolded, peering at her over his glasses while he worked on his laptop at the kitchen table. "I just bought some veggie patties. They're in the freezer."

She acknowledged his comment by saluting him with her bare foot over the back of the couch.

"Seriously. I'll make you one."

The door creaked open, surprising them both, and Ophelia sat up to see who it was. Adam walked in, offering her a brief smile, looking a little sunburnt as often happened when he decided he didn't need sunscreen on overcast days.

"Hi," she said as warmly as she could, but the delicate way he closed the door and stepped into the room told her that he knew this wasn't going to be anything like the last time he saw her.

Sticking his hands in his blue hoodie pocket, he studied her from the entryway, his thin eyes expressionless as he sighed. A beanie flattened his hair, yet he was still in shorts and flip-flops. An oddity she would miss about him.

Ophelia scooted to the edge of the couch, patting an empty cushion, but Adam didn't budge. "I'm guessing this won't take long," he said, his deep voice tight.

Alex's typing slowed in the kitchen but he didn't relocate, as if wanting to be present for auxiliary support.

"Adam," she began. "There's a lot to say."

He pursed his lips and shook his head. "Then let's hear it."

She rose with a spark of irritation at his nonchalance. "I never meant to hurt you. It just all happened so fast." The words left her lips, twisting their vowels until her voice was posh and English, and she was looking at Kent whose eyes shimmered with far more emotion than Adam's. "The engagement and... and then you were called up."

Kent's face flushed, his mustache quivering above his arched upper lip as he fought to maintain his composure.

"Your skill for deceit is unparalleled," he said hoarsely. "I thought you loved me." His words shifted into Adam's voice, and she was once more looking at the muscle-bound blonde. "I thought I could trust you," Adam continued.

Ophelia shook her head, a part of her panicking because the flickering in and out of lives while having the same confrontation wasn't helping any. "No, you didn't. You never trusted me. You did your best to control me."

"Someone damn well had to," Kent shouted, the shimmer in his eyes fading.

Amelia held her head up higher, though, try as she might, couldn't stop the tremor in her jaw over never having seen him so upset.

"Charles," she began.

"I suspected," he barked. "I prayed I was merely being paranoid but you..." He shook his head and took a step towards her, flickering back to Adam in his beanie.

"I tried," Ophelia retorted. "I tried as hard as I could. One day, you'll meet someone else, and you'll understand what it's like to brush against something—" Amelia finished voicing the thought for her. "—So much brighter than anything you've ever known. Like a star."

Kent closed his eyes. "This will pass, Amelia. He is a footman. They're peacocks. You are hardly the first woman to be seduced by—" his voice and image morphed into Adam's, "—a musician."

Ophelia took a deep breath and closed her eyes, grounding herself in her own body, even if sliding between lifetimes now felt as effortless as breathing.

Adam paused a few feet from her. "Lia?"

She opened her eyes and looked up at him, grateful Alex was nearby when she recognized the strain tightening his strong jaw.

"This is bigger than us," she said softly. "I don't expect you to understand, but I missed him even before I knew him."

Adam's blue eyes sharpened as he cocked his head, his sun-bleached brows twitching together, as if she just struck him in the chest or insulted his mother.

"What did you say?" he whispered, pointing at her with a limp finger.

Ophelia tensed, as if caught giving away a secret. She wanted to take a step back. A month ago she *would* have taken a step back. Wept. Instead, she stood taller, narrowing her eyes.

"I've done nothing with him while you and I were together." Her voice shifted into Amelia's as she stood her ground before her fiancé. "I have maintained my honor."

"Your honor?" Kent repeated, his voice rising an octave as his expression turned incredulous. "You *have* none. Talking back to your mother, corrupting your sister with novels." He twisted so that his shoulder was facing her, shaking his head, lowering his voice. "An Irish footman, at that."

Anger flared, moving her feet for her as she took two threatening steps towards him. "I wouldn't care if he were a Fenian rebel and I the Duchess of—"

"*Enough,*" Kent snapped, spinning to face her, but Amelia talked right over him.

"He is dearer to me than this life!"

Kent's face contorted in disgust and he looked upon her as if she were a vagrant off the street. Adam was now peering at Ophelia with the same expression and she allowed it to feed the roots of her resolve.

"There is no going back," she said softly. "It's better for us both to just... say goodbye."

"No," Adam groaned. "Not again."

"You were there for me when I needed you," she said with a smile. "I'll always love you for that."

Adam closed his eyes, his body trembling, and she had to resist the urge to hug him. When he opened his eyes, he was Kent. "You don't mean that."

"You have no idea," Amelia countered, and Kent looked upon her as if having feared her answer. "Though I wish this didn't cause you pain," she continued, her voice morphing into Ophelia's American.

Adam gritted his teeth before running a hand over his face. "You're ripping my heart out," he croaked, "and you don't even care. All for a fucking no good drug addict!"

"Just stop," Ophelia snapped. "And walk away now. We can talk again later when we're not so..." She shook her head, surprised when her vision blurred from unshed tears.

Adam gazed at her from under a weighted forehead, his nostrils flaring. When he spoke, his voice was English. "I was the one who had you followed."

Ophelia cocked her head, blinking away her tears and clenching her fists in a desperate attempt to remain in the present. Footsteps shuffled a few yards away as Alex walked into the room, taking off his glasses, his deep-set eyes fixed warningly on Adam.

"What did you say?" Ophelia whispered.

Adam shook his head. "You can't even admit to yourself what a loser he is."

"She said that's enough," Alex interjected calmly.

The blonde glared at him, his upper lip sneering before looking back to Ophelia. "Maybe it'll take years, but you'll regret this."

"Maybe," she replied. "But right now I don't."

Sighing and shaking his head, Adam stalked out, knocking a strand of Trea's sweet grass off the rickety end table as he went before slamming the door shut. Alex slipped around the couch and stood beside Ophelia, staring at the door with her. Ophelia's chest tingled, numb as the sound of the slamming wood reverberated in her mind.

Adam was gone. Her boyfriend, her lover, her sheltering arms. She had wounded him. Made him cry. And he was gone. For a moment, panic surged like an unleashed river and she took a step towards the door, only to stop herself with the memory of how he always seemed so much larger in her mind than he actually was. Shadowing her, even when she didn't need him to.

"You did good," Alex softly said.

Closing her eyes, Ophelia turned around to face him. The panic receded to a calm, tingling acceptance.

"It's over," she whispered.

"Yeah." Alex rested a hand on her lower back. "You did good."

She nodded, closing her eyes and forcing a smile, trying to gather up all of the grains of relief floating through her to make something solid to hide behind.

18

*N*ot wanting to be alone, Ophelia fixed herself a cup of lemon tea then sat beside Alex at the table as he worked on his assignment.

The wind picked up outside and she focused on the way it whistled through the screen of the cracked kitchen window as she replayed what just happened, struggling to separate her confrontation from Amelia's. While it felt very much the same, there was a major difference: she had never cared for Kent as much as she did for Adam. A part of her wanted to go to Brennan and lose herself in their newfound affection, but she cast aside the thought as impulsive and selfish. If she had any hope of building a relationship with the Irishman, they both needed to be sure not to rush a thing.

She took a long bath that night, letting the warm water soothe her, and then she and Alex opened a bottle of wine Ramiro had gifted him and drank it with dinner. The next day was school, and she was happy to have something to do to distract her.

Once at San Jose State in her moss green jacket over a yellow sundress with a pink floral print and her grey leggings tucked in boots that actually weren't galoshes, she headed to Dr. Douglass' office. He was with another student, so she waited for him to finish up with the undergrad who was having trouble picking which classes to take in the autumn. A few minutes later, the white-haired man smiled and waved her in before holding up a copy of her thesis that he had printed out.

"This is excellent, Miss Brighton."

Ophelia grinned, telling herself that she would remember this moment. "Really?"

"That section on his letter, Vale of Souls, is my favorite." He lowered his glasses and licked his thumb before fanning through the pages to find it. Once he did, he smoothed it over his knee then dragged his finger down the page before reading: *"This is perhaps the defining element of Keats to which readers respond. His poetry is felt—experienced—rather than dissected and taken at its literal value. Within that experience lies a spiritual acknowledgement of the eternal soul of both the poet and the reader. The act of reading a Keats poem stirs an innate connection that echoes with understanding, even if the* what *of what is being understood remains elusive. It is only by reading and re-reading the poems that knowledge surfaces, completely secondary to the original act of surrendering to 'negative capability': to accepting that understanding is not necessary to appreciate or edify. The immortality of the soul becomes negligible, for in this back and forth between words and reader, Keats succeeds in teaching from the page. We see parts of ourselves reflected in his work, opening our minds to mystery, and thus he has achieved the only true immortality: a thriving consciousness with which to engage long after his untimely death."*

Taking off his glasses, Dr. Douglass fixed her with a proud smile.

"It sounds better when you read it," she said with a little laugh, fidgeting in her chair under the weight of her own words.

"This is all you. See, you pushed yourself and look how far stepping outside of your comfort zone got you?" He smiled kindly.

Ophelia hesitantly nodded, remembering how Brennan once called books safe.

"Have you thought at all about teaching?"

"I have. But I think I'd like to live a little more, outside of school, first."

Dr. Douglass chuckled. "Fair enough."

Ophelia headed to her classes, surprised that her first professor was announcing the date and time of the final as a reminder. April had bled well into May without her paying much heed of the date. Caught up with her readings, she once again happily delved into discussions of Jack London and San Francisco at the turn of the century, a part of her imagination dancing about over remembering the era, albeit in England.

On the bus ride home, the happy glow of her success was only intensified when she received a text from Brennan that read, *I hope you haven't gotten your hopes up because... I'm already taken*, attached to a picture of him arching a brow with an unsure expression while Alex kissed his cheek, an arm around his neck in what appeared to be a bar.

Laughing softly, she saved the photo and took a minute to think up a shocking reply. She ended up sending him a picture of herself with a crooked mouth, flipping off the camera. His only response was gibberish until he started telling her that he wore a diaper and was going to try a diet where he was only allowed to eat toads and toasters, and she knew that Alex had stolen his phone. It was only fair, after all, given what he had done to Alex.

As such, she responded to every statement with, *That's hot.*

Realizing that she felt happy, genuinely happy, made the old, anxious side of her whisper that there was always something to worry about. She was going to silence the voice when she remembered the pain on Adam's face and felt a pang of guilt over having fun while he was so miserable. She had to fight off the urge to ask him how he was doing, reminding herself that it was no longer her business.

Opening up her latest text, she smirked when it read, *You're hot.*

Is this Alex or Brennan? She asked.

Ramiro.

BRENNAN!

Heya.

Rolling her eyes, she stuck her ear buds in and started listening to music, her twinge of guilt being replaced by longing to be with her friends. As the bus pulled into the metro, she noticed a familiar black leather jacket. Stepping out, she smiled, filled with rippling delight as she spied Brennan waiting for her.

He grinned at the sight of her and she forgot that she was surrounded by people as she darted over to him.

"Heya," he greeted before latching onto her in a bear hug, lifting her feet off the pavement.

"I was just going to ask where you were."

He set her down and smooched her, and she could taste the alcohol on his lips.

"I've missed you," he said.

"It's only been a day," she chuckled, not letting go.

"Aren't I allowed to miss ya, Girl?" he asked.

A question surged from the bottom of her stomach where she had banished her anxiety. "How do I know you're not just being a clingy drunk?"

"They call it mead because it means 'middle,' love." He pulled away to look her in the eye, and his were only slightly warmed from alcohol. The way they were dancing in the light of the streetlamps was because he was looking at her, and the sensation made her feel full. "It takes ya to that place between worlds where you're adrift and every-t'ing is muffled. Like where the fay live. You're not actually fully in your body, nor are ya fully a spirit."

"You should start a volume called *Drunken Keats*," she said, twining her hands with his and swinging them.

"It'd make a lovely coffee table book," he agreed.

He smiled softly, untangling a hand to brush her bangs off her forehead, and despite what they said the other day, she could see no harm in kissing him whenever she wanted. Resting her hands on the front of his jacket, she leaned up and—

"Hey," a deep voice called, and Ophelia halted and spotted Trea fishing aluminum cans out of the recycling nearby.

Her irritation at him ruining the moment was swept away by curiosity. "Why do you keep leaving—"

"Sweet," he chortled. "Hamlet."

Ophelia couldn't tell if he was looking at her or Brennan behind his shades, but the Dubliner seemed to have had enough and rested a hand between her shoulder blades, guiding her with him as he started to walk off. She followed his lead, wrapping an arm around his as he lead the way through the humid air to the Poet and the Patriot where Alex and Ramiro were waiting.

Ramiro greeted her with a bemused expression, wearing an old soccer jersey that had his surname "Morales" on the back, as if having come from a scrimmage. Alex was doubled over with cackles at his side, though at what, no one seemed to know. Brennan snagged another chair and dragged it over for Ophelia, waiting behind it, and she was reminded of Leander as she took a seat. He relieved her of her messenger bag and hung it on the back of the chair.

"What're you having?" he asked in her ear, and the scratch of his chin brushing against her cheek and the rumble in his throat made her breathing hitch pleasantly.

"The black stuff," she replied with a smirk.

"That's my girl," Brennan chuckled, ruffling her hair as he headed to the bar.

She watched him as he went, realizing that his snug dark pants were no longer a forbidden temptation, and she could stare at his hips all she wanted as he waltzed.

"Shit," Ramiro hissed, suddenly lunging.

Ophelia looked back just in time to see the larger man wrapping his arms around Alex as the brunette started to fall out of his seat.

"Oh my *God*," Alex gasped, looking around in surprise and latching onto the edge of the table with wide eyes. "That was totally just an earthquake, you guys."

Ramiro fixed Ophelia with a concerned expression until her lips curled in amusement, for the only thing that had shaken was Alex. Smiling in response, Ramiro shifted his gaze to the young man in his arms as he helped him right himself with a chuckle.

"Like, it could be a pre-shock," Alex slurred. "The Big One is coming."

Ophelia shook her head at Ramiro apologetically. "He usually doesn't do this."

"I don't mind," he replied, and the warmth in his eyes as he studied Alex tugged at her heart, reminding her of the way Mr. Meyer had looked at Lucy. While she couldn't explain her certainty in knowing, she now saw Ramiro and Mr. Meyer as one and the same.

He and Alex have also been together in two lifetimes.

"Here ya are, my lady," Brennan said, sliding a Guinness over to Ophelia then looking her in the eye and making a show of using a coaster to satisfy propriety. The sound of those words on his tongue jerked her mind, and for a moment she felt the pressure of a corset against her ribs. Resting a hand to her stomach, however, made the sensation fade as Brennan took a seat beside her.

"You all right?" he asked.

Ophelia nodded, about to misdirect him when she remembered that Brennan knew her secret. She didn't have to lie anymore.

"Long day?"

"A good day," she replied brightly after taking a sip. "Made even better now."

She latched onto the shoulder of his jacket and tugged him down so that she could hug his head, making him laugh as he wrapped his arms around her waist.

"Aww," Ramiro crooned.

Alex started slapping the table. "Take a picture! Take a picture of the happy Elephant!"

Ramiro grabbed Ophelia's phone and aimed it at the pair while Ophelia ruffled Brennan's hair until it frizzed, making him squawk and try to get away. She released him and he straightened, looking delightedly indignant as he tried to smooth it back down like ruffled feathers.

"Ready?" Ramiro asked, his full lips smiling as his thumb hovered over the button.

"Yes!" Ophelia latched onto Brennan, her head on his chest as he hugged her shoulder and they grinned. The ensuing flash nearly blinded them both and seemed to deeply offend Brennan.

"Mother of God," he gasped, clamping his hands over his eyes as Ophelia screwed her own shut, laughing.

"That was really cute, you guys," Alex slurred, his brows raised, sliding a hand across the table towards them. "I'm so happy for you both."

"No, sweetie," she said patronizingly as she patted his hand. "You're just drunk."

Alex rolled his eyes in exasperation. "I am *so* not dru—wait a minute." He peered around with a frown. "Where'd my drink go?"

Brennan let out a squeaky giggle, leaning back in his chair as if he were watching a show.

"In your stomach," Ramiro answered, eyeing his date skeptically.

"Seriously," Alex pressed, eyeing other tables as if thinking one of the other patrons stole it.

"I'm gonna have a wee," Brennan announced, giving her arm a squeeze as he rose.

Ophelia turned to watch him go. "You know, you don't actually have to announce every bodily function."

"I'm only being polite," he called over his shoulder.

She looked back to the table to find Alex drinking her beer while Ramiro checked the messages on his phone.

"Hey!"

Ramiro jerked his head up and tried to take the glass from Alex, but he didn't let go. A laugh bubbled up at the sight of her usually sober friend fighting over a drink, but it was cut off by a loud gunshot. Her body grew cold and her breathing stopped, yet the two men across from her didn't react.

How could they not have heard it?

A chuckle sounded behind her, rich and deep, and when she looked over her shoulder, she was gazing at Kent in Amelia's grand bedroom. The army captain quieted himself, seeming to savor her wide eyes as a tremor coursed through her from the rifle shot. Hurrying towards the window, she peered out at the stables and tack room while Kent leisurely approached.

"Dearer than this life, hmm? Seems your Leander felt the same way."

Icy chains wrapped around her torso and she had to grip the windowsill to keep from collapsing. "No…"

"As I was saying, I may be the one who had you followed," he snapped, "but your fool of a father was desperate enough to shove you off so as to acquiesce to my… methods."

Try as she might, Amelia couldn't stop her jaw from trembling as the gunshot rang out over and over in her mind, screaming Leander's name in the language of death. One palm still braced on the sill, she spun around to stare at her fiancé, forcing air into her lungs.

"My dear Lia," he said softly, cocking his head slightly. "You seem as if something is troubling you."

"You," she gasped, her voice wavering. "You paid Buchanan. You planned this whole sordid scheme?"

"No more sordid than what you were doing with that filth. So revolting that even your maid couldn't stand for it."

Amelia straightened, sneering. "I will turn you in and make sure every constable in the land knows—"

"Mr. Buchanan is old," Kent remarked with a slight shrug. "His eyes are failing. It would be quite easy for him to fire upon who he thought to be a horse thief or a bandit."

She closed her eyes as her knees threatened to buckle, keeping herself upright by sheer will alone. "Make other arrangements," she whispered numbly, repeating Buchanan's words to her in the tack room.

"Leander was a distraction from your true purpose," Kent continued, his voice sharp and firm.

Something ripped through her chest like fire and she clapped her blazing eyes on him. "And what would that be?"

Kent's shoulders relaxed as his expression softened. "We made each other happy once."

Her nostrils flared as she struggled to attach words to the primal barking tumbling around in her chest.

"Kent!" a voice bellowed from outside, and the fair-haired man's brows twitched together. It wasn't Buchanan's voice. "Kent!"

Shoving her aside, Kent hurried to the window and opened it.

Amelia spied over his shoulder, a shock of rejuvenation and relief coursing through her at the sight of Leander on horseback, galloping onto the lawn on a dapple grey mount in the moonlight. His livid face peered up at the window, looking more intimidating than she ever imagined.

"Damn that devil of a mick," Kent hissed, withdrawing a small pistol from the inside of his uniform.

"Kent, you coward," Leander bellowed, causing the horse to dance around in agitation. "Face me!"

Amelia's eyes darted from Leander to her fiancé as he extended his arm out the window, taking aim.

"Leander," she shrieked, shoving Kent's arm aside just as he pulled the trigger.

Snarling, Kent whirled around and backhanded her, hitting her cheekbone so hard that her teeth clanked together and she had to latch onto the bedpost to keep from losing her balance.

Leander's answering cry of her name told her that the other man's bullet had missed.

Slamming the window shut, Kent rounded on Amelia, his eyes darkening.

"Not again," he seethed. "Not again—I won't allow it!"

She could hear the horse's hooves fading as Leander galloped elsewhere and she backed up, pressing against the post, her resolve quickly flooding with cold panic as she realized that her bedroom being on the far wing meant that there was little chance of anyone downstairs hearing the commotion. Though surely, someone must have heard Leander's bellows and the horse's hooves.

"Papa!" She screeched as loud as she could. "Lucy!"

Kent surged forward and clamped a hand on her mouth.

Amelia sucked in a lungful around his palm and bellowed into his hand, prompting him to spin her around, pressing her backside against him as he clamped down tighter on her mouth. Heat radiated from his woolen tunic, spreading to her bare arms as she struggled.

"Do you know how long I have waited?" he growled in her ear. "Do you have *any* idea how many times I have tried? But always, the moment the whelp appears, you forget about me, don't you?"

She closed her eyes, remembering Lucy telling her that she was a terrible actress.

How did I ever think I could hide the truth from an officer?

"You never touched him," Kent said, anticipating her thoughts and revealing her tell. "Never even brushed his arm at a dinner."

Hammering sounds started in the distance but were difficult to hear over the rush of blood surging past her ears.

Kent eased his hand off her mouth then slid it down her neck, trailing his fingers over her collarbone.

"No matter. I know what to do. I know how to fix this. In the meantime..."

His hand tightened around her neck and the world spun as he shoved her over onto the bed, the pistol clattering to the floor.

"Liza," she screamed.

Kent struck her again, sending lights darting about in her vision and making her arms go limp as the mattress shifted around her from his weight. The hammering in the distance was louder, even when muffled by her pulse, and she realized it was footsteps.

"Amelia," Leander cried from the stairwell a story below.

"Leander," she murmured, blinking repeatedly to try to clear her vision.

She heard a jingle as Kent tossed aside his outer belt and tunic.

"Leander," she called louder.

The blonde man clamped a hand over her mouth as he struggled out of his suspenders, and the pain in her nose from the pressure helped clear the fog in her mind. She latched onto his shoulders and shoved him away from her. Kent grunted in surprise and she thrashed her legs, squirming out from under him and tripping on her lavender gown as she struggled off the bed.

The footsteps were closer.

"Leander!"

"Quiet," Kent hissed.

A hand clamped onto her arm and whirled her about. Her vision swam as she was shoved back down and pinned in place with bruising force.

"Stop," she barked, punching at anywhere she could reach on Kent and kicking his legs, even as her head made her feel as if she were floating on a raft. "Get off me, you brute!"

Kent had his trousers pulled down to his knees and yanked her skirts up before clamping a hand on her neck.

"I said, *quiet*," he hissed.

"Don't," she gasped against the pressure on her windpipe as the footsteps thundered in the hall, heading for her door. "Leander! Lean—"

She choked as Kent cut off her air then shoved at her legs.

Amelia could distantly hear Leander calling her name and pounding on the door, then ramming into it, until his cries were silenced by searing pain and a scream that Kent allowed out of her windpipe as he forced his way into her. The sensation of being stabbed between her legs made her go rigid and she couldn't have moved if she tried as he hurt her again and again. Gasping, choking sounds kept her from Leander's voice, and when tears warmed trails on her cheeks, she realized that they were coming from her.

"I deserve this," Kent snarled, his face red and sweating above her.

She screwed her eyes shut as her pulse surged, deafening her to all else, her back arched in a feeble attempt to escape the tearing pain coming from her loins. Then Kent's arms shuddered and he panted, shoving himself off her, taking some of the pain with him. Amelia didn't dare move and coughed, choking on her tears around her bruised throat. Her lower half trembled and her stomach contracted, as if trying to shove any remaining violation out of her. She gently pressed her knees together and shifted to study her fiancé with hitching breaths, terrified that he would do it again.

Instead, he was fastening his trousers and shrugging into his suspenders. Distantly, she noticed that the pounding on the door had stopped. Kent fixed her with a look of satisfaction before tossing his red tunic onto a chair in the corner. She trembled again and started to sit up, only to wince and gasp at the pain movement caused, as if a knife had been left in her loins.

Some of the satisfaction seemed to slide off his face. "Don't look at me like that."

"Like what?" her voice croaked. It sounded alien to her ears and seemed to unnerve Kent, so she used it again. "Like you haven't just betrayed the fabric of my being?"

The flush seemed to drain from his cheeks, followed by a brief tremor in his lower jaw. Then he looked away, tapping his thigh as if trying to work out some puzzle. After a moment, he sniffled and raked a hand through his hair, adjusting it, before striding to the door. Metal clicked as he unlocked it, and Leander nearly fell in as it swung open, as if he had been slumped against the wood. Kent immediately grabbed him by the scruff of the neck and hauled him to his feet, forcing him around to face Amelia.

Leander's eyes were red, his face flushed and miserable as he looked upon her, seeming to wilt in Kent's grip.

"You did this, boy," Kent growled, shutting the door. "This is your fault."

Amelia shook her head but Leander closed his eyes, tears escaping. "You failed her."

Growling as she shifted, Amelia hauled herself up against her pillows so that she could properly face the two. The broken grief in her lover's body seemed to complement her own.

"She is torn and bleeding because of you. Untouchable. Filthy."

"Don't listen," Amelia demanded, wishing her voice would stop warbling with her hiccoughing. "Don't."

Sneering, Kent yanked Leander over to her bedside, pinning one of his arms behind his back. The sight of him so vulnerable stirred the primal barking in her chest once more, dulling some of her pain as she narrowed her teary eyes at the blonde.

"Still got some fight in you?" Kent crooned. "Well then, I'm game for another round if you are."

Leander stomped on the larger man's foot, making Kent cry out and relax his grip. Jerking himself free, the Irishman spun about to face Kent. He brought up his knee, ramming him in the crotch. With a strangled gasp, the captain doubled over and Leander slammed him against the wall. He hastily felt at his sides, searching for the gun.

"Under the nightstand," Amelia gasped, spotting it on the floorboards.

Leander followed her gaze then lunged for the weapon. Amelia brought her knees up to try to move then screwed her eyes shut in renewed pain, her skin breaking out in a sweat. Leander's hand closed around the pistol at the same time that Kent recovered. The captain hurled himself, tackling Leander around the middle.

The dark-haired man wriggled about in Kent's grasp. He twisted to point the barrel right between Kent's eyes, stilling him. Leander sneered, his finger on the trigger, while Kent panted down at him, rigid.

Amelia bit her lip as she managed to climb to her knees, watching the two as Leander slowly inched out from under the larger man, scooting towards her. He sneered as he spat something in Irish, but what it was, she didn't know.

"Amelia?" he asked without taking his eyes off her fiancé. "*Mo chroî*? Can you walk, darlin'?"

She glanced at the door and it suddenly seemed so very far away.

"Yes," she whispered.

Leander nodded and used the bed as support while he slowly climbed to his feet, his eyes never leaving Kent's, whose skin was waxy as he watched the pair, still on his hands and knees. Blindly flinging out a hand, Leander reached behind him for his lover and Amelia latched onto his arm, leaning against his strength.

"Would it be terribly rude of me," Kent said quietly, "to inquire as to what happened to Mr. Buchanan?"

"Old man took a shot at me," Leander replied, side-stepping slowly towards the door as Amelia scooted along behind him on the bed, relieved that her pain was ebbing, clutching his free arm. "So I took his rifle and bumped him upside the head. I imagine he'll be right angry when he wakes up."

Kent leaned back on his haunches, chuckling softly. "I suppose that's what I deserve for relying on a Scotsman."

Amelia swallowed hard now that they were at the foot of the bed. Lowering one leg, she winced and hissed. Leander spared her a glance, slipping his free arm around her hip to help her off. His gaze darted back to Kent, who was watching calmly from the floor, his skin speckled with sweat. She hissed again as she shifted her other leg, inadvertently prompting Leander to turn his attention to her in worry.

It was all the opening Kent needed.

The larger man surged up from the floor, grabbing Leander's wrist with the gun and tackling him.

Amelia yelped as her lover was torn away from her.

Leander snarled as he hit the ground, Kent on top of him, ramming his hand against the floor over and over until he knocked the pistol out his grip. The smaller man immediately struggled, scrambling to get away. Kent yanked something out of his boot, and by the time Amelia recognized the glint, it was too late.

The sound of the knife plunging into Leander's chest reminded her of a bale of hay being stabbed, and the grunted gasp that followed chilled her blood. Leander's limbs fell limply to his sides as Kent sneered down at him before yanking out the blade.

Amelia clung to the bed post, feeling as if a part of her was tearing free, sending her spinning as Kent sank the blade into Leander's chest again and again. Rising with a grunt, he stood above the dying foot-man, and Amelia's arms and legs gave out. She fell against the foot of the bedframe with a choking gasp, her eyes unable to look away from the pool of blood sliding out from underneath Leander while he trembled, struggling to breathe.

Hooting gasps took ahold of Amelia's throat as Kent panted, peering down at his kill. Then the sounds started twisting out into a word as she squeaked "No" over and over again.

Kent turned, some of his blonde hair falling into his eyes, drinking her in with relish as she wilted.

Leander's blood surged across the floor, lapping at her foot, her calf, and her thigh. It was cold and smelled like barley. She stared down at it and instead of her bedroom floor, saw the dark wood of the bar, stained with beer that had splashed onto her leg.

"I'm so sorry," Ramiro said, lunging for the toppled glass that had sent liquid across the table and onto Ophelia and the floor.

She sucked in a gasping lungful of air as she realized that her drink had been spilled during Alex and Ramiro's fight over it, not blood.

Not blood.

"Leander," she whispered brokenly, her chest still clenched and her lungs aching. Taking another deep breath, her vision blurred with tears and she blinked them away. Alex was struggling out of his sweater and was trying to use it to mop up the spilled drink, wincing over just how much of it was on the table.

"Here," Ramiro said, offering her a pathetic cocktail napkin when the lap of her dress was soaked.

Her brown eyes darted to his as her chest clenched. "Where's Brennan?"

Ramiro glanced at Alex, thrown off. "Uh... Bathroom?"

"That was ages ago," she gasped before shoving away from the table and taking a step towards the back, only to pause and wait for a pain in her loins that didn't come.

"Elephant?" Alex called after her as she strode across the floor, weaving through the thinning crowd and bumping her shoulders into several patrons as she headed for the bathroom that was tucked into the side of the crowded dart room. The door was closed and when she tried the handle, it was locked.

Closing her eyes, she leaned her back against the wall beneath a framed old Guinness ad, reminding herself that not much time could have passed if Alex and Ramiro hadn't noticed her having an issue. Then again, it didn't take much time for something terrible to happen. She gasped, opening her eyes and feeling nauseas at the memory of how many times Kent had stuck his knife into Leander's chest.

Adam.

If he was anything like he had been in his past life, he could have hunted Brennan. The thought made her realize the true reason she had remembered: to save Brennan. Clasping a hand over her mouth, she whimpered and tried to rein in her panic as her arms trembled with the thudding of her heart.

The toilet flushed and she straightened, telling herself over and over that she just had to be patient because Brennan would come out. Brennan would come out...

Then the door opened and the bartender smiled confusedly beneath his flat cap at the sight of her wide brown eyes as he exited. Holding still against the wall, she waited until he was gone before surging forward and flinging the door aside. There was only one stall, a sink, and various band fliers. The bathroom was empty.

19

"Oh, God," Ophelia squeaked, hurrying back out as cold heat seemed to seep across her skin from her hairline with her surging adrenaline. Clutching the doorframe, she peered at the crowd, scanning every body for the Irishman's lanky frame. When she couldn't find him, she gripped the wood harder, her knees weakening.

What if he never made it to the bathroom? Or what if he never made it back?

Adam wouldn't hurt him in the bar. There would be too many witnesses. He would do it outside.

Shoving off the wall, she jogged towards the metal side-door with an electric exit sign, bumping into another girl on her way.

"Hey," the girl snapped after there was a splash but Ophelia didn't even look back after realizing she had spilled her drink. She shoved the door open with her shoulder, unable to breathe as she stepped out into the dark alleyway littered with black trash bags stacked around empty kegs and a dumpster.

A red glow burned a few yards down, near the wall, and the moment she recognized Brennan leaning against the side of the building with one leg up, smoking, she squawked and sprinted for him. He barely had time to turn towards her before she slapped the cigarette out of his hand and crushed him against the wall with a wail, her arms clamping around him.

"Jaysus," he squeaked, and she could feel his heart surging with surprise at the assault. Ophelia trembled and shook, feeling as if she couldn't hug him tightly enough. With a shove, she made him lose his footing and toppled down with him as he landed on the seat of his jeans. "Ophelia," he gasped in surprise.

Her only response was to suck in a squeaky lungful of air and yank him down until she was cradling him against her, tangling a hand in his hair. Brennan was stiff with irritation then seemed to give in to her forceful affection, warm in her arms.

"He killed you," she whimpered, resting her teary cheek on the top of his head. "He killed you."

Brennan straightened, untangling himself to study her in the ambient light from the street on the other side of the building.

"I ain't dead," he insisted, as if hoping that was obvious.

Ophelia shook her head, her face scrunching up with another sob.

"You were," she whispered.

"Hey, now," he soothed, sliding his fingers into her hair on either temple.

Another sob escaped and she rested her hand on his before curling in on herself. He let go to pull her onto his lap, hugging her to his chest as she wept. She knew he must be confused and burning with questions, but he didn't ask any of them. Ophelia was grateful, for all she could focus on was his warmth and the scent of leather and tobacco as she wrapped her arms around his neck and stained his shoulder with her tears.

"Hey," he tried again, attempting to rouse her, but she only clung tighter, loosing another sob, hearing the horrible sticking sound the knife made over and over, and the one time it crunched, as if hitting bone. The pain of her rape as Amelia skirted around the fraying edges of her mind with searing heat, and she doubted she could ever look at Adam the same way again, even if this was a different lifetime.

Something soft vibrated against her forehead, rumbling pleasantly, and she shifted her senses outward, focusing on the sound. Humming.

Brennan was humming. The tune was simple and familiar, even if she couldn't place it. The rumble in his throat built and her chest hiccoughed as she let the comfort of the sensation spread through her.

"*Someone within my heart,*" he crooned, his breath tickling her hair, his quiet voice raspy. "*To build a throne.*"

She closed her eyes, the lilt in his voice like a balm, sealing the tattered edges of her mind and quietly tucking them away.

"*Someone who'd never part...*"

He rubbed her side and she took in a ragged breath.

"*To call my own.*"

Sniffling, she relaxed her grip to hug him more gently, resting against his chest. Brennan's song once again drifted into a hum as he nosed into her hair, his lips vibrating against her scalp. She closed her eyes, relishing the touch as her trembling faded, leaving her with a tired calm that she welcomed. His humming drifted away and he kissed her head before straightening, resting his hands on her shoulders to gently peel her off him.

Ophelia looked up into his face, her eyes having adjusted enough for her to make out his features in the dimness, and he was never more beautiful and dear to her than in that moment. The curve of bone around his eyes, boring into hers with such concern, seemed softened, and the imbalance of his features that she had once found to be goofy was now the most precious thing about him. His coarse thumbs wiped the tears off her cheeks, making her brim with gratitude. Ophelia prayed for a thousand more moments and yet none, as if eternity and death were in the puff of his breath against her moist cheeks.

She fell against him in another hug.

"I'm crazy," she whispered.

"That's hardly news, love."

Closing her eyes, she sighed, noticing for the first time that the stench of sour milk was reeking from the dumpster. A plastic bag skittered on the wind of the gathering storm, rattling past them.

"What put the fear of the devil in ya?" he asked.

Having only just folded the raw, bleeding memories back into her mind, she wasn't eager to relive them. Later, she would have to. Brennan needed to know. But not now when she was so tired.

"I couldn't find you," was all she whispered.

Brennan sighed, giving her a squeeze before kissing her forehead. "Don't ya worry about that. You've found me now, and I've found you. The hard part is over, darlin'."

His words made her star in the night sky of her soul glow all the brighter beside his. She tilted her chin towards him, pressing her lips to his, allowing the kiss to anchor her to the alleyway. He didn't protest when she pushed her tongue against his lower lip and cupped his scratchy cheek, happy that he hadn't shaved. Brennan returned the pressure, teasing with such welcome tenderness that her whole body sighed, and she once again wondered what it would be like to make love with him.

Gentle, she thought. For even just kissing, he was more attuned to her than Adam ever was.

Focusing on the tautness of Brennan's fingers as they tensed on her back, she pushed her tongue into his mouth, sliding a leg over his hip to straddle him. He leaned back against the wall when she cupped his face with both hands, pleasure pulsing in her lips and tongue as it twined with his. One of his hands rested on her hip while the other slipped up the back of her dress, warm and coarse, pressing gently against her spine with the rhythm of their massaging lips. She didn't stop, even when she needed to breathe, opting instead to steal a few pants in unison with him now and again, moaning softly when her lips found his once more.

Odd sounds started to build around them, like something spilling, and it wasn't until cold seeped in through her jacket and scalp that she realized it was raining. Brennan seemed to notice at the same time and laughed softly, catching his breath, rubbing the skin of her back. Ophelia wrapped her arms around his neck, feeling his quickened pulse pumping past her wrists while the rain grew from a sprinkle to a cascade.

She arched her back, leaning her face out into the shower with a smile, his neck her anchor point. Brennan squawked a little when she almost pulled the two of them over, but his hand was still under her dress, cradling her back, as he grinned and supported her weight.

"I love the rain," she said.

"You are definitely going to like Éire," he chuckled.

Curling over her, he kissed her neck, and the trill of his chin scratching her soft skin made her open her eyes.

He rose, hauling her up with him, which surprised her for she wasn't exactly easy to lift. Once on their feet, Brennan swiped his damp hair back and kissed the tip of her nose before guiding her into the shelter of the bar, leaving the alleyway to be cleaned by the rain.

Ophelia hugged her body close to his as they wove through patrons and back to their table. Alex had Ramiro's hand in his, toying with their fingers as he tried to keep his words straight.

"See, time isn't a constant—it's an illusion—a means of processing our realities. We're just, like, machines."

Ramiro cast the two a smile in greeting, his eyes momentarily darting to the disheveled hem of Ophelia's yellow dress sticking to her leggings. She let go of Brennan with one hand to tug it back into place.

"Machines, huh?" he asked.

"Okay, think about it this way. The speed of light is faster than the speed of sound, so if you were across the room and I made a sound like this," Alex brought Ramiro's hand up to his lips and smooched it loudly, making the other man chuckle. "You *think* you're hearing and seeing it at the same time, but you're not. You're seeing it *before* you hear it, but your brain slows down the image so that it synchs up."

Brennan arched a scarred brow at the pair then at Ophelia, silently asking if she would like to leave. She nodded, hugging his arm to her.

"It's crazy trippy," Alex insisted, peering at the darker-skinned man as if it were imperative that he understood this. "It means we're all living in the past, even if it's just a few milliseconds or nanoseconds or whatever."

"Heya," Brennan cut in, reaching over to squeeze Ramiro's shoulder. "I'm walking her home."

Ramiro nodded with a, "Take care, guys," while Alex pushed forward, oblivious.

"It means we're all time-travelers."

Brennan had to ruffle Alex's hair to get his attention then waved. "Seeya, pal."

"Oh." He swiveled in his chair to smile at the two with unfocused, heavy-lidded eyes while Ophelia pulled the strap of her messenger bag over her shoulder. "That was a long piss."

Ophelia kissed Alex on the cheek then fixed a meaningful gaze on Ramiro. "Get him home safe."

"Of course," Ramiro replied then offered them a wave goodbye as Alex continued.

"Like, what if ghosts aren't dead people, but are just people in alternate realities, or parallel universes, doing their thing, every once in a while brushing up against ours?"

"I'm glad they closed the bar," Ophelia heard Ramiro mutter as she and Brennan stepped back out into the rain.

He zipped his jacket up tighter and kept her glued to his side with their linked arms as they strolled through the downpour, the scent of wet pavement filling the air. Hardly anyone else was about but she kept a weather eye open for anyone shady. With Adam she had always felt protected to the point that she hardly even noticed passersby. While she didn't feel more vulnerable now, something had changed, and for the first time, she knew that guarding went both ways. She would just as soon hurt someone threatening Brennan as he would for her.

As they approached the house, Brennan released her arm so that she could fish out her keys and unlock the door. Stepping inside with her, he flipped on the light and glanced over the place but didn't budge from where he stood, dripping in her doorway. Just like when they first met.

Something tightened inside at the thought of saying goodbye.

"You should stay," she said softly. "We can just sleep," she added in the hopes of stripping away any pressure.

"Don't tempt me to your bed, Girl," he teased, running a hand through his soaking hair. He gazed at her with a smile that dimmed a little as a thought entered his head. "You wanna talk about earlier?"

"Yeah," she whispered. "But not now."

He nodded and kissed her without pressing his wet body against her, as if she weren't already soaked. "No goodbyes. Just seeya later. Tomorrow evening?"

She nodded, smiling, and then pulled him into a hug, marveling over how the stench of his wet leather was now a comfort to her. He gave her torso a tight squeeze, as if imparting some strength to her before kissing her forehead and quietly slipping out. Sighing, Ophelia stripped off her wet jacket and bag, thinking back over all that had happened and wondering if it were really possible that it had only been one day. She could smell Brennan's aftershave on her skin and it warmed her with such simple pleasure that she cherished the earnestness amidst the turmoil.

Hanging her coat to dry on the cold woodstove, she headed upstairs, gathering up her wet curls, nearly flattened by the rain, into a ponytail, preparing to shower. When she was halfway up, she stopped in her tracks, for a light switched on upstairs.

Letting go of her hair, she latched onto the railing.

Trea?

Straining her senses, Ophelia heard the floorboards creak. A shadow fell on the wall, growing larger as a man approached. He had broad shoulders and short hair. Adam loomed at the top of the stairs.

She parted her lips to ask what he was doing there, but the fear that cranked tighter and tighter in her chest kept her from speaking.

Fight or flight, her brain screamed.

His features were tight as he held up the photo of her and Jack.

Shoving off from the banister, Ophelia darted down the stairs, heading for the door.

Adam's feet thundered down the steps. Her fingertips had just brushed the metal of the doorknob when he latched onto her arm, hauling her backwards and into his chest.

"Lia," he pleaded, trying to pin her in place as she struggled.

Mimicking Leander, she rammed the heel of her boot into his toes.

"Shit," Adam barked before throwing her away from him.

Ophelia stumbled but the back of the couch kept her from falling. She whirled around to face him, bracing herself against the furniture, her eyes darting to the door as she parted her lips to scream.

"Go ahead," Adam said, cutting her off. "Call for him. It'll only end like last time."

Last time...

Adam's long brows lowered as he panted and shoved the crumpled photo into her chest. She didn't move and let it flutter to the ground.

Last time...

"Leander," she breathed.

The tall blonde stiffened, as if he had mistaken her for someone else, then leaned his torso away from her body. "The footman?" he whispered. "How do you...?"

Her blood surged through her, pounding out a mantra of, *he remembers.*

"Jack," he said hoarsely. "Jack..."

Ophelia straightened, meeting his blue gaze that now seemed so much higher up than her own.

"What about Jack?" she asked, forcing a quiver out of her voice as her senses screamed at her to get away from her rapist.

Adam blinked several times, as if he had just surfaced after being tumbled by a wild wave while surfing.

"What else? Lia," the concern in his voice sounded like the man she had once loved, but as soon as he rested a hand on her shoulder, white fear shot through her body and she tried to jerk away. He held her in place. "Lia," he repeated, swallowing hard as sweat beaded on his brow, "what do you remember?"

"*You,*" she snarled, leaning into his face, wishing she could bite. "You raped me, you sick son of a—"

He shook his head violently, even if his jaw trembled. "That wasn't me. That was Kent."

"You *are* Kent."

"No—"

"And you murdered Leander," she snapped.

Adam released her, spinning away with a groan. He ran a hand over his jaw and Ophelia started to inch towards the door while he was distracted. He tilted his head towards her in warning and she knew she wasn't unnoticed.

Fuck it.

Shoving against the couch, she feinted for the door. As soon as he lunged to block her, she sprinted in the opposite direction, heading for the hall that led to the back yard.

"Ophelia," he shouted, chasing after her.

She didn't even make it to the threshold before his arm was around her waist, hoisting her backwards. Bellowing, she pounded against his arm and was about to scream with all her might. Then white lights danced in front of her when her head was slammed against the wall with a crack that made her teeth clank.

"Shit," Adam hissed. "Baby, baby, are you ok?"

His hands were pinning her shoulders to the wall, and with her blurred vision, she couldn't tell if he was Adam or Kent.

"I'm so sorry—I wasn't trying to hurt you."

"Everything," she breathed.

"What?"

"I remember everything," she pressed, forcing her world to come back into focus. "The dinner parties, the sneaking around, the fact that Lucy is now Alex."

Adam cocked his head, licking his lips like a nervous canine. "Alex is Lucy?"

The genuine surprise in his voice was all she needed to seal her words on the matter.

"You didn't count on me remembering, did you?" she snarled. "You followed me into this life and thought you could start all over again without me knowing what you did to me."

"Why would I?" he snapped, his hands tensing on her shoulders. "When it's always been only me? Only *me* remembering for more life-times than I can count."

The air fled from her lungs. "What did you just say?"

His jaw shook and after a moment, his eyes shimmered. "All this time… but now I'm not alone." He smiled faintly, and the hint of hope in his expression made her heart skip a beat. "Only…" Adam's eyes narrowed, as if he could hear the sounds of the knife popping out of Leander's chest. "I did what I had to do, Lia. For you. For us."

Ophelia shook her head. "If you knew me at all, you'd know I could never forgive you for what you've done."

Adam hung his head, sniffling, letting out a soft, "I know. But I can't change any of it now. Lia, even if I wanted to. I can't bring back Jack or Leander or—"

"Jack?" Her sweat cooled on her skin, chilling her far more than it should.

The blonde raised his head to meet her gaze, remorse fading into a dull numbness in his blue eyes. "I broke his back."

"No, no, that's impossible. If I was four then, so were you."

Adam smirked mirthlessly. "I was Ambrose."

She clapped her hands onto his pinning her shoulders, coiling inside. "That's *impossible*."

"I've come to learn that's the single most useless word in the English language."

"Now you're just making shit up," she snipped.

Adam pressed her against the wall with renewed force. She dug her fingernails into his skin but he didn't so much as flinch.

"I am strong, Lia," he hissed. "So much stronger than your fledgling consciousness can even comprehend. I'd left a string of dead little boys behind me as Ambrose and the cops were closing in. Deaths are so much more difficult to cover up these days than they used to be. So after they found your little playmate's body, I ended my life. *That* life. I couldn't risk my fingerprints."

"You don't expect me to believe you're Brennan's age?"

Adam's lips formed a tight line as his eyes seemed to darken. "It's like your poet said—not all souls are equal."

"You've never even read Keats."

"I played the surfer boy. The paramedic student. The frat freak because I knew you wanted simple. Stupid. Like that mick."

"Brennan isn't stupid."

Adam appraised her for a moment, his nostrils flaring. "I've killed him as a child in every lifetime since the trenches after Leander. If that won't retard a soul, I don't know what will."

He played a part. He deceived me. My life has been a lie. He hunted Brennan... since the First World War?

"After Ambrose, a five-year-old was pulled out in the riptide," Adam gushed, and she realized that this was the first opportunity he had ever had to share his truth with anyone. "The coast guard told his parents that it was a close call. That he had almost died. They don't know that he actually did. That the moment his soul fled, mine entered. I'd never tried such a feat before—I didn't even know it was possible—much less that me being in him would morph his body as I grew to match what I've always looked like. But Lia, this is what I mean. I'm a *god*."

Her mind felt like it was choking on all of the information he had just poured into it. Adam's grip softened as he felt her going limp beneath his palms and a hopeful light danced in his eyes.

"Now you can be a goddess. Don't you see what a pair we make?" His smile was so genuine that her breathing hitched. "My secret weapon."

She was still holding onto his wrists, so she gave them a gentle tug and he allowed her to pull them away from her shoulders. Swallowing past the tightness in her throat, she leaned away from the wall, straightening. Adam watched her all the while with a doting expression, as if they had both just said that they loved each other for the first time.

"Adam," she said softly, and he nodded. "Nothing has changed. You're a murderer."

"No, that's," he quietly argued, "that's such a primitive concept."

"Death is *death*," she insisted.

"I could've," he barked. "From the moment he showed up here, I could've killed him a hundred times over. But I thought you and I..." He paused, blinking as his eyes shimmered again. "I thought at last we were finally... but I was wrong. Every damn time, I'm such a fool.

Because every time that whelp shows up, you change. You forget who you are. It's like he bewitches you."

"You mean as Amelia and as myself, I've made a *choice* that you don't like."

He laughed, shaking loose a few tears. "This goes so much deeper than the footman and the Lady. This is older than most nations."

Older than... for how many lifetimes?

Ophelia felt dizzy. Her heart pounded in rhythm with a drum in the back of her mind, and, unbidden, she smelled wood smoke and brine.

"And you've followed me in every single one?"

Adam snatched up her hand, sniffling, his voice hoarse. "Lia, I didn't kill him. I know I tried to in Ireland, but that was a long time ago and I'm different now. I've grown as a person."

Tried to?

Her hand was limp in his.

"Oh my God," she breathed. "The car accident. His parents. You were the American on the wrong side of the road. You hit them on purpose. You found him and you... you..."

Adam nodded and squeezed out more tears. "But he lived. And I knew it. And I let him. Even when I recognized him at that dumb ass party where I jumped in the pool. I paid a guy to give him and his girl a free taste, sure, to keep them busy so you wouldn't meet him, but I didn't *kill* him."

Brennan was at the party?

She had ignored Adam because she had seen him talking to that boy from high school who was in and out of prison... A dealer.

Why didn't I trust my instincts? Why had I been fooled by a broad smile and the kiss of the sun on his skin?

"That *girl* was named Charlie and she died from an overdose," Ophelia hissed.

"And that paddy should've, too, but damn his—" Adam looked away, forcing calm into his demeanor. All the same, his face was flushed when he met her eyes again. "But don't you see? Doesn't it mean anything to you that I've changed? That I didn't—"

"Because you didn't want to get caught," she snapped, yanking her hand out of his. "Your precious fingerprints would've been all over."

Adam screwed his eyes shut before bellowing, "You don't know what it was like! I waited for you, and waited, but you didn't come back after Amelia. Because of what *I* did to you. And I wouldn't have had to do it if that fucking Irish bitch could've just left you alone. He deserved every death as a child from the Great War until now. *Every* one. And I'd do it all over again if it would teach him to stay away, but that little whore just won't..."

The blood rushing past her ears drowned out the rest of Adam's rant. Nausea filled Ophelia's stomach and crept up her spine, pooling in her shoulder blades. She had the wayward thought that she ought to have a quiver there, or some sort of weapon. But there were only her hands and feet and teeth. And Adam...

He raped me. Murdered Leander. Killed Brennan's parents and countless other child versions of Brennan for over a century. And Jack...

She could see the little boy with the wild black curls and the impish smile twisting her up in the swing as he sang. Jack's laughter made her feel filled up to the brim inside, like she was a night sky full of twinkling stars, or even just two brightly glowing ones. And Adam had broken his back.

The blonde's lips were still moving but all Ophelia could hear was the drumming of her heartbeat. Her body tensed, lusting for violence. Tears pooled in her eyes, making Adam's lips blur as they stopped moving.

Her glower made him freeze.

"You fucking piece of shit," she snarled before making a fist and swinging at his face as hard as she could. The pain that radiated up her arm from the punch made her bellow blend with his as Adam's head snapped to the side.

Hugging her hand to her stomach, Ophelia bolted for the nearby back door. She tried the handle but it was locked. Fumbling with her uninjured left hand, she unlocked the door and had just flung it open when Adam latched onto her hair. He yanked hard enough for her to stumble backwards. The next thing she knew, he had kicked the door shut and was hauling her down the hall.

"Lia, calm down," he snapped.

She tried to yank her head free but he had knotted his fingers in her hair. Spinning around to face him as much as she could, she rammed her elbow into his side. Adam released her with a cough. In the split second it took for her to regain her footing, she saw his face morph from panicked to eerily determined. Like Kent.

"Get out of my way," she snarled, "or I swear to God, I'll—"

Adam backhanded her hard enough to make her stagger. Her teeth rattled, sending a shock through her jaw. Hands shoved, knocking her off her feet and into the coffee table. The force of the impact shoved the air from her lungs and her body spasmed in pain. Before she could even suck in a wheezing breath, Adam was on top of her, his thick fingers around her neck, squeezing.

"Get off—" she tried to snarl but he pressed harder.

She thrashed her legs but his weight on her chest was like an immobile truth. Images raced through her mind of Kent standing above Leander. Adam tightened his grip and she couldn't even squeak.

He's going to kill me. Jesus, I'm going to die.

"You swear to 'God,'" Adam grunted. "You have no God. Only me."

Then Kent was scooping up Leander's body and placing it next to her on the bed.

Ophelia's limbs tingled and hummed as numbness settled in, and she could only faintly hear Adam over the blood rushing past her ears.

"I don't know what else to do," he was squeaking through what looked like tears. "We have to start over."

Then she was watching Leander's chest quiver and stutter on the bed beside her as the light dimmed in his eyes. Kent leaned over them both, having put on his red tunic to hide the bloodstains on his shirt. He placed his knife in the footman's dead fingers then pressed it to Amelia's throat. With a forceful swipe, he used her lover's hand to kill her.

The pain was nothing compared to the weight of him choking her now, and distantly, Ophelia wondered why she ever remembered anything if it was only going to end the same way.

A rush of cool air brought with it the scent of wet pavement and the pressure was suddenly off her neck, sending her into a convulsive coughing fit. The blood noise in her ears intensified as she wheezed for air, feeling warmth rushing back into her arms and legs and head. Something falling hit her foot, but all she could focus on was the will to breathe. Then her ears popped and she could hear again. Rain hissed outside and things were scuffing and smacking the floorboards.

Propping herself up on her elbows, she spotted a black blur wrestling with Adam, accompanied with the scent of wet leather.

Brennan.

She tried to call out, but her swollen throat wouldn't let anything exit.

Brennan hauled himself onto Adam's chest as the blonde blinked in confusion, the side of his head streaming blood. Pinning him in place with a knee on either bicep, the Irishman rose up and struck down with his fist, again and again, like an attacking raven. Adam gasped and gurgled, craning his neck to try to shield his face from the abuse. Brennan's chest heaved as he panted, hauling his fist back. He stopped himself once he noticed the other man's dazed state.

Wincing, Brennan snarled and grabbed his hand, cradling it to his chest as he staggered off the blonde. Glaring down at him, his whole face scowled as he stomped and shook his throbbing hand.

"Fock!" he screamed at Adam's chest.

Adam flinched the slightest bit but other than that, the only thing he seemed capable of doing was shifting his heels on the floorboards.

Brennan turned to Ophelia, stumbling towards her with his injured hand before falling onto his knees at her side. She sucked in a wheezing gasp as she met his eyes, and the wildfire blazing in their forest hues shifted directions with the wind in his heart when he took in the damage done. Her head felt like a river was rushing through it, sloshing at the sides and keeping her off-balance.

Run, she wanted to say. *Run before he kills you again.*

Brennan held his good hand towards her face, but it shook. His cheeks flinched and he pulled it away, as if afraid she would shatter.

He looked like he wouldn't breathe until she could, reminding her of Leander's broken gaze when Kent hauled him into the room after her rape, and she wanted to tear the hurt away and never see it again. Instead, all she could do was squeak and rest a hand on her chest while she struggled for air.

Rainwater jetted down Brennan's cheekbone, pooling on his lower lip in a tear while his brows lowered like a cowl. Exhaling through his nose, the forest fire returned to his eyes and he looked far wilder than Leander ever had. Feral. The water dripped from his lip onto her hand as he started to shake with each heartbeat, and Ophelia realized that he was fighting the impulse to kill the other man.

Adam propped himself up against the wall, spitting out blood, and through her haze, Ophelia inched out her hand to brush her fingers against Brennan's skin.

The light touch seemed to clear his head of the smoke and flames and war drums. He slid a hand under her back and another under her legs then scooted her towards him. The river sloshing around in her mind drained as she realized he was trying to pick her up. Wincing, she raised an arm to wrap around the back of his neck and Brennan ducked his head to help her.

"You coward," Adam mumbled around his swelling lip.

Brennan adjusted her arm on his neck before catching her eye to silently ask if she was ready. The squeak in her throat grew thin as she nodded, feeling anchored in her body once again. Setting his jaw, Brennan rose, lifting her with him, and the fluid motion made darkness creep on the edges of her mind, like black lace.

"Where is the killer?" Adam pressed. "The animal? The soldier?"

A breeze tickled her bangs and the crown of her head. She knew Brennan was ignoring Adam's taunts and carrying her towards the door. Sucking in a deep breath cleared her vision, and she focused on the dark stubble of Brennan's jaw and the way his eyes looked narrow from her angle as she rose and fell with each step, the rainwater in his hair dripping onto her face.

"Bran," Adam barked. "Bran, don't you shirk from me again. Look at me!"

The coolness of the outside air brushed across her skin and the rain hushed Adam's voice as he continued to shout after them.

"Bran!"

Brennan shifted her in his arms, bringing her head up to his shoulder where it bounced as he hurried down the stairs. Blood surged through his neck, thumping against her wrists as his breathing grew ragged. She was about to ask him to let her try to stand when he came to a halt and tensed.

"Shite," he hissed, and her world snapped into focus at his voice. "The car, Ophelia. Did Alex take it?"

Something broke in the house, making her heart clench. Brennan twisted to look then his entire body flinched. He dropped to his knees, making her bounce. The crack of a gunshot sounded at almost the same time that she heard the bullet stick into the pavement beside them. Brennan loosened his grip on her torso and she planted her feet on the ground, suddenly steady with instinct.

Her blood surged with the command to run.

A gun. Adam was going to kill them both all over again.

2 0

*B*rennan wrapped his arm around Ophelia's waist, hauling her onto her feet with him. The dark street grew even darker for a moment as her vision slipped, but she didn't hesitate as she shoved off the pavement. Brennan ran beside her. Her throat throbbed and she realized dully that she was leaning against him like he was a tree as he helped bear her.

Her back tensed with each step, waiting for a bullet to tear through muscle and bone. Imagining the gunshot filled her with primal strength, and she relaxed her grip on Brennan and bore more and more of her own weight.

Brennan skidded to a halt at the end of the street, his wet hair obscuring his face as he whipped his head around, hunting for an escape route. An engine revved to life and Ophelia looked over her shoulder towards the sound. She readied to lift an arm and flag down the driver for help. Yet when the headlights flared up, she recognized the rumble of the vehicle.

Adam's truck.

The Irishman started to pull her with him towards the railroad tracks, as if to head for the forest, but Ophelia shoved the opposite direction, away from the street. Immediately switching tack, Brennan shifted his grip to her bicep and broke into a run down the sidewalk.

Tires ground against the road as the red truck pulled away from the curb. The clack of their boots slapping against the wet pavement momentarily drowned out the rattling of the engine as Adam gained speed behind them.

Deaths are so much more difficult to cover up these days, Adam had said.

Oh, God, he's going to run us down, like he did to Brennan's parents. As if it was an accident.

Every raindrop was suddenly illuminated when the headlights beamed into the air around Ophelia and Brennan when the truck turned. Ophelia's legs grew heavier as her throat tightened, realizing that she couldn't possibly outrun a vehicle. Brennan's hand pinched her arm when the roar behind them grew louder, wheels churning on the slick street. She thought she could feel pebbles and grime from the tires pelting her calves and braced herself for the impact, but everything was growing sluggish.

Just then, Brennan hauled her to the side, dragging her into a parking lot. Her feet clanked against each other and he bore more of her weight as he forced her along. Tires hissed as the truck skidded to a halt. Then the blood rushing past Ophelia's ears grew so loud that she couldn't hear if Adam had slammed a door shut or not.

Is he after us? Does he still have a gun?

"Your mobile," Brennan barked as he wrapped an arm around her waist again, straining under her weight. "Do ya have it?" She shook her head no.

"Shite."

She tried to ask if Alex still had Brennan's phone back at the bar, but nothing was allowed out anymore. Burning built in her chest as her throat clenched, making her wheeze. Stumbling to a halt, she worked her jaw, trying to gulp down enough air to clear the pounding in her head. She couldn't stand anymore. Her limbs burned and Brennan sounded like he was underwater as he called her name.

Then his arm was cradling her neck and she was floating in the rain.

Floating? No, that's impossible.

Cold. Shivering, she heard the click of a lock then a door opened. The lights were so bright that she squeezed her eyes shut and the room smelled of starch. She wasn't floating anymore.

A door slammed and she cracked open an eye to see Brennan bolting it before glancing at her through his disheveled hair. He darted to a corded phone and held it to his ear but his hands were shaking so badly that he almost dropped it.

Motel. We're in his room.

"Brennan?" she hissed, surprised at the rasp of her voice.

He swiped his wet hair back as he peered at her. "I'm ringing an ambulance."

"No."

"You're passing out—"

"I'm fine," she squeaked, screwing her eyes shut as she sat up.

Brennan ignored her and punched in the numbers.

"Please," she whined.

He gazed at her, his jaw set as if to argue, but when the dispatcher picked up, he slammed the phone back onto the cradle. "Damnit, Girl!"

Ophelia's right eye felt as if it wouldn't open properly and she pressed her cold fingertips to her swollen cheek, testing the flesh where she had been hit. Brennan yanked the curtain aside and peered out at the street before tugging it back in place. Looking her over once more, he tugged off his jacket with unnecessary force while muttering, "You're soaked to the bone."

He seemed to change his mind about giving her his coat when he realized how sodden it was.

Tossing it aside, he strode into the bathroom and came back with a towel that he wrapped around her shoulders. She offered him a brief smile in thanks, the thrum of blood in her ears calming the longer she held still.

"How do ya feel?"

"Better."

Brennan fell onto his knees before her and his raven brows nearly touched as he examined the bruising on her neck, gently tilting her head to the side.

"Oh, darlin'…"

She closed her eyes as his fingertips brushed against her swelling cheek.

"I'm scared," he whispered.

Opening her eyes, she met his gaze, noticing for the first time just how pale and haggard he was. She rested a hand on his cheek, gently running her fingers over the tickle of his stubble.

"He was Ambrose," Brennan whispered, then his lower lip started to shake and he clamped his jaw shut.

The tightness in his eyes made her hesitate, focusing instead on the sensation of his cheek until her fingers stilled and she nodded. Brennan seemed to deflate, sagging down against her until his face was in her lap. Seeing Adam after remembering how much he had ripped from her chest as the upper class girl had irrevocably shifted something deep inside, even though she had been at least twenty when he had killed her as Amelia. She didn't want to look upon him through the eyes of a tortured child who'd had his back snapped. She rested a hand on the top of Brennan's damp head.

"Why?" he asked.

"I don't know," she whispered. "He's… I don't know."

Brennan straightened, sliding his hands down her thighs to rest on her knees as he peered up at her with reddened eyes. "I think I'm sick."

She parted her lips to ask what he meant when the phone rang, making them both jump. Brennan got to his feet and looked outside before answering.

"Yes?"

Ophelia could faintly hear a woman on the other side robotically saying that a call was logged from his number and asking if he needed assistance.

"There was a home invasion," he said in a rush. "I can tell ya the name of the fecker but send the guards here, as well. We're at the

Super 8—" He scowled at the phone when the woman asked him to please repeat what he had said. "I'm saying you've got to send someone to both places, ya gobdaw," he insisted, his face flushing. "It's not complicated!"

He caught his breath as he listened then picked up the base and carried it over to Ophelia, holding out the receiver as if it had insulted him.

"She can't understand me."

Under different circumstances, Ophelia would have laughed. As it was, she took the phone and spoke to the dispatcher, explaining to her what had happened in a whisper. When she had finished, her voice was threadbare.

Not having any dishware, Brennan washed out an empty beer bottle and offered it to Ophelia with some water. She sipped it on the bed, watching him pace by the door as they waited for the police to arrive, looking like a thin, caged animal, the front and back of his grey Henley darkened with either water stains or sweat.

"How did you know that he was Ambrose?" she asked.

One of Brennan's shoulders jerked up in a nervous shrug.

"Brennan?"

"He..." His pacing slowed and he hung his head, as if focusing on the cheap carpet. "The moment I saw him hurting ya, I understood." He observed her across the small room. "Like when you finally figure out a maths problem, or see one of those magic eye pictures. I just *knew*."

Ophelia nodded, wondering if remembering past lives was different for everyone. Her book-trained imagination had processed her memories as images, like scenes from novels, but Brennan was impulsive, and had always been far more accepting of the mystery surrounding them than she had. Perhaps he understood his past and Adam's identity from sheer instinct. She was about to share her thoughts when red and blue lights flashed on the walls.

Brennan immediately opened the door and peered out, and she knew he was tracking the police officers as they got out of their vehicle and climbed the stairs. Ophelia drank more water, happy that it was now easily sliding down her sore throat, knowing that she would have a lot of talking to do.

"His name is Adam Gunnar," Brennan started before the man and woman were even in the door. "He's about six-four, blonde—"

One of the cops waved a hand, cutting off his description. "I'm gonna have to make you backtrack there. What's your name?"

Brennan looked offended so Ophelia cut him off before he could insult the law enforcement of his host nation. He proceeded to pace the room while she answered her half of the questions. Brennan looked smug when the female officer informed Ophelia that she would have to be taken to the hospital to get checked out.

Ophelia didn't want to go anywhere. She just wanted to curl up and feel Brennan's heart beating beside hers and pretend that they were just a boy and a girl.

The ride in the police car was uncomfortable, and Ophelia pretended that she didn't notice when she and Brennan were split up at the hospital. A doctor inspected her injuries and the police photographed them. She was surprised to discover bruises on her back and a cut on her head until she remembered being slammed against the wall and the coffee table. At length, they finished their report and left her to rest.

Lying in a hospital bed with a neck brace was so strange that it made her feel as if she wasn't really in her body. Her life. The conversations in the hallway and the beeping from other rooms put Ophelia on edge.

Brennan wandered in, looking over his shoulder a few times, as if he wasn't supposed to be there, and as he approached, she noticed that his knuckles were bandaged.

"Heya," he greeted with a smile that didn't reach his eyes.

"Heya."

He tugged a chair out of the corner then draped his arms on the bed railing, peering up at the machines as if they were eavesdroppers. Sighing, he returned his attention to Ophelia and rested his chin on his folded arms, gazing down at her.

"You look tired, Girl."

"Tell that to yourself."

Brennan's eyes twinkled a little, even if they were puffy and pink with exhaustion. His hair had dried frizzy, sticking out every which way, as if he had been constantly raking his hands through it.

"You should sleep," he said. "It's half past t'ree."

"T'ree" instead of "three." Little things that had felt foreign at first were now such a comfort. Ophelia took a deep breath and let it out slowly, rolling onto her side to face him, inching her palm out. He shifted, unfolding one arm to rest his hand in hers, giving it a squeeze. The thought that she had woken up that morning and headed to school to talk about her thesis seemed ludicrous.

"How's your hand?" she asked, running her thumb over the bandages.

Brennan grunted. "Grand. It's you I'm fretting over, love."

His eyes drifted to the tear in her dress and the run in her leggings, and she realized she had no memory of when they had snagged.

"I'll be fine," she squeaked. "I can go home in a few hours. This is all just a precaution." She glanced at the drip feeding fluids into her arm and he followed her gaze. "The police are looking for him."

He nodded, hunched over her like a roosting bird. "Where do ya reckon the Fecker got the gun?"

The surfer who had brought her donuts and came over every Wednesday night to watch *Survivor* would never have had a gun. Her mind still felt like it bungee jumped every time she reminded herself that he was the same man who had tried to strangle her. Who could remember centuries.

"Never mind that," Brennan amended, squeezing her hand. "Let's not talk about the Fecker now."

Her lips quirked a little at the nickname, feeling that it was too flattering given all that he had done to her... and Brennan. "I'm sorry I dragged you into this... feud."

"I'm not," he said softly.

He studied her face then fixed her with a hesitant little smile that warmed her chest and made her want to hold him as tightly as she could, as if she could protect their bond by sheer will alone. Then he blinked as a distant flame flickered in the shadows of his eyes.

"Though I should've killed him so ya don't have to worry."

"That wouldn't have stopped him."

His expression tensed, but the time he would have argued or called her mad had passed the moment he recognized Adam as Ambrose.

"You know how I can remember a life in the Victorian era?"

Brennan lifted his chin a little as he swallowed, his shoulders tensing even as he adopted a playful tone. "Alex was a girl and I was a servant."

"All you'll ever remember is that Alex was a girl, isn't it?"

"Was he hot?" Brennan asked, raising his brows.

Ophelia tugged on their linked hands and the amusement in Brennan's eyes faded as he studied her. She was thankful for his ability to cut through strain and put her at ease.

"I was a lady, named Amelia. You were Leander." Her throat tightened around the name, but it had nothing to do with the bruises. "We tried to elope together."

Brennan straightened, cocking his head as he listened, as if trying to picture what she looked like as a society girl.

"But we were caught. By Adam. He was my fiancé."

"And you've dreamed all this?" he asked softly.

She shook her head. "I see it as clearly as I see you."

A corner of his mouth lifted a little in a smile but his eyes were distant. "Was I short?"

"You looked exactly the same as you do now. All of you did."

"Even Alex?"

She shook her head in exasperation. "Really?"

"What?" he insisted with a squeak. "It's an honest question."

"Lucy was still just Lucy, and I knew who she was... the same way you recognized Adam. I just *knew*."

Brennan sighed, resting his cheek on his arm, his eyes so distant that they almost looked like they belonged to someone else. "And I died."

A part of her was vindicated over having always fretted that something bad would happen now that she knew it stemmed from the very worst happening in the past. The fact that Brennan's statement wasn't a question chilled her a little as she nodded.

"For me."

Snapping back into himself, he held her gaze for the span of several heartbeats, pity lining his face. Then deep tiredness crept in and she felt guilty for being the one lying down.

Letting go of his hand, she scooted to the side, making room for him, and then patted the mattress. He eyed the narrow strip beside her skeptically then lowered the bed railing. As he eased down, she knew that she ought to keep talking and tell him that Adam said his grudge extended far beyond their Victorian counterparts. However, that would mean sharing what the blonde did to Brennan over the past hundred years in retaliation, and given the way the Dubliner reacted to knowing Adam had killed him as Ambrose, it didn't seem fair to add even more weight to his heavy mind. At least not yet.

Ophelia slipped her arm under Brennan's neck as he lay on his side, facing her, his breath tickling her chest. The fact that she was here, breathing and lying beside him, suddenly seemed surreal. She focused on his slow pulse bumping against her arm and a man chuckling in the hallway. The sheets were a little scratchy from so much washing and the sting of antiseptic kept wafting by her nose, blending with the tang of her dirtying hair and the milder scent of unwashed cotton clothing clinging to Brennan. None of it smelled very nice, but it was life, and she was in it.

"Thank you," she whispered. "If you hadn't come back..."

He kissed her forehead then held her free hand in both of his, hugging it to his chest.

"Somet'ing started pacing inside," he explained quietly, his eyes downcast. "By the time I got to your house, it was clawing at my ribs."

Ophelia took in the lashes and skin and sigh of a man who had knocked on her door as a stranger a month ago, yet was never a stranger at all. As determined as Adam was to hunt her down in each life, her soul and Brennan's seemed just as drawn to one another, no matter the era. And despite being murdered by Adam, over and over, Brennan still came back. Even when she didn't.

"I thought telling the police would change how I feel," he whispered.

She squeezed his hand, and being four years older than him suddenly seemed like it mattered, or maybe it was just knowing that there was a picture of his parents in his jacket pocket back at the motel.

"Yeah," she quietly agreed. "I don't feel safe, either."

Brennan seemed content not looking at her, so she quieted, her breathing evening out until her chest rose and fell in rhythm with his. She didn't realize that she had fallen asleep until she woke up to her parents' hushed voices in the hallway.

The weight on her arm was gone, as was the warmth at her side, and her heart stuttered when she opened her eyes and found her bed empty. Sitting up a little, she peered around the room for any sign of Brennan but found none.

"Ophelia?"

She looked out in the hallway at her name on her mother's lips as the woman entered the room, her tense eyes darting over her daughter with concern. The doctor nodded to her father out in the hall then he followed his wife in. Ophelia's lower lip trembled, not having realized just how much she had needed to see them until this moment. Her face clenched and she gasped as a small sob wracked her. Her mother's arms were around her before she could even try to rein in her tears.

The words tumbled out of Ophelia and she couldn't stop them, even as she registered that she wasn't making much sense and that her mother had stopped asking questions. She wept into the crook of her mother's neck until her swollen throat hurt. Her father's hand was on her shoulder, and her mother was rubbing her back, rocking her gently. Once, this would have been enough to feel protected.

Late that morning, the two drove her back to the old Victorian after having insisted that she stay with them, at least for a little while. The moment she stepped into the house, Alex yanked her into a hug that lifted her off her feet despite his slight build. She clung to him, not letting go even as his arms pressed the bruise on her back.

"I came home and there were cops all over," he murmured breathlessly against her. "They said you were ok but you were at the hospital." Pulling away, he straightened her hair that was a lank mess then his eyes caught the dark marks on her neck and cheek. "You don't look ok."

"I will be."

"Thank you for calling us," her father said, squeezing Alex's shoulder, and the younger man nodded. Dark rings were under his eyes and she doubted he had managed very much sleep, if any. To say nothing of the hangover he must've had.

"Have they caught him?" Alex asked.

"If they have, we weren't told," her mother replied, setting down her purse.

Alex nodded before ushering Ophelia into a seat and offering to get her anything. He knew better than to believe her when she said she wasn't hungry and fixed her some toast while her parents made small talk with him, catching up with his life. Her father disappeared upstairs and later headed down with a packed bag. All Ophelia wanted to do was sleep, so she didn't even check its contents as she said goodbye to Alex and got into the car.

"Ramiro's dad is a cop," Alex offered before she closed the door. "I'll have him let us know the moment he hears anything."

"Thank you, poo-face."

Ophelia told herself that this was just like the times she visited home on long weekends or holidays, however it felt anything but. Her parents hovered around her, as if worried she would break, and the strain of their eyes on her made her feel like she was living someone else's life. When she lay down on her childhood bed, surrounded by stuffed animals, she only intended to close her eyes, but wound up falling asleep.

In her dreams, she was pressed against Brennan's side, basking in his affection, but the firmness of his body kept fading until she was alone and cold. She woke up, her neck aching, surprised that it was still light out until she realized that she had slept into the following morning. Rummaging through her bag for her phone, hopeful of finding a message from Brennan, she was disappointed to only find texts from Alex until she remembered that Alex had Brennan's phone.

Her father coaxed her into watching documentaries with him all day and that night they had breakfast for dinner and feasted on buttermilk pancakes. Adam may have still been out there and plotting some new scheme to get her on his side or send her into the next life, but the thought didn't bother her as much as it should have. As if knowing who he was, and remembering what he was capable of, had stripped him of some power. He couldn't deceive her like he had. Not ever again, so long as she remembered.

Ophelia called Alex that night, and he told her that he had taken Brennan's phone to him at the shop and asked him to move back in, but the Irishman declined the offer. Worrying over what would make him turn down a free place to stay, she sent Brennan a text to ask how he was doing and received no reply. She had to remind herself over and over that Adam didn't want to get caught, and going after Brennan would surely snare him. From what he had said while strangling her, if he had succeeded in killing her, he would have taken his own life right after. That way, they could have been reborn on matching timelines, isolating them from Brennan. So it was in Adam's best interest to keep the Irishman alive.

Her sleep that night was fitful and as she laid awake and sent Brennan several more unanswered texts, she decided to go home the following day. A sick feeling had settled in her stomach, as if she had eaten too much rich food, and it lingered, intensifying whenever she thought of the raven-haired young man.

While her parents were hesitant to give her back up so soon, they complied, and her mother drove her over the mountains. The house was empty since Alex was at work, making the living room feel cavernous.

"I could spend the night," her mother offered in her husky voice.

"It's all right. But thank you for everything."

After several hugs and promises to let her know the moment she

319

needed anything, her mother left, and Ophelia was alone in the house. She wandered over to the wall where Adam had pinned her, tracing her fingers over the textured paint. A chill coursed through her and she checked the time. It was past five. The sick feeling in her stomach morphed into a cramp.

Wrapping a green scarf around her neck to hide her bruises, she headed out on the long walk to the motel, expecting that she was too early for Brennan to be home from work already. His room was on the second story and faced the street. The curtains were drawn and the interior was dark, yet she knocked anyway. Pulling out her phone, she was about to call him when movement by the curtain caught the corner of her eye. Moments later, the lock slid back and Brennan opened the door.

He was in a wrinkled white T-shirt and looked like he hadn't shaved in days, but his eyes lit up when he saw her.

"Back home, huh?"

"I told you. In a text."

"Ya did?" he stepped away from the door, wandering into the room, and she realized that he not only had a beer bottle in his hand, but several empty ones lined the windowsill and nightstand. Dirty clothes were on the floor and Brennan was barefoot as he dug around in his bag for his phone then grunted in surprise as he found her messages.

Ophelia cautiously stepped inside, feeling like she was entering a stranger's home.

"Must've had it on silent," he muttered.

She wanted to say that it had been two days and to ask why he never had the thought to call her, but the question seemed petty, even as the sickness in her stomach grew thicker. He ran a hand through his hair, scrolling through his texts before shutting off the phone and tossing it onto his duffel bag. Glancing around, he set down his beer and started gathering up the bottles.

"Sorry about the clutter," he muttered. "Alex would be proud. Lots of recycling."

He offered her a smile that she forcibly returned. As he stepped past her to the door, he paused and smooched the corner of her mouth, as if the action were robotic, then set the bottles down outside.

"How's your throat?"

"Better," she replied, kicking aside a pair of jeans so that she could walk over to the bed. "How did your bag vomit?"

"My what?" he asked from outside.

There was an odd scratching sound that she recognized as a lighter once she smelled the tobacco smoke.

"Your bag," she said softly, but the timing was off and she didn't want to repeat the joke.

Brennan toed the door open a bit more so that he could see her then took a drag. She eased onto the bed and folded her hands in her lap, momentarily wondering who might walk by and see them, looking like desperate people without roots. The smoke from his cigarette wafted in, stinging her nose.

Is this what I chose?

"Sorry," he muttered upon seeing her face then closed the door enough to block the tobacco fumes from drifting back into the room.

"I woke up and you were gone," she said to the door. "And now I see you again and your priority is to have a cigarette instead of talking to me?"

"It's not a cigarette, it's a rollie. And we're talking right now," his voice replied.

Ophelia shook her head, her jaw set, glad he couldn't see her when her eyes momentarily burned with tears.

"I don't know what I expected," she said so softly that she didn't think he could hear her.

Quietness settled over the two until Brennan headed back in, propping the door open with a few bottles.

"So no word from the *garda*?" he remarked, grabbing his beer then holding an unopened one out to her. She shook her head no. "The Fecker's probably in Mexico. Or Canada. They have good waffles in Canada."

"You've been?"

"No."

He took a swig then sat down beside her, picking at the label. In that moment, she realized he hadn't looked her in the eye since he let her in.

"You need to stop worrying about him."

Brennan shrugged, peeling off part of the sticker. There were pink marks on his knuckles from hitting Adam. "I'm not worried."

Sighing, she gave up and glanced around at the water stains on the ceiling. "How was work?"

"Grand."

"Grand?"

"Grand."

"What's wrong?"

He laughed softly, rubbing the glue off his thumb. "Not'ing's wrong."

"Then look at me," she snapped, making him flinch.

He hesitantly met her gaze, and when he did, his eyes were so blanketed with exhaustion that he would appear apathetic if not for the tremor of timidity in his expression.

"Because I'm leaving right now if you don't want me here."

Brennan shrank away from her gaze, hunching a little, and the sting of his response sent her to her feet and striding for the door.

"Wait," he called.

She stopped in the patch of sunlight but didn't turn around.

"Don't go, Girl."

Her throat tightened and she reminded herself that yes, she *did* choose this. She chose the orphan and the addict and had trusted that it would all be worth the roller coaster ride. Because with it came the strength and laughter and the easiest affection she had ever felt.

"Maybe..." he began quietly behind her. "Maybe somet'ing is wrong."

Ophelia turned around to face him and the sight of his thin, hunched frame made her feel thick and sturdy. "What?"

He shook his head and met her gaze, his eyes shimmering. "Can ya stay?' he whispered. "I don't want to be alone."

Nodding, she took off her cardigan and was unwinding her scarf when he crossed over and did it for her, his brows knitting at sight of her bruising.

"Don't look at that," she said, blushing without knowing why. "Look at my face."

Brennan ignored her and lightly kissed the edge of a bruise below her ear before planting another kiss on the fading swell of her cheek where Adam hit her. She closed her eyes at the brush of his chin, wanting to lean in to the sensation, but it was gone all too soon as he pulled away. Resting his forehead against hers, he sighed and closed his eyes. The stale alcohol on his breath made her wonder when he had gotten off work.

Brushing aside some of his wavy hair, she pressed her lips to his. His mouth was cool and dry and the only thing he seemed able to muster was a token kiss. When his lower lip stopped moving despite her gentle sucking, she gave up, reminding herself that this was the same boy who had kissed her with such hunger in the alleyway, even if right now he felt like dead weight.

When she pulled away, she was startled by the distance in his eyes, and wondered if he had drifted off in the middle of their kiss.

"What're you thinking about?"

His only response was a soft sound before shifting his eyes back to hers, and she watched as his pupils contracted in focus.

"Charlie?"

Brennan took a long breath through his nose then stepped away from her and back to his beer. "No."

Giving up on trying to force an answer out of him, she followed him to the bed, disheartened to see the glaze that had settled over his eyes again as he stared listlessly at the night stand. The stillness was so different than the young man she knew that she wanted to cry, but instead forced playfulness into her tone.

"Hey," she tried, lightly kicking his ankle. "I'm right here."

She was rewarded with a half smile as he peered up at her.

"You need to shave."

He laughed softly. "I need a lot of t'ings."

"Go." She gently shoved his shoulder, realizing that among all the bottles there wasn't evidence of any food. "We're going out."

"I don't—"

"You're forcing me to be your mam," she mock scolded, and the reminder of the old joke sent a spark of recognition through his eyes. "Now go. We'll eat and it will make you feel better."

Sighing, he shoved up from the bed and trudged into the bathroom.

Once the door clicked shut behind him, she glanced around at the mess then started gathering up his dirty clothes and tossing them into a pile. Hopeful that the domestic act would taunt him into carrying on the joke, she shook out his black jacket, surprised when a piece of paper fluttered out. Picking it up, she found the photo of him as a child with his parents. Water stains had all but ruined the image.

She held it up to him when Brennan stepped out of the bathroom a few minutes later, clean-shaven and looking like he had run a wet comb through his hair, taming it.

"Is this from the rain the other night?"

He merely glanced at it as he stepped past, taking his leather jacket from her and shrugging it on.

"It's just a picture."

With that, he brushed past and tugged on a pair of socks. Ophelia studied the damage done, nearly obscuring his parents' faces, feeling hollow inside at his response. He yanked on his boots and adjusted his pant cuffs over them before grabbing the keycard to his room.

"Ready?"

Ophelia nodded, setting the picture aside and grabbing her cardigan and scarf on the way out. They walked downtown and Brennan's gaze was sharp and on everything but her, his hands in his pockets. She tried to tell herself that he was just having an off day, and that the fact that he didn't seem to notice that she was actually a few steps behind his long-legged stride didn't mean anything. But a part of her whispered that maybe their charms had faded with her memories, leaving the pair of them like two shapes that wouldn't fit together the way Leander and Amelia did, no matter how she wanted to force them.

Then again, how well did our Victorian counterparts fit together? Even if they had survived, there was no room in their world for a noblewoman and a servant. Nowhere to go... for a grad student and a recovering addict.

At length, it became clear that the Irishman was merely wandering, so Ophelia tugged on his sleeve and directed him into a Thai restaurant. He sat down opposite her, drumming his fingers on the table as he took in the other customers.

"Are you still thinking about going home?" she asked, feeling like a silly little girl trying to get the attention of a disinterested boy.

"What?" He met her gaze as a curl sprang out of place and into his face.

"Ireland," she clarified.

"Oh." He blinked, as if she had just brought up something obscure that he had wanted to do as a child. Then he noticed the menu before him and started examining it.

"Have you?" she pressed, searching for at least a hint of the man she had known the previous week.

Brennan shrugged, shaking his leg, and she gave up. There was no use forcing him into something he didn't want to talk about. They ordered a plate of pad thai and shared it. Ophelia had to keep prodding him under the table with the toe of her rain boot to get him to eat.

"I visited Charlie today," he said quietly, looking at the food instead of her. "Well, not Charlie, but... ya know."

Ophelia nodded, delighted that he had at least spoken on his own. "How was it?"

"They just had this picture up in the community hall. Like a wake for anyone who knew her before the real funeral down south." He sniffled a little, his eyes fleetingly meeting hers. "I brought her daisies. She hated flowers and all that girly stuff." He smirked a little. "But... didn't feel right to come empty-handed."

"They say funerals are for the living. If the flowers helped you, then that's good."

"No one else was there," he whispered.

Brennan stopped chewing and didn't eat much after that. For the first time, Ophelia sensed that his distance had little to do with her, and the thought both comforted and alarmed her. While no affection may have been lost on his end, if her being back at his side after nearly dying couldn't snap him out of his apathy, she didn't know what would.

Brennan walked her home and she bumped her shoulder against his several times in an attempt to tease out even a spark of interest, but it didn't work.

Alex was playing a video game when they entered and greeted them with a smile. "Did you bring me anything?"

"I ate *chicken*," she taunted, delighting in the normalcy of their banter and making Alex stick out his tongue as he focused on battling a dragon, his elf riding a pegasus.

"Hey," Brennan said quietly in her ear, his hand resting on her hip as lightly as if it were a bird. "I'm gonna go."

"Okay."

She turned to kiss him goodbye but he had already stepped away from her. Instead, she followed him to the door and watched him trot down the stoop, thankful for the touch she did get.

"Brennan?"

He paused to look up at her once he reached the sidewalk. "I'm here. Whenever you're ready."

"I know, love," he said softly. "But sometimes here is still too far away."

Ophelia wanted to ask him what he meant but was also afraid of the answer, so she let him walk away. Slipping back inside, she spotted one of the strands of sweet grass that Trea had left weeks ago... no. Days ago. So much had changed in so little time.

"Did you have fun?" Alex asked as he defeated the beast.

"I'm really tired," she replied, for telling Alex of her worry over Brennan's altered state would make it too serious and real when she hardly understood it herself.

Ophelia showered, allowing silent tears to blend with the hot water, knowing that she was forever changed. She wept for her old self before the Irishman knocked on her door and before Adam jumped in a pool.

What happened to the girl whose biggest problem was that her mother wouldn't let her paint her walls yellow? The teenager who waited and waited for someone to ask her to prom but went anyway when no one did? The young woman who could curl up with a book at night and feel happier than she ever thought she would with a boy?

"For what it's worth," Alex said, pausing outside her door later that night. "He was off the other day, too. When I dropped off his phone."

"Off ?" she asked, pretending she was busy unpacking the bag she had taken to her parents'.

"Distracted."

Ophelia nodded then looked at him over her shoulder with a smile. "How're you?"

The most adorable light bounced around in his eyes as he prodded the mark left from his lip piercing with the tip of his tongue. He ran a hand over the paneling of the doorway, trying and failing to suppress his grin as he studied the moulding.

"Falling." He rested his temple against the frame as he met her gaze. "Hard."

Delight coursed through her at the confession and she darted over, pinching his cheeks before kissing him. Alex laughed softly, taking her hands in his and swinging them before sobering as his eyes drifted to her healing bruises.

"I wasn't here."

The look in his gaze made her think of Lucy and how terrible she must have felt when her sister was discovered dead.

"Let go of that," Ophelia said softly, running her thumbs along the backs of his hands. "Please?"

His shoulders rose as he took a deep breath and forced his gaze from her bruises to her eyes. "But what if he'd—"

"Then I'd still want you to let go."

Alex flinched slightly and she knew that some part of him that was still Lucy needed to hear this.

"And live as much as you could for the pair of us. Because your heart is big enough for two, anyway."

To her surprise, his lower lip trembled and he had to blink away tears. She could count on one hand the number of times she had seen Alex cry over all the long years she had known him, and the sight filled her with gentleness.

"Hey," she softly scolded, resting a hand on each of his smooth-shaven cheeks. Alex screwed his eyes shut and twin tears darted down his face. She wiped them away with her thumbs and quirked her lips.

"You're supposed to just say 'thanks for the compliment.'"

He laughed a little before pulling his face away with a sniffle, folding her into a hug. His embrace grounded her, and Ophelia held him for some time, letting his soothing presence wash over her like a balm.

As she fell asleep that night, she felt as if she could think clearer, and decided to give Brennan the space he needed by not contacting him. As such, the days slipped past with more nights spent playing board games and baking vegan cookies. Or at least attempting to. The first batch she pulled out was largely charred discs.

"Cookie?" Ophelia asked, offering one to Ramiro when he came over Wednesday night. His dark eyes lingered on the accident on a plate, and when he parted his lips to decline, Ophelia cut him off with a conspiratorial whisper. "Alex made them," she lied.

"In that case..." Ramiro examined the plate, hunting out one that looked the least burnt before taking a bite. The muffled noises that came from his mouth couldn't be construed as sounds of pleasure by any culture on earth.

Ophelia stifled a laugh as he forced it down. She waited until he was at the sink, cupping his hands under the faucet in a desperate attempt to rinse the taste out of his mouth, before she strolled into the other room and winked at Alex who was watching TV on the couch.

"He loves you," she mouthed.

Oblivious, Alex did a double take then peered into the kitchen, as if expecting an explanation, making Ophelia laugh.

Boarding the bus for school the following day made her nervous, but Ophelia told herself over and over that nothing bad would happen just because it was another Thursday. Not wanting to draw any more attention to herself than the healing bruise on her cheek already did, she kept her neck hidden by a handkerchief scarf. During a break in her first seminar, a quiet boy with glasses and chest hair peeking out of his shirt asked her if she would like to grab coffee after class.

Ophelia had just been biting into a banana and nearly choked on the fruit as she realized that he was asking her out.

"Um," she gulped down the bite before facing him properly. He was just a boy, and she was just a girl, and he was smiling a little, his brown eyes hopeful. How easy it would be to say yes. "I actually have another class after this."

"Okay." He nodded. "Maybe another time?"

"Sure," she said automatically, and then her breathing hitched as she remembered the way the sun seemed to shine in the forest of Brennan's eyes when he looked at her. She had given him enough space to help himself, and if he couldn't, then she would have to step in.

Ophelia distracted herself by listening to music on the ride back, trying hard to not think about what was waiting for her at home last week. When the bus pulled into the metro center, she peered out the window for any sign of the familiar black leather. There was none, even when she was out on the sidewalk, and though she wasn't expecting Brennan to be there, his absence still made her heart dip.

Alex was on the doorstep bidding Ramiro goodbye as she approached, and Ophelia bit her lip and milled about under the street-lamp on the corner once the two started kissing. Afterward, Ramiro walked past her, a goofy smile on his full lips. She raised her brows in silent question and he chuckled.

"Goodnight."

"Good*niiight*," she drawled before heading inside to find Alex hiding his face in his comforter over knowing that she had seen him kissing. His childish reaction spurred her to march in with her pillow and beat him until he fought back. In the midst of it all, a squeak that she hoped he hadn't heard came out of her rear end.

329

Of course, Alex immediately froze and straightened. "Was that a fart?"

Ophelia tucked her chin in to her neck until it disappeared, indignant. "Of course not."

His eyes brightened at her giraffe face. "It *so* was."

"Whatever."

"Sink!"

Ophelia remained where she was standing, feigning offense, hoping to throw him off, until she bolted down the hall, heading for the bathroom. Alex tore off after her and easily caught up, snaring her in a hug. She shrieked when his arms were around her and had to use all her strength to bear his weight and hers as she stomped inside, reaching a desperate hand out for the sink.

The following day, she waited until it was close to noon before readying to try to catch Brennan on his lunch break. The fog overhead was still heavy, so she donned her floral galoshes and skinny jeans then tugged on a snug, grey cardigan. Deciding to make a bit of an effort, she stuck in a pair of pearl earrings and a pink cloth headband to keep her hair back. She looked in the mirror as she combed her bangs to the side, pondering which scarf to wear, then stopped herself, for she was tired of trying to hide what happened to her and the marks were slowly on their way out.

As she walked to the repair shop, her stomach started to twist in knots. She told herself that she was being silly and that if they could find each other in at least three lifetimes, they could work through whatever Adam's attack had dredged up. Yet still, the tension inside persisted and the knots twisted tighter when the handlebar-mustached man behind the counter told her that John Brennan had quit last week.

"What?" she asked dumbly.

The older man shrugged. "Showed up late a couple times then just left. We've got his last payroll. We're just waiting for him to come in and get it."

Ophelia nodded stiffly before backing out of the lobby. "Thank you."

"You're welcome," the man said before returning his attention to his computer.

Once out on the street, a breeze picked up, and Ophelia watched an old receipt skitter past, feeling like the paper was her thoughts. Adrift.

Then it all made sense. Brennan's odd mental state, erratic work schedule, and his reclusiveness.

"Oh God," she breathed. "You're using again."

21

The thought weakened Ophelia's knees and she wanted to sit down, but cars were whizzing past and there was only the sidewalk. Anxiety curdled in her stomach, sharp and familiar, and with a jolt, she realized that she associated the dread with Adam. Because there was always something about him that was intimidating. Something she wanted to placate and please. And now Brennan was making her feel the same way. She grew so numb that she could scarcely feel the tears that slipped down her cheeks as she closed her eyes.

When you love someone, ya tether yourself to them, Brennan had once said. *And tethered people spend their time tripping and falling and stepping all over each other.*

A quiet gasp escaped, spilling more tears as failure seeped into Ophelia's limbs, creeping towards her heart like black ink. Pivoting, she scanned the skyline to orient herself, feeling as if she had to do something to stop the poison from reaching her heart.

She had to fight.

Ophelia broke into a run, the moisture on her cheeks stinging as her galoshes pounded the pavement. Several passersby shot her curious glances as she bolted past but right now, she couldn't care what they thought. A car honked and her lungs and thighs burned, but still she ran, new tears forced from her eyes from the wind as she cut through it. Every beat of her racing heart flushed the black ink further and further away until it gathered in her fingertips and the failure left her body.

They would overcome this. They *had* to overcome this.

She didn't slow her pace until she arrived at the motel, flushed and sweating and barely able to breathe.

Bottles were sat on the landing outside the entry and the curtains were drawn, making the place once again appear deserted. Climbing the stairs, her feet hot in her rubber boots, she moistened her lips and knocked on the door, panting. When there was no answer, she wondered if Brennan really was out then knocked again anyway. Tinkling came from within, like bottles knocking into each other, but no footsteps approached the door.

"Brennan," she said, then closed her eyes at the warble in her voice. *I will not let him fall.*

"Please, let me in."

She held her breath and listened as sweat cooled her, but nothing stirred inside. Resting her hand on the lever, she pressed, surprised when it gave. Straightening her shoulders, she eased the door open, knocking over bottles and cans.

The room was dark and reeked of stale tobacco smoke. The sheets on the bed were the easiest to make out since they were white and lumped in a pile. Clothing was once again strewn, left wherever it landed when Brennan took it off. Ophelia cautiously stepped in and looked around for the Irishman, switching on the lights when she couldn't find him.

A grunt rose from the corner on the other side of the bed. She eased the door shut behind her before stepping over. Brennan was slumped on the floor against the wall, shielding his eyes in the sudden brightness. Sweeping her gaze over the room now that it was illuminated, she searched for any clue as to his state but spied none other than what looked like a beer stain on his white, ribbed tank top. His black jeans were so wrinkled and stretched out that she knew they hadn't been washed in ages. The fervent hope that she was wrong screamed in her veins.

Brennan cautiously removed his hand and she scrutinized his face, something deep inside wrenching at the sight of him. The skin around his eyes was pink and puffy, as if he had been weeping or ill, and his face was pale, made to look even paler by the thick stubble on his unshaven jaw. The curls on the back of his head had been flattened while the flyaways on the sides were windswept from worrying them.

Swallowing hard, she reminded herself that everything she was noticing were fixable details.

"Let me see your arm," she gasped as her breathing evened out.

He arched a dark brow, his face still screwed up, making him look disgusted by the sight of her, his scar pink.

"Your arm," she demanded and he extended it.

Swallowing hard, she crouched and took his wrist, rotating his forearm. When she spotted the small puncture, like a displaced red freckle on the inside of his elbow, she stared at it for some time, as if to make sure she wasn't imagining the needle mark.

Ophelia's mouth was suddenly dry and nothing she could do would moisten it. She had wandered into the sea to reach his shore without a raft. She had thought she didn't need a raft. And now a storm was making the waves swell over her head. Her jaw quivered as she leaned back onto the seat of her jeans, her forehead cool with drying sweat.

"After everything?" she whispered.

Brennan wouldn't look at her, but his face smoothed as he adjusted to the lights, leaning his head back against the wall.

"Even after *Charlie*?" she barked, and he recoiled his arm. "You don't get to do this. Not to me. Not to *me*, you selfish bastard."

The words rang in her ears, stinging, but they were out now.

"*Why?*"

"Just...." He began so quietly that she wasn't even sure it was a word. Brennan shook his head listlessly. "Just go then." He sluggishly met her gaze, his eyes disturbingly dull. "Go," he continued a little louder. "And don't try to find me again. I won't look for ya. I can't. I understand now."

His lower lip trembled as his eyes focused, seeming alive for the first time, even if the sharpness in their depths came from a wound so deep that she knew it was not from this world.

"All I've ever done is bring ya harm," he croaked. "So much suffering."

A shudder coursed through him and he closed his eyes, tucking his arms in against some chill, though the room was warm and stuffy.

Ophelia's vision blurred and she realized that her eyes were filling with unshed tears. She clenched her fists, trying to will them away. Now was not the time.

"That's not true."

"Not'ing helps," he said through clenched teeth, his eyes still shut. "Not the drugs or the beer... there's no middle place. No fay..." His body flinched with a gasp, tightening his arms around his thin torso. "I'm just so tired. He's cold in my bones and I'm so tired..."

She swallowed, her tears spilling onto her cheeks as she cleared her vision. "I'll take you to a clinic. Somewhere they can help you get clean and..." She trailed off, for rehab sounded so very small in the scale of their lives. Just a drop in the sea between them that was drowning her. "If you mean Adam," she continued, forcing strength into her voice, "then you need to stop worrying, because he's going to be arrested and put in prison where he can't harm us."

"Of course he can," Brennan groaned, digging a palm onto his face. "He'll come back. He'll always come back. That's what I'm saying, Girl."

She shook her head, her nose tickling with her tears. "You won't even try for me?"

Brennan let his hand fall away from his face and fixed her with a hollow expression, the forests of his eyes charred and smoldered into nothingness. His tall form and broad shoulders spoke nothing of largeness when he was so crumpled before her. Like a broken-winged bird with crooked feathers who couldn't even find the strength to hop. Or a four-year-old whose back had been snapped over an adult's knee. Not an adult... far older than an adult.

One of the oldest men in the world, Ophelia had said to the police officer when she was a little girl. When she remembered without effort. Just like Brennan did now. Only he was recalling things he never should have remembered.

I've killed him as a child in every lifetime since the trenches after Leander, Adam had said. *If that won't retard a soul, I don't know what will.*

Even with a soul that could return, such brutality, such violation, would cause irrevocable damage. While she didn't understand where she had been between Amelia and now, she knew that the agony Brennan was going through in his mind was because of her. He had come back in each life hoping to find her soul, only to be tortured for his audacity. And all the while, she wasn't there... until now.

Scooting over to him, she rested a hand on his shoulder. A small tremor rippled beneath her palm but he didn't shrink away so she pulled him to her, wrapping her arms around his tense body.

"All right," she whispered, a tear dripping into his hair as she rubbed his back. "It's all right."

Brennan had risen again and again for her. Even after Jack. If he couldn't stand on his own now, then she would help him. She had to help him. His forehead dropped onto her shoulder like dead weight and he didn't uncurl his arms from his chest to hug her back, but she cradled him anyway, as he had once done for her when she was overwhelmed by the weight of remembrance in an alleyway.

"Remember what you said?" she whispered. "We've found each other now. The hard part is over."

Some of the tension left his frame and he untucked an arm to wrap around Ophelia, allowing her to bear more of his weight. She rested her chin on the crown of his head, closing her eyes as more tears escaped, and when her shoulder felt moist, she knew he was shedding his own. He sucked in a shuddering breath and she could feel his ribs under her splayed hand, more prominent than before.

Recovery would be a long road, but she would walk it with him, kicking aside any debris she found along the way. She owed as much to both of them.

Pulling away a little, she held his face in her hands and forced his teary gaze to hers. Sprigs of green were growing in the ashes of his forest eyes and the sight made her smile. Tilting her head, she pressed her lips to his, relief coursing through her when his dry mouth feebly kissed her back. It wasn't much, but she would gladly take it over his despondency days ago.

"You should know," she whispered, pulling away to take in his face, "that I love you."

The words sparked energy into his frame and his lips curled the slightest bit, as if he couldn't believe his luck. The green shoots in his eyes grew, and she grinned when the man who had charmed her with his impish light returned to the body before her, flooding her with relief.

We'll be all right.

Kissing the tip of his nose, she let him go and rose, grabbing the closest bottle, which was still nearly full, to empty. "You need water."

Brennan shifted his weight, peering up at her with tickling delight that seemed to erase the strain of his suffering.

"I love ya, too, Girl."

The words made her feel weightless and right and she stood taller, warmth blooming inside from the two stars that blazed in the night sky of her soul.

His eyes shimmered and his jaw trembled as he took in her reaction, then his features winced, halting the spread of warmth inside her. Brennan screwed his eyes shut, shedding the tears, and when he opened them again, all new growth was gone and the charred forest was back.

"Which is why ya have to go."

A dozen knots suddenly cinched in Ophelia's stomach, burning with the warmth that had just bloomed, and her fingers tightened on the neck of the bottle. "Brenn—"

"Loving each other isn't enough," he said, bracing himself against the wall and staggering to his feet.

K. M. RICE

Ophelia shook her head, rooted to the spot by how swiftly he morphed from the young man she adored to the hollow stranger.

Or have they always been one and the same?

Brennan pointed at the door, panting from the effort of rising.

"Get out," he said, eerily calm. "And I never want to see ya again. Not in this life, or the next. Not ever. We're done."

She stood taller, meeting his gaze with hers, silently challenging him to say it again. "You don't mean that."

"Damnit, Ophelia," he snapped as more tears sparkled in his eyes, clumping his dark lashes. "He's won. We're on our own. It *has* to be this way."

"Of course it doesn't," she snapped back. "We'll fight. We'll *always* fight."

Brennan shook his head, breathing hard through his nose. "I'm too tired to fight."

"You just need to eat and sleep and—"

"It's not my body," he shouted, knocking a bottle off the nightstand, startling her. "It's this t'ing inside me. I'm ragged and I'm done. I'm tatters."

Ophelia took a step backwards as the knots tightened, Brennan's yelling reminding her of Kent's. He took a step towards her and she didn't move because she was sinking in the swells and couldn't keep her head up long enough to see his shore. To think. She just needed a second to think, because he wasn't Adam, but he was advancing upon her, his fists trembling.

"Get out," he seethed through clenched teeth, his teary face flushed as he latched onto her shoulders. "Ya have to."

Ringing sounded in her ears at the contact and she tensed, waiting for his grip to become bruising. Instead he shoved her back a few steps towards the exit. He hesitated, as if gauging her reaction before twisting his features.

"Get out, or I swear to God, I'll make ya," he croaked.

He's not Adam, she told herself as she shook her head, tears blurring her vision. *He's not Adam. He won't hurt me. I'll stand my ground.*

338

Brennan grabbed her shoulders again and shoved, making the bruise on her back twinge.

But oh, God, he's touching me.

She latched onto his wrist with a gasp, trying to pry him off as he shoved her towards the door. Brennan wasn't Leander. Brennan was broken and had been put back together wrong and she didn't doubt that the man whose hands were on her was capable of great harm. After all, she had trusted him, just as she had trusted Adam.

He's going to grab my neck. He's going to hurt me.

"Go, Ophelia," he barked in her face. "And don't look back. Never look back for me."

A white beam of panic whined in her limbs as instinct kicked in, telling her to fight or flight. She shoved his chest. Brennan stumbled a few steps backwards, surprised at her strength, his gaze aching. Then his brows lowered over his eyes like a dark cowl, and the look on his face cinched her lungs until she couldn't breathe. He had only ever looked at Adam that way before. Adam when he had wanted to kill him.

"Stop it!"

"Get out," he snarled. "For your own good, Girl."

Her healing throat clenched with a throb as he stalked towards her.

Get him away. Get him away. Get him away.

She raised the bottle in her hand.

Brennan lurched his right shoulder towards her middle, as if to knock her over. She yelped, swinging hard. The butt of the bottle connected with his temple before cracking. He stumbled sideways as beer leaked out, the door lever slipping out of his hand. He fell to his knees with a growl. Blood slicked the side of his face, impossibly fast, and Ophelia panted down at him, leaning against the door, the twang of the metal reverberating in her mind.

The lever. He was lunging to open the door... not for me. Not for me.

"Jaysus Christ," he wailed, curling in on himself, his hands clamped to the injury.

"Oh, God," she gasped, her eyes darting over the cracked, leaking bottle in her hand and the blood running down his arm in rivulets.

I got him away from me. What have I done?

"Oh, God..."

She tossed aside her makeshift weapon, hearing it crack completely as it hit the floor, and then kneeled in front of Brennan. Her arms shook at the sight of the damage she had caused, her eyes wide while her entire body shuddered with sick terror. Brennan had his eyes screwed shut and she was relieved to see that the gash on the side of his head missed them.

"Brennan, I'm so sorry," she gasped, holding her trembling hands out to him but not knowing what to touch.

"Jaysus," he gasped again, curling in tighter.

"I'm so... so..." She said breathlessly before resting her fingertips on his bare right shoulder, tracing them down his bicep past the tattoo, silently asking if she could look, startled by the unnatural rigidity of his muscles.

He gasped as a tremble shook him. The sight of him in such pain on her account made her stomach churn. She had to swallow hard to keep from vomiting.

"Let me take you to the ER," she said, her voice firmer. "Let me..."

She tugged on his arm but it was stiffly in place. So stiff. Blood dripped steadily from his elbow onto his thigh and ran in another rivulet down his neck, staining the side of his tank top and jeans.

"Head wounds bleed a lot," she stumbled, breaking out in a clammy sweat. "It'll be okay. We'll get you some stitches and... and it'll be okay."

Brennan straightened, his teary eyes latching onto hers, and they were green and brown and betrayed, oh so betrayed. As if he couldn't believe she had hurt him so terribly and was afraid she would do it again. In that moment, the strength his gaze had always gifted her cracked irrevocably.

"I'm so sorry," she wailed, blinking to clear her vision. "I thought... I thought..."

His head twitched and he closed his eyes, flinging out his bloody hands as if losing balance. He fell onto his side before she could react, his neck crooked at a painful angle as he rolled onto his back. The paleness of his skin and his sheen of sweat frightened her. She tried to remember everything she ever learned about how to treat shock.

"An ambulance," she gasped, crawling towards him, the fabric on her knees soaking up the blood. "I'm calling you an ambulance."

She gently took his head in her hands and straightened his neck. The glassiness in his eyes startled her, sending a wind through her night sky, making one of the stars flicker like a candle.

"Brennan. Brennan?"

His eyelids fluttered and with an effort, he focused on her face. She felt his hand flop onto her thigh, leaving a bloody handprint. Snatching it up, she hugged it to her chest while she gazed down at him, blinking again to clear the tears from her eyes.

"Ophelia?" he said softly, his lips so stiff that his voice was limited to the faintest imitation of words. "I can't... move my other arm."

"Okay." She nodded, even as the confession sent burning terror through her. "That's okay. We'll fix you. You'll be good as new."

He tilted his chin as if to nod then screwed his eyes shut as his body flinched. His arms and legs jerked involuntarily and he gagged. She was about to tell him that she just saw his other arm move when he whimpered. The seizure convulsing his body froze her organs with primeval understanding.

No. No, this is not happening. This can't be happening.

"Brennan," she commanded, squeezing his slick, limp hand in hers and bracing her other on his shoulder. "Brennan look at me, sweetheart. Stay focused."

When he opened his eyes, they looked as if they had been put back in his skull the wrong way, and no matter how much he blinked, they wouldn't roll back into place. His back arched and he gasped, struggling for air, then relaxed with a short cough. Cupping the uninjured side of his face, she smeared blood on his cheek as she tried to still his head.

"Brennan," she barked.

His eyes were half-lidded and their pupils blown, but he directed them at her while one of his legs jerked.

"Just keep looking at me," she continued. "You're my colors."

Brennan squeaked and she forced her panicked breathing to slow as she focused on the sounds, realizing he was speaking. She could feel his body relaxing under her hands, troubled only by small tremors, and his placid expression was peaceful. The dull ghost of a sun appeared in the forests of his eyes, warming her. For a moment, she felt that everything would be all right, even as he quietly slurred.

"A...Lia. Aelia, you're..." he squeaked. "Head up. Don't let them..."

Ophelia's eyes latched onto his pale lips, trying to decipher his words, clinging to his hand so tightly that hers hurt.

"Tame... don't...don't...."

She held her breath, waiting for him to finish, but his jaw trembled then stilled. A film passed over his eyes when the ghostly sun disappeared, as if was never there at all. Ophelia worked her jaw, looking over his face, willing a muscle to twitch or something to move to dethrone the cold, wicked understanding in her heart.

"No..." she whispered then shook his hand, trying to stir him into moving again. "No..."

Letting go, she pressed her fingers to his neck, nearly jumping when she thought she felt his pulse. But it wasn't his. It was hers, pumping blood through her thumb.

Gone.

The understanding coursed through her as something far more significant than four letters. Far more primal than a word.

Gone.

It was an ancient knowing and left her as vast and empty as the night sky. She wasn't drowning anymore, or drifting. Just suspended like a cold star, knowing that the star that used to warm her was sent barreling to the earth, shattering on impact.

Her breathing hitched as something deep inside shifted. It howled and bayed, its sounds that weren't sounds at all ripping at her from within. She let it carve her out with its claws until the hollowness was crushing her and she thought she would implode.

Ophelia didn't want to see the gash on the side of Brennan's head or the way his skull dented in at the temple, yet she couldn't look away, terrified she would forget.

Come back to me, please.

But he was gone and the aching vastness inside was shriveling her. She collapsed on his chest, her body breathing for her as she wept. Her fingers dug into the soft fabric of his shirt, as if by holding tightly enough, she could will his soul back into his body. His body that she broke, taking his star with it.

Realizing that she didn't need her heart anymore, she dug her fingernails into her chest, trying to gouge it out to bury it with him. But her flesh was too firm, and even as her blood mixed with Brennan's on her fingers, she couldn't get to it, no matter how she carved.

Then there were other legs in the room and shiny badges. Hands snatched at hers, stilling her mutilation.

"I killed him," she gasped over and over. "I killed him."

What happened next would never be clear to her. She suspected it was because some part of her succeeded in ripping out her heart and placing it on Brennan's chest to thump for him. She could picture the misshapen muscle, nestled in a pink halo of blood on the middle of his undershirt, humming away, as if to keep him warm.

Handcuffs were placed on her wrists but all she saw was the steadiness in Leander's gaze as she fastened them as Amelia. She was informed that there were no marks left on her from Brennan's hands, but the officer's eyes darted to the old bruises on her neck.

Self-defense.

Alex was waiting for her when she was let out of her cell. His eyes were already shimmering, but his face crumpled when he looked her up and down. Wondering if he could see right through her in her hollowness, she followed his gaze. Instead, she saw that her clothing was still stained with blood. And a browning handprint.

She couldn't remember when her mother arrived at the house, or when she agreed to stay with her parents while she awaited her court date. As she readied to go, Alex had his head in his hands, sobbing so hard that he was hyperventilating. The sight reminded her that there were other stars in her sky, even if they were distant. Ramiro rubbed the other man's back then yanked him against his chest. Just as she had held Brennan before killing him.

Killing him.

The betrayed look in his eyes haunted every thought; their teary, wounded depths emblazoned on her brain like a brand.

"Baby," her mother asked in the car on the drive home. "What did he do to you?"

"He loved me," Ophelia whispered, her forehead resting on the window.

If she closed her eyes, she could see Brennan's cold chest on the coroner's table. Her pink heart was beating wildly, nestled upon the blue lines and staples of the autopsy wounds, like Frankenstein's creature.

22

In her room, Ophelia felt Brennan's hand on the small of her back. When she turned around, nothing was there. If he had a ghost, she hoped it would push her down the stairs or drown her in the tub. Anything to dig out the memory of her lover's broken eyes. But she was so vast and empty inside that she knew he had no ghost, and that, for the first time in hundreds of lives, he was gone.

Where is Adam when I want him to kill me?

Ophelia ate and drank and went to school because people asked her fewer questions when she performed and acted and pretended that she was alive. She even smiled when Dr. Douglass hugged her goodbye after the last day of class. But always, always, she was cold inside. The sensation reminded her of when she was a little girl and lost her Jack, but this was so much worse than that, because now she knew what was missing, and it wasn't coming back.

Her fingernails had left purpling, scarring marks on the skin of her left breast, above her heart, and she adored them.

"Elephant," Alex whispered, resting his hand on hers while she sat on her bed. His nostrils were flaring and his eyes were sparkling.

Is he crying?

"I miss him, too. So very much. He knew it was an accident. He wouldn't want you to torture yourself like this."

Her only memory of Brennan was the betrayal in his eyes and it had charred her out, like the hollowed redwood trees explorers used to live in.

"And besides," Alex continued softly. "He could already be back as a baby. You could find him again."

She pursed her sandpaper lips. "There's nothing left of him to come back. Not for ages."

Alex shook his head and she knew he thought she was just feeling sorry for herself rather than telling the truth. That Brennan had left like she did after her death as Amelia.

Gone.

A lawyer told her that based on the coroner's investigation and the trace amounts of heroin found in Brennan's blood, her case had been classified as self-defense and domestic violence. Added to that was the fact that Brennan's fingerprints matched those associated with multiple acts of larceny from a year ago and that he was wanted by the Irish police for possession of an unregistered firearm. The lawyer doubted she would face any serious charges.

Ophelia broke down in the office, digging her fingers into her ratty hair as she sobbed. Because Brennan had been reduced to a thieving drug-addict who tried to kill her, and he was watching her with those horrible, horrible betrayed eyes.

"He'd never have hurt me," she gasped. "He was just opening the door."

Opening the door.

That night, she felt her heart smoldering. The pain was wonderful. Then it crumbled into ash with the rest of Brennan's body. She wished he had hit her with all his might.

She lay in her bed, her cheeks tight with dried tears, gazing at the picture Ramiro took of them at the Poet and Patriot, the other of Alex kissing Brennan's cheek, and their snapshot from the Giant Dipper. Three pictures. That was all he had left her.

For the first time in weeks that had felt like years, she could remember the Irishman as something other than the last look he gave her. As something more than the sum of her faults. As the man who was afraid of roller coasters, saluted crows instead of magpies, and could try her patience like no other. Who played and loved with such unparalleled gentleness. The man who pulled her out from Adam's crushing weight.

Adam.

Brennan was never going to touch her like Adam. He was only trying to scare her away. He thought he could protect her by not loving her anymore, when in reality, nothing was his fault. It was hers. Adam killed him again and again because she had chosen Brennan over him.

She could never shed enough tears.

Her parents argued in the kitchen one morning when they thought she couldn't hear them, saying how Nana refused to believe Adam would hurt anyone and had accused Ophelia of lying. They asked each other where they went wrong, and how had they raised a daughter who could date a criminal.

"He trusted me," she whispered in response. "And I failed him."

Because she knew now with certainty that her only purpose in remembering Leander was to save Brennan.

The days grew warmer and the fog didn't always reach her parents' house on the other side of the Santa Cruz Mountains. The streets were quiet as Alex peered out her window.

"They gave me his ashes. I'm... I'm not sure..."

He took a moment to collect himself before facing her. Ramiro's voice echoed downstairs, chatting with her parents about authentic Mexican dishes.

"Should we bury them? Would he want that?"

Ophelia closed her eyes. She could no longer picture her heart with Brennan's remains, for its ashes were now entombed with his. It felt like a violation.

Who would want their killer's heart trapped with them?

"He would want to be alive," she whispered.

Alex was quiet so she opened her eyes, forcing herself to meet his troubled gaze.

At length, he nodded. "We can talk about it later."

He gave her a hug and a kiss on the cheek then stepped out of her room. She rested her hand on the patch of skin that his lips had touched, realizing that the tenderness of her bruise was gone. Healed.

"She seems a little better," she heard Alex say to her parents downstairs. "But nothing like…"

"I know," her mother softly agreed, as if the weight of the world was in the two words.

Ophelia shoved their concern out of her head. They had no right to worry over her. She deserved no pity. She ran her fingertips over the thin, dark marks on the left side of her chest where she had tried to dig out her own heart.

Days later, she was back at the old Victorian with her parents, Alex, and Ramiro. The pile of firewood that Brennan collected that cold night after the Boardwalk was still on the back porch. A handful of other men were there and she wanted to tell them to leave and thank them for coming at the same time, for they were Brennan's band mates and co-workers, including the man with the handlebar mustache.

Muppet conspirator…

An urn rested on the coffee table, and as Ophelia forced herself to circle it, she heard Brennan's voice whispering from the tomb, telling her that she had failed him. Only it wasn't his voice after all. It was hers.

Brennan was silent.

"So, um," Alex began, wearing his black sweater and dark jeans as he held up a glass of Guinness. "I did a little reading on Irish wakes. They aren't always done anymore, and we've already screwed things up, but he wasn't religious and I thought…"

He paused, swallowing past a memory in his throat, lowering his voice.

"I thought it would be nice to remember the good times and have a drink for him. I'll start by saying that if it weren't for John Brennan, I would never have met the most wonderful man I've ever known."

Ramiro tried to hold Alex's gaze but his eyes were full of tears and Ophelia made her mother grow new lines on her face by slipping into the kitchen. For once, Alex was cleaning up one of her messes, and she couldn't bear it. She wrapped her hands around her Artemis mug then faced the table. Trailing her fingers over the wood, she thought of how many conversations she and Brennan had had, and how they had first kissed in that very spot.

She had thought there would be time for a thousand more kisses. A thousand more moments.

"Brennan didn't do anything half-assed," Alex was saying. "He went into every situation with his heart blazing. We could all do with more of that courage."

"*Love is my religion,*" Ophelia whispered, quoting her favorite poet, feeling a tingle of warmth at the knowledge that Brennan's eyes and mind may have once traced the words. "*I could die for it.*"

A loud caw sounded at the open window, startling Ophelia into dropping her mug, shattering the moon goddess on the floor. When she felt a muscle beating wildly under her hand, she remembered that her body was alive. Approaching the kitchen window, she peered at the bird. It was young and black and still had some of its down feathers, making its head look wild and unkempt. Its dark eyes glistened in the sunlight under what looked like thick brows as it cocked its head.

"Good morning," she whispered, lightly touching her forehead, "Mr. Magpie."

She knew it was a raven and not a magpie, but greeting the bird made something shift deep inside, like the echo of a star.

Laughter rumbled in the other room as a band mate said how annoyed Brennan got when everyone and their dog felt the need to come up to him after a show and tell them that they had either been to Ireland, had Irish blood, or met an Irish person once. She recognized him as Brian and realized that he had no idea that Brennan had once sent her a picture of his butt crack.

The raven cawed again then flew away and she smiled as she

watched it go. A black down feather drifted in the air, settling on the sidewalk. She stepped into the living room and past the broken end table that Brennan had tried to fix. Brian paused in his story while everyone watched her dart out the door. Picking up the tuft of down, she ran her fingers along the feather's soft edges and it reminded her of the touch of Brennan's curls. Behind her, Brian finished his story then sang "The Parting Glass."

> "Of all the money ere I had, I spent it in good company.
> And of all the harm that ere I've done, alas was done to
>   none but me.
> And all I've done for want of wit, to memory now I
>   cannot recall.
> So fill to me the parting glass. Goodnight and joy be
>   with you all."
> Of all the comrades that ere I had, they're sorry for my
>   going away,
> And of all the sweethearts that ere I had, they wished me
>   one more day to stay..."
>
> But since it falls unto my lot, that I should rise and you
>   should not,
> I will gently rise and softly call, 'Goodnight and joy be
>   with you all!'"

More than anything, Ophelia wanted to hear Brennan sing in that moment.

---

*O*phelia told her parents over and over that she didn't want to go out, but her father forced her by shedding tears and saying that they would never be a family again. They had fed her and clothed her and kept her safe, loving her despite what she had done. She owed it to them to make an ounce of effort, so she tucked the legs of her blue skinny jeans into her well-worn floral galoshes and tugged on her favorite lavender tank top. It was still stained with grease above the hip from when Brennan had tried to wipe away the coffee he had spilled on her, and she resolved to never wash it again. Before she left her room, she tucked the raven's down feather into her bra beside her scars.

Heading downstairs, she forced a half smile for her mother, who returned it in full.

"It'll get cold," her mother cautioned.

Ophelia snatched a wide grey scarf off a hook by the door, wrapping it around her neck and shoulders when she felt the chill in the evening air. The fog was finally reaching over the mountains, reminding her of her other home. Her father worried it would obscure the fireworks and Ophelia reminded herself that it was her country's birthday.

How is it already July fourth?

Time seemed to have stopped the moment she carved her heart out and gifted it to a corpse.

"Your father and I were talking," her mother said, peering at her in the rearview mirror. "Now that you're done with school, we can travel in the fall. Wouldn't it be great to finally take that trip to Trinidad to visit our cousins?"

"Yeah," Ophelia replied.

It would.

The idea of looking forward to experiencing something new, however, immediately reminded her of the betrayal in Brennan's eyes and she killed her own excitement. She had taken his life from him. She didn't deserve to live her own.

The parking lot was full so it took the three a while to find a space. They had to walk several blocks and Ophelia stuck close to her parents, feeling as if the gaze of every stranger whispered "It's the murderer" when they looked at her.

Snaring a patch of grass in the park, her mother spread out a blanket while the crowd roared and cheered over the lyrics "*...and the home of the brave.*"

351

Booms echoed overhead as the first of the fireworks were launched.

"Will you look at that?" her father gushed, whistling in appreciation as red lights illuminated the sky, like so many faeries. Like falling stars. The sight of them made the night sky inside Ophelia feel less vast. A tree was blocking part of their view so she began wandering to the side.

"Lia?" her mother asked.

"I want to see," she replied. "I need to see."

Her mother nodded and Ophelia could tell she was resisting the urge to remind her to be careful. The thought made her wonder why her parents weren't in her past life. The idea of leaving them for her next life made her sad, but then again, she hadn't known them before yet loved them now no less. After all, most of the souls in her life were random, brushing up against hers without the intensity of her boys'.

Pops echoed from the air as the speakers blasted upbeat military tunes and Ophelia wandered through the crowd. The fireworks reflected in her eyes and she smiled, really smiled, for the first time in weeks. Because they were green and beautiful and reminded her of the sun that would shine in the forests of Brennan's eyes when he looked at her.

"*Bright star,*" she whispered, quoting Keats as she meandered through the grove of strangers. "*Would I were steadfast as thou art, not in lone splendor hung aloft the night... Pillow'd upon my fair love's ripening breast, to feel for ever its soft fall and swell, awake for ever in a sweet unrest... And so live ever—or else swoon to death.*"

She paused, the light breeze tickling her curls, and she wondered if Brennan was gone to wherever she had been after her life as Amelia. Pulling out the feather, her fingertips danced over the soft edges.

Is he finally in the in-between place he so often sought, amongst the fay?

White lights blazed in the sky like a massive, glowing dandelion. The military song ended and a young woman on the stage began an impassioned violin solo of the National Anthem. The smoke from the explosions in the sky painted a backdrop for the next burst of blue lights and Ophelia watched with a wistful smile.

A hand rested on her shoulder and she didn't have to turn around to know who it was. In fact, she was happy he was there and she tucked her feather away against her breast.

He gave her shoulder a gentle squeeze, silently asking her to come with him.

"They're beautiful," she whispered.

"Yeah," he agreed huskily. "They are."

Then his hand slipped into hers and tugged. Tearing her eyes away from the bright lights, she followed Adam as they wove through the crowd. He slowed in the parking lot behind a dumpster.

"I'm taking your wallet," he said. "It'll look like a robbery."

She shook her head. "I don't have one."

"It'd be a courtesy to your parents. I'm following you, you know. Not here. I'll make it look like I ran after killing you and hit a tree." He pulled out a switchblade. "But I'll make it quick. It's the least I can do to repay you." His narrow blue eyes sparkled, reflecting the burst of red overhead. "You did what I never could. You destroyed him."

Ophelia felt Brennan's betrayed eyes watching as Adam leaned her against the hood of a car, forcing her to expose her neck by brushing the scarf aside. She wondered if she would remember this death when she came back. If Adam would have the same body. If he would have dared challenge Brennan if he knew the other man remembered who he was. If he would be crippled without being able to manipulate them. If he had any idea what he was getting himself into now that all three *knew*.

"Adam," she gasped as he pressed the blade to her throat.

He dug the metal in then yanked, and a brief burn was all she felt before it grew hot with the blood surging out.

"You and I," she choked, "aren't the only ones who remember."

The blonde's brows came together in confusion until the significance of her words clicked in his mind. He shook her, asking what Brennan told her, if he knew who he was, but she ignored his voice and couldn't answer anyway. The last thing she heard was the tail end of the violin "Star Spangled Banner" and the popping of the fireworks.

Like guns.

Her mind sucked inward until she was the night sky that filled her. The darkness wrapped around Ophelia, enveloping her in its presence that was nothingness and everything all at once. It hugged her curves and tickled her curls then surged through her from the slice in her throat. But she didn't have a throat. The dead didn't have bodies.

Then how can I hear?

A scratching hiss came from somewhere nearby, soothing in its age and white noise. She was on something hard and twitched her fingers, feeling cool linoleum under her skin. Frowning, she opened her eyes and saw the ceiling of the old Victorian.

The sight startled her and she squawked, shoving herself upright and grabbing her neck, feeling for a wound that wasn't there. In fact, nothing was anywhere. The house was completely empty, as if vacant. Except for the phonograph that stood in the center of the living room, playing a gramophone record that seemed to be blank for it merely hissed and crackled.

"Liiiaaa," a deep voice drawled, as if tasting her name. "Lia, Lia, Ophe-lia."

Ophelia hopped to her feet at the sound, surprised by her own agility.

Or is it just that I feel lighter?

Trea shuffled out of the kitchen, shaking his head with a disappointed sigh as he dipped a teabag into her Artemis mug that was as whole as could be.

23

"*W*hat... what are you doing here?" Ophelia asked, hugging herself as Trea approached. He took a sip of the liquid despite the fact that it was hot enough to steam up his shades. "And I didn't say you could use that."

Shrugging, the large man went to set the mug down then seemed to notice that there was no furniture. Ophelia followed his gaze and realized what else seemed off about the house: it looked new.

"How's the neck?" he asked, shaking a dread out of the way after setting the mug on the ground. "He seems to always go for it."

Her hand flew to her throat under her scarf, even though she already knew she wouldn't feel anything there. "How do you know about that?"

"Like, you've just gotta take some time to adjust." He held out his arms in a half Hula movement. "You know, allow yourself a little room for some breathing space." He crooked his nose. "That may have been a poor choice of words."

Ophelia blanched and let her arms fall to her sides. "So... I'm dead."

Trea giggled. "Nah, man. That's like, such a modern way of interpreting existence." He shuffled over to the phonograph then jerked his head back when he reached it, as if not realizing it was so close. "I mean, you could be, if you want to."

She furrowed her forehead, watching him as he peered at the device, inspecting it. "If I'm not dead... what am I?"

"Whatever happened to Negative Capability?"

"That's Keats."

"Hell yeah."

Ophelia studied him for a moment before cautiously approaching the phonograph as he circled it. "So I've... transcended the borders of my...?"

"Context," Trea finished for her. "Parameters. Capacity."

She arched a brow, wondering if this was one of those weird things that happened in a dying person's mind when their neurons started firing and they thought that they were discussing the universe with Rasta scarf-wearing, bathroom-dreaded transients before they were snuffed out completely.

"In short," he continued with a smile, "you're like me now. At least, for the moment. And without a physical form. So come to think of it, not that much like me at all."

"And... what exactly *are* you?"

"Dude, don't hate. I've been trying to define that for a few thousand years now. Like, the easiest way I can describe it without, you know, breaking your brain, is to say that I'm pretty much an inter-dimensional being."

Ophelia stared at him for some time, and he looked so out of place next to the phonograph that she immediately turned towards the stairs.

"Alex?" she shouted, starting up the steps. "Alex!"

"Brother can't hear you," Trea said. "He's on a different plane."

"I'm serious," Ophelia threatened, whipping around to face him. "Take me back."

"Whoa, like, chillax there. It ain't happening."

"Then what the hell is an inter-dimensional being?" she snapped, kicking lightly at the base of the railing.

Trea sighed and took off his shades, fixing her with eyes that made her heart jump. They were purple. Unnaturally, impossibly purple.

"And here I just thought you were high all the time," she whispered.

"Your boy Adam thinks he's old," Trea said, "because he was spawned in the Agricultural Revolution."

"He's not my boy," she said quietly.

"He's a pain in the ass is what he is, man. I mean, why's he gotta be like that?"

Ophelia swallowed hard and stepped down off the stairs. "So you're older than him?"

"Sister, I'm older than most rocks." He pursed his lips then darted his eyes to the side in thought. "That might be a *slight* exaggeration."

She looked him up and down, hunting for any sign of his age and finding none. He looked like the same college hippie in denial of his weight gain that she had met in the café, other than his eyes, which were always kept covered. Now that she could see his whole face, she realized that she had never before noticed that he was actually handsome.

"And you can remember your past lives?" she asked.

"Totally."

"That must drive you crazy."

"Nah man, it gives me perspective."

The blank record continued to hiss on the phonograph behind them, giving her goosebumps. "Why am I here with you?"

Trea sighed. "That shit that went down..." He shook his head regretfully. "That wasn't cool. And I realized that now that you remember, too, I could finally do something about it."

"You?"

The man studied her at length then pulled an apple out of his pocket that was too small to have held one and offered it to her. "The thing about perspective is that it gives you *perspective*."

Ophelia waved the apple away and sat down on the bottom step.

"Like, you've been feeling guilty over what you did, and it sucked monkey balls, but you were just a pawn. You both were. Victims of outside circumstances. Ophelia and Hamlet. Hero and Leander."

"Brennan used to call me a hero." Her throat tightened.

"It's a myth," Trea continued, taking a loud bite of the fruit. "See, Hero was this beautiful priestess who lived in a temple, and Leander was across the water from her. Every night, she would light the beacon of the lighthouse and he would swim across to be with her, where they would make sweet, sweet love. Then one night, a storm kicked up and blew out the light. The water grew so rough that brother Leander drowned. His body washed up on shore the next morning and she was like, crazy sad, you know what I'm saying?"

Ophelia studied her hands, wondering if such myths were based on star-crossed souls like hers and Brennan's.

"Want a bite? I mean, we don't need to eat, but it's small farm organic."

Ophelia shook her head. "No, thank you."

"You probably didn't know this, but crab apples were actually considered by the Celts to be among the chieftain class of trees. Can you imagine that? No one pays attention to trees anymore, yet the people who set up the first sophisticated legal system of Europe included trees among those protected. And the apple represented fertility, immortality... rebirth."

She closed her eyes, remembering the scents of the redwoods and the cries of the stellar jays. If her walk on the tracks was her last in the forest, then she was happy to have shared it with Brennan. A Celt.

"Anyway," Trea continued. "I've been watching that mythic story unfold for years with you two. I mean *years*. Except the water would've had to have been played by Adam to make sense. Talk about a guy who can hold a grudge."

"What are you, like, some sort of immortal voyeur?"

He let out a laugh that sounded like it was lacking in all mental faculties.

"If you've somehow known me for this long, then why haven't you ever helped?"

"I tried. There was a time the sweet grass would've worked and repelled him, but I guess he's beyond that now." He chomped loudly as he spoke. "Anyway, that was before I knew sister Ophelia had started to remember."

He winked as he chewed crudely.

"Why did I?" she asked.

He scrunched up his face, picking at a molar with his tongue before replying. "That shit, like, comes when you reach a certain stage in your development, but don't ask me when, because that was light years ago for me. Literally."

Ophelia took in a deep breath and let it out shakily. She found it hard to believe that someone as fanatical as Adam had reached a knowledgeable stage of development before she did. Though given what remembering had done to Brennan, maybe it was more of a curse.

"You three are freaks," Trea said as he swallowed. "You keep coming back in the same bodies you were in when you first met. As if you're trying to make it easier to recognize one another. No one's ever noticed because everyone didn't have cameras in their pockets back in the day, and then you've been gone for a century and Brenny Boy was always killed before he ever reached six after the Great War. Like, how fucked up *is* that?"

Trea jerked his head to the wall behind her, beside the stairs, and what had appeared there made her hold her breath. Stiffly rising, she climbed the steps, her eyes roving the wall that was now covered in newspaper clippings about dead and missing little boys. The first was yellowed with age. The date was 1924. The descriptions of the child on the gruesome wallpaper were all the same. Black hair, dark eyes, Irish. There were more than she could count. Descending the stairs, the most recent clipping was a picture of Jack. She could hear Brennan's laughter in the child's smile.

Cold settled inside at the reminder of the fear he had felt as he died over not being able to move half of his body.

"What happened to Brennan?" she whispered. "Where is he now?"

Trea sighed, tossing aside his apple core. "He went back."

"Back?" Ophelia turned to face him, hugging herself. "Back where?"

"To where he came from. Sometimes we need to rest and heal, like you did after Kent killed you."

Her eyes drifted around the familiar house. "Was I here?"

"Not like, here specifically, but sure."

"So this is… some sort of Purgatory?"

Trea chuckled. "No way, Jose. This is bigger than any religion. It's the Afterworld. We can exist in it, in this state, without anyone in the world of the living seeing us, but we're not really dead or else we'd come back. We're in-between."

"The Afterworld…." She repeated in a whisper, remembering how Brennan had once mentioned such a fay place as they walked along the railroad tracks. She looked around. "So, Alex is actually here, in this house, we just can't see each other?"

"No, no, no, no. We're not actually *in* your house. I just picked this setting to help keep you calm. We're not actually anywhere." He paused, his purple eyes boring into hers. "But I can guide you somewhere."

"Like Virgil?" she whispered. "In Dante."

"Exactly. See, you always knew your knowledge of the Classics would come in handy, didn't you?"

"But what do you mean 'guide'?" she asked.

"Like I said, sister, you remembering has changed you. We wouldn't be able to have this conversation in this place if you weren't different now. If you weren't *awake* in the Afterworld."

Ophelia ran her fingers over the scars above her heart. Aside from having no craving for food, water, or rest, she felt very much alive. Awake.

"I don't understand."

"Ophelia," Trea said in the softest tone she had ever heard him use, and she couldn't help but meet his gaze. "Most souls don't remember as much as Adam's because it isn't right. It upsets the balance of things and gives him too much power."

"But you're the same. You must remember even more than he can."

"Knowledge itself is a tool. It's what we *do* with that knowledge that can make it a weapon."

Her gaze drifted downwards, worrying that she was fated to become as scattered as Trea, or worse. Yet despite all of the ages in their words, only one question persisted in her mind.

"Wherever he is, does Brennan know how much I wish I could hear him sing? That I could change what happened?"

"What if I said that you could go back?"

Ophelia's head snapped up.

Trea shuffled towards her until he was only inches away.

"Lia… what if I sent you to him in his life after Leander? Before his child blood was spilled?" He jerked his head towards clippings covering the wall. Trea's eyes searched hers and she was captivated by their lavender circled by darker purple, glittering like nebulae. "You could fill your own gap in time. And your presence…there's no telling what you would change," he continued quietly. "Wouldn't it be worth it if there was a chance?"

She didn't dare blink, her eyes welling up.

"Yes," she whispered, her heart that shouldn't be there anymore hammering in her throat.

"If you do this," Trea continued, "it will cost you. And I can't make any promises."

Ophelia nodded, causing the tears to spill from her eyes. She wiped at her cheeks, still holding his gaze, even as she felt the temperature around them plummeting. "I don't need any."

"You'll have to be like this, sister. Unborn. In the Afterworld. No need for food or water or rest and…" he hesitated, wincing slightly, "and no need to be seen."

"How?"

"When we're in our bodies, we think of time as numbers on a ruler, marching forward." Trea licked his lips but didn't react to the cold enveloping them, even as it made his breath cloud. "It's way more complicated than that, man. Especially in our form. You know how when you're in a dream it all makes perfect sense until you wake up

361

and try to explain it? That's what time is like, and being in a body is waking up. But right now, in the Afterworld, you're still dreaming."

Her tears diminished as she tried to wrap her mind around what he was saying, distracted by his mesmerizing eyes.

The phonograph switched to a song behind them, startling her with an upbeat, old timey military tune.

"Johnny get your gun, get your gun, get your gun," a tinny, male voice sang from the record as "Over There" started playing. The song pricked her skin, giving her goose bumps, for the music was alien in its age.

What am I getting myself into?

"Not what. *When.*" Trea corrected for her, making her wonder if he could hear her thoughts.

He held up a crab apple and Ophelia's eyes settled on the fruit between them. A chill pooled in her stomach for she was reminded of the sea washing over her head as she tried to reach Brennan's shore. She was adrift again where nothing made much sense, but she had to try. No matter what happened to her, she had to try. She owed him that much.

Trea smiled, tilting the apple. "It'll be an experience, man. An *experience.*

"Take it on the run, on the run, on the run..."

"Ophelia," Trea continued. "Are you ready?"

She could smell the stale weed on his breath and closed her eyes as the record skipped and started over again. Folding her hands around the small apple, she nodded.

"I am."

"Johnny get your gun, get your gun, get your gun."

Trea closed his hands around her fingers and the apple then pressed his forehead against hers. In that moment, she recognized the cold around them as space and didn't need to open her eyes to orient herself. She was weightless, and even though it made no sense, she could breathe. The stars that surrounded her were felt rather than seen, millions of them, stretching as far as her thoughts could take her. They swirled in their galaxies that were the most glittering, beautiful things she had ever beheld. The nebulae spun in gaseous hues of purple and blue and orange, bejeweled with the white lights of stars.

Or are they souls?

Either way, it didn't matter, for Ophelia could feel herself expanding, like spilled water spreading out on a table. She forgot her name. She forgot her species. She knew only the humming of the stars around her and the exquisite clouds of color that reminded her of Trea's eyes.

Trea...

The warmth of his forehead was still against hers, and the realization made her suck her tendrils back into herself with a snap. Blood rushed past her ears with a deafening flood that soon quieted with her thoughts, allowing her to hear once more.

The music was still playing, albeit distantly, when the noise of the blood rushing past her ears fully receded, like a retreating wave. She could no longer feel Trea's forehead pressed against hers but instead became aware that her back was supported by something lumpy and covered in cloth. Taking a deep breath, she jolted as smoke stung her nose, forcing her eyes open to face a cracked plaster ceiling. "Over There" still played in another room on the phonograph.

How?

Something colorful caught her eye and she turned her head to find the crab apple sitting on the nightstand, its reds and yellows in stark contrast to the greys of the walls that surrounded her. Beside the fruit was the black down feather from the raven that she had tucked against her breast before she was killed.

Why?

A window was to her left and through it she could hear birds singing, though their songs and cadences were unfamiliar. Sitting up,

Ophelia realized that the window was just broken glass revealing the green of a thriving countryside as far as she could see. Trees, grass, and quaint stone and wood fences stretched towards what appeared to be fields in the distance, though she couldn't make out what the crops were amidst the shifting rays of light, as if rainclouds kept passing by and blocking out the sun.

"Johnny get your gun, get your gun, get your gun..." the phonograph continued to play, only the song was no longer scratched and hissing with age, but instead was crisp and sharp as it looped.

The needle must be stuck...

A muffled boom, like a tree falling in a gorge in the distance, startled Ophelia into stillness and caused the birds to quiet.

"What?" she breathed.

Something cool shifted under her hand and when she looked down, she realized that it was a shard of glass from the broken window. A shard of glass with a jagged edge that should have pinched her skin, if not sliced it, but instead all she felt was an odd pressure, as if she had gloves on. She turned her hand over and inspected her palm, running the fingers of her other hand over the lines that were supposed to tell her life and fate but were really just creases. Creases, because nothing about a life or a death could actually be so simple as to be predicted.

A life or a death?

Another boom sounded in the distance, closer this time. Ophelia sucked in a lungful of air as she straightened, peering around at her surroundings once more as she let her palm fall into her lap, settling onto her dress.

Dress? Hadn't I been in jeans?

Rising, she felt her head swim for a moment and closed her eyes to steady herself before smoothing her hands over her hips. Her dress was white and covered in a layer of lace that loosely frilled just before her elbows, leaving her forearms exposed. Buttons ran down the V-necked front, disappearing beneath a cream satin sash.

Amelia? No, no that is over and done with. Amelia is dead, and so is Ophelia Brighton. Then who am I and why am I here?

The question made her mind feel tight and slippery at the same time.

The breeze rattled something over the bed. Twisting around, Ophelia caught sight of a calendar pinned to the wall. Though it was in French, the word *Mai* for May was easy enough to understand. The date of 1917, however, was not.

GLOSSARY OF IRISH TERMS

- Arseways – Doing something wrong/the wrong way.
- Babby – Baby.
- Baltic – Freezing cold.
- Banjaxed – Broken or tired.
- Bladdered – Very drunk (with a full bladder).
- Bloody – An equivalent to "damn."
- Blubbering – Crying/weeping
- Bollix – A variation of "bollocks" (testicles), meaning contempt or annoyance.
- Cheers – Thanks.
- Codding ya – Fooling someone.
- *Craic* – Irish (Gaelic) for fun, good times, laughter, good conversation, entertainment, news. Pronounced "crack."
- Dead on – Exactly right.
- Deadly – Excellent.
- Dote – Cute, as in a child.
- Eejit – An idiot, a stupid person.
- Feckin' – A version of a rude word that is acceptable in polite society.
- Gobdaw – A foolish person.

- Grand – All right, fine, mediocre.
- Guards – The police.
- Hurling – An ancient Gaelic sport poplar in modern Ireland.
- Knickers – Ladies' underwear.
- *Mo chroí* – Irish (Gaelic) term of endearment, literally meaning "my heart." Pronounced "mo kree."
- Right ya be – You're very correct.
- *Slán* – Irish (Gaelic) form of goodbye, short for *sláinte*. Pronounced "slahn-cha" in full, "slawn" in short. Wishing health to another.
- Twig and berries – Male genitalia.
- Wee – Urinate/Pee
- Winding up – To annoy or intentionally provoke someone.
- Woozy – Dizzy and/or nauseous.

IRISH EXPRESSIONS/PHRASES

- "A brick shy of the load" – Not possessing all of one's mental faculties.
- "Off your nut" – Crazy/Insane.
- "You'd think butter wouldn't melt" – Used when someone puts on a harmless front but you suspect they are not.

ACKNOWLEDGMENTS

I would like to thank the many friends and family members who helped bring *Ophelia* to life. First and foremost, immense gratitude is owed to my sister Alex who is by far the biggest Afterworld fan. Her excitement over hearing each new chapter kept me skipping along as I wrote, and her continued enthusiasm bolsters me every day, both as a writer and a person.

Thanks is also do to Ophelia's tribe who helped her along in her early days, including Tanya, Leanne, Ashley, Julie, Aaron, Max, Agnes, Kipp, Kimberly, and of course, my parents.

My linguistics consultant Rónán O Conchubhair, who is a boon to me in many ways, came through time and time again as I tweaked the Irish slang.

I kneel to you, my most devoted readers, the Wildling Warriors, who are bravely introducing this series to the world.

Last but certainly not least, I owe CJ Henderson a great debt for allowing me to use him as a canvas to create Trea, and for his contribution of, "It's like Tea… but with an R." The character was originally introduced for a cameo as an inside joke, and, well, the rest is history… or is it?

ABOUT THE AUTHOR

K.M. Rice is a national award-winning screenwriter and author who has worked for both Magic Leap and Weta Workshop. Her four-part Afterworld series continues with the second book, *Priestess*.

Her first novel, *Darkling*, is a young adult dark fantasy that now has a companion novel titled *The Watcher*. Her novella *The Wild Frontier* is an ode to the American spirit of adventure and seeks to awaken the wildish nature in all of us. She also provided additional writing and research for *Middle-earth From Script to Screen: Building the World of The Lord of the Rings and The Hobbit*.

Over the years, her love of storytelling has led to producing and geeking out in various webshows and short films. When not writing or filming, she can be found hiking in the woods, baking, running, and enjoying the company of the many animals on her family ranch in the Santa Cruz Mountains of California.

ALSO BY K. M. RICE

Darkling

The Watcher (A Companion Novel to Darkling)

The Wild Frontier

The Country Beyond the Forests

COMING SOON

Priestess (Afterworld Book Two)

Afterworld Book Two

PRIESTESS

Coming in Spring 2019

Stay up to date with everything Afterworld by
following K.M. Rice on social media @KMRiceAuthor

and by subscribing to her mailing list
Wildling Adventures!

www.afterworldbooks.com

www.kmrice.com

Made in the USA
San Bernardino, CA
02 June 2018